PRAISE FOR *THE GIRL NEXT DOOR*

"The grittiness of northern New Jers[illegible]ealities of newspaper work, and the hard [illegible] hers has been a winning formul[illegible] reader] who enjoys a gritty mys[illegible]

—W[illegible] *nt Review of Books*

"With his third featuring bras[illegible] reezy, unflappable Carter, Parks propels himself to a niche shared by only a handful of others: writers who can manage the comedy-mystery." —*Kirkus Reviews*

"A tantalizing tale . . . [Parks] impeccably depicts newsrooms and their denizens. A combination of grit and wit, *The Girl Next Door* honors the mystery genre, a noble profession, and—not least—its author." —*Richmond Times-Dispatch*

"Brad Parks has crafted another complex and satisfying mystery, full of suspense and newsroom intrigue."

—*The Star-Ledger* (Newark)

"[Parks's] chatty style, quick pace, and trademark team efforts make this series a refreshing tonic for the mystery soul."

—*Library Journal*

PRAISE FOR *EYES OF THE INNOCENT*

"*Eyes of the Innocent* is the complete package. With wonderful prose, witty observations, and a relentless drive, this book held me hostage until the last page. Well done, Brad Parks!"

—Michael Connelly

"Zany characters, witty dialog, and a plot that races to a bang-up finish are guaranteed to have readers cheering for the good guys. Parks's sequel to his acclaimed debut, *Faces of the Gone,* is as good if not better. Think Lisa Scottoline meets Richard Yancey."

—*Library Journal* (starred review)

"An engaging personality . . . Carter Ross [is] the New Jersey investigative reporter narrating Brad Parks's *Eyes of the Innocent* . . . a capable follow-up to this author's award-winning debut mystery."

—Tom Nolan, *The Wall Street Journal*

"A breezy, entertaining sequel to Parks's well-received debut."

—*Kirkus Reviews*

PRAISE FOR *FACES OF THE GONE*

"Impressive debut . . . Carter's fresh voice, his willingness to be entertained balanced by honest sympathy and some sharp editorializing, is the book's considerable strength. The action, including a string of bombings, is brisk; the villain's identity is elusive; and the settings (from the projects to the Office of National Drug Control Policy) ring true. How could this be better?"

—*Houston Chronicle*

"This is the most hilariously funny and deadly serious mystery debut since Janet Evanovich's *One for the Money.* Former journalist Parks has learned the art of making words flow and dialog zing."

—*Library Journal* (starred review)

"A first-rate crime thriller . . . gritty and hard boiled, but with a sly sense of humor. This strong and confident debut is sure to make an appearance on many 'best of' and awards lists. Parks is a bright new talent whom readers will hopefully be able to enjoy for years to come." —*Chicago Sun-Times*

"Commanding, entertaining debut . . . Parks, former reporter at *The Star-Ledger* in Newark, shows he's made the transition to becoming a novelist with this impressive debut."

—*Sun-Sentinel* (South Florida)

"The story and characters make *Faces of the Gone* a success; the plot plays out with twists, and the characters are drawn with realism. Parks has begun his projected series with a bang."

—*Richmond Times-Dispatch*

ALSO BY BRAD PARKS

Eyes of the Innocent
Faces of the Gone

To Judy,

Thanks for having me at the Women's Club!

THE GIRL NEXT DOOR

Brad Parks

www.minotaurbooks.com

The Library of Congress has cataloged the hardcover edition as follows:

Parks, Brad, 1974–
The girl next door: a mystery / Brad Parks.—1st ed.
p. cm.
ISBN 978-0-312-66768-9 (hardcover)
ISBN 978-1-4299-4999-6 (e-book)
1. Ross, Carter (Fictitious character)—Fiction. 2. Reporters and reporting—Fiction. 3. Murder—Investigation—Fiction. 4. Newark (N.J.)—Fiction. I. Title.
PS3616.A7553G57 2012
813'.6—dc23
2011040880

ISBN 978-1-250-01340-8 (trade paperback)

First Minotaur Books Paperback Edition: January 2013

10 9 8 7 6 5 4 3 2 1

To the smart, strong, wonderful boy who makes his father want to be a better man every single day. This is for you, pal.

For three mornings, he merely observed. With a clipboard on his lap and an eye on his car's clock, he tracked her from house to house, logging every movement.

Her consistency was remarkable. She tackled the streets—and the houses on those streets—in the same order. Her time for each road never varied by more than a few minutes. Her time for each house never varied by more than a few seconds. By the end of the third morning, he felt he knew her route almost as well as she did.

And so, on the fourth morning, a Friday, he struck. He decided his best opportunity, there among the tightly packed postwar suburban houses of Bloomfield, New Jersey, was on Ridge Avenue, which seemed to have been expressly designed for a hit and run. It was long and straight and slightly downhill, which would make for easy acceleration. It was narrow and packed with parked cars, which would allow her little room to dodge him. And it was close to the Garden State Parkway, which would provide him ample opportunity to escape.

He had studied his notes the night before, memorizing the order and spacing of her stops. There were twelve houses on Ridge

Avenue that subscribed to the Newark Eagle-Examiner. *On the three previous mornings, she had reached the first one at 5:25, 5:24, and 5:27, respectively.*

So he was ready for her at 5:26 when she rounded the corner of Ridge Avenue and started working her way down the block. The sun had not yet pushed over the horizon, but there was enough dawn that he could make out her car and the small smudge of her body as she scampered toward each front porch, dutifully delivering that day's edition. It was just the right amount of light—too bright for the streetlights to illuminate much, too gloomy to make out a license plate—in which to commit the perfect crime.

He felt the smoothness of the steering wheel on his Cadillac Escalade, sliding his wedding ring on the wrapped leather. When she reached the midpoint of the block, he twisted the ignition key. The engine quietly came alive and the dashboard lit up. The car pinged at him to fasten his seat belt, which he did. He pivoted his right foot a few times, stretching and flexing his calf like a sprinter about to settle into the starting block, and placed it on the brake pedal. Then he shifted his transmission to Drive. Timing was everything. For as many mental rehearsals as he had staged, he knew real life would give him only one chance.

He peered once more into the murkiness of daybreak. When he saw the brief flash of white in her brake lights—signifying she had put her car into Park—he pressed down on his accelerator, gently but firmly. His eyes briefly tracked the speedometer as it leaped from twenty-five to forty to fifty. Then he turned his attention toward his target.

She had just stepped out of her car, grasping a rolled-up newspaper in her right hand and closing the door behind her. She was too preoccupied to pay attention to the SUV hurtling toward her. Up until a quarter second before impact, he was just another car going a little too fast down a residential street in too crowded

New Jersey—hardly unusual in a part of the country where everyone was always in a hurry.

She didn't notice him until his grille plate was practically on top of her sternum. He was going at least seventy by that point. She had no chance to get out of the way.

That's when she rewarded him with the look that briefly flashed in his headlights—total shock mixed with complete misunderstanding mixed with utter horror. In the nanoseconds that stretched out before he made contact, his only wish was that she could know this was no accident, that he was the driver, and that she was getting what she deserved. Tussle with me, will you, bitch? *he wanted to scream as his bumper crushed into her side.*

He heard the impact, a solid chunk, but didn't really feel it. There was nothing to feel. The force of his car—all that mass times all that velocity—was so much greater than her hundred ten pounds of squishy humanity. Her body flew forward, directly into the path of the still-accelerating SUV. He did not even tap the brake pedal as he drove over her, his suspension absorbing the jolt as if she had been nothing more than a worn speed bump.

When he reached the end of the block, he allowed himself one glance in the rearview mirror, where he could see her crumpled form in the middle of the street. Then he concentrated on his getaway.

The number one mistake most hit-and-run drivers make is jamming on the brakes—the squealing alerts would-be eyewitnesses. The second mistake is continuing to drive like maniacs after leaving the scene.

He was not going to commit either blunder. He gradually slowed to a reasonable speed, following all posted signs as he put distance between himself and that bloody, lifeless heap. Eventually, he slid onto the Garden State Parkway, joining that unending stream of fast-moving traffic and reveling in its well-traveled anonymity.

CHAPTER 1

To anyone who says newspapers only print bad news, I say: read the obituaries.

For the most part, obits are the uplifting stories of people who led long and full lives, enriched communities with their accomplishments, died at peace with the world, and left behind many loving relatives. And sure, the subjects of these articles have to be more than just slightly dead in order to appear in our pages—that part is, admittedly, a bit of a buzz-kill. But otherwise, obits are some of the happiest news we print.

My paper, the *Newark Eagle-Examiner*—New Jersey's largest and most respected news-gathering and content-producing agency—organizes its obits alphabetically, last name first, followed by the deceased's town and age. And I defy anyone, even the most jaded cynic, to read one day's worth of obits without feeling at least a little bit better about the state of the world.

Sometimes all you have to do is read one letter's worth—like, say, the *M*'s. You start with a guy like Milazzo, Vincent, of Elizabeth, 92, the high school football star who served his country in World War II, then worked his way up to foreman at a lawnmower parts manufacturer before enjoying a long retirement. You work your way to Monastyrly, Jane C., of Wharton, 81, the beloved mother of four, grandmother of ten, and great-grandmother of eight, who was an avid gardener and won the Wharton Elks Club pie-baking contest five times. Then you finish with Muster, Edward L., of Maplewood, 77, the son of South Carolina sharecroppers who earned scholarships to college and law school, set up his own practice, and became the first black treasurer of the Essex County Bar Association.

All the wrinkles of their days on this planet have been smoothed away and turned into one seamless narrative. All their trials and struggles have taken on the aura of parable. All their successes have been magnified, while their failures have been forgotten.

And by the time they "passed on"—or "made their transition," or "entered into eternal rest," or any of those other wonderful euphemisms for the Long Dirt Nap—they seemed to have achieved some kind of understanding of why they walked this planet in the first place.

Or at least that's how I like to imagine it.

There's also something about obits that, as an unrepentant newspaperman, I find comforting. Over the past dozen years or so, my business has ceded its dominance in any number of areas—classified advertising, national and international news, sports scores, and so on—to the Internet. But we still have a monopoly on obits. So while you can go anywhere to find out if the Yankees won, you have to come to us to learn if your neighbor is still breathing. It makes the obit pages a throwback to a better day for newspapers, one part of a crumbling industry that has somehow held strong. For me, it's just one more reason to love them.

Some folks, especially the older ones, scan the obits each day to see if anyone they know has died. Me? I'm only thirty-two. So hopefully it will be a good fifty years or so until anyone has to read about Ross, Carter, of Bloomfield. And it will probably be forty years until my high school classmates start popping up with any regularity.

In the meantime, I read them strictly for the inspiration.

So there I was one Monday morning in July, sitting at my desk against the far wall of the *Eagle-Examiner* newsroom in Newark, getting my daily dose of good news—once again, from the *M*'s—when my eyes began scanning the entry for Marino, Nancy B., of Bloomfield, 42.

I read on:

> Nancy B. Marino, 42, of Bloomfield died suddenly on Friday, July 8.
>
> Born in Newark, Nancy was raised in Belleville and graduated from Belleville High School. She was a popular midday waitress at the State Street Grill in Bloomfield. Nancy also had one of the largest delivery routes in the *Newark Eagle-Examiner* circulation area and was proud to serve as a shop steward in the International Federation of Information Workers, Local 117.
>
> She is survived by her mother, Mrs. Anthony J. Marino of Belleville; two older sisters, Anne Marino McCaffrey of Maplewood and Jeanne Nygard of Berkeley, Calif.; and many other friends and relatives.
>
> Visitation will be held today from 1 P.M. to 3 P.M. and from 7 P.M. to 9 P.M. at the Johnson-Eberle Funeral Home, 332 State Street, Bloomfield. A Funeral Mass will be offered Thursday at 10 A.M. at St. Peter RC Church, Belleville. Interment will be at St. Peter Parish Cemetery following the service.

In lieu of flowers, please make a donation in Nancy's name to the IFIW–Local 117 Scholarship Fund, 744 Broad St., Newark, N.J. 07102.

Even though we were employed by the same newspaper, I didn't know Nancy Marino. The *Eagle-Examiner* has hundreds of carriers, all of whom work at a time of day when I try to keep my eyelids shuttered.

But I have enormous respect for the work she and her colleagues do. The fact is, I could spend months uncovering the most dastardly wrongdoing and then write the most brilliant story possible, but we still rely on the yeoman paper carrier to get it to the bulk of our readers. That's right: even in this supposedly all-digital era, our circulation numbers tell us the majority of our daily readers still digest their *Eagle-Examiner* in analog form.

So every morning when I stumble to my door and grab that day's edition—always one of life's small pleasures, especially when it contains one of those stories I busted a spleen to get—I receive a little reminder that someone else at the paper, someone like Nancy Marino, takes her job just as seriously as I do.

I leaned back in my chair and considered what I had just read. In obit parlance, "died suddenly" was usually code for "heart attack." But that didn't seem to fit. A just barely middle-aged woman who delivered newspapers and waited tables was probably in fairly good shape. Something had taken Nancy Marino before her time, and the nosy reporter in me was curious as to what.

By the time I was done reading her obit a second time, I had concluded that the newspaper she had once faithfully delivered ought to do something more to memorialize her passing. Most of our obits are relatively short items, written by funeral home directors who are following an established formula. But each day, our newspaper picks one person and expounds on their living and dying in a full-length article. Sometimes it's a distinguished citizen. Sometimes it's a person who achieved local fame at some point, for reasons good or ill.

Sometimes it's a Nancy Marino, an ordinary person who spent her life serving others—whether it was with newspapers or coffee refills—and whose presence had graced the world for far too brief a time.

After eight years with the *Eagle-Examiner*, I had reached the stage in my career where I was afforded a fair amount of latitude to write what I wanted. Sure, I received the occasional assignment, but otherwise I was left to my own devices. It was a trust I gained the hard way. After earning a job at the paper thanks to a philandering state senator named Lenny Ryan—his girlfriend crashed his car into a go-go bar at what turned out to be a very opportune moment for my career—I put in several years' hard time in a suburban bureau. After working my way to the main city newsroom, I finagled a coveted spot on our investigations team, where I had won the right to pursue the things that interested me.

Not that it meant I had some kind of blank check. Yes, I could write what I wanted. But if I actually wanted it to run in the newspaper, I had to make sure I cleared it with my editor.

And there, my life had recently become a little more complicated. My previous editor had been Sal Szanto, the assistant managing editor for local news and a gruff old-time newsman. We had forged a relatively easy understanding: he had high standards, and as long as I worked tirelessly to meet them, we got along famously.

Unfortunately, Sal had been "invited" (read: forced) to take a buyout in the latest *Eagle-Examiner* herd culling. In the consideration of the fiscally constipated bean counters who had been given full rein over our newspaper, Sal was "overpaid" (read: fairly compensated). His long experience and many contributions to quality journalism actually counted against him because he had accrued so many raises during the good years. Now, with the good years long gone, he was rewarded with a one-way trip to early and unwanted retirement.

His replacement was Tina Thompson, the former city editor and my former . . . something. I would say "girlfriend," but that wasn't right because she made it clear to me she wasn't in it for that. I would say "lover," but that was also inaccurate because we never quite did that, either.

My interest in Tina was that, in addition to being fun, smart, and quick-witted—in a feisty way that always kept me honest—she's quite easy to look at, with never-ending legs, toned arms, curly brown hair, and eyes that tease and smile and glint all at the same time.

Her interest in me was more . . . chromosomal. Tina, whose age might best be described as forty-minus-one, is keen on trying motherhood. But she doesn't want to bother with the kind of pesky annoyances some women take prior to childbirth—meeting a man, courting him, perhaps even marrying him.

Tina had explained to me, quite matter-of-factly, that she long ago abandoned the idea of actually having feelings for the opposite sex. She claimed her approach was now more practical. She was looking for a tall, blue-eyed, broad-shouldered man of above average intelligence, all in the hopes he would pass on some of those traits to her yet-to-be-conceived child. As I possessed these characteristics, I had an open invitation to jump into her bed three days out of every twenty-eight.

Still, I had never taken her up on the offer. For whatever you may read about the male animal, I don't believe in emotionless sex—and, even if I did, I'm quite sure I would find it somewhat less interesting than a game of one-on-one basketball. Plus, I never wanted to have to tell my son that his mother chose me primarily for my nucleotides.

Tina's promotion had eliminated that possibility, at least for the time being. Newspaper policy dictated an editor couldn't sleep with one of her reporters, even if it was strictly for reproductive purposes. So Tina had gone elsewhere in her search for Mr. Right Genome.

Nevertheless, I couldn't shake the suspicion that Tina's claims to romantic imperviousness were a false front, and that behind them was a woman who really did want to be loved, just like any other human being. And if I was being honest with myself, I regretted that we hadn't at least provided ourselves a chance to figure out what we could be together—a failure I hoped to rectify at some point in the future.

As I slid into her office with a copy of Nancy Marino's obituary in my hand, those unresolved feelings were floating around, somewhere above her desk but below the fluorescent lights.

"Hey, got a second?" I said.

Tina was a yoga fanatic and could usually be found sitting in one contortionist position or another. This time, she had a knee drawn up, with one arm wrapped around it and another stretched at an odd angle while she read something on her computer screen. Call it an Ashtanga Pixel Salutation.

"Please tell me you have a big story for me," she said, already looking defeated by the day. "If Lester runs another floater photo of some bikini-clad, Snooki-wannabe bimbo on the pretense of it being a slow news day, I'm taking a baseball bat to the morning meeting."

I grinned. Lester Palenski, our photo editor, was a notorious pervert who dedicated no small amount of resources to documenting the young, female population that migrated toward the Jersey Shore at this time of year.

"Well, it's a story. Maybe not a big story. But it's one I'd really like to do," I said, then slid the obit page at her. "Read Marino comma Nancy."

Tina moved her attention to the newspaper, frowning as she scanned it.

"You want to write a story about a dead waitress?" she asked.

"A waitress and a newspaper delivery person, yeah."

I grabbed the obit from her desk as she narrowed her eyes at my mouth.

"Were you sleeping with her?"

"Tina! Have some respect for the dead!"

"Well, were you?"

"Oh, yeah, I was shagging her rotten," I said. "I'd throw a quick one in her every morning. Her customers complained their papers were late if I took more than five minutes, so it was always wham-bam-thank-you-ma'am."

Tina often claimed I had certain tells when I was lying, though she would never say what they were. For a while I tried sticking to the truth, but it just made me feel even more self-conscious. Since she became my editor, I had changed course and lied to her whenever possible. She knew this, of course. But I had to keep her off balance somehow.

She scrutinized me for a moment, then said, "Okay, so you didn't know her. Why do you want to write about her again?"

"I don't know. It would just be a nice story about the kind of everyday person you don't miss until she's gone—call it a Fanfare for the Common Woman."

"All right there, Aaron Copland, knock yourself out," Tina said. "What killed her, anyway? Anything good?"

Only a newspaper editor would describe a cause of death as potentially being "good." Only a newspaper reporter would know exactly what she meant by it.

"Don't know yet. I'm sort of curious about that, actually."

"Well, unless she died of some exotic and heretofore undiscovered strain of swine flu, you're not going to get more than sixteen on this. So don't go crazy and file forty or anything."

We measure stories in column inches, and the Incredible Shrinking Newspaper had a lot less of them than it once had—especially in the middle of July, the absolute doldrums of the news calendar. It was a bit of a problem for me, as I was notorious for writing as if we still published a paper as thick as a phone book every day.

"I won't go so much as a word over budget," I promised.

"How many times do I have to tell you," she said, as I departed her office. "I know when you're lying."

There's no easier way to report a story about the newly dead than to attend a service in their honor. You have to be somewhat discreet—since leaning on the casket, flipping open your notebook, and asking for comment as people pass by is considered a tad gauche. But if you show the proper respect and make it clear you're just there to write a few kind words about the deceased, you generally get a line of people waiting to chat with you. It's cathartic for the aggrieved, and it gives you everything you need to write a glowing tribute.

My trip to Bloomfield for Nancy's visitation included a change-of-clothing pit stop at my house, which was not far from the Johnson-Eberle Funeral Home. Then again, since Bloomfield is only about five miles square, more or less everything in town is not far.

On a map, Bloomfield looks like a bowling alley—a long, narrow chunk of land with the Garden State Parkway running through the middle of it. The town was carved away from Newark sometime in the early 1800s and now serves as the unofficial dividing line between the parts of New Jersey that scare white people and the parts that don't. To the north and west are well-to-do towns like Montclair and Glen Ridge, where people are mostly concerned about sending their children on to their first choice four-year college. To the south and east are rough-edged cities like Newark and East Orange, where people are mostly concerned about their children getting shot.

In the middle is Bloomfield, which doesn't always know what to make of itself. Case in point: when you get off at the Bloomfield exit, you see a BMW dealership on one side of the street and a check-cashing place on the other.

It's not quite urban, inasmuch as there are no high-rise buildings; yet it's not quite suburban, either, inasmuch as the houses are packed together so closely you tend to know if your neighbor has a cold because you can hear the sneezing.

The citizenry consists of some young professionals like me, some blue-collar folks, some senior citizens, and a lot of guys named either Tony or Vinnie who like to pretend *The Sopranos* was really about *them*.

The Realtors trumpet the town's diversity because otherwise they'd have to talk about the property taxes, which are levied by the local chapter of the Barbary Pirates. I pay $11,000 a year in tribute, in exchange for which I am spared from having to walk the plank *and* I enjoy curbside leaf pickup.

Oh, and just to get the New-Jersey-What-Exit thing out of the way: 148 off the parkway.

I pulled into my driveway and waved to my neighbor, Constance, who was watering her lawn. Constance lives alone, having divorced Mr. Constance long ago. She spends a lot of time watering her lawn. She also prunes her roses, weeds and reweeds her flower beds—not that they have any in them—and generally makes my yard look like it is tended by wild rabbits.

Constance is, at most, sixty-five. But she has one of those old-lady perms that ages her appearance a bit. She has two grown children who live in Colorado (I think) and Florida (perhaps), but have not seen fit to give her any grandchildren. I think she plans to move in with whichever one spawns first, which is perhaps part of what dampens their urge to procreate. But, in the meantime, she likes to keep an eye on the neighborhood and inform people about things they already know, starting conversations with, "You came back late last night" or "You were visited by a lady friend." (Though, sadly, I haven't had many of those lately).

My house is a tidy, two-bedroom ranch that is perfect for an on-the-go bachelor like myself: one bedroom for me and one bedroom for my extraneous stuff, so the rest of the place can stay relatively uncluttered in the event I do get to entertain a member of the fairer sex. Or at least that's the theory. Most of the time, I share my home with just one other living creature, a black-and-white domestic short-haired cat named Deadline.

Granted, it's not always readily apparent that Deadline actually is living. The act of sleeping all night exhausts him so much he can only compensate for it by sleeping all day. He has some brief periods of activity in the late morning and early evening, during which time he mostly eats and uses the litter box. Then it's straight back to dreamland. Some people describe their cats as curious or playful or affectionate. Mine is best described as dormant.

"Don't let me wake you," I said, as I slipped into my bedroom, where Deadline was snoozing on the radiator cover by the window, bathed in sunlight.

I opened the door to my closet and selected a charcoal gray suit. Not that it was much of a choice. I only own one suit, which is still one more than a lot of newspaper reporters. I bought it my senior year at Amherst College for job interviews. Now that there are no jobs left in print journalism, I use it exclusively for weddings and funerals. I couldn't begin to count how many people that suit has married or buried.

I dressed quickly. It helped I had already been wearing my usual reporter uniform, which included a white shirt and half-Windsor knotted tie. It's a bit formal by the standards of my profession, which went business casual sometime around the invention of printed type and slowly degraded from there. I get teased by my colleagues for my stodgy attire, but I don't think that's fair. I mean, hey, sometimes I wear a blue shirt. Sometimes it even has stripes.

So, yeah, my wardrobe isn't especially hip. But neither am I. Over the years, I have resisted the flat-front pant revolution, the slip-on shoe insurrection, the hair product revolt, and a host of other rebellious fashion movements I felt would take me further away from what I really am: an upstanding, prep-school-educated, clean-shaven WASP with freshly cut side-parted hair and absolutely no interest in changing styles.

"Try to keep it down," I told Deadline as I departed. "I don't want the neighbors calling in a noise complaint on you."

Deadline signaled his acknowledgment by keeping his eyes screwed shut and his body unmoving. "Good boy," I said.

I went back outside to my car, a five-year-old Chevy Malibu that often turns women's heads—but sadly, only because it keeps getting holes in the exhaust line. I've been told that driving an aging Malibu isn't good for my "image," to which I usually have two responses: one, it doesn't make sense to spend money on a car in a place like New Jersey because even if the tailgaters don't get you, the potholes will; and, two, people who judge others based on what car they drive are idiots.

It took four minutes to get to the Johnson-Eberle Funeral Home, a pristine white Victorian with immaculate landscaping. I parked on the street because the lot behind the building was already full of cars driven by people who had come to pay their last respects to Nancy B. Marino.

If you want good attendance at your funeral, die young. Almost everyone you ever knew is still alive and mobile enough to make it out. It's only the people who hang on to ninety or one hundred—and outlive their would-be funeral audience—who get the lousy crowds.

As such, the Johnson-Eberle Funeral Home had put Nancy in the largest of their three viewing rooms, and it still wasn't big enough. Some of the mourners sat in the rows of white folding chairs set up in the middle of the room. Others stood around the edges. Still more spilled outside into the lobby and down the main hallway that split the center of the building.

I'm sure some of them were fellow employees of the *Eagle-Examiner,* but I'd have little chance of knowing them—the distribution arm of our operation is so separate from the newsroom, they might as well be different companies. The Belleville High School Class of 1987 also appeared to be well represented, as was the staff of the State Street Grill. It was, all in all, a nice cross section of regular folks from Essex County, New Jersey.

Really, there was only one person in the crowd who didn't fit. He was a tall, patrician-looking man standing self-consciously against the far wall, looking like he'd rather be anywhere else. From his perfectly coiffed ash-blond hair to his waxy pale skin to his insincere blue eyes, I'd know him anywhere: Gary A. Jackman, the not-so-esteemed publisher of the *Newark Eagle-Examiner.*

It was a nice gesture for him to show up, and I might have even given him credit for it if I didn't otherwise detest the man. He had come to us from a chain of smaller papers in Ohio or Michigan or something similarly Midwestern. His lone qualification for the job appeared to be that he knew how to cut a budget better than anyone else. He did not have a background in newspapers before that—I think he operated a national chain of sweatshops, or something like that—and I held it against him every chance I got.

In the newsroom, where he was universally despised, he was known by a variety of nicknames. The features desk, with its appreciation of alliteration and poetry, called him "Greedy Gary" or "Scary Gary." In sports, where the locker room influence tends to make them a little crude, he was "Jackoff." In my corner of the newsroom, where we're more direct about things, he was "Jackass."

In the two years he had been at the paper, he had made it clear to us that he cared deeply about how much money we spent but very little about anything else we did—those forgettable things like telling great stories, uncovering grave injustices, or holding powerful people accountable for their actions. He actually admitted he did not read the newspaper each day, an unforgivable sin in the minds of the people who toiled so assiduously to produce it. Yet his most despicable act may have been that, at a time when he was sacking editors and reporters with lunatic glee, he kept three secretaries. What he did to occupy them was a source of constant speculation.

His personal appearance only made him easier to dislike. He was perhaps best described as foppish, with his expensively tailored clothes, monogrammed cuff links, and—his personal calling card—a predilection for pocket squares. It was also rumored, though never confirmed, that he had a manicurist come into the office once a week to keep his nails trim, as if he couldn't just buy nail clippers like everyone else.

As I approached him from the other side of the room, he had those well-manicured hands crossed in front of him. He was talking with a man who had stubbornly refused to give in to his male-pattern baldness, with one of the worst comb-overs I had ever witnessed: the piece of hair stretched across his shiny head had come loose and was sticking up and to the left, sort of like a single horn on a lopsided unicorn.

Jackman and the unicorn were having a rather animated conversation—correction: the unicorn was animated, while Jackman just seemed to be tolerating him—and I observed from a distance. The unicorn kept gesturing broadly, occasionally pointing a finger at Jackman, like he was accusing him of something dastardly. Maybe he didn't like pocket squares? Tough to tell.

I finally got curious as to what had the guy overstimulated, so I closed to within eavesdropping range. But I was too late. All I heard was Jackman end the conversation with, ". . . I'm sorry, this just isn't the time or place. We'll have to talk later. Now, if you'll *excuse* me."

Jackman rather pointedly turned his body away from the unicorn, who forced out an exasperated sigh and then walked in the opposite direction. A small part of me wondered, Not the time or place for . . . what exactly? Was the unicorn asking Jackass to dance the polka? But a much larger part of me had a story to write and a deadline to respect. I gave Jackman a moment or two to clear his head, then sidled up to him.

"Mr. Jackman, Carter Ross, we've met before," I said in a low voice, extending my right hand.

He looked at me disdainfully and did not uncross his arms, leaving my hand hanging in the air. We *had* met before, on several occasions. He had even presented me an award for outstanding reporting once. Yet he was examining me like I was something that fell out the back end of one of his foxhunting dogs.

"I'm doing a feature obit about Nancy Marino for tomorrow's paper and was hoping I could get a quick quote from you," I continued, undeterred by his aloofness. "Could you just say a quick word or two about her?"

Having tossed him the mushiest of all softballs, I slid my notepad out of my pocket to capture whatever dribbled out of his mouth next.

"If you want to talk to me, you'll have to call my secretary and set up an appointment," he said in a cool, clipped tone.

During my long career in journalism, which began when I was a freshman in high school and was now nearing twenty years, I had been blown off for interviews plenty of times, and by people far more important than Jackass. But I had never been blown off by someone who, at least in theory, was supposed to be on the same team as me. I did my very best to keep my voice down and remind myself that the man had the authority to fire me on a whim.

"Sir, with all due respect, this will just take a minute or two," I said. "I'm sure it would mean a lot to the family to have the publisher saying something nice about someone who worked very hard for our newspaper."

I stressed the "our newspaper" part, but it did not seem to move him.

"Call my secretary," he said, then turned his back on me and started walking to another part of the room for no other reason than to get away from me.

"Which one of the three?" I shot back, a little louder than was perhaps needed.

"Just call my secretary," he said again.

I frowned. I'm a big boy. I've been spurned before and will be spurned again. It was just annoying that it would have taken this man absolutely no effort to say something that would comfort a grieving family, but he still wouldn't do it. He had taken perhaps three more steps when I momentarily lost my filter.

"What a douche bag," I said, in a voice I hoped was loud enough so he could hear it. But he kept walking. My childish insult was lost in the din.

It's a peculiar thing, being a reporter at a wake. Because you have absolutely no reason to be sad—after all, you're the only one in the room who never knew the guest of honor—and yet, hanging around a bunch of people in mourning, you're something less than human if you don't start feeling a little melancholy, too. Empathy is a burden that way. You start to feel like you actually did know the deceased. And it wasn't long until Nancy—if you'll pardon the phrase—started coming alive to me.

The family had assembled some photos of Nancy, who was petite and, while not a knockout by any means, pretty in a girl-next-door kind of way—or at least she was the girl next door if you happened to live in an Italian neighborhood. She had olive skin, brown eyes, dark hair, a nice smile full of white teeth.

The pictures, which had been mounted on poster board and

displayed on easels, basically told Nancy's life story. There was Nancy as a carefree kid at the Jersey Shore, with skinned knees and a summertime tan; Nancy at her first communion, looking like the starch in her white dress was chafing her very soul; Nancy with a face full of braces, wearing a softball uniform that bore the name of a local podiatrist; Nancy as a teenager with a head full of eighties Jersey hair, teased up to elevations that could only be described as alpine; Nancy at her graduation, trying to act like a woman in a cap and gown but still looking like a kid.

After high school, there were fewer photos. It was never Nancy alone after that, just Nancy with family at holiday time, the obligatory Thanksgiving-and-Christmas shots. There wasn't a single picture of her waitressing or delivering newspapers, the things she spent the majority of her time doing. No one had deemed those activities important or noteworthy enough to permanently record. Such was the life of the common woman.

I pulled my eyes away from the photos and focused on the rest of the room. Nancy's family was up front, accepting a stream of visitors by the casket, a highly polished—and conspicuously closed—oak-colored box adorned with large sprays of flowers on either side. A closed casket meant one of two things: a long, slow wasting disease that left the deceased withered beyond repair; or a quick, violent end that left the deceased shattered beyond recognition.

Whichever it was, it had obviously taken a toll on the mother. She was sitting in the front row, looking frail and aged. I wondered how many of the years on her face had been applied in the last few days. According to the obituary, forty-two-year-old Nancy was her youngest. You never expect to bury any of your children, much less your baby.

Seated to the left of Mrs. Marino was another woman, and I could guess it was one of Nancy's sisters. She was dabbing her face with a tissue and swaying gently to some unheard music while she clutched her mother's hand, patting it occasionally. I surreptitiously slid Nancy's obituary out of my pocket to refresh my memory with the names of the survivors and immediately pegged this one as Jeanne Nygard, the sister who now lived in California. She had long, salt-and-pepper hair tied into a braid; wore a loose, floor-length floral-print dress; and had those photochromic glasses that turn darker in sunlight but still appear to be semishaded even indoors. Then there were her feet. Anyone who wears Birkenstocks to a funeral home has to be from Berkeley.

The other sister, Anne Marino McCaffrey, was standing, and had assigned herself the job of greeting each successive group of mourners as they came to pay their respects. She was the take-charge sister, the strong one who was holding it together because neither her devastated mother nor her hippie sister were capable of playing that role. She looked businesslike in a black skirt suit and white blouse, with nude hose and sensible pumps. Her hair was short, dark, and bobbed. The three women shared a certain family resemblance, with dark features and curved noses that left little doubt about their Mediterranean ancestry.

The line continued to shuffle forward. Each successive group offered the obligatory hugs and handshakes, paused to stumble over a few kind words, then moved on, relieved to be done with the whole uncomfortable thing.

I waited for a slight break in the action and then made my move, aiming for take-charge Anne. I introduced myself, finishing with, "I'm writing a story about Nancy for tomorrow's paper."

The woman considered me for an instant, then greeted me with all the warmth of gazpacho.

"Thank you, but we're not interested," she said, articulating every consonant so there was no misunderstanding.

It took me a second to register that I was being blown off again—and again by someone who should have been quite happy to speak with me. I was beginning to wonder if perhaps, on my drive over to the funeral home, I had developed a pronounced case of leprosy. Was my ear falling off or something?

"Maybe I didn't explain it right," I said, feeling off balance. "I'm writing a feature obit, which is—"

"We don't want any more written about the accident, thank you," she interrupted.

Accident. Of course. That explained the closed casket and, depending on the circumstances, her reluctance to chat with me.

"I'm sorry, I have to apologize, I don't know about any accident," I said.

This seemed to surprise her. She studied me for a moment and I returned her gaze. Most people—Tina Thompson notwithstanding—tell me I have an honest face. And since I really was telling the truth, I let my earnest blue eyes do the convincing.

"You don't?" she asked.

I swiveled my head left-right-left. She took four short steps and bent down, reaching under a chair to pick up her purse. She twisted open a small clasp, pulled out a newspaper clipping that had been folded in half and handed it to me.

It turned out to be a six-inch brief from Saturday's newspaper. And before I could even begin to read the article, the headline told me most of what I needed to know:

"BLOOMFIELD POLICE INVESTIGATE HIT AND RUN."

• • •

It took only a few more seconds to read the story and pull away the pertinent details. Nancy Marino had been struck by a speeding car while delivering newspapers on Ridge Avenue early Friday morning. An anonymous caller had tipped off the police about the accident but had provided no further details. The Bloomfield Police Department was asking anyone with information to call their tips line, which is cop speak for, "Yeah, we got nothing."

I was embarrassed I hadn't seen the story the first time around. Sure, it was a mere six-inch brief buried in the guts of the Saturday paper—an easily ignored spot in our least circulated edition of the week—but that didn't excuse my ignorance. A reporter doesn't have to know everything, but he ought to know what's written in his own newspaper.

Now I understood why Publisher Jackass didn't want me quoting him. Nancy was killed in the line of duty. He was worried about the paper's exposure to a lawsuit and feared if he said anything it might be used against him later.

My cynical side—a not insubstantial part of any newspaper reporter—also wondered if that's why we hadn't written a bigger story about it. Wrongful-death lawyers read the newspaper like everyone else. An unknown hit-and-run driver is impossible to sue and probably wouldn't be worth much even if you could find him. But the state's largest newspaper is a juicy target, one with considerable assets.

All it would take was some lawyer making the argument that because the paper didn't provide reflective vests for its carriers—or didn't give them proper training in how to dodge oncoming traffic, or didn't give them car-repellent deodorant, or whatever—the paper was therefore legally responsible for Nancy's death. That would open up the possibility of damages for pain and suffering, loss of survivorship comfort, and a host of other things that juries just loved to award suffering families. Jackass didn't want any more attention given to this than was absolutely necessary.

At least in theory, the publisher has no say over how the paper covers the news—a division we take so seriously we refer to it as the separation of church and state. But Harold Brodie, the seventy-something executive editor who had run the *Eagle-Examiner* newsroom for the last quarter century, was inexplicably deferential to Gary Jackman. It was a curious thing, something most of us wrote off as a sign the old man's Corn Flakes were going a bit soggy. Nevertheless, if Jackass were to make a phone call and apply some gentle pressure . . . well, let's just say that while there's separation of church and state, priests still tend to listen when they get phone calls from congressmen.

I refolded the clipping and handed it back to Nancy's sister.

"I'm so sorry," I said. "I had no idea."

Anne kept her head bent as she stowed the piece of paper in her purse. I glanced over at Mrs. Marino and sister Jeanne, who was still moving her head back and forth to some disjointed rhythm, one she alone could hear. They were receiving visitors and seemed to be paying no attention to either of us. I turned back to Anne.

"I really just want to write a tribute to Nancy. From reading the obit, she struck me as the kind of hardworking person most folks probably don't appreciate until they're gone."

The sister looked up from her purse, her eyes suddenly moist.

"Nancy hadn't missed a day of work in nineteen years," she said, then bit her lower lip. The unflappable sister was struggling to keep her composure.

Not wanting to push her over the edge, I eased back on the emotional throttle.

"You're her sister, yes?" I said.

"I'm Anne McCaffrey, yes." She blinked a few times, glanced up at the ceiling for a second, then looked back at me. "I'm sorry I gave you a hard time. This has just been so difficult for . . . my mother."

"I understand. And I didn't mean to be a bother."

"You're just doing your job."

"No, actually, this isn't my job," I corrected her. "Normally I'm an investigative reporter. This is something I'm doing on my own initiative. If you really don't want a story done, I'll walk away right now. Otherwise, I'd like to talk to the people here and get them to say some good things about your sister, which I'm sure won't be difficult. Would that be okay?"

Anne actually smiled for the first time.

"We'd really like that," she said. "What did you say your name was again?"

"Carter Ross. Let me give you a card," I said, reaching into my back pocket for my wallet. I was just pulling out one of my business cards when Nancy's other sister—who, as far as I knew, hadn't been following our conversation—suddenly spoke up.

"I'd like one, too," Jeanne said.

I looked at the woman, with her semidark glasses and groovy, Berkeley-esque head swaying. Suddenly, I recognized she wasn't dancing to any music. She had some kind of neurological disease—Parkinson's, perhaps—which meant she had little control over her head's wobbling. The movement made her hard to focus on, and I realized my attempts to do so might create the impression I was staring.

"I'd like a card, too," she said again, reaching out a trembling hand.

"Jeanne, no," Anne said, gently but firmly.

"I'm her sister, too, and I have a right to say what I want to the reporter," Jeanne said. Her voice had a monotone quality to it—another Parkinson's symptom?—yet she was clearly growing agitated, and her volume was rising to indicate it.

"I know you have a right," Anne said, making her tone softer as Jeanne's got louder. "I'm not here to debate your rights."

"She's a *lawyer;* she's always debating people's rights," Jeanne told me, spitting out "lawyer" in a way that made it clear she wasn't a friend to the American Bar Association. "Could I have your card, please?"

I acquiesced, if only because I wanted her to be able to put her hand down—the longer she kept it outstretched, the more it shook. Anne looked disapprovingly at the transaction. The family dynamic was becoming clear to me: there was Anne, the oldest sister, the controller, always trying to maintain order; Jeanne, the middle sister, the free spirit, trying to keep things disorderly; and Nancy, the youngest sister, the worker bee, who had probably just tried to stay out of the way and keep the peace.

"Jeanne, I don't know if it's the best idea for you to—"

"She doesn't want me talking to you," Jeanne told me, ignoring her sister. "She's afraid I'll say something embarrassing that will hurt her reputation."

"Jeanne, that's not fair—"

"Fair? We're going to talk about fair now? Was it fair that you stayed in law school when Daddy died?"

Anne's face flushed red and her jaw locked.

"About as fair as you running off to *California,*" Anne replied tersely, saying "California" with the same kind of vehemence as Jeanne said "lawyer."

There's nothing like a funeral to rip open old family wounds. And this was evidently not the first time these two sisters had gone for blood on this particular topic. I wished I hadn't stumbled into the middle of it. I needed a few nice quotes about Nancy for my obit, not a reprise of some ancient sisterly squabble.

"That is *not* how it happened, and you know—" Jeanne started until Anne's low-but-fierce voice drowned her out.

"If you could have just stayed around for *one year* instead of going back to your cult—"

"It was *not* a cult, it was a—" Jeanne started, but again her voice lacked the strength to compete with Anne, who turned her attention to me.

"I was in my final year of law school when our father died," Anne said, apparently trying to win me over because Jeanne was beyond convincing. "I couldn't quit at that point, not when I was that close. Nancy had just started college and she shouldn't have had to quit, either. But she dropped out to be with our mother because my sister here felt it was more important to spend time with a bunch of strangers in—"

Jeanne was drawing breath to dispute that point when the fight was abruptly halted by a terrible noise:

Their mother began bawling.

There's nothing like an old woman wailing at a funeral home to send people, particularly the guys, scurrying to action. Men in suits were suddenly diving in from all directions with handkerchiefs and offers of support. At a WASP wake—the kind with which I was more familiar, given my ethnicity—the grieving woman would have been shushed. This being an Italian affair, Mrs. Marino was allowed to moan as loudly as she wanted, but she was not going to do so alone.

In the meantime, two men—cousins or husbands, it was unclear—dove in between Anne and Jeanne, ostensibly breaking up the fight by driving the women into their respective corners. As the jerk who started it all, I found myself trying to slink away quickly so no one could identify me as the culprit.

Chastened, I retreated into the hallway, where I eventually began interviewing a representative sample of the people who had been in Nancy's life: high school classmates, fellow *Eagle-Examiner* carriers, coworkers from the State Street Grill.

I got a good dose of the usual clichés—everyone liked her, she never said a bad word about anyone, she didn't have a single enemy, and so on—but also managed to ferret out some of the details of Nancy's life.

She had been an outstanding student at Belleville High, graduating in the top ten percent of her class and making All-County in softball. After high school, she enrolled at College of New Jersey, then known as Trenton State, a well-regarded small public college. Her father died a few weeks into her freshman year, and Nancy moved back home to be with her mother. And, somehow, that's where she stayed. She got a job as a waitress. A few years after that, she took over the newspaper route.

And that became her life: she worked two jobs, kept her mother company, and maintained her friendships from high school and the neighborhood. She didn't have much time for anything else. She was never married. She dated occasionally, but there hadn't been anyone special in that capacity for quite some time. Friends said she seemed content, never considering what life might have held for her if her father had stayed alive or if she had gone back to school.

Eventually, she saved enough money to buy her own house, a source of pride. It was just a few blocks over from her mother's place, but in that part of New Jersey—a jigsaw puzzle of tiny towns fitted next to each other—a few blocks crossed a municipal boundary. So it was she ended up living in Bloomfield, not Belleville.

Beyond those biographical details, I mostly heard about Nancy's kindness and generosity of spirit. She not only had two jobs that involved serving others, but she did it in her off-time, too. It seemed Nancy was everyone else's biggest fan, the kind of person who always knew when someone had done something good and was the first to congratulate them for it.

"She just existed to cheer on other people," one of her friends told me. "It's like her hands were made for clapping."

It was the perfect first quote. And since it was nearing three o'clock, the end of the afternoon session at the funeral home, that made it the perfect time to get back to the office and start writing.

I was on my way out the door when I recognized one last person who could make for a useful interview: Jim McNabb, the executive director of IFIW–Local 117 and a well-known figure on New Jersey's political scene.

Local 117 was a large conglomeration of unionized employees, encompassing workers who could loosely be considered in the communications business—everything from newspaper deliverers to bulk mail assemblers to cable TV installers to the people building the latest wireless network. All told, it claimed something like a hundred thousand members, which made it a force in the state capital, where vote-hungry legislators remained cognizant of the need to pander to its leadership.

For as long as anyone could remember, that leader was Jim McNabb, who greatly enjoyed being the recipient of said pandering. His primary talent was knowing all the players and, more important, where they buried the bodies. (And this being New Jersey, I mean that literally.) He was a gregarious guy with a full head of silver hair and a stocky frame, and he was like the politicians he lobbied, in that he enjoyed working a room.

Unlike the politicians, though, he was actually likable. He had a gift for names and faces, and once he met you the first time, he treated you like a long-lost best friend every time he saw you thereafter. To some that might seem disingenuous, inasmuch as he reacted to everyone that way. But to me, you couldn't be that enthusiastic about other human beings unless somewhere, deep down, you really liked them.

Plus—and this always counted for something in a newspaper reporter's estimation—he was a colorful quote, the kind of guy who was always available for comment and could be relied upon to say a bit more than he probably should.

So we had some good history, and as I approached, he greeted me with a quiet-but-enthusiastic "Carter Ross! How is the star investigative reporter!"

"Hey, Jim, pretty good. Wish we were seeing each other under different circumstances, but—"

"Is there something to investigate here?" he interrupted, not bothering to hide his intrigue.

"Not a thing. I'm just doing a little appreciation piece about Nancy for tomorrow's paper."

"Are you sure there's no smoke here?" he quizzed. "Because you know what they say about places where there's smoke."

His natural friendliness aside, McNabb was the kind of guy who was always looking to exploit any angle that might help the union cause or, at least, get his name out there. If I told him I was doing a piece on businesses that refused to let their workers eat hot dogs, he would launch into a windy sermon about the health benefits of the roasted wiener—all of which he would have invented on the spot—and rail against anyone who deprived employees of their right to life, liberty, and the pursuit of Oscar Mayer.

"Nope," I said. "No smoke, no fire."

"Okay, okay," he replied. "Well, it's real kind of you to do a story about Nancy. She was a terrific kid."

We chatted for a few minutes about Nancy, whom he

described as one of his best shop stewards. He said the obligatory nice words about her, sharing the opinion that she was a loyal employee and a trustworthy friend. Then, as we began to wrap up, he jerked his silver mane in the direction of her coffin.

"Hit and run. Hell of a way to go, huh?" he said. "I just hope they catch the bastard that did it and tie him to the center lane of the Turnpike so we can run *him* over."

By the time Jim and I parted, it was after three and the funeral director was gently shepherding the crowd out onto the street. He was subtle about it—a funeral home can't exactly announce last call—but people were getting the hint.

I climbed into my Malibu, feeling my reporter's notebook pressing against my thigh. I don't know what it is, because ballpoint-pen ink barely weighs anything, but a full notebook just feels heavier than an empty one. And I knew I had filled this one with enough good stuff to easily get me to sixteen inches.

My favorite anecdote was shared by one of Nancy's fellow paper deliverers. As any longtime resident of New Jersey knows, one of the *Eagle-Examiner*'s nicknames is "the bird." For one of her shop meetings, Nancy made T-shirts with a picture of a guy tossing a rolled-up *Eagle-Examiner* onto someone's front porch, Frisbee-style. Underneath, it read, IFIW–LOCAL 117: PROUD TO FLIP YOU THE BIRD!

I wasn't sure whether I could get that line past some of our prissier editors. But as I returned to the newsroom and started writing, I figured I owed it to Nancy to try.

The words were just starting to flow onto my computer screen when my cell phone rang. The caller had a 510 area code, which was neither a New Jersey number nor one I recognized.

"Carter Ross."

"Mr. Ross?" said a monotone female voice on the other end, and I knew who it was before she could say her name. "This is Jeanne Nygard, Nancy Marino's sister. We met earlier today."

"Hi, Jeanne. Thanks for calling."

The line hissed with the sound of no one talking, though I could faintly hear her breathing. I shifted my weight, and my chair creaked in response. I cleared my throat and soon found myself talking, because I felt like someone ought to be.

"I'm sorry if I triggered a little bit of a spat at the viewing," I said. "I didn't mean to stir up ill will."

"My sister and I don't always get along," Jeanne said, and I fought the urge to reply, *No, really?*

"She's not a happy person," Jeanne continued. "She seeks fulfillment in worldly things, in money and power. They will never lead her to enlightenment."

Okay there, Siddhartha, I nearly replied. But again I resisted. And since I didn't want to enter into a conversation about Anne's self-actualization or lack thereof, I asked, "So what can I do for you, Jeanne?"

"My sister would be angry if she knew I was talking to you," Jeanne said, which didn't exactly answer my question. "She said I should keep my mouth shut. But I gave up trying to please my sister a long time ago. Do you have siblings, Mr. Ross?"

"An older brother and a younger sister."

"So you know what it's like."

"Family can be a joy and a pain," I confirmed.

The line hissed silence.

"I'm sorry, is there something I can help you with?" I said, trying to prod the conversation toward . . . wherever it needed to go. "The story about your sister is going in tomorrow's paper, so I'm on a bit of a deadline."

"I wanted to call you because your card says you're an 'investigative reporter.' Is that true?"

I put my hand over my mouth so I wouldn't say something like, *No, Jeanne, I'm actually a taxidermist with an active fantasy life.*

I gave myself half a beat, then removed my hand and said, "Yes, it's true."

More faint breathing was followed by "Don't you think it's odd, her being killed in a hit and run?"

"I'm not sure I would choose the word 'odd.' I would just say it was a terrible tragedy."

"The police said it was probably a drunk driver. What do you think about that?"

"That people shouldn't drink and drive?" I said, trying not to sound like a smartass.

"I'm told bars around here close at two. Would anyone still be drunk at six in the morning?"

I sighed. Where was she going with this? "People get drunk places other than bars, so there's—"

"And there were no skid marks," Jeanne interrupted, her voice managing to rise above the flatness of Parkinson's disease to gain some inflection. "The police said they didn't find any skid marks on the street. Don't you think the driver would have slammed the brakes after hitting something as large as a person?"

"Depends. The guy might have been so bombed he didn't even realize he hit someone. It happens."

Jeanne took a moment to consider this. She was nothing if not deliberate.

"Your card says you're an investigative reporter," she repeated. "Are you going to investigate the accident any further?"

"I'm not planning on it, no."

I tilted forward in my chair and rested my elbow on my desk. The bottom right corner of my computer read 5:17. Obits, which are not considered breaking news, have to be filed by six, no exception. I wanted to be considerate to Nancy's grieving sister, but I had to find a way to gracefully exit this conversation.

"I need to know if I can trust you, Mr. Ross," Jeanne said.

"And why is that?"

"Because I have something I think you should investigate," she said.

"Okay."

Another pause. Then:

"It wasn't an accident."

"You mean Nancy's death?"

"Yes. It wasn't an accident. I believe Nancy had reason to fear for her life. I believe someone killed her."

"What makes you think that?"

"She's my sister. Sometimes sisters just know things about each other."

"Yes, but do you have any proof?" I asked.

"No," she said. Then, after a pause, she added: "And yes."

"I'm listening."

"I was the last person to talk to my sister before she died. She called me at ten on Thursday night—that's one in the morning, her time. Mr. Ross, my sister went to bed at seven-thirty and woke up at three-thirty. She *never* had trouble sleeping like that."

"So what was bothering her?"

"She was having . . . problems at work."

"What kind of problems?"

The line went quiet again, causing me to press my ear to the phone. From somewhere in the background, I heard a door open. Jeanne drew in her breath sharply.

"Jeannie, whatchya doin'?" I could hear a male voice inquire.

And at that, Jeanne promptly hung up.

There had been a dent in his SUV, a roughly human-sized crease just to the right of the midpoint of the hood. That Friday morning, he spent an hour at one of those do-it-yourself car wash places making sure there were no traces of blood, skin, or muscle hanging stubbornly into one of the crevices.

Then he took the car to a local body shop, to a place that would do the work quickly and without comment. He explained he hit a deer while driving through South Mountain Reservation. The only question he received in reply was whether he had gotten some fresh venison steaks out of the deal. No, he said, the deer got away.

Then he started worrying about his own getaway. He knew all it would take was one citizen with quick eyes looking out the window at the wrong moment. For as fast as he was going, for as dark as it was, for as suddenly as it all happened, he still couldn't rule out the possibility he had been spotted.

So that afternoon, he set up down the street from his house, where he could see the traffic coming in and out. And he waited. He waited for an unmarked car with a grim-faced detective to roll past on the way to his house. He waited for someone from work to phone and say the cops were there and asking questions. He waited for his lawyer to call and say there was a warrant for his arrest.

But none of it happened.

He relaxed a little when the story appeared on the Eagle-Examiner's *Web site later in the day on Friday. The Bloomfield police were already begging the public for information, which was a good sign. It meant they had canvassed the neighborhood, come up empty, and were now tossing up one last Hail Mary before they completely forgot about this case and moved on to one they could actually solve.*

He relaxed more when the same small, empty story appeared in the paper Saturday morning. He had worried the death of an employee might cause the paper to react more strongly, to run larger stories that would keep the news in the public's eye—and therefore in the cops' eyes. But the paper had treated it with yawning indifference. Ultimately, she was just another papergirl, nothing special after all.

Two days later, he went to the wake. He went to keep up appearances, because people would expect to see him there. But he also wanted to monitor the conversations. If people were still buzzing about the accident, talking about it like it was a suspicious event, then he'd know he had to keep his guard up.

He was momentarily concerned when he became aware there was a reporter at the wake, interviewing seemingly everyone. But no. The reporter didn't suspect anything. And neither did any of the other attendees. They were trading in all the same empty aphorisms people always did when they were around death. It didn't seem to occur to anyone that this might have been anything other than a tragic, stupid accident, no different than if she died in a plane crash or a head-on collision or any of the other capricious ways a life can suddenly end. Soon her body would be in the ground and her death would be forgotten by all but a small handful of friends and family.

By Monday afternoon, he finally allowed himself to relax completely. By early Monday evening, he was celebrating with a stiff drink. He had gotten away with it.

CHAPTER 2

In the forty minutes I had to write the remaining three hundred words of my feature obit on Nancy, I mostly ignored the thought that I ought to be writing a story about a homicide instead.

I told myself that, in all likelihood, wacky old Jeanne was just letting her imagination get the best of her. Sure, Nancy was having "problems at work." News flash: we all have problems at work. The only people who don't are the unemployed.

If Nancy was still among the aspirating, Jeanne wouldn't have given that late-night phone call another thought. Death has this tendency to take ordinary words and mundane conversations and magnify them ten-thousandfold, because it makes them the *last* words and the *last* conversation. Really, how many times have you heard someone say, with utmost gravity, "That was the last thing she ever said to me."

So Jeanne was just taking those final utterances—which Nancy never intended to be profound—and blowing them out of proportion, letting them lead her mind to some frightening place. Grief does strange things to people's heads. And hippies are notorious for being predisposed toward conspiracy theories.

Then again, so are newspaper reporters. So, yes, I was a little curious what made Jeanne think Nancy's death was something other than what it seemed.

I studied that 510 number in my phone for a few seconds, debating whether I should call it. In my younger days, I was the kind of hard-charging reporter who probably would have. But now, in the dotage of my early thirties, I had finally gained the wisdom necessary to let it rest for a while. Wooing sources is not unlike Friday night at the bar. Sometimes you have to play a little hard to get.

So I mentally shelved Jeanne Nygard and concentrated on writing Nancy the send-off she deserved. Naturally, it ended up being a bit long, but I had a reputation for overwriting to uphold. With exactly three minutes to spare, I hit the button that sent it over to the copy desk, where my elegant prose would have to withstand the ritualistic assault known as "editing."

Then I stood and quickly surveyed the newsroom. Unlike most workplaces in America, newspapers have eschewed cubicles, partitions, walls, or any other attempts to divide space into discrete units. The *Eagle-Examiner* newsroom—sometimes called "the nest," because of the whole, you know, eagle thing—is just a great plane of desks. It's set up that way so we can yell at each other, unhindered by any barriers that might break up the sound.

Only a handful of editors get actual offices, and even those are walled-in glass for maximum transparency. I selected the fourth office from the left and ambled over to find the assistant managing editor for local news sitting in her chair, tucked in a convoluted ball, engrossed in her computer screen.

"Hey, I'm filed," I said.

"I'm overjoyed," Tina replied. And although she didn't appear to remove her attention from the screen long enough to look at me, she added, "It's a good thing you're wearing that suit."

"And why is that?"

She finally lifted her eyes.

"I got free tickets to the symphony tonight and you're my date."

"I am?"

"Yes. You may now express your pleasure."

"I'm . . . so pleased?" I said, raising my pitch at the end so she wouldn't miss the question mark.

"Next time, you will express more pleasure than that," she said, then unwrapped herself with a series of quick, sumptuous little stretches.

When Tina isn't doing yoga, she's jogging. She couples those twin obsessions with an aversion to carbohydrates. It's not a lifestyle I would recommend for everyone, but she seems to enjoy the discipline. It certainly had rather admirable effects on her physique, which she showed off with a wardrobe that tended toward the form-fitting, sleeveless, and short-hemmed side of the fashion spectrum. It led to complications in my life that didn't exist when my editor was a pear-shaped, middle-aged Italian guy.

"Who says I don't already have plans tonight?" I asked.

"What, like a hot date? Come on, I already heard you struck out with Sweet Thang."

"Sweet Thang" was the nickname bestowed on a former intern at the paper. She and I had engaged in a brief flirtation that never went anywhere, and it was now an entirely moot point—she had departed newspapering in favor of a job at a nonprofit in New York City, which was probably a better fit for her philanthropically oriented soul.

I held my chin high and said, "I'll have you know I happen to be highly sought after by a great variety of women."

"Who . . . the cougars from Montclair?"

"Well, them, yes," I said. "But I also happen to have caught the eye of a rather fetching younger woman."

Tina reached around to the back of her head and released a hair clasp, allowing a cascade of thick, brown curls to fall on her shoulders.

"One, you're lying," she said. "Two, do we really have to play this game?"

"What game?"

"The one where you pretend you actually *have* a love life."

She had me there. My last serious relationship was now several years in my rearview mirror, and it had ended rather poorly. The lady and I had been living together at my house in Nutley—the house also ended poorly, but that's another story—and we were entering that period in our late twenties when we spent a lot of time going to friends' weddings. I thought we were heading in the same direction, even thought I was happy about it. Then she explained to me I wasn't, then explicated all the reasons. The short version: she didn't like anything about me, after all. I'm not even sure I had digested the long version by the time she was off shacking up with someone new.

And now? I seemed to have become a rather committed bachelor. I had sporadic and nonrecurring dalliances with the opposite sex, though nothing that stuck. My life pretty much consisted of deadline (the job) and Deadline (the cat).

"Well, okay, fair point," I said. "I'm just not a big symphony guy."

"Come on, I'll wear a dress and pretend not to notice when you stare at my legs all night."

"Tempting offer."

"Perhaps you missed the point earlier," she said. "It's not an offer. It's an order."

• • •

As promised, Tina changed into a regulation-issue Little Black Dress, one that stopped several inches above the knee. She coupled it with a dash of perfume, a thin gold choker, and four-inch heels. And it was a good thing we were leaving the building because she was starting to set off all the smoke detectors.

We took her car—a Volvo being a better fit for the symphony than a used Malibu—and scooted across town to the New Jersey Performing Arts Center, a handsome brick edifice that really shines when lit up at night. Built in the late nineties, NJPAC was trumpeted as the catalyst that would bring nightlife roaring back to downtown Newark in a way not seen since the city's long-ago heyday.

And while those expectations had perhaps been unrealistic—they were building a concert hall, not a miracle machine—there was no disputing that the surrounding area, while still a bit grungy, was far better off for its presence. In a lot of ways, it was typical of the urban renewal process. People somehow thought it should happen instantly, simply because you poured money into a shiny new building. But the fact was, it had taken America many long decades of concerted effort to systematically destroy its cities. It would take at least that long to build them back up.

And sure enough, Newark was getting better. A new arena, the Prudential Center, had eventually joined NJPAC downtown. A cultural community was slowly taking hold. New restaurants were cropping up. So now at least when suburbanites announced they were going to Newark for the evening, their peers looked at them only slightly crookedly.

Tina and I arrived at seven-thirty for an eight o'clock show. The *Eagle-Examiner* was one of the event's sponsors, which meant we were invited to a special, preshow cocktail party. Once inside the building, we found the gathering simply by following the sound of overly boisterous chatter.

"Well, I don't know about you, but I've been sober long enough today," I announced as we entered.

"Yeah, why don't you do something about that for both of us," said Tina, who didn't seem to notice or care that she was being ogled by every man in the room with usable eyeballs.

I elbowed my way toward the bar, procured a Sam Adams for the gentleman and a white wine for the lady, and returned to find Tina alone but still not lacking for attention.

"Wow, that was a tough choice," I said. "They had both of my favorite beers up there."

"What are those?" Tina asked.

"Free and Free Light."

"You can dress him up, but you still can't take him anywhere," Tina said, shaking her head.

We scanned the crowd, which was decked out in its finery, as if the orchestra would refuse to play if a single person wore jeans. There was nothing like the symphony to bring out the heavy-duty pretense in people, and it was being layered thickly in every corner of the room: men acting more important than they really were, women masking insecurities in catty comments, wannabe aristocrats hoping not to be outed as members of the proletariat.

As a newspaper reporter, I'm required to move in all strata of society. I get to observe human behavior everywhere, from the meanest housing projects to the gilded symphony hall. And what always strikes me is that when you strip away the superficial differences in clothing, setting, and dialect, groups of people everywhere are more or less the same. We all have our pretenses. We all posture to a certain degree. But, ultimately, most of us are just trying to find a way to fit in.

Still, in any crowd, there's always one guy who—in a strictly symbolic sense—thinks his dick is bigger than everyone else's. And in this crowd, that man was the guy in the middle of the room with the pocket square: Gary A. Jackman.

"Speaking of people you can't take anywhere . . ." I said, pointing Tina's attention toward our publisher.

We studied him for a moment. Something was obviously off. His face was flushed, as if he had just been running. His hair, which I had never seen even slightly out of place, was mussed in a haphazard way. His tie was askew. His voice was too loud. His posture, much like the amber-colored beverage anchored in his right hand, was sloshing from side to side.

"Is he . . ." Tina started, giggled, then finished: "Oh my God, Jackass is drunk."

"Correction: Jackass is *hammered*," I said.

Tina tittered some more, putting her hand in front of her mouth to hide her giggling.

"That is just so regrettable," she said. "He's not a very subtle drunk, is he?"

I didn't find it quite as funny as Tina. For better or worse, this was the man charged with being the public face of the *Newark Eagle-Examiner.* And here he was, surrounded by some of the finer members of polite New Jersey society, totally inebriated. He wasn't just embarrassing himself. He was embarrassing all of us.

"About as subtle as a car alarm," I said. "It just makes me . . . Oh, would you look at that!"

At that moment, Jackman was in the midst of spilling his drink on the unsuspecting woman standing next to him. She was wearing a red cocktail dress, which immediately acquired a dark stain down the front. The woman was mortified, but it was about to get worse: Jackman removed his pocket square and started attempting to dry her off, essentially groping her breasts in the process. The woman twisted away to free herself from molestation, but he didn't seem to understand and clumsily pursued her for several steps until she finally got away.

The entire group around Jackman was politely pretending nothing had happened. For his part, Jackman was too oblivious to know how ridiculous he looked. In the meantime, a waiter had supplied him with a fresh drink. I noticed everyone was now giving him a wider berth.

"What a fool," I said.

"Oh, give Jackass a break," Tina said. "He's under a lot of pressure these days. He's just blowing off some steam."

I rolled my eyes. "Yeah, I guess ruining a perfectly good newspaper can be tough on a guy."

"Say what you want. I know he's not exactly beloved in the newsroom, but he's doing everything in his power to save our paper right now. It's got to be a strain."

"Yeah, why don't you run over and give him a backrub to relieve the tension?"

"I'm serious," Tina said. "Those negotiations can't be easy."

"What negotiations?"

Tina was about to answer when she was interrupted by a chiming sound being piped in from somewhere above us. The show was about to start.

"Drink up," she said. "Let's go find our seats."

I drained my beer as Tina finished her wine, then she grabbed my arm and escorted me into the concert hall, where she made for the front of the orchestra section.

"Not exactly the cheap seats, huh?" I said.

"My best reporter is worth every penny I paid for these," she replied.

"I thought you said they were free."

"Exactly."

"Ouch. Now you're hurting my feelings."

"If you're nice, I'll make it up to you later."

She gave me a flirty smile and a quick peck on the cheek. Tina had a long history of being all bark, no bite. So I mostly just dismissed the comment as the wine talking. Still, as we made our way to our seats, she pulled more of her body against my arm, bringing me in close enough that I fell under the spell of her perfume. Before I could exert any control over my brain, I began wondering what she might or might not be wearing under her dress and, more to the point, how I could get myself in a position to find out.

We had to break contact when we made it to our row, which snapped me out of it. I reminded myself Tina was, essentially, my boss. And as nice as it might be to temporarily ignore the prohibition on reporter-editor fraternization, we both knew it would make things too weird in the long run.

Or at least I think we did.

"Anyway, you were asking about the union negotiations," Tina said as we settled into our seats. "Have you really not heard about them?"

"Sorry, I don't sit in meetings all day where these sorts of things are discussed, remember? You'll have to enlighten me."

Tina stared straight ahead for a second, as if she needed to summon the strength to explain it all.

"Gosh, I don't even know where to start," she said. "You know we're losing money, right?"

"Buckets of it, yes."

"Well, one of the reasons is that a lot of the contracts we signed with our unions date back to better days," Tina said. "So, for example, even though our revenues have plummeted, the guys who drive our distribution trucks are still working under a collective bargaining agreement that guarantees them a three percent raise."

"No kidding. Damn, where do I sign up for *that*?"

Our newsroom wasn't unionized. Once upon a time, it hadn't seemed all that necessary. As reporters and editors, we fancied ourselves highly specialized, highly skilled, highly mobile workers who did not need group representation: if management didn't keep wages competitive, we would—in the fine tradition of LeBron James—take our talents elsewhere. We told ourselves unions were for auto workers and factory linemen, people who worried their jobs would be outsourced to Bangladesh, not for stars like us.

Then our business collapsed, taking those illusions with it. Suddenly we were no different from employees in any other contracting industry. And we had grown so comfortable during the good ol' days, we didn't have any kind of collective bargaining to give us some shred of leverage.

So I hadn't had a pay raise in six years. The pay *cuts* started three years ago. And really, I was just happy to have hung on to my job. Szanto and a lot of my other (now former) colleagues weren't as fortunate.

"Yeah, well, we'll go out of business if we can't renegotiate those deals, and Jackman obviously knows that better than anyone," Tina said. "And it's not just the drivers. It's the delivery people, the press operators, pretty much all the unions. None of them want to give in. But they're also realistic enough to know that if the paper goes under, they won't have jobs."

"And a three percent pay raise doesn't do much for you if you're no longer getting a paycheck in the first place," I said.

"Exactly," Tina said. "So it's like this big game of chicken. We tell them we need concessions. They say they'll go on strike if we keep pressing for them. We say we'll go out of business if we don't get them. And round and round it goes."

The audience was getting settled in, as were the musicians, who were fiddling with their instruments and readying themselves for the appearance of their concertmaster and conductor.

"I guess it just bothers me that all I ever hear about is how we need to cut costs. You never hear about new revenue initiatives," I said, as a drummer tested the timpani. "It's going to take a pretty bright person to figure out how a newspaper can monetize the Web, and I don't have a lot of confidence Jackass is the guy."

Just then, as if on cue, Jackman came stumbling down the aisle toward us. He was being loosely steered by an usher, who led him to a row two ahead of ours, where there was just one empty seat. Naturally, it was in the middle of the row. And Jackman, whose dexterity was several scotches behind him, began falling over people on his way toward it.

"Jackass is made of tougher stuff than you think," Tina said, keeping her voice lower now that he was in the vicinity. "I know he plays the part of the dandy. But at the paper he worked at in Michigan, he pretty much broke one of the unions he was negotiating with. He just refused to blink. Supposedly it got pretty nasty."

"Nasty . . . how?"

"Well, he bashed some guy's brains in, for one."

"What!"

"I've heard this story from a few people, so I'm pretty sure it's true. The union was trying to intimidate Jackass and sent some muscle to his country club, just to scare him, show him they meant business. The story I heard is that Jackman took a seven-iron and buried it in the guy's skull."

"Holy crap! Didn't he face assault charges or anything?"

"Apparently the guy who came at him was carrying a concealed gun. He hadn't pulled it, but it was on him, so Jackman was able to claim self-defense, and his golfing buddies backed him up. There were no charges."

I shook my head as I watched Jackman find his seat and sink heavily into it.

"All I'm saying is, don't underestimate Gary Jackman," Tina finished. "The man has brass balls."

I was about to comment on Jackman's balls when suddenly, from two rows ahead of us, there was a commotion. A woman let out a horrified shriek. Two men jumped up from their seats, as if there were debris falling on them from above. Another man stood up and was staring down at a whitish mess dripping from his tuxedo pants. It was difficult at first to discern what, exactly, had happened.

Then it all became clear: Gary A. Jackman, the *Newark Eagle-Examiner*'s dandy, brass-balled publisher, had thrown up on the guy next to him.

Once Jackman was escorted out and order was restored, the actual performance began and things got a lot less interesting. The orchestra was from somewhere in Europe—the Netherlands, perhaps, or maybe Belgium . . . I honestly don't know how anyone (besides the Dutch and the Belgians) keeps those two countries straight.

After the first piece, Tina was chirping about how some well-respected music magazine—not *Rolling Stone,* apparently—had named the orchestra the best in the world. They certainly passed the Carter Ross Classical Music Test: I drifted off during the first movement of the second piece. Call me boorish or uncultured, but I've always found falling asleep at the symphony to be one of life's greater pleasures. And if you look around at any of your finer concert halls, you'll see I'm not alone.

At intermission—or, as I delighted in calling it, "halftime"—I convinced Tina we had received enough refinement for one night and that, as newspaper people, it was time to get back in touch with our more populist roots. So we snuck out and made our way down the street to Kilkenny Alehouse, a comfortable establishment with a beautiful wooden bar, an array of flat-screen televisions, and a plethora of beer on tap. My kind of place.

Tina stuck with white wine as I bounced between ales. We put away several rounds, yammering about the miserable state of our chosen profession. But, at the same time, Tina and I had long since decided that if the ship was going to take us down, we might as well keep dancing on the decks until it slipped under the water.

Then we started trading war stories, remembering our brushes with disaster, recounting our triumphs. Even though the bar was all but empty on a Monday night, Tina and I had pulled our chairs together as if a crowd of people had forced us into close quarters. The contact was delicious. Tina's legs kept brushing against mine. Her hands took turns resting on various parts of my person. And her brown eyes, which had gone just slightly watery as a result of the wine, glowed with particular intensity.

I wasn't sure how many hours had passed by the time we teetered out. But a hot July day had given way to a pleasant, temperate summer evening. The air was so perfect—neither too hot nor too cold—it was almost like it didn't exist. And a nearly full moon hung above us, large and lanternlike.

As we made our way down the street, toward a car neither of us had any business driving, Tina had draped herself on my right side, with one arm wrapped tightly around mine and a hand on my chest.

The next thing I knew, we had veered into the darkness of a small alleyway and we were kissing. It was unclear whether I had pinned Tina up against the brick wall or she had pulled me there. Either way, I had one arm wrapped around her, cushioning her against the bricks. My other hand was running up and down her side, making the wonderful journey from her upper thigh, to the curve of her hip, to her rib cage and then back again.

Her hands, meanwhile, were planted on my ass, which she was using as a handle to draw me even closer to her.

I had no idea what was happening, nor did I care to stop and examine it. Our mouths just felt too good together. She started letting out these little moans and I heard myself doing the same. My hand had reached her firm, small breast, which I could easily feel through the thin fabric of her dress. Tina had been grinding our lower bodies into each other, with the expected results, then separated just enough to begin fumbling with my belt buckle.

Then suddenly she wasn't.

"Oh my God, this can't happen," she said, turning herself perpendicular to me and taking perhaps two steps away.

"Sure it can," I said, moving toward her and putting both arms around her shoulders. "Neither of us should be driving anyway. Let's just get a hotel room and enjoy this."

"No, I . . . That can't happen," she said, breaking out of my grasp.

"Why the hell not? We seem to do this all the time. Maybe that ought to tell us something."

She looked down at herself to make sure her dress was properly adjusted, then started walking purposefully—if drunkenly—back toward the NJPAC. The show had obviously been over for a while, but there were still a few police officers around directing what traffic still lingered in the area. I let her stalk away for a moment, then caught up to her as she crossed Broad Street.

"Hotel," I said.

"We can't. I'm your editor."

"Great. I'll find a new one."

"That's not the point," she said, walking faster.

"Then what is the point? We've been doing this dance for a while now. You keep telling me you want to have a baby with me. I keep telling you I don't just want to be a sperm donor daddy. Let's compromise: we'll have the baby and do all the other stuff that goes with it, too."

"You're just drunk and horny. You don't mean that—"

"I do, too," I cut in.

"And even if you did, I don't want that. I've told you that. I'm not the girl you or anyone else is falling in love with."

"And why not? I have feelings for you, and I know you have feelings for me. Why don't we give them a chance?"

She was making bad time in her high heels, and finally, in one remarkably fluid motion, she took them off and transferred them to her left hand. She broke into a fast jog. It was all I could do to catch up with her and gently grab hold of her arm.

"Tina," I demanded. "Why not?"

She wheeled around and, for a moment, I thought I was going to get eight inches worth of high heel embedded in my face. Instead, I heard:

"The first guy I fell in love with was a total jerk. The second guy I fell in love with was even more of a jerk. And then, just to confirm it wasn't a fluke, the third guy I fell in love with turned out to be a jerk, too. After a while, I started thinking maybe it wasn't them. Maybe it's me. Maybe I'm toxic. Maybe I just turn them into jerks."

"Now you're the one who's sounding drunk. Let's get a hotel room and—"

"I'm toxic. Don't you get that? You're a great guy, Carter. I want to have a baby with you more than anything, and I hope it's a boy who turns out to be just like you. But I don't want to fall in love with you, and I don't want you falling in love with me. I don't want to turn you into just another jerk."

With that, she ran to an idling taxi, leaving me standing on a sidewalk just outside NJPAC, a small cadre of bored cops looking at me like I was prize idiot for letting a beautiful woman get away.

I remained there for a little. Then I flagged down my own cab, giving the driver my address in Bloomfield. I arrived home to find Deadline in his usual spot (the exact, geometric middle of my bed) and shoved him aside so I could begin the predictable tossing and turning.

Strangely, though, it wasn't the thought in the front of my mind that kept me awake. It was the one wedged off to the side. Of all things, I kept playing over my conversation with Jeanne Nygard:

She was having problems at work . . . Nancy had reason to fear for her life . . . It wasn't an accident.

Could someone really have wanted to kill a waitress/delivery girl? Somewhere in the midst of my fitfulness, I resolved to indulge my curiosity by looking into it for a day, maybe two, if only so I could put it to rest.

The next morning, I saw that Jeanne Nygard had been thinking about me, too. When I retrieved my phone from the pants I had been wearing the night before, it told me I missed a call from her 510 area code number. She didn't leave a message, so

I decided—in keeping with my hard-to-get tactic—I wouldn't call her back.

Instead, I shook off a minor hangover, quickly ran through my shave-shower-breakfast routine, and caught a bus into downtown Newark. In addition to retrieving my car, I had to go into the newsroom and make an appearance in Tina's office. I was entered in an event at the Awkward Olympics: the About-last-night-athalon.

Tina was obviously gearing up for the competition as well because I was still on the bus when I received an e-mail from Thompson, Tina. The subject: "Good Morning." The body: "Come see me when you get in.—TT."

I considered dawdling but then decided to get it over with. As soon as I arrived at the nest, I forced myself toward her office.

"Hey," I said, tapping on the glass but not wanting to enter without being asked.

"Come on in," she said.

I complied. Figuring we had parted ways around midnight, and it was now ten A.M., it had given us both ten hours to sober up and start feeling abashed about the evening's events. Tina was wearing a subdued light blue blouse, a chagrined expression, and puffy dark smudges under her eyes. Plus, the woman who never drank coffee—she told me caffeine wasn't good for developing fetuses and she didn't want any coffee in her system when she conceived—had an extra large Dunkin' Donuts cup in front of her.

"I'm sorry I just ran off without thinking of how you were going to get home," she said. "That was awful of me. I—"

"It's okay, Tina. I took a cab, too."

"Still," she said. "I was halfway back to Hoboken by the time I realized what I did. I almost told the cab to turn around, but then I thought you'd probably rather walk than see more of me."

"It's okay, really."

Tina smiled weakly, then took a long pull on her coffee. I glanced at the side wall of her office, which contained a dry erase board filled with story ideas we would probably never get around to doing. Then I stared at the small stack of newspapers behind her. Tina, meanwhile, was straightening paper clips on her desk.

"So you, uh, made it home okay?" I said, just to say something. Obviously, she did make it home okay, because otherwise she wouldn't be sitting in her office, making pointless small talk while an eight-hundred-pound gorilla was doing jumping jacks in the corner.

"Yeah," she said. "You?"

"Yeah."

I coughed gently into my hand and stretched out my legs. Tina twisted to her right until two of her vertebrae made a popping sound, then twisted back to her left. The gorilla switched from jumping jacks to mountain climbers. I guess he was working on his core strength.

"See?" Tina said, finally breaking the silence. "This is why we can't sleep together."

"I meant what I said last night," I blurted. "I think we should give our relationship a chance."

"We're not having that conversation right now."

"Tina, that kiss—"

"We're definitely not having *that* conversation right now."

"Okay, when are we having that conversation?"

"I don't know. Maybe never."

"Tina . . ."

"No," she said sharply. "We're not doing this. *Please.*"

She punctuated the "please" with an emphatic jerk of the head, like she wanted to create a page break between that conversation and a new one.

"So how do we move forward from here?" I asked.

"The same way we did yesterday. I'm your editor. You're my reporter. That's the real reason I called you in here. I have a story I need you to work on."

"Oh," I said, a little taken aback. It was the last thing I expected to hear. Tina plowed forward:

"We're getting word there's a bear in Newark."

"A what?"

"A bear. As in the furry, forest-dwelling creature. Except this one isn't in a forest. It wandered into Newark overnight and is now rambling around Vailsburg."

"I actually have something I'm working on at the moment. Mind putting someone else on it?"

"Have you looked around the newsroom lately, Carter? I would put 'someone else' on it, but 'someone else' took a buyout three years ago, and 'the other guy' got laid off last year," she said, not bothering to hide her annoyance. "We need a writer on this thing. If we get the right art, this could lead the paper. You know how Brodie loves animal pictures."

I did. It had just been a long time since that particular partiality—which ran the gamut from bears to dogs to escaped pet alligators—had been my problem. Those kinds of stories were generally farmed out, as it were, to bureau reporters or interns, not members of the investigative team. And yeah, maybe it was a little bit of a diva move, trying to duck this assignment. But I didn't get into journalism so I could write searing exposés on zoo animals.

"What about Hays? Can't he do it?"

"Hays is the only full-time reporter we have covering every crime between here and Morristown. And besides, he'd end up writing this as straight news."

"What about Whitlow?"

"Whitlow is on vacation."

"What ab—"

"Stop it, Carter," she snapped. "You don't make the staffing decisions around here, and you certainly don't get to second-guess them. I'm your editor and I'm telling you this is your job. End of conversation."

"You've got to be kidding me. This is the stupidest—"

"End of conversation. Go."

Tina buried her attention in her computer screen, as if to emphasize our dialogue had, indeed, come to a close. I couldn't help but feel this was personal. I had crossed some kind of boundary with Tina last night, gotten a little too close to someone who preferred to maintain a rather generous buffer zone. Saddling me with a stupid daily story was her way of planting me firmly back on the other side of the line.

"You can take an intern with you if you want someone to help with the legwork," she said, without making eye contact. "I don't think Lunky has anything to do right now."

"Aww, come on—Lunky?"

"Yeah, you know, the big—"

"I know who he is. I've also heard he can't walk and chew gum at the same time."

"Probably true," Tina said. "So I suggest you don't share your Bubblicious with him."

If Tina thought I was going to waste my day dodging piles of bear scat in Newark, she had another think coming. Fortunately for me, I wasn't beneath using interns to do my work for me. And so, in giving me Lunky, she had unwittingly provided me an escape from this lowly task.

"Lunky" was the clever nickname the editors had given to

Kevin Lungford. He was one of the newest members of the ever-rotating battery of indentured servants who have become increasingly predominant in most newsrooms, mostly because of their remarkable ability to subsist on salaries that qualify as human rights violations.

Our editors thought of the interns as packages of ramen noodles: cheap, portable, and surprisingly filling, but not something you put a lot of care into making. I, on the other hand, tried to take an interest in their personal development. I guess it's because I don't have time to volunteer at animal shelters. I push for the humane treatment of interns instead.

Our interns come in all shapes, colors, and talent levels. Some of them are actually quite good, or at least have the potential to become good.

Others are like Lunky. In the few weeks he had been here, the only thing that had distinguished him at all was his size, which was, to be sure, quite impressive. He was about six foot five and had the kind of heft to his chest and shoulders that suggested his weight was somewhere in the neighborhood of 275. He had an abundance of bushy hair protruding out of a massive skull, with a sloped forehead a pronounced ridge above his brow, all of which made it tempting to surmise he had some Neanderthal DNA floating around in him. Combine his general, hulking appearance with the last name Lungford, and it didn't take long for his nickname to originate or stick.

The rumor was Lunky had played defensive end on his college football team—probably at one of those jock schools that had majors like "Personal Communications"—and that the sports department had hired him without much vetting, mostly with the intention of having him bat cleanup for their softball team.

But for reasons that were still unclear, sports promptly

shipped him over to news, where he wasn't considered much of a value-add, either. His byline had, so far, been suspiciously absent from the newspaper. From what I gathered, people tried not to talk to him. So he hung around the newsroom, all day and halfway into the night—long after most of the other interns had gone home—with apparently nothing to do.

As I approached him, sitting in a chair that looked too small for him, alone in the raft of desks where we stick the interns, I actually felt sorry for him. Poor Lunky, dim, dull, and friendless, was reading a thin paperback that more or less disappeared in his massive hands. I couldn't tell what was on the cover, but it was about the size and shape of a comic book.

"Hi, Kevin," I said. "I'm Carter Ross. We've been assigned to work on a story together."

He held up a finger, as if he didn't want to break his concentration from the exploits of the Green Lantern. I watched him read for a second—at least I couldn't see his lips moving—then he finally looked up.

"Sorry, I just got to a good part," he said, then turned his attention back to his reading. "Listen to this: 'The invariable mark of wisdom is to see the miraculous in the common. What is a day? What is a year? What is summer? What is woman? What is a child? What is sleep?' "

I felt my head cocking to one side.

"What . . . What are you reading?"

"Emerson."

"Excuse me?"

"Emerson."

"As in Ralph Waldo?"

"Of course," Lunky said. "I actually started out with Thoreau—he was going to be my 'summer beach read,' if you will. But I just wasn't getting the most out of my Thoreau because I wasn't as current as I wanted to be on my Emerson. Trying to understand Thoreau without being solid with Emerson would be like"—he paused, groping for the right analogy—"trying to make sense of a baby without having ever met its mother."

"Uhh," I said, mostly because it expressed the sum total of my knowledge about the subject. As an English major at Amherst, I should probably have been a little more conversant on all things transcendental. But I put in more hours at the student newspaper than I ever spent in the stacks. I usually just tried to fake my way through these kinds of discussions.

"This is some incredible stuff," he continued, fanning back pages in what I now recognized was no comic book. "Check this out, '. . . why should we grope among the dry bones of the past, or put the living generation into masquerade out of its faded wardrobe? The sun shines to-day also. There is more wool and flax in the fields.' "

Lunky leaned back, blown away. "*There is more wool and flax in the fields!* Can you imagine writing that in 1836? The *nerve* it took."

His eyes were fixed on some far-off point, his thoughts weighted with profundity.

"Kevin, I thought you . . . played football in college."

"Huh? Oh yeah."

"Where did you go to school again?"

"Princeton."

Oh. Yeah. A real football factory, that place.

"I finished my undergraduate degree in the spring," he said. "I'm actually starting my Ph.D. in English there in the fall. I'm planning to write my dissertation on Philip Roth. He grew up here in Newark, you know."

"Yeah, I, uh, knew that."

"I visited his boyhood home yesterday—81 Summit Avenue, as any good Roth fan knows. I spoke to a lady who lives there now. She was so nice. She let me look around the house and everything. I'm endeavoring to better understand his milieu: see the things he saw, learn about his influences, get some real-world Newark experience before cloistering myself in academia."

"Yeah, well, speaking of real-world Newark experience . . . We, uhh . . . We've been assigned to work on a story about a bear."

"Bears are highly symbolic in Eastern European literature," Lunky lectured.

"Yes, I'm sure they are. But right now there's a bear—not a figurative bear, an *actual* bear—wandering around Newark. Which is sort of unusual because Newark is, you know, kind of urban."

"Ah yes, indeed," Lunky said philosophically, considering this information. "I guess I can see how that would be newsworthy—in a certain voyeuristic sense."

I smiled with what I hoped was insincerity. "Yes, the philistines get quite a charge out of this sort of thing."

Missing my attempt at irony, he said, "Okay. So where is it?"

"Well, that's part of the challenge."

"I see. How do you suggest we go about finding it?"

"It's a bear in Newark, New Jersey," I said. "We head down South Orange Avenue and listen for the sound of screaming."

"Oh," he said, then after a thoughtful pause asked, "Where's South Orange Avenue?"

Realizing Lunky was going to need a little more mentoring than the average intern, I got him armed with a notepad and a pen—things he might have forgotten, if left to his own devices—and walked him out to the parking garage. We got into our respective cars, and I gave him instructions to stick to my bumper like the elbow patches to his professors' tweed jackets. We wound our way out of downtown toward the Vailsburg section of Newark and what I hoped was a rendezvous with something dark and furry.

Vailsburg is a small chunk of western Newark that, a century ago, was actually considered the countryside. These days, approximately 87 percent of its surface area is covered by man-made substances—primarily concrete, asphalt, and discarded chewing gum. It is not easily confused with grizzly country.

As I trolled down South Orange Avenue with my window down, I kept my eyes and ears peeled for something that would suggest the regular order of things was askew. Not long after passing over the Garden State Parkway, I found what I was looking for: a teenaged kid—who appeared to be a member of the Junior Gangbangers League—had shimmied up a light stanchion and was clinging to it like he planned to still be there the next time the census came around.

I hand-signaled to Lunky to pull over, and soon we were on foot, approaching the kid. He was whip thin with a big head of braids, and his clothing choices suggested he frequently consulted the league's fashion manual, "31 Ways to Dress Like a Blood," which advocated a lot of red accessorizing—red bandana, red shoes, red hat, and so on.

"Excuse me," I said, "you haven't seen a bear by any chance, have you?"

He looked at me like he couldn't understand how white people managed to do so well on the SAT.

"You think I'm up here 'cause I like *the view*?"

"Which way did it go?"

He pointed down a narrow side street with a shaky finger.

"The *one day* I come down here without my piece and look what happens," he said, shaking his head.

I looked in the direction he pointed. "I don't see anything. I'm guessing it's probably safe to come down now."

"Helllll no!"

I grinned. Here was a kid who probably stood out on this busy street corner all day long and half the night. In a state where there are roughly 150 pedestrian fatalities a year—and exactly zero people killed by bears—a fast-moving Chevy was, statistically speaking, a far greater threat to life and limb. But this youngster didn't look like he wanted to engage in a breakdown of the mortality and morbidity tables with me.

"Aw, come on, it's just a little bear," I teased.

"Yeah, but what if he likes dark meat? *You'd* be all right. But I'd be lunch."

"Skinny guy like you? You wouldn't be much more than an appetizer."

"Laugh it up, white boy. I ain't going nowhere."

I listened for sirens but didn't hear any. So I turned to Lunky and said, "This young man has seen the bear. Interview him. I'm going to go find the little critter."

I bid them good-bye and started jogging down the middle of the side street. A few houses in, I saw an old woman on her porch, looking wary, clutching a broom—as if that would give her all the defense she needed when the bear decided to climb her front steps. She was craning her head to the right.

"That way?" I asked.

"I think so. You with animal control?"

"No, ma'am, I'm with the newspaper."

"And you *chasin'* that thing? You some kinda crazy?"

I kept jogging, which I suppose answered her question.

About midway down the next block, I found the source of everyone's excitement on the left side of the street: a mass of black fur roughly the height of a Great Dane, with tulip-shaped ears and dirt-covered hindquarters.

In my entirely inexpert opinion, I judged this to be a young adult male *Ursus americanus,* maybe 150 or 200 pounds and well fed. He had knocked over a garbage can and was having a fine time pawing through its contents, his nose eagerly exploring the various odors. Banana peels. Potato chip bags. Chicken bones. It was bear manna.

Every once in a while, he'd take a nibble at something and I'd get a glimpse of his rather well-developed incisors. So I kept a safe distance, probably a hundred feet or so, though I wasn't particularly worried. This fella was so happily engaged in yesterday's dinner he was oblivious to my presence. Bears have good hearing and an excellent sense of smell but notoriously bad eyesight. As long as I kept quiet and stayed downwind, he'd never know I was there.

Then, to my horror, I felt a sneeze coming.

It started as a mere suggestion, a small tickle somewhere in my sinuses. I thought I could keep it at bay until the feeling passed, only it kept getting more insistent, like it wouldn't be denied. I held my finger under my nose to try and stop it, because isn't that what they always did in cartoons? But that only made it worse. So did a variety of other efforts: Lamaze-style breathing, biting my lower lip, making funny faces.

None of it worked. The more I fought it, the greater the urge to sneeze became. Plus, I could tell my resistance was only going to make the inevitable explosion that much more percussive. When I finally succumbed to the sneeze and let it loose, it sounded roughly like a shotgun.

The bear immediately looked up.

I froze.

He regarded me with interest, no longer engrossed by the balled-up diaper he had been sniffing. He held his nose in the air and then, in an ominous development, reared up on his hind legs, with his front paws dangling, like he was some kind of circus bear.

Except, of course, I don't think he was planning to dance around on a giant beach ball for my amusement. I'm no park ranger, so I didn't know what this signified. Mere curiosity? A display of aggression? A challenge to his hegemony over the Jones family garbage can?

I once read a wilderness safety pamphlet that said if you ever encountered a bear in the wild, you were supposed to be big and noisy—the idea being that bears are naturally shy and would easily be scared off. So I went up on my tiptoes, raised my arms in the air, and said something that sounded like, "Raaaarrrr!"

But I guess this bear was more of an extrovert than most, because he just tilted his head and sniffed at me some more, thoroughly unimpressed by my version of big and noisy. I let out my roar again, though perhaps it was less convincing this time, because it sounded more like, "Rarrr?"

The bear dropped back on all fours and I felt my shoulders relax.

Then he charged.

For a second or two, I just stood there as he lumbered toward me with a pigeon-toed gait, making a guttural noise that was somewhere between a woof and a bark. I seemed to recall the wilderness safety pamphlet counseled that you should never turn and run, that you should hold your ground. Running doesn't work, the pamphlet advised, because bears are faster than people. Plus, bears were big into what it called the "bluff charge," meaning he would pull up before he reached his target.

So this was a bluff. Just a big, nasty, snarling, drooling, growling, menacing, intimidating, teeth-baring . . . bluff.

As he narrowed the gap between us from a hundred to perhaps seventy feet, I told myself he would stop short any second, just put on his bear brakes and come to a skittering halt. This was all about the sound and nothing about the fury.

I just wished the sound—which was throaty and primal and utterly believable—wasn't making my sphincter tighten.

I couldn't really just stand there, could I? I began to question the wisdom of the pamphlet. What if it was misinformation put out by the bears themselves? Some kind of slick, bear propaganda? Shouldn't I, as a trained journalist, weigh the veracity of my source a little more carefully—and, more to the point, weigh the possibility the source might be hungry?

The rational part of my brain kept repeating those simple safety tips. *Don't run. Stay calm. Running only makes matters worse. This is a bluff.*

Then a different part of my brain, a more instinctive part, took over. *Hey, stupid,* it said. *This bear is about to bluff your head off. Run, stupid. Run!*

So I ran.

With my imaginary tail tucked between my legs and a frightened yell escaping my throat, I began desperately scrambling up the street, back in the direction of South Orange Avenue, hoping perhaps that when the bear saw I had dropped all claim to his garbage bag, he would return to his rotting vegetables in peace.

But no, as I allowed myself a quick peek back, I saw he was still after me. And he was getting closer. Apparently, that damn pamphlet was right about only one thing: bears *are* faster than humans.

I dashed through the first intersection without bothering to look for cars, gaining new appreciation for the wisdom of my young gangbanger friend. Fast-moving Chevys are a lot less scary, after all.

As I continued up the next block, I passed the old woman on the porch, still clutching her broom. She started yelling encouragement.

But not at me. At the bear.

"That's right! Get 'im!" she hollered. "He crazy. We got enough crazy 'round here already!"

"Aw, come on!" I protested, through ragged breath. "Can't you at least root for your own species?"

I looked back again and saw I was at least not losing any more ground. As long as I kept sprinting, I'd be fine. Too bad I'm not a world-class half-miler. As I got closer to South Orange Avenue, I was starting to feel the burn in my legs and lungs, and I didn't know how much longer I could keep it up. I rounded the corner, with the bear in hot pursuit, and saw my gangbanger buddy, still high up in the air.

"Run, white boy, run!" he crooned. "I'm the appetizer, but it looks like you the main course!"

I glanced up at him covetously and began calculating whether there was room for two up in that light stanchion. Then I spied a much better, much larger safe haven.

Lunky.

My hulking intern was just completing his interview, and I don't want to say I hid behind him, but, well, I hid behind him. Lunky seemed confused by what I was doing. I just grasped his back and positioned him so the full breadth of his body was between me and the bear.

This turned out to be the smartest thing I did all day. The bear took one look at Lunky and dug his paws into the asphalt, coming to a stop so quickly I thought he was going to roll over on himself. Even in Newark, the call of the wild has a pecking order. And Lunky was definitely the biggest bear on this block.

"Mister Ross," he said, "are you okay?"

I was. But only because the bear was now dashing toward the nearest tree, a stout-looking sycamore. He clambered up with surprising agility, flaking off large chunks of exfoliating bark as he went, only stopping when he got to a branch about fifteen feet in the air. Then he turned and warily eyed Lunky.

"I'm fine," I said, still panting.

I bent at the waist, put my hands on my knees, and spent a minute or so sucking whatever oxygen I could ply from the humid July air. Finally I straightened and said, "Well, that was a nice jog. I'm going to take my leave of you now. You got this situation under control?"

Lunky cocked his head to the side and considered me with the same kind of empty-headed curiosity as the bear. I filled in the blanks for him.

"You talk to some of the people who have seen the bear and get their reactions," I said. "Get some old people, some young people, some people in the middle. Then come back later this afternoon with a nice full notebook and we'll make a story out of it."

"But what about the bear?" he pleaded.

I glanced up at the tree and said, "Put him down as a no comment."

As I walked back to my car, I whipped out my phone and placed two calls. The first was to the photo desk, which would love a picture of a treed bear in Newark for A1. The second was to animal control, which would have the unenviable task of figuring out how to get the thing down.

Then, feeling reasonably confident in Lunky's ability to shag a few usable quotes, I set about my own work. That began with a call to Detective Owen Smiley of the Bloomfield Police Department. I'm always a bit leery about working on stories in the town where I live—what I write doesn't always win me popularity contests, especially with the authorities—but there are certain advantages, like when the third baseman on your rec league softball team is a cop.

As I merged with the northbound traffic on the Garden State Parkway, I called his cell phone and immediately heard, "Smiley here."

"Hey, Owen, it's your left fielder."

"Wuzzup, lady-killer!" he greeted me. Owen is married with either two or three or four small children—I'm not sure how many, as it seems like his wife is perpetually pregnant. He thinks that because I'm single, I must be hooking up all the time. I don't disabuse him of the notion, if only because he enjoys living vicariously through my bachelorhood.

"Not much," I said. "You playing this Thursday?"

"You bet."

"Good stuff," I said, then went for the subtle shift in topic. "Say, did you catch that hit and run by any chance?"

"Which one?"

"The one with Nancy Marino, the papergirl."

"Marino . . . Marino . . . You mean the one *last Friday*?" he said, like I was asking him to recall a cold case file from 1978.

"That's the one," I said.

"Yeah, I caught it. Why, you interested?"

"Maybe. Call it a case of morbid curiosity. Her family thinks there might be something more to it."

"Oh well . . ." he said, like he was struggling with how to say something. "We're off the record, right?"

"Yeah."

"Okay, off the record, you got to find a way to tell this family to move on," Owen said. "Hit and runs like this, if we don't get something right away—an eyewitness who snags a plate, a surveillance camera, a suspicious repair shop visit, something like that—we aren't going to get anything. Unless the guy who did it gets some kind of attack of conscience and turns himself in. Forget it. If the family wants us to, we'll put out a reward for information. I can get that approved pretty quickly."

"Reward, huh? Does that work?"

"People are motivated by all sorts of things."

"So you don't have any other leads?" I pressed him. "Our story mentioned an anonymous caller. Were you able to track that down?"

"I tried. Prepaid cell phone. Could be anyone."

"What about the tips line? Anything come in on that?"

"Nada."

"Huh," I said. "Well, thanks anyway."

"Sure. If you hear anything, let us know."

"Will do. See you Thursday," I said.

"Thursday," he confirmed, then ended the call.

I drove in silence the rest of the way to Ridge Avenue, just me and my Malibu. There are some reporters who don't feel compelled to visit the scene of a crime they're writing about, but I'm not one of those. Even if days have passed since the event in question—and the ambulances are gone, the blood is cleaned up, and the police tape has blown away—I still want to walk the ground where it happened and give my senses a chance to work for me.

Sometimes I jot down some notes. Sometimes not. Sometimes I want to just feel the place.

In this instance, the feeling I got from Ridge Avenue was one of utter ordinariness. It was an archetypal Bloomfield neighborhood, with that not-quite-city, not-quite-suburb feel. The single-family houses were small, neat, and cozily packed together. They were all at least fifty years old, built for the waves of workers who were fleeing the city two generations ago. I could hear the rush of the Parkway from a few streets away—the Jersey equivalent of a white noise machine—but it was otherwise quiet.

The street, while called an avenue, was really more like a lane. Cars parked on either side further constricted traffic flow. So while it was technically two-way, there was really only room for one car to pass.

I pulled my Malibu to the curb midway down the block, where Nancy had been hit, and looked for some small piece of evidence a life had ended there. But, of course, there was none. The residents of Ridge Avenue had been temporarily disrupted by the accident Friday morning, probably talked about it for the next day or two, but had otherwise gone on with their lives. The victim was no one they really knew.

Cutting the engine, I sat there for a moment, imagining I was a paperboy, quickly rolling out of my car to deliver that morning's edition. I opened the door like I was in a hurry, without really bothering to see if anyone was coming, as Nancy Marino had likely done. That's when I realized how little chance she had: the street was so narrow, I was in the middle of it by the time I stepped out of my car. Had some drunkard been barreling down the street behind her, he couldn't miss.

I was standing in the middle of the street, notepad in hand, scribbling down these and other thoughts when something caught my eye. It was just a brief fluttering in my peripheral vision, but there it was again: a curtain in the house to my right, being drawn slightly.

Someone was watching me.

This, of course, happens all the time to newspaper reporters. Stand out in the middle of the road with a notepad, writing furiously, and folks tend to want to know what you're up to. Are you an insurance adjuster? A tax assessor? Are you casing the neighborhood?

Sometimes people get edgy and call the cops, which always turns out to be a hassle. I try to defuse the situation before it gets to that point by simply introducing myself. Most people are actually relieved when they learn you're a newspaper reporter, because it means you're not there to jack up their taxes or steal their flat screen.

I walked up the short driveway of the house, which had dark red clapboard siding and a down-on-its-luck vibe about it. There were weeds where there had once been flower beds, unkempt shrubbery and high grass in the yard. Whoever lived there wasn't all that concerned about competing in the neighborhood garden competition. I bounded up a small set of concrete steps, then knocked on the door. I could hear movement inside that sounded like small children, but no one answered. I knocked again. More movement. Still no answer.

"Hello?" I said. "I don't want you to be concerned. I'm just a reporter with the *Eagle-Examiner.* I'm writing about the accident that happened here last week."

The house went quiet. The children had finally been shushed, and the adults were hoping I'd take the hint and go away. But there are times when common courtesy is something a newspaper reporter has to leave at home, so I knocked again.

"The woman who was killed delivered newspapers," I said. "I was wondering if you or anyone else on the street might have seen anything."

Finally, a reply: "*No habla.*"

• • •

I retreated from the front stoop, wondering if I had just found my anonymous caller. On that hunch—and because I like bothering him—I pulled out my phone and dialed my on-staff Spanish interpreter. Tommy Hernandez is second-generation Cuban-American, the son of immigrant parents who insisted the family speak Spanish at home. He's also our Newark City Hall beat writer and one of our finest young reporters. He has been with the *Eagle-Examiner* two years now, and while he was still technically an intern—our paper had long ago stopped granting full-time status to new employees on the fear that they might actually expect to be paid a living wage—his internship has been rather indefinitely extended.

Tommy has a keen eye for detail, a well-developed sense of story, and an easy way of chatting with people that made them want to talk back. If I felt like kidding myself, I could say I had been a role model for him and helped him develop these skills. But it's more accurate to say Tommy came out of the box with these talents and I had, on occasion, exploited them for my own purposes.

Sort of like I was doing right now. He picked up on the third ring.

"Are you at a clothing store?" he demanded. "If so, I want you to drop the plain blue shirt, put down the penny loafers, and step away from the cash register."

Tommy is as gay as taffeta and chintz, and he's got some rather pointed opinions on matters sartorial. He finds my WASPy fashion sensibilities a bit on the starchy side.

"But what am I supposed to wear to the lawn party in the Hamptons I'm going to this weekend?" I asked, playing along. "Veronica and Muffy are expecting me."

"Come out and salsa with me instead. It wouldn't hurt you to discover that people's hips can actually move while dancing."

"That's just a rumor being spread by you Puerto Ricans in an attempt to bring my people down," I said.

Tommy said something in Spanish that I assumed was an insult.

"Yeah, right back at you," I replied. "Anyway, as charming as it is to swap pleasantries, I was hoping you could help me out with a quick interview *en español, por favor*."

"I'll do it, on one condition."

"Shoot."

"Please don't *ever* try to speak Spanish around me again. It hurts my ears."

"Deal," I said, giving him the red house's address and extracting a promise that he'd hurry.

I spent the next twenty minutes pacing up and down Ridge Avenue, knocking on doors, getting the same load of nothing the police had gotten. The neighborhood busybody, a nice white-haired lady, assured me that she had talked to *everyone* on the block—just because she felt so bad about what happened to "that poor girl"—and neither she nor anyone else had seen anything.

"What about the people over there?" I asked, pointing to the red house.

"Oh well, they're Mexican," the woman said, as if being Mexican rendered them sightless.

"Yes, I know, but they still might have seen something. Maybe they're the ones who called it in."

The woman glanced furtively to the left and right.

"They're illegal aliens," she said, pronouncing each syllable very deliberately so it came out as "*eee*-lee-gal *ale*-eee-ans."

Which likely explained why they didn't want to open the door for a nicely dressed, officious-looking white man or give their names to the police. I thanked the woman and resumed my wait for Tommy, who eventually pulled up behind my car, parked, and got out.

Tommy is small, dark, and wiry. He works out, but only for tone, not for bulk. So I'm not sure he would have cracked 140 pounds on the scale. His clothes—which today consisted of black chinos, a snug-fitting gray shirt, and shoes that were undoubtedly the height of queer couture—are always quite dapper.

"Make it quick," he said. "I've got my own stories to work on, you know."

I gave him a rundown of what I knew, ending with my suspicion that someone in the "Mexican" family was the anonymous caller.

"That's the place," I said, pointing to the house. "You want me to come with you, or would I get in the way?"

"You might as well come. They probably just pretend not to speak English so they don't have to talk to dumb *americanos* like you."

"Can't blame them," I said, as I repeated my walk up the driveway and concrete steps toward the house, this time with Tommy at my side.

Our approach had been watched from the front window, from behind the slightly drawn shade.

Tommy knocked, coupling it with two sentences in Spanish. Whatever he said must have disarmed the inhabitants somewhat because they stopped their we're-not-home act. The door opened slightly, and a short, barrel-chested, dark-skinned man with wide eyes and distinct meso-American features appeared behind it. He was wearing a clean white T-shirt and khaki pants splattered with a dozen different paint colors.

Tommy immediately unleashed a burst of rapid-fire Spanish. The only words I understood were *"Newark Eagle-Examiner."* The man listened, then returned the volley with one of his own. They went back and forth a few more times, and I got the sense the exchange was becoming friendlier. Then suddenly Tommy was smiling and nodding, while gesturing at me and saying something through grinning teeth. I was the butt of some joke, which was fine by me. I was here as the straight man, after all.

"Do you have a press pass?" Tommy asked me.

"Yeah."

"Show it to him."

I dug my press pass out of my wallet and passed it through the crack. The man studied it for a moment, handed it back to me, and said, *"Un momento, por favor."*

The door closed.

"So what's the deal?" I asked in a not-quite-whisper.

"I think you've found your caller."

"Yeah, what'd he see?"

"Not sure yet. That's why we're doing the interview, remember?"

"Oh, right," I said, looking down to the street, at an elevation drop of perhaps five to ten feet. All of Ridge Avenue was on a gentle slant, and we were on the high side, which would have provided a good view of whatever happened below.

"And by the way, they're from El Salvador, not Mexico," Tommy added.

"They here legally?"

"Don't know, don't care. So don't ask."

"Yeah, but . . . it seems like the cops interviewed everyone on the block except them. And I'm sure the Bloomfield police have some Spanish-speaking officers. So they must have hid from the cops. And if they hid from the cops . . ."

Tommy fixed me with a flat stare.

"You figure that out all by yourself, did you?" he asked.

I cracked my best winning smile. "Young man, I'm a trained newspaper reporter. I'm capable of making logical deductions beyond the reach of most ordinary citizens."

"Yeah, well, in case I haven't made it clear: don't ask. Don't even ask anything that might sound like a roundabout way of getting at their status. We don't want them getting spooked."

"Got it."

"Oh," Tommy added. "And stick with 'mister' and 'missus.' El Salvadorans are very formal."

Before I could reply, the door opened wide.

"Please," the man said. "Come inside."

We entered to find a plump, round-faced woman sitting on a folding chair with a roughly three-year-old boy on her lap. An older sister who was perhaps five stood obediently beside her mother. The furnishings were sparse, just a couch, a folding table, and a few plastic chairs. Children's toys were scattered across the floor. The Virgin Mary smiled down at us beatifically from one of the walls. Next to Mary was a cross, with Jesus still hanging there—which, of course, meant this family was Catholic. We Protestants let poor ol' J.C. come down from there several hundred years ago.

"This is Mr. Felix Alfaro," Tommy said.

"Hi, there," I said, sticking out my hand toward the man. "Carter Ross."

"Hello, Señor Ross," Mr. Alfaro said, smiling widely as we shook. "I sorry, I no speak the English so good. But I learning."

"Your English is already better than my Spanish," I assured him. I nodded in the direction of the woman, who I assumed was Mrs. Alfaro. "Good afternoon, ma'am," I said.

"You like drink? Some coffee?" Mr. Alfaro asked.

I was drawing the breath to say "no, thank you," but as my

tongue reached toward the top of my palate to form the *n*, Tommy saved me from that faux pas.

"*Sí,*" he said. "Yes, please."

Tommy shot me a glance that might as well have been a jab in the ribs. Mrs. Alfaro had already risen, deposited her son in front of some trains, and headed toward the kitchen to get the coffee. I don't drink coffee—can't stand it, actually. But this was clearly an instance when I would pretend otherwise.

As the honored guests, we were invited to sit on the couch, which had a horrific plaid pattern that dated back to a more disco-intensive era. Mr. Alfaro sat in a folding chair across from us, and soon words I could not understand began pouring out of his mouth. Tommy listened, grinning at first, then getting serious. He added a word here or there, asked a question or two, then laughed twice at the end.

"He says he hopes we like the coffee," Tommy said. "Mr. Alfaro's family grew coffee for generations. He was raised on a small coffee plantation. Then his family got chased off in the civil war. But he says coffee beans are still in his blood. He hopes to be able to save enough money to someday return his family to its land."

Mr. Alfaro listened to Tommy's translation, pleased with what he heard.

"And he says most American coffees are blends that ought to be lining garbage cans," Tommy said.

Mr. Alfaro nodded enthusiastically at this sentiment.

"Maxwell House," he said, making a face like he had just swallowed a heaping mouthful of sidewalk grit. "Baaah."

We all laughed heartily at this—everything is funnier when you're trying to be polite—and Mrs. Alfaro returned with four mugs, serving me first. I took a small sip, feeling like I was being watched the entire time. I acted like I was considering the brew for a moment, as if my taste buds were searching for the gentle hint of peach, the almond subtext, the caramel finish.

"Excellent," I said,

Mr. Alfaro smiled proudly. I had just complimented ten generations of Alfaros in one word. Mrs. Alfaro seemed pleased. Tommy looked relieved. The Virgin Mary smiled some more. And I tried not to grimace when the bitter, acidic taste flooded into my mouth.

As everyone else helped themselves to their mugs—milk, no sugar, for all—Tommy began chattering, and I could tell we were getting down to business. Mr. Alfaro listened gravely, his eyebrows moving closer together as he concentrated. Still, I surmised he liked what he was hearing. When they completed their negotiations, I looked at Tommy expectantly.

"He said he feels a . . . a"—Tommy groped for the right word—"a duty to do the right thing and tell the truth about what they saw. But he said he doesn't trust the police. It sounds like no one really trusts the police down in El Salvador. So I assured him we would not go to the police."

"Right," I said to Mr. Alfaro. "No police."

He nodded. Tommy continued:

"He said we can quote them, because I explained they wouldn't be helping at all if we can't quote them. But we can't use their name. We can identify them as 'a resident who asked not to be named.' "

"That sounds fair," I said to Tommy, then gave Mr. Alfaro some good eye contact as I said, "No names."

Mr. Alfaro immediately turned to Mrs. Alfaro, speaking in a low and rapid voice. It became obvious Mrs. Alfaro was the witness to the accident. She just wasn't going to say anything without her husband's permission. He finished by barking a quick order at the children who, led by the older girl, scampered upstairs.

Mrs. Alfaro waited for the children to clear out, then began telling her story. I removed my notepad from my pocket and Tommy—speaking in the first person, as if he were Mrs. Alfaro—provided the translation in short bursts:

"I'm an early riser . . . I often wake up before the children . . . I like to look out the window and watch the sun rise . . . It reminds me of home . . . One morning, I saw a black . . . a black, sorry . . ."

Tommy interrupted Mrs. Alfaro with a question, which generated a response, then another question, then another response. There were some hand gestures, and I heard automobile brands being discussed.

"It was a black SUV, but she doesn't know what kind," Tommy said. "She said she first saw it on Tuesday morning. It was large and black and had a big, shiny grille plate, which sounds like just about every SUV out there to me. But I think that's going to be as good as she can do."

"Okay," I said.

Tommy returned to being the voice of Mrs. Alfaro: "I had never seen the truck before Tuesday, and then it appeared several mornings in a row last week . . . It would park and wait, park and wait . . . Always following the girl who delivers the papers . . . Then it would drive away when she drove away . . . I kept thinking, 'What is he doing here? What does he want?' . . ."

I could imagine that a black SUV casing the neighborhood in the early morning would be of some concern to her—whether she was here legally or not.

"Then Friday morning last week, I saw the SUV parked up the street again . . . And the woman who delivers the papers was there, in front of our house . . . Then the car was driving . . . It was driving . . . no, it was speeding actually, very fast down the road, very fast . . ."

Mrs. Alfaro's voice was accelerating as well, her face flushing from the excitement. Tommy was concentrating on her mouth, almost like he was lip-reading rather than translating.

"I saw the woman getting out of her car . . . The black SUV was going very fast . . . I could hear the roar of the engine, but the woman didn't seem to be paying attention . . . The driver, it was like he was pointing, no, aiming toward the woman . . . I could see the SUV was going to hit her and I wanted to scream, but I knew she couldn't hear me . . . And then the car hit her . . ."

Mrs. Alfaro was shaking her head, then she finished:

"It hit her very hard, without stopping . . . Her body flew into the air, almost like it weighed nothing . . . And then the car ran over her . . . I screamed to Felix, 'She got hit by the car! She got hit by the car!' . . . And then Felix called the police . . . We were hoping that if an ambulance got there fast enough, they could save her . . . But she was dead . . . She was dead . . . It was terrible . . . May God rest her soul."

Everyone thought they knew him, or at least thought they could guess his story. They looked at him, looked at what he had achieved, saw how important he was, and they assumed he had been born to it.

He never bothered to correct them. Some men who grow up poor are proud of where they came from, constantly bragging about their lowly beginnings and how bad they had it, because they feel it makes their glorious climb to the top all the more impressive. He wasn't one of those. To him, that was the whole point of outgrowing humble beginnings—it meant you never had to revisit them.

But the truth, which few people knew, was that he started at a low station. His family was filled with totally unremarkable types, the kind of people who were born, lived, and died without the wider world ever being aware of them. They were cogs in the machine, nothing more.

His father was an off-the-docks immigrant who worked for a grocery distributor, loading and unloading produce trucks—tomatoes, oranges, whatever was in season. The man never complained about it, until one day he just wore out. He was a few months short of retirement when he suffered a massive heart attack, right there on the loading dock. The forklift he was driving at the time slammed into a wall, spilling a couple skids of lettuce. One of his coworkers said it looked like he was dead before the lettuce even hit the ground. Within a half hour, the mess was cleaned up and someone else was driving the forklift.

His mother, who had come with his father from the old country, was a homemaker, living in the same fifth-floor walk-up apartment from the day she got married until the day she died. Her husband wouldn't let her take a job, and in some ways it didn't matter: she never wanted one anyway. She was content to raise her children, spend time with the other women in the neighborhood, play her bingo, and smoke her Pall Malls. After her husband passed, she got by on their meager savings and a small Social Security check. Then lung cancer got her. She didn't so much wear out as she wasted away.

He never talked about his parents. He loved his mother right to the end but, in truth, was always ashamed of his father, with his lack of ambition. His father had never pushed him, never demanded he do anything in school besides show up, never insisted he better himself in any way.

No, all his motivation was strictly internal. He pushed himself, mostly so he didn't end up like his old man. He worked and schemed and angled. He took shortcuts now and then, cheated when he had to. He did anything he could to move up life's ladder. And he'd do anything he could to stay there.

He wasn't going to be another cog.

CHAPTER 3

Having finished with her story, Mrs. Alfaro brought the back of her hand to both sides of her face, wiping away the small tear tracks that had formed. Tommy gave her a moment to compose herself, partly out of kindness and partly because he needed to catch his breath. Mr. Alfaro stood rigidly by his wife, a hand on her shoulder in a small-but-important gesture of consolation. I paged back in my notebook, filling in key words while they were still fresh in my mind. My self-invented shorthand hadn't quite been able to keep up, and I wanted to get as much of it as I could.

Of course, the details only mattered so much. The main point was that it was now undeniable: Nancy Marino's death was no accident.

Unwitting hit-and-run drivers don't stalk their prey for days on end, wait patiently down the block and then accelerate when someone gets out of her car. This was a homicide, as cold and simple as if someone had brought a gun to her ear and pulled the trigger. This weapon just happened to take unleaded gasoline.

Eventually, Tommy started asking Mrs. Alfaro some follow-up questions, providing me the short version of the answers. No, she never got much of a look at the driver. No, she didn't catch the license plate. No, she couldn't say for sure the make and model of the SUV. No, she had nothing else to add to her story. She had told us everything she remembered.

When we were done, I thanked the Alfaros for their hospitality and for their willingness to talk, reiterating my promise not to go to the police or print their names in the newspaper. Soon I was following Tommy back down the front steps to our cars. It was getting toward the middle part of a hot summer afternoon, but it felt like Antarctica in my guts.

"So what now?" Tommy asked as we reached the sidewalk.

"I don't know exactly. At risk of stating the obvious, someone killed this woman and the Bloomfield police sure won't be able to figure out who or why."

"And you can?"

"Well, I certainly have to try. This may sound strange, but I feel like I owe it to Nancy. She was one of the good guys. And who am I as a newspaper reporter if I don't look out for the good guys? Besides, I've gotten to like her. And whether I knew her or not, she was a colleague."

"It would be a hell of a good story, too," Tommy added.

"Well, yeah, and there's that," I conceded.

"Can I do anything?"

"No, no. I got this," I said, knowing it would only make Tommy more eager to help. "You have your own reporting to do."

"Yeah, but it's just some stupid city council stuff. I can make time for something like this."

"I don't know," I said, setting the hook a little more. "If Tina found out . . ."

"Tina doesn't need to know anything about this," he assured me. "Come on. You know you can't do this all by yourself."

"Well, okay," I said, smiling inwardly as I thought about what task my newly recruited assistant should tackle.

Nancy's sister obviously knew something. But after a quick glance at my phone—no missed calls from the 510 area code—I decided I could continue playing it cool and let her come to me.

In the meantime, I had to learn more about Nancy Marino. Because while I could fake my way through her obituary, that didn't mean I really knew her. Sure, she seemed like a reliable newspaper deliverer and could apparently keep a lunch order straight. But it was also entirely possible Nancy Marino was a hopelessly addicted gambler, a hundred grand in debt to a bookie who finally lost his patience.

Was it likely? No. But put in enough years as a journalist, exploring life on the margins of society, and you start to realize how cunning humankind can be. The gentle Little League coach turns out to be a vicious mobster. The humble parish priest is an embezzler. The prim kindergarten teacher has a raunchy Internet site. It happens.

I'm not saying I assume the worst about people. But it also doesn't make sense to assume the best. That's what being a reporter teaches you: don't assume.

"Hello?" Tommy said, pantomiming like he was knocking on a door. "Anyone home?"

"Sorry. How about you head back to the office and see what kind of paper you can find on Nancy Marino," I said. "Pull her mortgage, search the court filings, look for liens against her house—the usual."

"Okay."

"Oh, and if you bump into Tina, remember: you didn't see me, you aren't working on this, you don't even know me. I'm supposed to be off chasing a bear in Newark."

"Oh," he said, as if this made perfect sense. "So what's your plan while I'm doing all the boring work?"

"I'm heading to the restaurant where Nancy worked and

asking some questions. Call me if you learn anything interesting."

"You, too," he replied and we parted ways.

I climbed into the Malibu, the interior of which was only slightly cooler than the surface of the sun. The Malibu's air-conditioning may once have worked well, but that was many years and several owners ago. So it was still sputtering lukewarm air when I reached the end of my two-mile-long journey to the State Street Grill.

The restaurant just in from the corner of Bloomfield Avenue and State Street used to be one of those prototypically scuzzy/wonderful Jersey diners, named after its original proprietor—Willy? Henry? Something ending in a *y*—until the current owners decided the best way to renovate was with a wrecking ball. They tore down the old diner and in its place raised the State Street Grill, an attractive stucco-faced building with Art Deco metal awnings and a hip, retro look.

I had been to the new place a couple of times since moving to Bloomfield two years earlier. So I knew that while it looked the part of the modern eatery—and had gone somewhat upscale as compared to its greasy spoon days—it was still a Jersey diner in its soul, with a twenty-four-page menu, neon signage, and a keepin'-it-real vibe. Visit during a busy lunchtime, and you'll see an America the Founding Fathers could only have barely imagined, with people of every different hue and ancestry dining next to each other. Old Italian men. Young Hispanic families. Blacks and whites and ambiguously browns.

I entered and was immediately greeted by the hostess, whom I recognized from my previous visits. I'm also pretty sure I had seen her at Nancy's wake the day before. She was in her late twenties and attractive in that way that hostesses tend to be, with dark hair, green eyes, and nice curves, all put together in a neat, medium-sized package. Her nose announced her Greek heritage, but her accent was all Jersey. So when she asked me if I wanted to sit at the "bar," it came out sounding like "baw."

"Actually, I'm not here to eat today," I said. "My name is Carter Ross. I'm a reporter with the *Eagle-Examiner*, and I'm working on a story about Nancy Marino."

As soon as I said the name, the hostess went stiff, as if she was reliving the shock of Nancy's death. She took a moment to collect herself, then motioned to one of her colleagues.

"Jen, could you cover for me? I need to talk to this reporter," she said, then turned in my direction. "Come with me, please."

I hurried to keep up as the hostess walked briskly toward the side of the restaurant, through the kitchen and toward a wooden door, which she held open for me. We walked into a small office decorated with sports memorabilia, pictures of the Parthenon, and posters of women eating gyros.

"I'm sorry, this is still so weird, you know?" she said, closing the door behind me. "My family owns this diner, and Nancy had been working here since I was a kid. She was like my older sister. I can't believe what happened."

We made eye contact and I found myself momentarily swept into a sea of green iris. In that instant, something clicked between us. And I'm pretty sure it wasn't merely my overly active male imagination, because she was gazing back at me with unusual intensity. Call it pheromones or whatever, but sometimes you just know you like someone, and it comes with more than an inkling that the sentiment is returned. There were future possibilities between us, even if the current circumstances would not allow it.

After a pause—more pleasant than awkward—she recovered and walked over to the desk, where she began picking through a pile of invoices, order forms, and time schedules.

"Did you see the story about her in the paper today? We got it here somewhere," she said.

"Yeah, I saw it." Then added with perhaps false modesty: "I wrote it."

"You did?"

I had long since reconciled myself to the extent to which readers ignored bylines. Even people who knew me—and knew where I worked—would come up to me and start telling me about my own stories. No one ever bothered to read the first three words: "By Carter Ross."

She found my story, which had been tucked in the upper-right-hand corner of that day's obituary page. I walked toward her and pointed to my name at the top of it.

"That's me," I said.

She studied it, seemingly in some kind of trance.

"So that's my name. What's yours?" I prompted.

"I'm so sorry, I'm just out of it today. I'm Nicola Papadopolous. But call me Nikki."

"Hi, Nikki, nice to meet you. Do you mind if we sit down and talk?"

"Yeah, sorry, yeah, have a seat," she said, sitting behind the desk while pointing to the chair on the other side. "This whole thing is just, like, wow. It's thrown me for a loop, you know?"

"I understand," I assured her.

She nodded, and I had a brief debate with myself about how much to tell my new friend, Nikki. Past mistakes had taught me to be cautious with information when you don't know quite who you're dealing with. Even people who seem benign—or at least neutral—could turn out to be malevolent. And you never want to give those malevolent types too much notice about what you're up to.

But in this case my gut—and maybe those aforementioned pheromones—told me Nikki was safe. At a certain point, a reporter has to decide to trust someone. It might as well be the pretty Greek girl.

"So, Nikki, this is going to be hard for you to hear, but I think Nancy was murdered."

The look on Nikki's face confirmed her guilelessness. She was registering the kind of authentic surprise—slack jaw, stunned mouth, astonished eyes—no one would have been able to fake.

"That hit and run was no accident," I continued. "I talked to a reliable eyewitness who told me a black SUV appeared to have been following Nancy for several days. It was that same black SUV that ran her over."

Nikki was shaking her head.

"But I don't . . . Nancy was like . . . She was like the nicest person in the world. Who would do that to her?"

"That's what I'm trying to figure out. Did she mention being worried about anything? Fearful of anyone? Was she having any problems that she told you about?"

"No," Nikki said, thought about it for a moment, then added more definitively, "I mean no."

"What about boyfriends? Was she having trouble with any guys?"

"No. Definitely not. She didn't . . . I'm not saying she was a dyke or anything. But I've known Nancy—sorry, I knew Nancy—for, like, twenty years, and she never had a serious boyfriend. She never even talked about guys like that. And that's kind of different, you know? I mean, say a good-looking guy like you walks into the restaurant."

I tried desperately not to blush as Nikki continued:

"All the other waitresses would be like, 'Oh, check out Mr. Handsome at Table 17 . . . I got myself a stud,' stuff like that. It's just what we do to pass time, you know?"

"Sure," I said, as if I had long experience in waitress small talk.

"Well, Nancy wasn't like that. It's like she didn't notice or didn't care. I mean, she was nice to good-looking guys, but she was nice to ugly old ladies, too, you know?"

"Got it. Okay, not boyfriends. So what about after work? What did she do after work?"

"Nancy? My God, I think all she *did* was work. She got up to deliver papers at, like . . . I don't know, but it was early. Then she was here doing the seven-to-three shift. She did the busy part of breakfast *and* lunch. Then she did, I don't know, church stuff. Family stuff. Sometimes she would go to meetings at night for her other job."

"What kind of meetings?"

"Oh, I don't know. I guess they were like union meetings or something. It was all about the newspaper."

It made sense a union shop steward would have some nighttime obligations, probably ones that stretched close to midnight. Nancy must have been an expert in sleep deprivation.

"Did you guys ever hang out after work or anything?" I asked.

"No. I mean, we were close, but Nancy kind of—"

Nikki was interrupted by the office door swinging open with enough force that the resulting wind scattered some of the papers on the desk. A round-faced, balding Greek man stormed in behind it, his fists clenching tightly enough that I could see his forearm muscles tensing where his rolled-up shirtsleeves cut off.

And he looked angry enough to shoot fire out his nose.

• • •

In my (albeit limited) experience with Greek women, they are masters at manipulating the tempers of their menfolk, stoking them or soothing them as the situation warrants. And that is what Nikki immediately, and perhaps instinctively, began doing with her father: turning on the charm in an effort to pacify him.

"Babba!" she said brightly, putting the accent on the second "ba." She gave him the kind of heart-melting smile that Daddy's Little Girls have been using to wrap their fathers around their fingers for eons.

But Babba wasn't buying it this time.

"What's going on here?" he asked angrily, in a thick Greek accent slanted with the sound of accusation. He shot glances back and forth between us. I knew I had seen the man before, though I was having a tough time placing where.

Then a small piece of his comb-over broke loose from his bald head and started dancing in the air, and it hit me: he was the lopsided unicorn I had seen chatting up Jackman at Nancy's wake, the one Jackman had told to get lost. And now he was looking like he wanted to gore me with his hair horn.

"Babba, this is Carter Ross from the—"

I was standing up to introduce myself, but Nikki's father was having none of it.

"I don't want you talking to no newspaper reporter," he interrupted. Nikki had never gotten the chance to say I was a reporter. Somehow, Babba already knew.

"But, Babba, we were—"

"It's time for you to go," he said, turning toward me, his fists still balled. I could tell he was considering whether to grab me by the arm and physically throw me out of his restaurant. I'm not the most menacing-looking guy in the world, but I'm just broad-chested enough that most guys think twice about trying to manhandle me. Besides, I was a head taller and at least twenty years younger than Babba. It wouldn't have been a fair fight.

"Leave, now," he said. "Or I call the police and tell them you trespass."

"Sir, I'm not trespassing. I'm conducting an—"

"It's time for you to go," he said again, finding new inspiration for his anger.

As best I could tell, my options were as follows: confront the fuming Greek man and attempt to calm him down, an act that would likely only enrage him further; or make like Alexander the Great and get the heck out of Macedonia, which is the course I chose.

"Nikki, it sounds like I'm not welcome here," I said, deliberately addressing her rather than Babba. "I think I'll leave now."

"I'll see you out," Nikki said.

Her father started to protest, but Nikki fixed him with a glare every bit as effective as if she had dropped a piano on his head.

"He is a *customer,*" she spat. "We are *not* rude to our customers."

The old man could hardly object to that logic. And it was clear an unspoken deal had been struck. She would acquiesce to his demand that the newspaper reporter depart, but he would allow her to coordinate my retreat in a way that preserved her dignity. As if to underscore the fact that she had resumed control of the situation, she slipped her arm in mine—clearly an unpopular move with Babba—and escorted me out of the office and back through the kitchen without so much as another glance at her father.

As we entered the dining area, my mind was already

churning. Whenever a reporter gets asked to leave someone's home, business, school, or place of worship—and I've been bounced out of all four on many occasions—it inevitably raises the question: What do they have to hide?

"What was that about?" I asked, when we were finally out of range.

"Oh, that's just my dad being my dad," she said, shaking her head like she'd seen it a thousand times before. "He's old-school."

"But why wouldn't he want you talking to a reporter? We're not discussing state secrets here."

"When he doesn't understand a situation, that's how he reacts. I'll explain it to him once he calms down, and he'll be fine."

I thought back to the debate I had earlier with myself, the one involving how much to tell Nikki. I had decided she was harmless, and I hoped I was still correct in that judgment. As for her father? There was no telling about him. Jeanne Nygard had said Nancy was having "problems at work." It was dawning on me she never specified which workplace.

Was it possible this man had something to do with Nancy's death? Was that why he didn't want me snooping around? It wouldn't immediately make sense that a diner owner would want to get rid of one of his most popular waitresses, but there was no telling what might have been happening beneath the metal awnings at the State Street Grill.

As we reached the front of the restaurant, where Nikki's pal Jen was still faithfully staffing the hostesses' station, I attempted to do some quick damage control.

"Do me a favor and don't tell him what I told you about Nancy," I said, then added quickly, "I don't want to upset him further."

"Oh, no problem," she said, holding the front door open for me. "Believe me, I stopped telling my dad everything about my life a long time ago. I mean, I'm twenty-eight years old and he still thinks I'm a virgin."

I brushed past her just as she said the word "virgin," and felt a charge rush through me. I walked out into a small anteroom, then to another door, which I held open for her.

"Anyway, sorry he freaked out," she continued as we reached the front porch.

"No problem."

I suddenly felt like I was being watched. And, sure enough, Babba was monitoring our interaction from inside the restaurant, his arms crossed, his unicorn horn at the ready. Nikki either didn't notice or didn't care.

"And thanks for writing that nice article about Nancy. That was really sweet."

"I was happy to do it."

Uncrossing his arms, Babba started making for the door. He had apparently lost his patience for our little farewell scene. This time Nikki noticed.

"You're a nice guy," she said quickly, and before I knew what was happening, she stood on her tiptoes, gripped my shoulders to propel herself upward, and kissed me on the cheek. It was one of those innocent-but-not-so-innocent kisses, the kind that involved a little too much body contact to be considered sisterly.

Without another word, she disappeared back into the diner, leaving me standing on the patio, just slightly dazed.

By the time I came to my senses, my empty brain had stopped calling the shots and my empty stomach had taken over. It guided me a block and a half down Bloomfield Avenue and into a hole-in-the-wall pizzeria, where I found myself ordering two slices and a Coke Zero.

This, of course, is one of the great pleasures of living in New Jersey, as compared to other parts of this vast, pizza-starved nation of ours. Walk into nearly any pizza place in my part of the state, and you will find better pie than you will in, say, the whole of the American South. People offer all kinds of theories for why this is so, citing the quality of the water (something in the aquifer that supposedly makes for good dough), the pollution (something in the air makes the sauce taste better), or the density of Italian-Americans (something about having a last name ending in a vowel just brings it all together).

I think it's a kind of natural selection. A pizzeria in, say, rural Virginia merely has to outperform Pizza Hut, which is about as tough as besting a week-old baby at arm wrestling. A pizzeria in New Jersey has to take on some of the toughest competitors in the pizza world. Offering anything less than outstanding pie puts them out of business within six months. Only the strong survive.

I was into my second slice when my phone rang. I recognized both the number and the inflectionless voice on the other end:

"Mr. Ross, this is Jeanne Nygard, Nancy Marino's sister. We met yesterday at the funeral home," she said, as if she feared I suffered advanced amnesia.

"Of course, Jeanne, I remember."

She wasted little time getting to the point: "Have you decided whether you're going to investigate my sister's murder?"

The word choice—"murder"—was an obvious attempt to be provocative. And even though I agreed with it, I didn't let on. I wanted to see if she could convince me.

"What makes you think it's a murder?" I asked.

I watched a bead of sweat drip down the side of my soda cup as I waited for her answer.

"Mr. Ross, I need to kn

"You've mentioned that

you're of the mind not to trust

to get past it. It will probably wo

a little trust and see how it works

"But I need to know whose si

People are always asking me v

to say, but in a world overstuffed with

person essayists, the true reporter—o

willing to let go of his ideological slant

shed closer to extinction every day.

"Ms. Nygard, I don't even know what the sides are yet," I said. "All I can tell you is that I have no agenda other than to find the truth. And if it turns out there are two sides to that truth—or three sides, or more—I will treat them equally."

My soda cup had created a small circle of moisture on the pizzeria's Formica tabletop. This time, as I waited for her reply, I lifted the cup and started making patterns with the rings.

"What if the truth . . . doesn't reflect well on *your* newspaper?" she said at last.

"Then my newspaper ought to be the first to report it. I don't know what experiences you've had with other newspapers or other newspaper reporters. But at my place, we insist on transparency from the people we cover, so we hold ourselves to an even higher standard of self-disclosure."

"So you're not . . . *with* management?"

"I'm neither with nor against it. Why don't you tell me what's going on and we'll worry about who looks bad later."

This seemed to satisfy her.

"I don't like having long conversations on the phone," she said. "Can we meet in person?"

"Sure. Where can I find you?"

La Quinta," she said, as if there were only ... d it turned its nose up at shoddier establish- ... e Ritz-Carlton.

...hich La Quinta?"

"Hang on," she said, lowering the phone for a moment, then returning to rattle off an address on Route 3 in Clifton.

"I can be there in fifteen minutes," I said. "I'll meet you in the lobby?"

"That would be fine," she said, and we hung up.

I finished my pizza in two large bites, then drank what remained of the Coke Zero on my way out, tossing it in the trash by the door. Before long, the Malibu was pointed north on the Garden State Parkway, then east on Route 3, a thoroughly obsolete divided highway with short exit ramps and nonexistent merge lanes. To drive it is to invite early death to do the merengue with you. Yet, judging from the traffic that was always on it, roughly four billion people somehow survive the dance every day.

The La Quinta was just beyond a Shell station and a merging panel truck that nearly relieved my Malibu of its bumper. The hotel, which shared a parking lot with an egregious theme restaurant, looked like it had gotten a much-needed face-lift sometime in its recent past, and I'm sure somewhere there was a manager using the phrase "newly refurbished" whenever he got the chance.

Jeanne was waiting for me in the glass-enclosed lobby when I arrived, bobbing and weaving involuntarily as she sat in an armchair just inside the entrance. She was wearing a slightly different floral-print dress than the day before, but she still had on the same photochromic glasses. Her brown-and-gray hair, now out of the braid, fell halfway down her back. Any hairdresser would have told her it was far too brittle to be worn so long, but I could guess Jeanne Nygard probably wasn't one to solicit opinions from the local salon.

"My husband doesn't want me talking to you," she began as I sat down, not bothering with preamble. "He thinks the stress is bad for my disease. I have Parkinson's."

She stopped dramatically, like I ought to have some kind of reaction—pity, dread, horror—or like I should be shocked and appalled by her condition.

"My sister doesn't want me talking to you, either," she resumed. "She thinks I'm just imagining everything. She . . . she doesn't believe in negative feelings, so she thinks no one should be allowed to have them."

Jeanne threw another pause into the conversation, so I filled it with an "uh-huh" because it felt polite.

"But I feel it's important for me to talk to you, for *Nancy*'s sake," she said.

Jeanne had obviously rehearsed this little speech and needed me to believe she was speaking to me at great personal peril and only out of considerable devotion to her late sister. The amateur psychologist in me recognized she was most likely a narcissist who was creating a self-serving fantasy in which she, Jeanne Nygard, was the heroine. The reality was that she was probably just using me to get back at her older sister, the disapproving lawyer.

But hey, if it got me the story, I was happy to play along.

"Yes," I said. "For Nancy's sake."

With that matter settled, Jeanne paused—there were a lot of those in a conversation with Jeanne—and drew strength for what she needed to say next.

"I believe my sister was murdered because of her views," she said.

Murdered for her views. Jeanne was turning her sister into

the classic hippie martyr. *She was making the fascists in the military-industrial complex nervous, man, they hadda get rid of her!* And I might have dismissed it as ridiculous paranoia—too much peyote on the commune back in the day—except, of course, I knew someone *did* want to get rid of her, based on what Mrs. Alfaro had seen.

"What views?" I pressed.

"They were . . . unpopular . . . with certain people," Jeanne said, and I didn't know if she was being evasive on purpose or if this was just how she talked.

"Yes, but what views? Are we talking political views? I'm confused."

"I suppose you could say they were political."

"So . . . Nancy was killed by . . . Republicans?" I asked. Didn't hippies blame Republicans for everything?

"No, no, not like that," Jeanne said. "I mentioned to you she called me the night before she was killed."

"Right. You said she was having problems at work?"

"Well, not at work, exactly."

"Then where, exactly?" I asked, feeling my patience easing away. Talking with Jeanne was like being trapped in a car that only made left turns.

"You know my sister was very involved with her union, yes? She was a shop steward."

"With the IFIW. Right."

"You know it was in the midst of negotiations with . . . *your* newspaper."

"I'm aware, yes," I said, even though I hadn't known about any of that until Tina had brought it up the night before. She never mentioned the IFIW specifically, but it stood to reason that if all the paper's other unions were being asked to renegotiate their deals, the IFIW would as well.

"So my sister called me that night. Thursday night."

"Right. The night before she was killed."

"I think maybe there had been a meeting that night, a union meeting."

"You *think* there was a meeting, or there *was* a meeting?"

She stopped to consider that question. I watched as a vacationing family—ugly dad, pretty mom, two elementary-school-aged kids who looked like they could end up going either way—checked in for a night of thrills and excitement at the Clifton La Quinta.

"My sister didn't say, specifically," Jeanne said, eventually. "But I . . . It stands to reason that she got home late from the meeting and then had trouble getting to sleep."

"Okay," I said, feeling like I was in another one of those left turns. "So what was keeping her awake?"

"She was very worried about the negotiations with the paper. She made it sound like they were going poorly. Nancy was . . . quite steadfast in her position."

"And what position was that?"

"That they shouldn't settle."

"Settle what?"

"I'm not sure," Jeanne said. "But she said the union couldn't afford to give in, because if they did, management would assume it could do anything it wanted to them. She felt if the union wavered at all, it would lose any leverage it had in the future."

"Okay. So who would have disagreed with her?"

"Maybe people in the union. Or maybe management. She could be very strident, in her own way. And as a shop steward, she would have been seen as . . . a leader. People were drawn to my sister. She was very smart."

There was another pause, so I filled it with: "I know she was."

"So if my sister felt one way, a lot of other people would have felt the same way. She would have convinced them of it. And if the way she felt was . . . counter to what other people felt . . ."

She let that statement linger for a second.

"She might have been seen as . . . getting in the way of what they wanted," Jeanne finished.

"So," I said, trying to straighten out all the left turns. "What you're suggesting is that perhaps Nancy was seen as an impediment in the negotiations, so someone wanted to get rid of her?"

"It seems very stark when you put it that way . . ."

"So how would you put it?"

She ducked and swayed, the unheard music—her constant soundtrack—quickening by a beat or two. Then she made the effort to hold herself very still.

"My husband was out here on business not long before Nancy was killed," Jeanne said. "He saw her at my mother's house. And you know what she told him? She said, 'If these talks get any rougher, we're going to have to start bringing guns to the table.' "

As if summoned, we were soon being approached by a man who was apparently Jeanne's husband, a large, pale doughy guy I recognized as one of the men who helped break up the funeral home fight between Jeanne and Anne. He wore square glasses that reminded me a bit of safety goggles, a bushy mustache, and a checkered button-down short-sleeve shirt that stretched tightly over a belly that had gone paunchy years ago. I had him pegged as an engineer before he even opened his mouth.

"Hon, dontchya thinkya had enough now?" he said with an accent that came from either Wisconsin or Minnesota.

"Mr. Ross, this is my husband, Jerry Nygard," Jeanne said.

"Nice to meet you," I said, but didn't stand up or acknowledge him further, because he wasn't even looking at me.

"Hon, why dontchya come up to the room and have a Coke with me."

"I don't *want* a Coke," she said testily.

"Jeannie . . ." he said, raising his voice as much as a guy from Minnesota ever would in front of a stranger like me. She ignored him.

"So, Mr. Ross, do you intend to investigate my sister's death?"

She was a little too eager. And in keeping with my hard-to-get strategy, I wanted her to stay that way. Besides, she didn't seem like the type who needed to be told there really *were* monsters under the bed. She imagined enough of them on her own. So I summoned my best nonchalant air.

"I'll look into it a little," I said. "I don't want to make any promises. I can't charge around tossing out allegations on a hunch."

"Yes, of course. I can understand your need to be . . . prudent."

"Yes, prudent," I said, even though I was the kind of reporter who usually stayed at least ten highway exits away from prudent.

"Thank you," she said, and started to rise slowly from her seat.

"I'll see you at the funeral on Thursday," I said.

She nodded slightly. She really did look quite spent. Maybe Jerry was right. Maybe she did need a Coke.

Still, she sloughed off any aid from her husband as she made her way toward the elevator. Jerry waited until she had rounded the corner, then suddenly the dorky, mild-mannered husband was standing over me, in an apparent attempt to be intimidating.

"Back off," he said sharply. "This family has been through enough."

"Mr. Nygard, I—"

"Just back off," he hissed again. "This doesn't concern you."

I was so surprised by the sudden show of aggression from the mild-mannered engineer, I just sat there as he stalked off. There was suddenly yet another man who didn't like the newspaper reporter.

As much as I might have enjoyed spending more time in the La Quinta's lobby—it was newly refurbished, after all—I returned to my car and nudged it back onto Route 3, putting myself on a course to visit IFIW—Local 117 Executive Director Jim McNabb in his downtown Newark office.

Once I had gotten myself up to the speed of the surrounding traffic—only slightly slower than the Daytona 500 and just as likely to use a turn signal—I put in a call to Buster Hays, the one reporter at the paper who would likely know about the *Eagle-Examiner*'s ongoing labor negotiations with Local 117.

Buster was the kind of reporter who knew stuff about things like that, in the way that he knew stuff about more or less everything. He had been at our paper so long, I'm pretty sure he started when Johannes Gutenberg was the press foreman. Through his many, many, many years of employment, Buster had developed the kind of institutional knowledge that made him a go-to guy on all happenings at the nest.

I certainly don't like him, inasmuch as I consider him an archaic, cantankerous, condescending pain in the ass. He also doesn't like me, inasmuch as he considers me a snot-nosed, spoiled, overeducated pretty boy. Other than that, we get along great.

Still, I think if you strapped us down, dosed us with all the surplus truth serum left over from every Cold War–era spy movie ever made, and asked us what we thought about the other, we might—after several hours of interrogation, water-boarding, and forced viewings of *America's Next Top Model*—actually admit to having respect for each other.

He answered the phone by saying "Hays."

"Buster, it's Carter."

"What do you want?" he said. Buster grew up in da Bronx—and had the accent and attitude to prove it—so it came out sounding like "whaddauwant?"

"How much do you know about our negotiations with the International Federation of Information Workers?"

"Why do you care, Ivy?"

I had repeatedly tried to convince Hays that my alma mater, Amherst, was not part of the Ivy League. Those efforts had been a failure.

"Let's just call it idle curiosity for right now," I said.

"Fine. How much does an Ivy boy like you know about labor law?"

"Umm . . ."

"Right, okay, here goes," he said, inhaling. Hays pretended otherwise, but nothing gave him more pleasure than lecturing me on one of the (many) areas where his knowledge outstripped my own. "There's a key distinction in labor law between independent contractors and employees. If you're an independent contractor, an employer doesn't have to do squat for you, because you don't technically work for them. So there's no benefits, no worker's comp, no paid holidays, no stuff like that. And independent contractors can't unionize. That's why a lot of newspapers use independent contractors to deliver their papers. It saves a lot of headaches."

"Okay," I said, merging onto Route 21 and following the highway as it snaked alongside the Passaic River.

"Now, a long time ago, there were two papers in this town, and the *Eagle-Examiner* was locked in a battle for survival with the *Newark Express*," Hays continued. "We were using independent contractors to deliver our paper, which meant the contractors could actually deliver both papers—the *Eagle-Examiner* and the *Express*. Well, the *Eagle-Examiner* had gained a small advantage in market share and was really trying to turn the screws on the *Express*, so it told its carriers, 'We don't want you doing both, you've got to pick,' thinking that most carriers would pick the *Eagle-Examiner*. And they did. Hang on, I got another call."

Hays put me on hold. I had accelerated to sixty-five miles an hour, which meant I was puttering in the right lane, being passed as if I were motionless by traffic doing eighty.

"Where was I?" Hays asked.

"The independent contractors were only delivering the *Eagle-Examiner*," I prompted him.

"Oh, right. Well, it all seemed to be working out pretty well for the *Eagle-Examiner*, but then the IRS stepped in and said, 'Wait a second, if you've told them what they can and can't deliver, they aren't independent contractors anymore. They're employees and you've got to start treating them that way.' Well, once they became employees, they were no dummies. They organized lickety-split. You still with me?"

"Got it. So they formed a union," I said, having hit the Newark border and the first of a series of traffic lights.

"Yep, and the *Eagle-Examiner* hasn't been happy about it since, because once a union gets formed in this state, good luck getting rid of it," Hays said. "It's become a real problem for Mother Eagle, a huge problem. When you look at some of our other unions, we've got maybe fifty guys running the presses that print this paper, and maybe a hundred guys driving the trucks that distribute this paper. I'm making these numbers up, but you get the point—if push really came to shove and they went on strike, we could replace them.

"But the carriers? Fuhgeddaboutit. You're talking about more than a thousand people—men and women, boys and girls—all over the state delivering this paper. Each of them knows their route and their neighborhood like the back of their hand. And if they decided to go on strike, it would literally shut the paper down because there's no way we could find enough people and be able to train them to do those routes. The subscribers would be getting their morning papers at five in the afternoon."

"So they got us by the short hairs," I said.

"Yeah, and they know it. In the early days, they threatened to strike pretty much every time their contract came up. So sometime in the late nineties, the publisher got tired of dealing with it. He signed them to a twenty-year contract."

"*Twenty years?* I've never heard of that. I thought most collective bargaining agreements were three or, at most, five years."

"Yeah, no one else had heard of anything like that, either. But, remember, this was the late nineties. Owning a big paper like the *Eagle-Examiner* was still a license to print money. So the publisher figured it was no big thing giving a few paperboys a sweetheart deal. But as the years went on and those guaranteed raises kept kicking in, suddenly we were grossly overpaying our carriers. At other places, carriers are independent contractors, driving their own cars, paying for their own gas, not making much more than minimum wage. Here they're employees making I-don't-know-how-much, plus we reimburse them for miles. It's killing us, and every publisher since has wanted to strangle the publisher who signed that deal. It's gotten to be a real albatross."

"So what's going on with the negotiations right now?"

"Well, they don't exactly give me a seat at the table, Ivy," Buster said. "But from what I'm told, they're stuck."

"Stuck?"

"Yeah, stuck. Normally management coerces concessions by promising not to furlough people or lay them off. But you can't furlough people you need 365 days a year, and you can't lay them off, either. So management has been going with their hat in their hand, saying they won't survive unless they get givebacks on their contract—basically, pay cuts instead of pay raises. And the union has been telling 'em where to shove it."

"You heard anything about a shop steward at Local 117 being particularly difficult?" I asked. "Maybe she was getting in the way of progress at the table?"

"Oh, I don't get that deep with it. But if you really want to know, call Jim McNabb. He's always looking to get cuddly with another *Eagle-Examiner* reporter."

"That's actually where I'm heading right now," I said.

"Good," Hays said. "He'll try to spin you a little. But his information is reliable. Once you take off the spin, what you're left with is usually pretty good."

The headquarters of the International Federation of Information Workers–Local 117 were housed at 744 Broad Street, also known as the National Newark Building. Of the two skyscrapers that dominate the Newark skyline—744 Broad and the Prudential Building—744 is the one that *doesn't* look like an architecturally bereft marshmallow.

I found parking in a garage and made my way inside. Having seen on the directory that the IFIW's offices were located on the twentieth floor, I announced myself at security in the lobby. By the time I made the elevator ride up and walked through a pair of smoked-glass doors with the IFIW logo stenciled on them, Jim McNabb was waiting to greet me at the front desk. He was wearing tan slacks, a golf shirt, and a wide smile.

"Carter Ross!" He practically shouted, like I was there to shower him with winning lottery tickets.

"Hiya, Jim," I said, knowing his overly chummy welcome was merely the first part of his act. I actually have no problem with sources who try to spin me. For a guy like McNabb, it's part of the job—just like it's my job to have done enough homework to see through it.

"Let's go back to my office," he said, then turned to the receptionist and added, "Janet, hold my calls. Mr. Ross is a very important reporter for the *Eagle-Examiner* and I don't want any interruptions."

He led Mr. Ross the Very Important Reporter through a maze of cubicles and hallways. I could only imagine that the IFIW's hundred thousand members generated no small amount of paperwork, all of which funneled to these desks. McNabb was overweight, but he was more thick than fat. So he was still able to walk fast, and at times all I could see was his bushy silver head peeking above one of the partition walls.

"We call this the nerve center," Jim said. "We're protecting the rights of hardworking New Jerseyans all across the state, right here in this office."

I said nothing. Replying would only encourage him, and I'd end up wasting a half hour listening to an IFIW infomercial.

"Like this beautiful young lady right here," he said, stopping suddenly at one of the cubicles. It was occupied by a mousy, low-rent, bleached blonde whose eye makeup might charitably be described as whorish. She was in her early forties, desperately trying to cling to her youth, and looked up at Jim like she was grateful to be in his presence.

"Do you know what this beautiful young lady does for a living?" Jim continued. "She makes sure the dirtbag insurance companies aren't denying coverage to our workers. Isn't that a wonderful thing? You should write a story about her someday."

"Hi, Big Jimmy," she said in a singsongy voice.

"Around here they call me 'Big Jimmy,'" he said, in case I had missed the point that he was a man of great status. "Keep up the good work, honey."

With that, we were moving again. "Love that kid. We got her, what, six months ago?" he said, like she was a pound puppy who had eagerly taken to paper training. "She works her sweet little ass off."

Not wanting to engage in a discussion about the flavor or size of her ass, I kept my mouth shut until we entered Big Jimmy's lair, a corner office with ten-cent furnishings but a million-dollar view of Manhattan.

"Nice," I said.

"Not bad, huh?" he said, following my line of sight across the Hudson River, and we both got lost in the view for a second.

"Anyhow, take a seat," he said, and I did, selecting a wire-framed plastic chair, the only kind he had. Jim settled into his one piece of nice furniture, a high-backed, ergonomically correct, cushy executive chair. "What can I do for the *Eagle-Examiner* today?" he asked.

"This is going to sound a little strange, but I'm hoping you could tell me a little more about your negotiations with my newspaper."

I thought this might trip him up a bit, but he rolled with it, the friendly smile still in place.

"And why would I do that? You some kind of spy for Gary Jackman or something?"

"Gary Jackman," I said, not bothering to hide the grinding

of my teeth, "has, in the last two years, been responsible for both cutting my salary and giving me involuntary furlough, which is the same thing as a pay cut. Plus, he's making me pony up a lot more for my health care, which eats further into my take-home pay. I'm not exactly in the mood to do him any favors."

"Yeah, but he still signs your paycheck. I've been doing this union thing for a long time. People have all sorts of strange loyalty to the guy that signs their paycheck."

"Okay, so let's do it like this: don't tell me anything that Gary Jackman doesn't already know. Does that work for you?"

He rubbed one meat-hook hand over his face for a second, then said, "Yeah, okay. I can play that game. What do you want to know?"

"Well, I'm told the negotiations are stuck. Where, specifically, are they stuck?"

"It's pretty simple. They're telling us we're way overpaid and that they need an across-the-board fifty percent pay cut *and* a freeze on future wage increases. And we're telling them to go pound sand."

"Fifty percent? Wow. That's a lot."

"Tell me about it. They keep saying our pay scale needs to be put back in line with the rest of the industry. But that's ridiculous. These people rely on that money to pay their bills. They shouldn't be punished just because deliverers at other papers don't have as good a deal."

"Has there been any give-and-take at the table?"

"Not really," Jim said, grinning sardonically. "They're making threats, and they think it gives them leverage on us, but they got nothing. And even if you *are* a spy from Jackman, you can tell him I said that. Find your savings somewhere else. Don't balance your books on the backs of the paperboys. They're not exactly making six figures here."

"You think your membership knows my paper is just rattling the saber?"

Jim leaned back in his throne, his eyes scanning south to the Verrazano Narrows. "Some of 'em do," he said.

"But some of them need convincing?"

"They always need convincing."

"Was Nancy Marino one of the chief convincers?"

The breezy smile Big Jimmy had been wearing since I first came through those smoked-glass doors vanished off his face.

"What's she got to do with it?" he asked, like hearing the name brought up the hurt of her death all over.

"Well, she was your shop steward there."

"Yeah, so?"

"So what was her role in the negotiations?"

"What does it matter now?"

I shrugged, like I didn't know, like I was trying to play it off as no big deal either way. "Not sure. I'm just asking."

"I thought you said there was no smoke with the whole Nancy thing," he said, turning his head to the side but keeping two leery eyes locked on me. In typical McNabb fashion, he was on the lookout for a handle on this situation so he could turn it for his own use.

"Well, there might be a bit of smoke," I admitted. "Or maybe it's not really smoke, just steam. Definitely not convinced there's fire. It's still sort of hard to tell."

"Well, what are we talking about here? You're beating around the bush."

"I am, I know, and I apologize for that," I said, feeling myself shift on the hard plastic chair. Time to lay at least a few of my cards on the table: "I'm told Nancy had taken a very hard line that the union shouldn't give in. I'm wondering if someone—maybe within management—might have taken exception to her line and decided to . . ."

I let that thought linger out there. Jim knew what I was saying without me filling in the blank.

"I thought it was an accident," he said.

"It was. But maybe it was more the intentional kind of hit and run than the accidental kind?"

"Who's saying that? The police saying that?" Jim asked, his dirt-groping antennae clearly extended as far as they went. But I wasn't sure I wanted to give Big Jimmy too much information to work with just yet.

"Not the police. The police are done with the whole thing. Let's just call it a reporter's hunch at this point."

"So you got a hunch maybe someone killed Nancy because of something to do with the negotiations?" he said, not bothering to hide his disbelief. "Boy, I don't know."

"I don't know, either. At this point, I'm really just indulging my curiosity," I said, deliberately soft-selling it. "For all I know, it could have been something at her other job, at the diner. Or, heck, it could be some boyfriend no one knows about. I'm really not sure, to be honest."

He stopped himself like something had just occurred to him. I shrugged again, trying to stay as noncommittal as possible.

"Let me think about it," he said. "Make some calls."

We small-talked a bit more but were clearly done with the meaningful part of our exchange. I was soon being escorted out of the IFIW nerve center. And really, it was just as well. It was nearing five o'clock. I retrieved my car from the garage and made the short drive across town, cognizant of the need to get back to the nest and babysit Lunky. I hoped he had managed to get a few decent quotes from bear-scared Newarkers over the last few hours.

My main challenge upon entering the newsroom was to elude Tina until after I had found Lunky. Otherwise, she'd inevitably start asking me questions about my afternoon with Smokey the Bear, and I couldn't just make up my reply. She'd get suspicious when my answers didn't end up remotely matching the story I handed in.

So I crept along the outer wall of the newsroom, a long distance from the glass office where Tina would be lurking, and worked my way toward the intern pod by way of the men's bathroom. I needed the pit stop anyway, with the Coke Zero I drank several hours earlier now pressing quite urgently against my bladder. I was just taking aim at a particular piece of white porcelain when, from the next urinal over, I heard Tommy's voice.

"Doing some of your best work?" he said, having sidled up next to me to take care of his own business.

"Excuse me, haven't you ever heard of the Men's Bathroom Code?" I said, keeping my gaze straight ahead—another part of the code. "Don't you know there's a prohibition against talking to a guy when his Richard is out?"

"Is that true? In that case, I've had whole relationships where neither one of us should ever have said a word."

I sighed and shook my head.

"For that matter, what about the entire institution of anonymous gay sex?" Tommy continued. "That's not my scene or anything, but those poor guys would be out of business if they couldn't talk to each other in men's rooms."

"Yes, but think of how much better off Larry Craig would be right now if he had just stuck to the code," I said as I stowed my equipment.

"Oh, that old queen? Someone would have outed him eventually."

We flushed simultaneously—sort of like synchronized swimming, only in reverse—then I went to the other side of the bathroom to wash my hands.

"So how are things coming?" I asked. "Learn anything new, interesting, or heretofore unknown about Nancy Marino?"

"That depends. Did you know she was perhaps the most boring human being on the planet?"

"I was unaware of that."

"It's true," said Tommy, who had started an elaborate handwashing routine that began with turning on the water and leaving it running while he rolled himself a length of paper towel. "She doesn't have a car loan. She pays her mortgage on time. She pays her tax bill on time. She pays everything on time—her credit score was a 740."

"You got her credit score?" I asked, impressed.

"I have ways," he said, lathering his hands for what seemed like an inordinate amount of time while I was drying mine.

"So what else?"

"No bankruptcy. No divorce. No lawsuits. No criminal charges. I couldn't even find a speeding ticket."

Tommy left the water running as he went over to his prerolled towel.

"I'm sorry," I said, gesturing at the sink, "but what the hell are you doing?"

"Do you know how many germs there are on that thing?" he said. "Everyone takes their dirty hands and turns on the faucet. Then they wash their hands and what's the first thing they do? Turn off the faucet with their clean hands—except they're not clean anymore because they've just touched the dirty faucet."

He used his wet paper towel to turn off the water.

"It's much more sanitary this way," he assured me.

"I'm so glad I have other things to worry about."

"Suit yourself. The next plague is coming. Only the clean will survive."

"I'll take my chances," I said. "So nothing at all stood out about Nancy Marino?"

Tommy threw his sodden towel in the trash. "Well, I don't know if it means anything, but she just took out a $50,000 loan against her house."

"Huh," I said, trying to make it fit with the rest of her financial profile. And it didn't. This woman had worked her sneaker treads off to buy that house. When it came to money, she seemed about as daring as an elderly shut-in on a fixed income. People like that generally don't take out home equity loans. They're too busy pressing leftover shards of soap together to make a new bar.

"She's probably just redoing her kitchen," Tommy said.

"Yeah, maybe. Well, it's something to file away, at any rate. Thanks for doing all the scut work for me."

"Don't I always? Give me a jingle if I can do anything else. City Hall is dead right now."

We parted ways and I continued to slink across the newsroom toward Lunky's desk. I had made it most of the way—still undetected—when I was interrupted by having to answer my phone.

"Carter, it's Jim McNabb," I heard.

"Hey, Jim."

"Look, I didn't want to say anything about this while you were still in the office because I just had to think about it for a little bit. But now . . . Well, I still don't know, but I guess I'm going to tell you anyway."

"Okay."

"We're off the record, right? Way, *way* off record. I'll help you get it on the record later if I can. But for right now, this just has to be you and me talking, okay?"

"Okay."

"So, I was . . . I can't believe I'm about to say this . . . are you sure you want to hear this? It's kind of a bombshell."

"I'm a big boy, Jim, I can handle it," I assured him.

Then he dropped it:

"I think Gary Jackman killed Nancy Marino."

He considered himself a good judge of people, the kind of man who could size up other men at a glance. That was the whole issue with Nancy Marino. She wasn't a man.

So he never really saw it coming with Nancy, never thought she'd be trouble, never thought things would be different with her than they were with everyone else. Maybe he had grown a little too used to having his way prevail, sure. But that happens to most men of import. He didn't feel he needed to treat Nancy with any special deference.

He actually liked her for a while. She was cute, like the proverbial girl next door, with that brown ponytail and quick smile. She had a lot of spunk and a nice little body. He liked watching her move. He was married, sure. But they could have something on the side. Just some casual fun. It wouldn't have been the first time for him.

Then Nancy Marino started to become a problem. Then she started to become an even bigger problem. She kept getting . . . emotional about things.

And that really gored him. It was just like a woman to make it emotional, to make a big deal out of something that should have easily been sloughed off. Deep down, although he dared not say it, he thought all women should be like his mother and stay home. The workplace really was a man's world. His father's generation had been better off in that respect.

Eventually, he knew he'd get her under control the same way he got everything else in his life under control—by being smart, patient, and, more important, tougher than everyone else around.

But he was surprised to learn he wasn't tougher than Nancy Marino. She kept coming back at him, kept pushing her claims. Didn't she know ultimately he would win—correction, that he had *to win?*

It got so she was in his head, distracting him from his other work. And that simply wouldn't stand. He had more important matters to deal with than her petty concerns.

He was respected in the community, a man who pushed the buttons of the machine. He didn't have time for this little cog jamming things up.

It was the visit from the regional director of the National Labor Relations Board that really threw him over the top. The NLRB wanted a sworn affidavit. It was taking Nancy Marino—Nancy Marino!—as seriously as it was taking him, treating the two parties as if they were on the same level. He could stall the NLRB, but only for so long. It could subpoena him. And, ultimately, there was no arguing with a subpoena.

Yes, once the NLRB was involved, it changed everything. It meant he wasn't really in control of the game and he certainly couldn't make up the rules anymore. With the NLRB, things would be by the book. It would put everything out in public, because any document generated by the NLRB became part of the public record. There would be some kind of settlement negotiated or some kind of mediation. There was no way he could tolerate all that.

Something had to be done. He wasn't going to risk losing everything he worked for because of the girl next door.

CHAPTER 4

There are places where a reporter can enter into the rather delicate discussion of whether his publisher is, in fact, a murderer. But the middle of the newsroom is not noted for being one of them. I had colleagues on every side of me, and while reporters are accustomed to hearing one side of some strange interviews—most of which they knew to ignore—I might attract a little too much attention if I started hollering questions like, "You really think Gary Jackman killed someone?"

So I started making for the first unoccupied glass office I saw while trying to ignore the pounding in my chest.

"Hang on a second, I got too many ears around," I said, walking in and closing the door behind me. "Okay, I'm in a spot where no one is listening. You're going to have to give this to me again."

"I know, I know, it's crazy," Jim said, talking faster than I had ever heard him before. "But I was with him the night before Nancy was killed."

"What are you talking about?"

"Well, you may not know it, but Gary likes to tie one on now and then, and I don't mind knocking back a few myself. So we went to a bar to do a little away-from-the-table negotiating. Sometimes you get a lot more done with a drink in your hand than you do sitting in a conference room, you know?"

"Right, of course."

Outside the door, Lester Palenski—our bikini-obsessed photo editor—stopped and looked at me curiously, sitting in an office that wasn't my own. He seemed perturbed, mouthed the words "I need to talk to you" and held up a printout of a picture. I flashed him a thumbs-up, then pointed to my phone. He frowned and moved on.

"And . . . look, you can't tell *anyone* about this," Jim continued. "I could get in deep water with the membership, negotiating on my own like this. They'd skin me alive. I'm just telling you this because you're a good enough reporter, you'd probably figure out it was Jackman sooner or later. I'm just helping you along, you know?"

"Sure."

"Okay, okay," he said, inhaling and exhaling loudly. "So, anyway, I had suggested we meet at this bar for a friendly get-to-know-you drink. But he and I both knew what I really meant was I wanted to be able to talk without all the lawyers around. You can make more headway in thirty minutes without the lawyers around than you can in thirty days with 'em, you know?"

"Uh-huh."

"So it's just him and me at this bar, and we're kind of getting into it. We'd both had a few—more than a few, maybe—and he was getting kind of pissed off. Some guys are like that when they drink."

And, I wanted to add, some guys throw up on the gentleman next to them at the symphony. But I just said, "Yeah, sure."

"So Jackman keeps pushing and pushing, saying we should just give in. And I . . . I feel really awful about this, given what happened . . . but I kept using Nancy as, like, I don't know, a block or something, like I was good cop and she was bad cop. Because he knew she had been a hardliner. So he'd say, 'We could maybe go for a thirty percent cut.' And I'd think about it and say, 'I don't think *Nancy* would go for that.' And he'd say, 'Well, what about a rolling cut, ten percent this year, ten percent next, ease people into it?' And I'd think about it some more, pretend to really be wanting to do it, and then say, 'I'm not sure *Nancy* would like that.' "

"Had Nancy told you she wouldn't cave, no matter what?"

Jim hefted another sigh.

"Well, she had and she hadn't," he said. "I was really just winging it, trying to tweak him. Sometimes negotiations are like that. You got to get under a guy's skin. In the end, we probably had to give in a little. I just didn't want to have to give in a lot. I feel so bad about what happened. I never knew he really meant it when he was making all those threats."

"Threats?"

"Oh, well, I kept telling him *Nancy* wouldn't go for this, *Nancy* wouldn't go for that, and it really got him going. Suddenly he was saying things like, 'I can handle *Nancy Marino*. I'm not going to let *Nancy Marino* get in my way.' I thought he was just blowing off some steam. I had no idea."

"So it got personal," I said.

"Oh yeah. Big-time. Real personal. There was this vibe to it like he was big Gary Jackman and she was just little Nancy Marino and how dare *she* get in his way. You can imagine a guy like Jackman is making, what, five hundred, six hundred grand a year? Maybe more. And here some papergirl making eighteen bucks an hour is telling him where he can get off? He just wasn't having it."

Lester wandered past again and squared to look at me, emphasizing his impatience by waving the photo at me. I gave him a palms-up, nothing-I-can-do gesture. He shot me a dirty look and stalked off.

"So how did you guys leave it?" I asked.

"We didn't. He just stormed out."

"What bar were you at?" I asked. I was thinking about how I was going to get this on the record in some way. If they were having that loud an argument, there would have been a bartender who heard it.

"I . . . Look, I can't say," Jim said, having already guessed my intentions. "I can't have you charging in there and asking questions. I'm known there. I go there a lot and so do some of my members. Word'll get out."

"Okay, so think like a journalist for a second, Jim. You know I can't just run with a single off-the-record source on something like this. This is my smoking gun, but I need more than just one person seeing the smoke. How am I supposed to prove this without a little help?"

"I don't know, I don't know," he admitted. "I just sort of hoped if I put you on the right track, you'd be able to figure it out."

I plunked my elbow on the desk in front of me and rested my chin in my palm. It was a lot to absorb, and I had a thousand questions, the first of which was:

"Why not take this to the police, Jim?"

"Look, I'd like to, and I thought about it. But I just can't. Think about it from my angle. I'm locked in a tense negotiation with this guy right now. Just say it turns out Jackman didn't have anything to do with it, that he just happened to get ticked at Nancy the night before she had an accident. The cops might decide I was out to frame the guy and hit me with charges of making a false statement or something. Or Jackman could sue me personally, say I was slandering him to get some leverage. It could wreck our whole negotiation, one; and, two, the union board would fire me for screwing it up. I can't risk getting involved when the whole thing could just be one big coincidence."

It wasn't a coincidence, of course. Nancy Marino really was murdered. I knew that for certain. Jim McNabb didn't, but I wasn't sure I wanted to tell him. Not yet.

The fact was, McNabb had reasons to want Jackman to be the killer. And a source with an agenda like that had to be handled carefully. If all these circumstantial pieces pointing toward Jackman turned out to be true, it would be an epic scandal. Jackman would be fired immediately, of course, and the paper's owners would appoint an interim publisher while they tried to find a replacement, which could take months. Then the new publisher would come in and take a few more months to figure out which way was up. In the meantime, IFIW–Local 117 would skate along with its current contract in place and no one would be bothering to press for pay cuts.

Plus, I'm pretty sure killing a shop steward qualified as an unfair labor practice. There might be ramifications there that would further help the union. So I would definitely be aiding Jim's cause.

But I'd also be bringing a murderer to justice and breaking a career story, both of which felt like fairly noble goals. Was Jackman really the guy? Was a man who once went after someone with a seven-iron capable of something even more brutal?

I took a deep breath and said:

"Okay, Jim. I'll do some digging."

Emerging from my borrowed office, I shot a quick glance in the direction of Lunky, who seemed to be concentrating on his story and not, I hoped, daydreaming about the fishing on Walden

Pond. Judging him momentarily innocuous—not a harm to either himself or others—I decided I had a few spare moments to start some of the aforementioned digging. Not enough to require a backhoe or anything. Just a little garden trowel would do fine.

I took the elevator to the third floor. It was not normally a place in the building I had any need to go, and I didn't know anyone up there—the whole separation of church and state thing—but I knew that was where Jackass wasted space alongside his harem of secretaries. It being nearly six o'clock, I thought they would all be gone for the day, allowing me to pry into his stuff without interference.

Instead, when I rounded the last corner, I was startled to discover one of the three desks in the secretarial pool still occupied. They must have staggered their shifts so one was on duty both before and after regular business hours.

I almost turned away, thinking I would come back later when all three of them would be gone. Then I noticed Jackman's door was closed and his office was dark. He had gone home. It was just the third secretary, a cute-if-somewhat-chunky brunette who probably spent a few too many Saturday nights at home with her Netflix account. There was always the chance she might be chatty.

"Hi," I said, then spied her nameplate and added, "Courtney," before it sounded like too much of a stretch.

Courtney's attention had been fixed on a piece of paper on her desk, and she looked up at me with utter bewilderment, like I had walked down the hallway with a giant bird of prey perched on my head. Seeking to set her at ease and perhaps build some rapport, I rewarded her with a winsome smile (because my mother tells me it's quite charming), fixed my blue eyes on hers (because my mother tells me I have nice eyes), and tried to look cute (because my mother thinks I'm cute).

And maybe it would have worked if Courtney really was my mother. Instead, she struck a businesslike tone and said, "Hi, can I help you?"

I laughed for no reason.

"That's so funny," I said. "*I* was just about to ask *you* if *you* could help *me*. And then *you* asked *me* the same question. That's wild! Do you have ESP or something?"

Courtney looked at me like the bird on top of my head was now talking to her. And she still wasn't buying . . . well, anything.

"No," she said.

"No? No psychics in the family?"

"No."

"Palm readers? Fortune tellers? Tarot card specialists?"

"No," she said again, more firmly this time.

"Oh well, I just thought that maybe . . ."

My voice trailed off. I was the comedian whose act was totally dying. Courtney was getting even less amused by the second.

"Did you need something?" she asked.

Time to take a stab.

"Yeah, I . . . uhh . . . I'm told Mr. Jackman gave a very important speech last Thursday night and I've been asked to get a . . . a video of it. You know, put it on YouTube, tweet it, Facebook it, hope it goes viral, that kind of thing. So I just need to know where he was last Thursday night. I think it might have been the, uh, Morristown Rotary Club, but the person who told me wasn't sure. Would you mind checking his schedule to see where he was that night?"

I said I'd take a stab. I didn't say it would be a good one. I was uncertain whether Morristown even had a Rotary Club. And even if it did, I wasn't sure if Rotarians met at night. Courtney was eyeing me like the bird on my head was now warbling Queen's classic rock anthem "Bicycle Race."

"Ah, okay." Courtney glanced down at her desk. "Mr. Jackman has us keep his appointment book by hand—he doesn't like using the computer. Let me just look for you."

"Thanks," I said, beginning to understand why he needed three secretaries.

"I was just about to leave, so I locked the drawer, hang on," she said, standing up and crossing the secretarial pod toward a small metal lockbox atop a filing cabinet. She worked the dials to the proper position, pulled out a round desk key, returned to her chair and started opening the drawer. I was almost at pay dirt when, as an afterthought, she said, "And, I'm sorry . . . who needs this video again?"

I didn't want Jackman to have any way of knowing I was snooping around his office, so I said, "Ted from accounting."

"Who's Ted from accounting?"

"I am."

She jerked her head up from her desk drawer. "No you're not," she said. "You're Carter Ross. I saw you on TV that one time."

I had made an unscheduled and unfortunate appearance on all the local networks a few years back. It had so thoroughly haunted me the first time around it didn't seem fair it was now haunting me in reruns.

"Ha ha," I said. "Yeah, that was . . . hoo . . . you remember that, huh?"

Courtney was now appraising me as if the bird had stopped singing and simply loosened its bowels on my face. Yet just when I thought things were going quite poorly enough, they got worse: Gary Jackman walked out of his office. He hadn't gone home, after all. He was just working with the lights off.

Looking at him as a potential murderer for the first time, I had to admit there was a certain fit to it. Who else would have benefited more from the death of an uncompromising shop steward than the man locked in a stalemate with her union? And who would have had access to the addresses on her paper route and known when she'd be delivering? All signs continued to point to Jackman.

Meanwhile, he was regarding me with his usual mild disgust.

"Are you here for that interview about, I'm sorry, what was her name?" he asked.

So that's how he was going to play it: like he couldn't even remember the name of the woman he had killed.

"Nancy Marino," I prompted, and watched him carefully to see if the mention of her would change something in him. But he was far too cool for that.

"Right, right. Nancy Marino," he said. "I really don't have time right now. But maybe Courtney can schedule you for first thing tomorrow?"

"Why, does it make you uncomfortable talking about her?" I challenged him, trying to give him a good stare down, only to be interrupted by Courtney.

"He told me his name was Ted and he was from accounting," she said.

Jackman tilted his head. "Is that true? Why would you do that?" he demanded.

I was so intent on staring down Jackman it took me a moment to realize I had been totally and completely busted. It was time to sound the retreat. This wasn't the right moment to confront Jackman anyway, not when I still had so many gaps in my story. So I started backtracking as best I could.

"Yeah, uh . . . Ted," I said, forcing out a laugh. "Just a little reporter's humor for you."

Jackman pursed his thin lips, crossed his arms, and looked at me condescendingly—a well-practiced posture for him.

"But how would that be funny, a reporter misrepresenting himself?" he asked. "I would call that unethical, not funny."

Oh great, the man who wouldn't know an inverted pyramid lede from an inverted nipple was suddenly a journalism expert.

"Yeah, I . . . uhh . . ." I said, groping for something that felt like an emergency exit. "Look, to be honest, I was just trying to hit on Courtney here, and I thought if I made her laugh, it would help my cause."

I turned to Courtney and said, "I'm sorry. I'm such a clod. Please accept my apology."

I expected Courtney might send a paperweight flying in the direction of the bird on my head. Instead, her face flushed and she looked down at the translucent floor mat under her chair.

"Oh, that's . . . that's okay, really," she stammered. "Maybe we could . . . grab some coffee sometime."

Jackman looked distinctly uncomfortable, like he had come to the television studio to be a guest on *Hardball with Chris Matthews* and stumbled onto the set of *The Dating Game with Chuck Woolery* by mistake. My previously wounded male ego experienced a moment of pure triumph—Mom was right after all!—then I decided to make my getaway while the situation was at the peak of confusion.

"That would be great," I said. "Anyhow, I'll just be moving on now."

I turned and walked briskly away before either of them had a chance to comprehend the strangeness of it all.

Back on the second floor, I made it off the elevator about five steps when I was accosted by Lester Palenski, who was waving a photo printout above his head. In addition to his fondness for bikinis, Lester was known to run a little hot. If one of his photographers failed to get the shot he needed—and it happens to even the best photographers on occasion—Lester took it personally, as if everyone was conspiring to thwart him.

"There you are!" he seethed. "You want to explain *this* to me?"

Lester handed me the piece of paper he had been brandishing. It was a picture of Lunky, our hulking intern, with his arms wrapped around a bear, which appeared to be dead. It had this vaguely Paleolithic feel about it—Lunky, with his latter-day Neanderthal eyebrow ridge and bushy hair, lugging his kill with him, wearing a goofy grin all the while.

"Brodie wants this story for A1," Lester said. "But *this* is the *only picture* I have of that damn bear."

And, of course, our newspaper couldn't very well run a picture of its own intern, especially when he was engaged in an act that didn't look much like journalism.

"My shooter told me the scene was roped off and the animal control truck was blocking his view. So *this* was all he could get," Lester said.

I looked at the photo some more, because I couldn't quite believe what I was seeing. It was our bear, all right, all two hundred pounds of it. Yet Lunky had the thing cradled in his arms like a massive, furry infant, and appeared not to be exerting himself at all as he carried it.

"I see" is all I could say, still staring at the printout.

"Your intern *ruined* my picture," Lester said, spicing the accusation with a pair of unrepeatable adjectives before the words "intern" and "picture."

"I, uh, wow," I replied.

The veins on either side of Lester's neck were starting to

bulge. "A bear wanders into Newark for the first time since the dawn of industrialization and *your intern* ends up carrying it. You want to explain that to me?"

I couldn't, of course. When I left, that stupid bear was fifteen feet up a tree, and it looked like it would take a cherry picker to get him out. I couldn't begin to fathom the circumstances that would have ended with Lunky cradling the thing in his arms. But I would have to figure it out, and fast. Lester had likely lodged his complaint with everyone in the newsroom—everyone who had functioning eardrums, anyway—and as the adult assigned to babysit Lunky this afternoon, I would be expected to account for what happened. I started inching my way around Lester, who was standing between me and any hope I had of mitigating this disaster.

"I'm, uh, going to have to, uh . . . I have to take a leak," I began, then, as soon as I had clearance, elongated my strides. "I'll get back to you, Lester."

I could sense Lester was gathering himself to begin some serious caterwauling, but I scooted away before he could gain too much volume. I made a straight line for Lunky, who was seated in the intern pod, happily typing away. He dwarfed everything in his workstation—the chair was made for someone roughly half his size—yet he seemed quite content, unaware of the calamity he had caused.

"Hi, Kevin," I said, gently. "How are things going?"

He looked up from his screen and studied me with his usual detached, academic manner.

"Oh, hello, Mister Ross," he said, and before I could correct him on the "Mister" part, he added, "I'm doing real well with the first draft."

Apparently, no one had explained to him that in this business, all we get is a first draft.

"That's great," I said, then slid the photo onto the desk so he could look at it. "You, uhh . . . want to tell me about this?"

I thought I'd get an apology, or at least an embarrassed explanation. Instead, he smiled at it. "Oh, cool picture! Can I keep it?"

"Kevin, you . . . uhh . . . you picked up the bear," I said, as if the problem with this should be self-evident.

But Lunky didn't get it. "It's okay, he wasn't that heavy. It was basically like doing a power clean, and I can power-clean a lot more than that."

I wanted to be mad at him but somehow couldn't summon the anger. It would be like getting ticked off at a two-year-old for wetting the bed.

"It's not . . . It's not about the weight," I said. "It's . . . I'm sorry, *how* did you end up carrying a dead bear?"

"He wasn't dead, just tranquilized," Lunky corrected me. "Animal control arrived after you left, and the officer decided the only way to get Ben out of the tree—"

"I'm sorry, Ben? Who's Ben?"

"Well, the bear, of course. The animal control guy told me I could pick a name for the bear. So I said 'Ben,' because my favorite book as a child was *Gentle Ben* by Walt Morey."

I was rendered speechless, which Lunky took as a cue to continue.

"Anyhow, the animal control guy had to shoot Ben with one of those darts. That got Ben out of the tree, all right, but then he was just lying there on the sidewalk. The guy from animal control couldn't lift him, so he asked me to help. But I knew it'd be easier if I just did it myself. So that's what I did."

"Did you tell the animal control guy you were a reporter?" I asked, when I finally found my voice.

"Why would that matter?"

Mindful of the fact that we are given only so much enamel in this life, I made a concerted effort not to grind my teeth. "Kevin, has anyone ever told you that reporters aren't supposed to become part of the story they're covering?"

Lunky pondered this for a moment.

"So I shouldn't have named him?" he asked.

"Actually, you shouldn't have picked him up to begin with."

"Hmm. Sorry about that. I won't let it happen again."

"That'd be peachy," I said and, as usual, Lunky missed my sarcasm.

I was about to continue my little journalism lecture when, out of the corner of my eye, I saw Tina Thompson closing in on me.

"You," she said, pointing one finger at me, her eyes narrowed, her voice quietly dripping poison. "Yoooouuuu. My office. Now."

While I would never consider myself an expert on the speech patterns of the adult female *Homo sapiens*, it is my general experience that when they lose the capacity of articulating in full sentences, it's an indication they might possibly be angry.

Either that, or they're having a stroke. In Tina's case, it could have gone either way. But since she was still walking upright—and was puffing out her cheeks like Dizzy Gillespie reincarnated—I took it that she was fairly incensed.

"I'll be right back," I told Lunky, who was typically oblivious.

I made the force march to her office, where she gestured for me to enter. She followed me inside, then slammed the door loud enough that half the heads in the newsroom jerked our way.

"Sit," she said, pointing to one of the two chairs in front of her desk.

I thought she would go behind her desk, like she usually

did. Instead, she selected the chair next to mine. I was alarmed by the choice. Not only did it increase our physical proximity—and the chance she'd wind up cuffing me on the ear—it made me feel more vulnerable to what was about to come. I've been subjected to what feels like a lifetime of editors yelling at me face-to-face, to the point where I've become inured to it. Sal Szanto, my previous editor, was particularly instrumental in increasing this tolerance.

But side to side? That's not something I had ever been conditioned against. My defenses were much lower from that direction. And even if I twisted my body toward her as much as the seat allowed, she still had a clear flank attack.

"I'm not sure where to start with you right now," Tina said, her voice alarmingly hushed. I definitely would have preferred yelling.

"Would you like me to get you something to drink while you think about it?" I asked, sounding much more flip than I intended.

She answered not with a word but with a soul-withering glower.

"Okay, so that's a 'no,' " I said, and hunkered down to wait for the coming storm.

She paused for ten seconds—it felt longer—then said, "When we last spoke, I was of the understanding that you would be working on a story with Kevin Lungford about the bear that was traipsing through Newark. Am I correct that was also your understanding?"

This was clearly one of those situations where it would be advantageous to say as little as possible, lest my mouth get me in any more trouble. So I just nodded.

"Well, in that case, it would be great if you could explain to me why you were talking with"—she interrupted herself to lean forward and grab a scrap of paper off her desk—"Nikki Papadopolous. She called here looking for you but didn't want to leave a message on your voice mail, because she wasn't sure if you checked it. She was explicit that she talk to someone who could get you a message. So the call got forwarded to me because, well, it seems I'm your boss. You *do* remember I'm your boss, right?"

I nodded again, though a bit more meekly this time.

"Well, good ol' Nikki said she was from the State Street Grill in Bloomfield and said she had spoken to you earlier in the day but had forgotten to get your phone number," Tina continued. "So you can imagine my curiosity as to how you ended up in Bloomfield when I thought I had sent you to Newark. You can imagine that, right?"

Another nod. Even smaller.

"And do you know what she told me?"

Head shake.

"Well, first she told me she thought you were an excellent reporter, and very cute on top of that, so kudos to you there, stud. Then she told me you had been asking questions about Nancy Marino. Now, I'm sorry, is the bear I asked you to track down named Nancy Marino?"

"No, his name is Ben," I said, immediately regretting it.

"Really? Really. Ben, huh? Well, so you know *something* about the bear after all," she said, her volume rising for a brief moment.

She stopped herself, did some strange breathing thing—yoga stuff, I imagined—then continued in her softer, scarier voice.

"Well, then perhaps you can explain this," she said, reaching for another piece of paper on her desk and producing a printout of the dreaded Lunky-and-the-bear photo.

"The, uh, animal control guy asked Lunky, to, uh . . ." I

started, and realized it was sounding lamer the more I talked, so I finished with: "He was just trying to be helpful."

"Helpful? Really? And where were you, his supposed mentor, while he was being so helpful?"

I looked out Tina's window, which offered a panoramic view of a brick wall, like the right answer might be written in the grout. Alas, there was nothing but graffiti.

"Were you in Bloomfield?" Tina prompted.

I considered saying that, at that point, I might have actually been in Newark—albeit downtown, several miles away from the bear, chatting with Big Jimmy. But that didn't seem like it would aid my cause.

"Look, Tina, obviously I wasn't with the kid," I said. "We found the bear and the thing was up in a tree, and I really thought Lunky could handle it from there on his own. I was wrong. I apologize."

Tina was making the kind of face I only thought was possible if someone was actively sucking on a lemon, but I continued:

"But, I've got to tell you, the story I'm working on instead is really—"

"I don't want to hear it," Tina said immediately.

"No, I'm serious, I think—"

"I don't want to hear it!" she said, now in full crescendo. "What you did today was totally inexcusable."

"Tina, it involves—"

"*I don't care.* Look, we'll talk about this more later. For right now, it's"—she looked at her watch—"quarter after six. I better have a story about a bear in my basket by seven o'clock. And if it's not the very best bear story I've ever read, you're going to ride the copy desk for a month."

Tina knew there was no greater threat to a free-range reporter such as myself than a month chained to a desk, scouring for typos. I'd rather do time as a galley slave. At least the boat is going somewhere.

With no time for moping, I returned to the intern pod, feeling the usual charge of adrenaline that accompanies being on deadline. There are people in our business who can't handle the stress: tender souls who eventually wind up following gentler pursuits, like public relations. Me? I love the rush. There's nothing that focuses your concentration like knowing you have forty-five minutes to write six hundred words.

"So," I said as I arrived, "what do we have so far?"

I scooted a rolling chair next to Lunky, who puffed out his mile-thick chest and proudly turned the screen toward me. I began reading.

> By Kevin Lungford
>
> In William Faulkner's acclaimed story "The Bear," which is rightly gaining its place as one of the finest works of twentieth-century American short-form fiction, the hunting and ultimate slaying of a lame-pawed bruin becomes a powerful symbol of European encroachment into the Native American way of life, and the tragic consequences therein.
>
> In John Irving's quixotic, madcap romp *The Hotel New Hampshire,* the strength and sorrow of bears are an important and continuing theme; and the character of Susie the Bear, a young woman so ashamed by her appearance she wears a bear costume, deserves greater scrutiny within the field of LBGT literature as an example of the ways in which lesbians are forced to, in essence, cloak their sexuality.

> And, of course, most schoolchildren can identify Ursa Major and Ursa Minor—literally "big bear" and "little bear"—by their more common names, the Big Dipper and the Little Dipper, yet do not know the names hearken to a classic story in Greek mythology that has been echoed in the canon of nearly every literary movement since.

I kept myself absolutely still for a few extra moments, pretending to be reading while I was actually trying to think of how to respond. My humane-to-interns policy was being rather sorely put to the test, but I was determined to stick with it.

"How is it? Pretty good, huh?" Lunky asked.

All I could think of was an article I read once that found the lowest-performing workers—people identified as being in the bottom twenty-five percent by their bosses—consistently rated themselves in the top twenty-five percent. While it seems to be a testament to the power of human self-delusion, the researchers concluded the real problem was that low-performing people lack the skills and training to know how bad they are.

Lunky clearly fit in that category, and I actually felt sorry for him. Princeton didn't have a journalism program. No one had ever told him how to write a newspaper article. He just applied for an internship—to our sports department, no less—and the sports guys hired him because they thought a Princeton kid was probably smart enough to figure things out (and because they hoped he could hit a softball ten miles). No one had even given this kid Remedial Journalism, much less Journalism 101.

So I had to treat this as a teachable moment. And the best teachers start by building on strengths.

"Okay, so that's a fine treatment on bears in literature," I said, and Lunky grinned. "Now what about the, uh, bear in Newark?"

"Oh, I'll be getting to that."

"Yeah, you might want to consider moving that part up a bit," I suggested.

"I didn't want to rush the reader too much."

"That's very thoughtful of you. Did anyone ever tell you about the five *W*'s?"

"Wilde, Wells, Wordsworth . . . does Walt Whitman count as one or two?" he asked.

"Never mind," I said, and started scrolling down.

Except below those three paragraphs was a cursor, blinking slowly and insistently, waiting for more copy that had not yet come. And below that was a fat little black bar that told me I had reached the end.

"Where's the rest of it?" I asked.

"What do you mean?"

"This is maybe five inches. We're on the schedule for eighteen."

"Oh, I figured I'd get maybe half of it done tonight, then finish it tomorrow morning."

"Tomorrow morning," I repeated. "By tomorrow morning, this thing is supposed to be in a newspaper, lying on front porches throughout New Jersey. It's due in"—I looked up at a clock on the wall—"thirty-nine minutes."

"Really?" he said, as if this was the first he'd heard of it. I was beginning to grasp why the words "By Kevin Lungford" had not yet appeared in our newspaper.

"Okay," I said. "Let's review some basic concepts: when all else fails, make your story start with a kid. Editors love stories with kids in them almost as much as they love stories with animals. So if you have a kid *and* an animal, they'll be so happy they'll wet themselves. Did you interview any kids?"

"Oh, sure," Lunky said, opening to a page in his notebook and showing it to me. "You told me to interview the young and the old, remember?"

I grabbed the notebook and flipped a few pages until I found what I needed.

"Start typing," I said, clearing my throat and dictating: " 'Before yesterday, the only bear six-year-old Newark resident Tashee Cunningham saw on a regular basis was Winnie-the-Pooh—and then only if he went to the library.' "

"Winnie-the-Pooh?" Lunky asked, horrified. I sensed his concern he would lose credibility at the next faculty tea.

"With all due respect to John Irving, Winnie will be a little more familiar to our readers than Susie the Bear," I assured him.

I continued my dictation: "That changed abruptly yesterday when a two-hundred-pound male bruin came ambling outside his kitchen."

I went back to Lunky's barely legible scrawl until I found the only usable quote from Tashee, who was, after all, only six. I read it aloud: "I yelled, 'Mama! Mama! It's a bear!' "

Lunky looked up from the keyboard. "Don't you think that's a little, I don't know, obvious? Wouldn't you rather be more oblique? Maybe we could craft an allegory of some sort?"

"You know we're supposed to write this at an eighth-grade level, right?"

"Oh right," he said, then added, "The eighth grade is when I started reading Joyce."

"You better let me type," I said.

For the next thirty-four minutes, Lunky read to me the contents of his notebook, which I attempted to translate into something that resembled a newspaper article. I suppose it was sort of like Joyce, in that it was pretty much stream-of-consciousness crap. In the world of Princeton Ph.D. candidates, they call that literature. In my business, we have a different term for that kind of writing: meatball surgery.

Nevertheless, we reached our eighteenth and final inch at exactly two minutes to seven.

"Aren't you going to put your name on it?" Lunky asked.

"No, this is your first byline, and I want you to have it all to yourself," I said.

"Aw, that's great. Thanks. And hey, if you ever need me to lift anything heavy for you, just give me a call."

I assured him I would, then went back to Tina's office to tell her the story had been filed. She wasn't there, so I wandered toward the copy desk, expecting she would be harassing someone there. Instead, I saw her curly brown head poking out of Harold Brodie's office.

"Carter," she said, then added the five words that turned my legs into spaghetti: "Brodie wants to see you."

At least outwardly, there should have been nothing remotely intimidating about our executive editor. To begin with, he was a small man, and ever since his seventieth birthday, he seemed to be shrinking even further. He had this high-pitched voice, these flyaway eyebrows, this near-constant need to urinate—all things that afflict men of advancing age and shrinking vitality.

Yet on the very rare occasions I was summoned into his office to discuss a story, my usual glibness was replaced with stumbling uncertainty. The instincts that served me so well elsewhere turned out to be false, as if Brodie's domain was some kind of opposite world. Every note that came out of my mouth sounded off-key.

Something about the guy just frightened me. He had been

the supreme ruler of the *Eagle-Examiner* since I was in diapers, and while most of the time he reigned with a velvet fist, he was still known to enforce discipline when and where necessary. There was always talk that in his younger days he had been so ruthless—diminishing hardened reporters to whimpering toddlers with the ferocity and precision of his attacks—that my older colleagues still referred to his office as "the woodshed."

Still, up until now, I had never experienced Brodie as anything more than a kindly old man. I didn't know what he looked like when wielding the paddleboard. And I guess that's what scared me most: the unknown.

As I entered the office, Tina had her head bowed, like she didn't want to look at me. I was a little miffed at her for running to Brodie with this bear thing. The cardinal sins of the newspaper world, transgressions that will get you fired immediately and without further comment, are things like plagiarism and making up sources. Insubordination doesn't come near that list. We are, after all, reporters. Lack of respect for authority is part of our job description.

Still, I obviously had some kind of punishment coming my way or I wouldn't have been summoned into the woodshed. Brodie gestured toward a chair in front of his desk, and I gingerly lowered myself into it. Some bit of classical music, heavy on the violins, poured from a set of small speakers next to his computer. Brodie closed his eyes and rested his tented fingers against his lips. He was either settling into deep contemplation or had fallen asleep. It was always hard to tell. He was famous for doing this—it was known as the "Brodie Think"—and it lasted as long as was needed for the old man to get his head around a situation.

For a long minute, I sat there in dreadful silence, waiting for whatever I had coming. Somewhere during that time, I decided that, since this was opposite world, I should do the reverse of what I normally did in Brodie's office. So whereas I ordinarily would have sat quietly, waiting for the Brodie Think to end, this time I started talking.

"Look, before you start, let me just say I owe Tina an apology," I said. "I know I should have just done what she asked. What happened with the bear is entirely my fault, and I accept full responsibility."

Brodie opened his eyes and I could immediately tell that, as usual, I had said the wrong thing.

"Bear?" he said. "What happened with the bear?"

I looked to Tina for help, but she shook her head.

"Uh, never mind," I said, now totally confused. Brodie settled back into his pondering, and I shifted in my seat. The violins had given way to something more ominous, something involving low brass. Brodie let another minute—or maybe it was a year—pass before speaking.

"Carter, I'm very disturbed by several things I've heard about you," he said. "I just received a phone call from Gary Jackman."

The name hit me with a jolt. What did this possibly have to do with him? The sinking feeling in the pit of my stomach told me this conversation was not going to end well.

"Gary has been a friend to this newsroom during difficult times," Brodie continued. "I don't need to tell you how much worse things could have been had he not been an ally."

I clenched my jaw. A friend? An ally? Why, because he hadn't insisted on rolling a guillotine into the newsroom every time we had another round of layoffs?

"Now," Brodie said. "He tells me you made a scene at a funeral home yesterday. Do you care to respond to that?"

"I . . . I wouldn't call it a scene," I said, my words foundering as usual around Brodie. "It was . . . We . . . We had a little run-in, I suppose."

"He said you called him a name," Brodie said. "Is that true?"

I scanned my memory and, oh shoot, it was. I just thought he hadn't heard me.

"Yes," I said timidly.

"What name did you call him?"

This was getting torturous.

"Dshbg," I mumbled.

"Say again?"

"Douche bag," I said, louder this time, and I could tell Brodie was unimpressed by my word choice. "But, in my defense, he really *was* being a douche bag."

Tina, head still bowed, actually groaned. Brodie pointed a long, thin, old-man finger at me and raised his already high voice another octave.

"You are way out of line, young man," he yelped. "Way out of line."

"Sorry. Sorry, it was just—"

Brodie glared at me and I stopped talking.

"He also said you were sexually harassing one of his secretaries . . ."

"I didn't harass—"

". . . and that you misrepresented yourself as not being a reporter," Brodie said, talking over me. "Is that true?"

"I . . . I was just . . ."

"Is it true? Did you misrepresent yourself or not? Yes or no? Did you say you were"—he looked at some notes he had kept—"Ted from accounting?"

Brodie was still on the other side of the desk, but if he leaned forward any further, I was going to be able to smell the Werther's Original on his breath. Tina had raised her head just slightly to see me answer. I thought about explaining myself, telling them the reason I was skulking around Jackass is because I suspected he was a killer. But in the moment, it felt like some kind of desperately invented story—especially when I had nothing but coincidence and supposition to prove it, and when I wasn't totally convinced myself that's what happened.

I was trapped.

"Yes," I said.

Tina's head sank again. Brodie leaned back, closed his eyes for a moment, then opened them again.

"You've always been one of my favorite reporters, but I don't know what's happening with you right now," Brodie said. "We can tolerate a lot of behavior around here, but we still have standards of professional conduct. I can't have you running around higgledy-piggledy, treating the publisher of this newspaper with such blatant disrespect.

"I'm afraid I have no choice," he concluded. "As of this moment, you are suspended without pay until further notice."

He was the kind of man who moved quickly from one challenge to the next. There was no time to dwell on things. So he had actually already started to forget about Nancy Marino within a few days of killing her. Sure, he went to her wake, and he would go to her funeral. But he thought he had put the problem squarely behind him—with his tracks well covered—when, suddenly, that reporter showed up, snooping around.

He didn't like reporters, not at all. He found them disrespectful and constantly overly familiar, saying things they had no right to say, asking questions with such rash impertinence. He detested that they seemed to consider themselves his equal in some ways. What gave them the nerve to act like that? They would be nothing without the newspaper behind them. That was the only reason anyone paid them any heed. Didn't they realize that? They fancied themselves essential components of the machine—unique and vital—when really they were just replaceable, interchangeable parts.

He had to pretend he thought otherwise, of course. He pandered to their inflated egos, made them feel justified in their self-importance. He never let on what he really thought about them, and they never would have been able to guess how much he despised them. But even on their best days, he considered them pests.

He wasn't quite sure what to make of Carter Ross at first. Ross was clearly bright, which was cause for concern—dumber reporters were easier to manipulate. Then again, Ross seemed nice enough, harmless actually.

But it's the nice ones you have to look out for. And as soon as Ross came around, throwing about the name "Nancy Marino," it was clear he was anything but harmless. To have a reporter like Ross asking questions about her, clearly curious about her, dredging her name up like there was something to be discovered about her. That brought a new and ominous twist to the Nancy Marino Problem.

It was possible—not probable but possible—that Ross would be able to put everything together. It depended on just how smart he was, of course, and how dogged he would be in searching. But if he managed to talk to the right people, hear certain things from the NLRB, from the IFIW, from any of the places there might have been small shreds of evidence left behind . . . well, it could become an issue.

It could not be allowed. Carter Ross was now, officially, a threat.

CHAPTER 5

They didn't call security on me. I guess I wasn't considered that much of a threat. I was allowed to stop at my desk and collect my things, albeit under Tina's supervision.

Somehow the newsroom gossips already knew what had happened—I swear, one of them has Brodie's office wired—and by the time I had collected my briefcase and was ready to depart, half of them were giving me looks generally saved for death row inmates in Texas. Tommy shot me a mournful glance, surreptitiously formed his fingers into the shape of a phone and mouthed the words "call me." Buster Hays was shaking his head sadly. The rest of the faces were a blur of pity, concern, and confusion. I'm sure in repeated retelling on the office rumor mill, I would emerge as an idiot for having lied about my identity, as a hero for having affronted Jackass, but as a cautionary tale that no one is safe in this day and age.

If they knew the truth—that I was being railroaded—they would undoubtedly view this spectacle differently. I would be seen as a martyr, a noble sufferer who was willing to lay his career on the line in his quest for the truth, a reporter's reporter.

Instead, as I made my condemned man's walk out of the newsroom, I merely hoped I looked brave rather than pathetic.

Tina and I rode the elevator down in silence at first, mostly because I wasn't sure what to say to her. I never knew where, exactly, our relationship was supposed to head, but whatever the optimal direction, this was clearly a wrong turn. Her eyes stayed fixed on the numbers above the door as they ticked from two to one.

"I tried, but I couldn't save you," she said quietly. "His mind was made up."

"How long am I gone for?"

"He wanted six months, but I talked him down to three," Tina said.

"Three months!" I blurted. I had been thinking I'd be out for a week or two.

"You're actually lucky," Tina said. "Jackman wanted you fired outright."

Of course he did. I was that pesky reporter who kept asking him questions about Nancy Marino.

"Carter, when you come back, you can't give them *anything* to use against you," Tina said. "Jackass would use any excuse to jettison another newsroom salary."

"Tina," I said, wanting to tell her some of the things I had learned about Jackman.

Then I pulled myself back. Before she became my editor, Tina had always been my confidante. I could tell her when I was going behind another editor's back and why I was doing it, and she supported me every time, often running interference for me. But that dynamic had changed. She kept trying to tell me, but now I finally got it: she wasn't my friend anymore; she was my editor.

So I just said, "Sorry about the bear thing."

"Oh God, that doesn't even matter."

She was inching back toward the elevator, and I knew she had work to do. We would, as usual, leave a lot unspoken.

"I'll see you around," I said.

She gave me a quick kiss on the cheek and scampered back on the elevator. She had a newspaper to put out. And it was a strange feeling to know I wasn't part of that anymore, at least for the time being. I had been working for one newspaper or another since high school. Being a reporter was the only thing I'd ever done, the only thing I ever wanted to do. It was much more than an avocation for me, even more than a career. It was my identity. My friends, my family, my neighbors, every person in my life knew me as a reporter, first and foremost. I couldn't imagine being without it for three months.

I also couldn't imagine being out of a paycheck for that long. With all the pay cuts and furloughs having whittled away my income, I was barely keeping up with my mortgage as it was. I could maybe afford to be out of work for three weeks but not three months.

I was beginning to have visions of being forced out onto the street or, worse, moving back in with my parents at the age of thirty-two. It would be an indignity for me, but it would be even harder on Deadline. Mom's allergic to cats.

So, as a responsible pet owner, I had little choice. I had to prove to Brodie and everyone else that I was, in fact, merely being an intrepid reporter; that Jackman was a nefarious killer; and that Ted from accounting—sorry, Carter Ross—deserved to be reinstated.

Which meant there was no time to mope. I had to make like Fred and Ginger: pick myself up, dust myself off, and start all over again.

And heck, I wasn't starting *all* over. Were this a cop drama, I would have been asked to lay my gun and my badge on the desk before I left. But you can't very well take away the tools of a modern reporter's trade—Internet, cell phone, devious brain—and in this case, they didn't even bother collecting my company laptop. So I retrieved the Malibu from the parking garage, pulled it up on the street alongside the *Eagle-Examiner* building, and tapped into the newsroom's wireless network.

I soon learned Gary A. Jackman, formerly of Michigan, was now a resident of Mendham, a bucolic bedroom community tucked in the hills of Morris County. He was a registered Republican—big shock there—and lived in a home assessed at $2.27 million, which set him back $35,000 a year in property taxes alone. Not a bad little shack.

I got the address and plugged it into my GPS, which told me it was forty-four minutes away. If I got started now, I would be at the Jackman manse just after dark, which would suit my purposes quite nicely.

Any lawyer, detective, or courtroom junkie knows that to prove a murder, you need to establish means, motive, and opportunity. In this case, I felt good about motive—Jackman wanted to erase an impediment to a business deal. Opportunity was clearly there as well—he would have been able to look up her route and lie there in wait for her.

Now I just needed to see if he had the means—a black SUV with a large grille plate, perhaps one with a suspicious dent in it. Finding a vehicle fitting that description parked in Jackman's driveway would be as good as finding the murder weapon.

With the setting sun disappearing behind the Watchung Mountains—we call them mountains because it sounds better than the Watchung Inclines, which is what they really are—I drove west toward Mendham, arriving just as the world was switching from daytime running lights to real headlights.

I made the turn on Jackman's road, then found the number for his house in stainless steel digits, bolted to a brick pillar on one side of the driveway. There was a matching brick pillar on the other side, and in the middle was a gate made to look like wrought iron, the kind with tops just pointy enough to reinforce the idea that the inhabitants would prefer you not just pop in for a visit. There was also a call box on the left side of the driveway for deliverymen, plumbers, and other members of the servant class.

The entire front of the property was shrouded by a line of tall shrubs. Beyond them was a front yard filled with trees. So it was a little tough to make out much of Jackman's house from the road. But it appeared to be your basic McMansion, a boxy monstrosity erected sometime during the go-go nineties and meant to look like some postmodern mash-up of Victorian and contemporary. I could already imagine what the interior looked like, with rooms that were a little too spacious to ever be cozy and at least one bathtub that could seat six adults comfortably.

I drove past twice at cruising speed but couldn't make out much. Privacy had obviously been a selling point for the Jackman family. There was only going to be one way I could get a full look at Jackman's fleet of cars, and that was to creep up to his house and peek into his garage. Under New Jersey Code of Criminal Justice 2C:18–3—a statute that deals with trespassing, and therefore a part of the law not unknown to an enterprising reporter such as myself—the act of peering into a dwelling place for the purpose of invading the occupant's privacy is explicitly defined as a fourth-degree crime, which can land you in county jail for up to eighteen months.

But only if you get caught.

So I killed a little more time driving around, gawking at the big houses owned by the wealthy capitalists, the inventive entrepreneurs, and, of course, the members of the lucky sperm club. Not that I have a problem with any of them. Some reporters hold a grudge against the well-to-do—primarily because we are not and will never be one of them—but the fact is the good ol' You Ess of A needs rich people, too. The more the better, frankly.

When it was sufficiently dark, I parked perhaps a quarter of a mile away and took off toward Jackman's place on foot. As I reached the driveway, I spied something I hadn't noticed while rolling along at twenty-five miles per hour: a small security camera bolted to the top of one of the brick pillars. It had a wire coming out the back that appeared to feed down into the ground.

I have a general theory about security cameras. The ones that you can see—that are made obvious for the whole world—are most likely fakes. Those wires led to nothing more threatening than a few hungry earthworms. It's the ones you can't see that are real. So I spent a minute or two scanning the trees and other possible hiding places, but there were no lenses looking back at me.

So I proceeded, albeit with caution. The shrubbery along the edge of the property was basically impenetrable to a person of my size, leaving me no choice but to vault over the faux wrought-iron fence, which I did with all the agility of a sake-stoked sumo wrestler. I landed heavily and felt a jolt in my knees—dress shoes not being known for their shock absorption—but determined that I was otherwise unscathed.

Before heading toward the house, I took one last look at the surveillance camera, inspecting the back side for telltale signs of authenticity, like blinking LED lights or the soft whirring of a motor. But there was none of that. It was a fake for sure.

So I moved ahead, quickly walking along the side of the Jackman driveway, trying to stay in the shadow of the trees. I wasn't exactly dressed in commando clothes—unless there's some unknown elite military unit that prefers khakis and white button-down shirts—so I felt a little exposed as I neared the house. Anyone who happened to be glancing down at the driveway would easily make me. But, really, how often do people look outside of their suburban McMansions? That's the whole point of them. They're fortresses of solitude, insulating the owner from the intrusions of the world at large.

The end of the driveway had a decent-sized area of asphalt—all the better for maneuvering large black SUVs—and I skirted the edge of it, staying somewhat concealed in a fringe of trees. The Jackman garage was of the three-car variety, though unfortunately there were none of those little windows that garages used to have. There was also a regular door, painted beige to match the siding on the house, but that was also windowless. They certainly weren't making it easy on the would-be criminal trespasser.

Above the garage was what appeared to be a living room. The lights were on and I could glimpse the top of a wall-mounted flat-screen television, also powered up. If there were any people in the room, I couldn't see them—which hopefully meant they couldn't see me, either.

Each of the three garage bays had a set of floodlights, now dark. But they had little boxes above them that told me they were motion sensitive. So I gave them a wide berth as I continued edging around the driveway, slowly getting closer to the house.

That's when I finally saw my in: the beige door had a small white rectangle at the bottom, so Fifi the cat could get out for her nightly exercise. If I could find a way to reach the cat door without setting off the lights, I'd get my needed glimpse inside the garage.

Completing my circumnavigation of the driveway, I stayed outside the range of the motion detectors, then dashed quickly to the side of the house, so I was flush up against it—and, I hoped, out of the line of sight of anyone inside. I tiptoed along until I got to the corner of the garage, went down on my hands and knees, and made like Fifi.

I nudged the kitty door open with my hand and peered through it, but that didn't allow me to see much more than a patch of concrete floor a few feet in front of me. No, I soon realized, my only way to see inside would be to stick my head through and look around.

So in I went. It was a tight squeeze: I had to get my head perfectly parallel to the ground and then push to squeeze it through. To make matters more difficult, the door was at an awkward height. It was too low for me to stay on my hands and knees but too high for me to lie flat on the ground. So I had to support myself on bent arms, with my legs splayed out behind me. I'm quite sure I looked ridiculous, but, then again, the whole point of this is that no one would ever notice.

With my head fully inside, I craned my neck to the right. At first, I saw nothing. It had been brighter outside than it was in the garage, and my eyes weren't adjusted to the darkness. But I was a patient trespasser, so I gave my pupils time to fully dilate.

Sometime during the next minute, as I waited for more distinct shapes to emerge from the darkness, I thought I heard a noise. I told myself it was nothing, maybe just the hum of a storage freezer that had been stuck out in the garage. But it got louder and, with a sudden sense of doom, I realized what it was:

a car engine, coming up the driveway. The Jackmans were home. Time to disappear.

But as I went to pull my head out of the door and make my escape, I lost that perfectly parallel angle I had upon entry. I kept yanking, but either the back of my head or my chin was getting caught every time. The geometry just wasn't working anymore. I twisted. I tugged. I pulled. But the more I struggled, the more it felt like the door itself was getting in the way.

Short of decapitation, there was no way out.

I was stuck. And screwed. The floodlights had already come on. The car was at the top of the driveway and was now idling in the turnaround. The occupants were probably trying to figure out why a headless human shape was sprawled by the side of their house. Then I heard a car door slam and a very official-sounding voice say:

"Sir, I'm with the Mendham Borough police. I'm going to have to ask you to take your head out of the garage so I can place you under arrest."

Getting myself unstuck turned out to be something of a trick. When it became apparent I had reached an impasse on my own, the cop started offering some helpful tips, going about the thing with a calm, professional demeanor I found impressive, given that I doubted he had ever come across a suspect with his head jammed in a cat door. Finally, after some exertion, I worked myself free and, relieved, faced my arrester for the first time.

He was a veteran whose buzz cut was going white, and he looked at me with a certain amount of resignation. After all, here I was, a nearly middle-aged man—not some stupid kid—and on top of that, I was well dressed, apparently sober, perhaps even educated. Shouldn't I have known better?

"We're going to do this the easy way, right?" he said, taking his cuffs out of his belt.

"Yeah, I've had enough," I assured him, sticking my hands out in front of me.

"Nope, got to do it behind," he said apologetically, and I turned around.

"Sorry about this," I said, because he seemed like a genuinely nice guy and I felt bad for putting him through the trouble of arresting me.

"I'm sure you are," he replied as he secured the cuffs.

"I assume someone inside the house called you?"

He didn't answer, and I began going over all the things I probably did wrong before arriving at the obvious conclusion:

"I guess that camera out front wasn't a fake," I said.

"Nope," he said, allowing himself a small guffaw as he opened the back door to his patrol car and helped me inside. I never knew this before—this being my first arrest—but it's not easy to get into a car without the use of your hands.

"Aren't you supposed to read me my rights or something?" I asked as I settled in.

"Don't have to," he said. "You need two elements for Miranda: custody and interrogation. I'm not planning on asking you any questions. Frankly, I don't even *want* to know what you were doing in there."

He shut the door and I thought we'd soon be on our way to the station. Instead, he went up a walkway that led to the front entrance of the house. It left me alone in the idling car, giving me some time to gain perspective on this entire episode.

On the one hand, it was a bit embarrassing. Okay, *a lot* embarrassing. I suppose technically, now that I had been suspended,

I was an amateur. But did that really mean I had to go *acting* like an amateur?

Mostly, though, I just found it funny. I realize this is not, perhaps, the prevailing attitude among men who have just been unfairly suspended from their jobs and then gotten their heads stuck in cat doors. But one of my core beliefs, while not necessarily found in any major world religion, goes like this: one sign of a well-led life is that you have great stories to tell when it's over.

And there was no doubt that, someday, this would make for a hysterical story—assuming that I didn't end up having to tell it to fellow inmates during my daily hour of yard time.

After ten minutes, the cop came back out, followed by Jackman, who ventured as far as the end of the walkway, close enough to take a look at me. Next came his wife. She was a brittle-haired blonde who actually looked a lot like Jackman, except *her* manicured nails had colored polish on them. She stared at me with this look of horror on her face, like I was a dangerous animal that had been captured and caged. If I had just a bit more sense of theater, I would have started slobbering and thrashing around like the Tasmanian devil. Instead, I just grinned and waved.

Once the Jackmans were done gawking at the deranged criminal, they turned away and spoke briefly to the cop, who nodded and followed them back inside. Clearly, there was some irony to this: the perhaps-murderer was free to return to his home while the trespasser was in handcuffs. I thought about saying as much to the cop when he returned to the car. But really, what would that accomplish? You know, other than get me evaluated by a prison psychologist.

So I just asked, "Is he going to press charges?"

"Looks that way," the cop replied. "He doesn't seem to like you very much."

The feeling is mutual, I thought but did not say. Even if I hadn't been Mirandized, I didn't want some loose, wiseass comment like that coming back at me if there was a trial.

We made the drive to the Mendham Borough Police Department, a brick building with a peaked roof and glass doors that looked more like a gynecologist's office than a police station. Once inside, I was led through the booking process, which included fingerprinting and photographing. I gave the photographer my best smile, if only because I knew—if I ever got myself reinstated—some wiseacre like Buster Hays would get his hands on my mug shot and plaster it around the newsroom as a gag. Or at least that's what I would do to Buster if he ever got arrested.

I could only hope my mother's golfing group never heard about this.

Eventually, I was tossed into one of the two small holding cells they had in back. In the cell next to me there was a guy who looked dead and smelled worse. My belongings had been taken from me when I came in, so I had no idea what time it was. But I would guess an hour or more passed by the time my cop came back to me.

"This is your summons," he said, handing it to me on a clipboard with a pen. "Your court date is on there. You sign at the bottom to say you received it. It's not an admission of guilt."

"Okay," I said.

"I charged you with trespassing rather than breaking and entering. You got the 'breaking' part, but I'm not sure you ever quite got to 'entering.' "

Great. I was such an inept criminal even the cop was making fun of me.

"Now the good news," he continued. "I was able to get the judge on the phone to set bail for you. I suppose you know whose house that was and so did the judge. So, given the circumstances, he couldn't R and R you"—release me on my own recognizance—"but he set it pretty low, five thousand."

"That's the *good* news?"

"The alternative is I couldn't get the judge on the phone and you would have spent the night in the county jail."

"Good point," I said. "So what do I do now?"

"Well, a five-thousand-dollar bail means you have to post ten percent. You got five hundred dollars on you?"

"That depends: Will you let me run to an ATM machine?"

He shook his head.

"Then I think I need to make a phone call."

Before long, he set me up at a phone. I ran through my options—Mom and Dad definitely not being among them—and realized there was really only one person I could call without needing to do a whole lot of explaining. And fortunately, I had Tommy's cell phone number memorized.

"Mmph?" he said sleepily. I didn't know what time it was, but guessed it was now after midnight.

"Hey, Tommy, sorry to wake you up but I need a Venti-sized favor."

"Wha . . . you woke me up because you need coffee?"

"No, no. I'm at the Mendham Borough police station and I need someone to post bail for me."

This instantly brought Tommy to life. Of course, rather than express heartrending concern for my well-being, he just laughed at me.

"Oh! My! God! The clean-cut prep-school boy gets locked up with all the rough-and-tumble outlaws," he cackled. "It's like gay porn come true!"

"Nice. Very nice."

"Are the fellas being gentle? Remind them you're thin-boned and that you've never done this before. Maybe they'll give it to you tender instead of rough."

"Sorry to inform you and your dirty imagination, but this is

Mendham. They have zoning ordinances that ban rough-and-tumble outlaws. Besides, I'm in a cell by myself."

"Oh, too bad," Tommy said, sounding genuinely disappointed. "Well, what can I do for you?"

"Think you can scrape together five hundred bucks and come post bail for me?"

He thought for a moment. "If I max out my ATM and get a cash advance on my credit card, I think I can get to five hundred. Oh, and I'm going to need to stop at an all-night drugstore, too."

"Why?"

"So I can get you some soap on a rope."

Sometime during the next hour or two, they rousted my comatose neighbor and sent him off to the county jail. And not a moment too soon: his body odor was starting to seep into my clothes. Still, even after he departed, his scent lingered, which was among the things thwarting my efforts to grab a nap—along with the thin mattress, the dank air, and the constant squawking coming from the dispatch. In the end, I just engaged in a staring contest with the wall. The wall kept winning, but I felt like I was gaining on it.

By the time Tommy arrived and completed the necessary paperwork to secure my freedom, it was after two A.M. I had been a guest of the Mendham Borough police for roughly four hours. And while that should have been long enough for me to reconsider my life of crime, all it really did was redouble my resolve to ensure that Jackman spent a lot more time—like, the rest of his life—staring at prison walls.

After receiving my belongings, I entered the lobby to find Tommy slumped in a chair. He was wearing the same clothes as he had been earlier in the day—black shirt, gray pants—but they were far more rumpled.

"I suppose a mere 'thank you' probably doesn't cover this one, does it?" I said.

He stirred and gave me an up and down.

"You look almost as bad as I feel," he said, then wrinkled his nose. "And you smell worse."

"Yeah, I'm planning to lodge a complaint with management about the pillow mints, too," I said. "And, you know, they don't even give reward points here?"

"You sure? From what it sounds like, they're looking to give you a free extended stay sometime soon."

"We'll see, I guess. It's a fourth-degree crime and I don't have a prior record."

"Yeah, and you might get off when they decide you're too nuts to stand trial. When I announced I was there to post your bail, the desk sergeant goes, 'Oh, you mean the Peeping Tomcat?' I'm sorry, what the hell were you doing with your head stuck in a pet door?"

As we walked out to his car and started driving back toward mine, still parked down the street from Jackass's place, I gave Tommy a full recap on what I had learned about Jackman, finishing with how finding a large black SUV would be a potentially crowning piece of evidence.

"Why didn't you just do a little stakeout in front of his house and see what he drives to work in the morning?" Tommy asked when I was done.

"Everyone knows you don't commute in the same vehicle you use to commit vehicular homicide," I replied. "Besides, I'm impatient."

Neither Tommy nor I knew Mendham very well, so it took

us a few wrong turns before we got on course. He had to drop me off at my Malibu, which meant we ended up cruising past Jackman's black-gated driveway.

"That's his house," I said.

"Looks dark."

"Yeah, I'm sure everyone is fast asleep after the excitement of the evening."

Tommy said nothing, but a small kernel of an idea had suddenly plopped itself down in my head. It quickly germinated, dug in its roots, and started reaching out its stalks, and before I knew it, I was opening my mouth to give voice to it.

"You know, you could sneak in there right now and have a little look," I said.

Tommy's head whipped in my direction.

"What?"

"It'll be easy. I've already scoped it out and made every possible mistake. We know about the camera, and besides, there's no one awake now to be looking at it. It was just bad luck I got caught in the first place. It's not like you'd be breaking into the Louvre."

"Forget it."

"C'mon, if you get caught, I'll have them wrangle up some of those rough-and-tumble outlaws you were fantasizing about."

Tommy made a face like someone replaced his entire shoe collection with white Reeboks—the kind with Velcro.

"Haven't you broken the law enough for one evening without being an accomplice to another crime?" he asked.

"I've got a flashlight in my car. You can shine it in there, take a quick look at the bumpers, and be out before anyone knows you were ever there. You're much sleeker and stealthier than I."

"That's true," he said, letting the thought drift along for a second before swatting it down. "No. No! Are you crazy? Absolutely not. I'm not getting my head stuck in some stupid cat door."

"No way you get stuck. Your head is much smaller. Look at this big coconut of mine. It's practically Jupiter. Yours is more like, I don't know, Mercury or something."

"That doesn't mean I'm going to go along with an idea you're pulling out of Uranus."

We both stopped to snicker. Hard to resist a Uranus joke.

He pulled up alongside my car. Decision time was here.

"I'm going to get my flashlight. When I get back, I want you to be in the passenger seat."

I climbed out, expecting that as soon as I was clear, Tommy would gun the engine and put down a fresh layer of rubber in his haste to get away. But no, as I retrieved the small flashlight from my glove compartment, I heard the driver's side door open and close. And when I returned, he was riding shotgun.

"Hurry up before I change my mind," Tommy said. "I'm only doing this because of those pocket squares Jackman wears. He gives pocket squares a bad name, and I'll not have anyone besmirching an otherwise wonderful accessory."

"Thanks ag—"

He held up a hand. "Just drive. Go by slowly so I can get a good look at it, then drop me off down the street."

I did as instructed. Before he departed, I reminded him about the security camera and the motion-sensing lights over the garage.

"Don't worry," he replied. "I don't plan to screw this up like you did. Just stay here."

"Leave your cell on. I'll keep a lookout for cops."

He didn't answer, taking off at a brisk jog before I even killed the engine. I waited in the dark, staying alert for Mendham's finest.

But there was no traffic of any sort. New York may be the city that never sleeps, but Mendham likes to get its shut-eye.

Ten minutes later, Tommy jogged back and jumped in the passenger seat.

“Nothing,” he said, panting a little.

“What do you mean *nothing*?”

“No SUV.”

“Are you sure? Could you see that well?”

“Sure I could see. I walked right inside and turned the lights on.”

“You what?”

“While you were busy playing cat burglar, you missed the most obvious fake rock in the world just to the left of the door. It had a key inside with the security code written on it—8331, in case you care. So I used the key, shut off the security system, and walked inside. There’s a silver Lexus and a tan Ford. Neither one is an SUV, neither one is black. Would you like their license plates and VIN numbers? I got those, too.”

I started the car, rolling past Jackman’s still-dark house.

“So, what, I guess he must have had someone do it for him? A hired hit?”

“Or a rented car,” Tommy said. “Either way, it’s not in his garage. Can I go home now? If I miss too much REM sleep, my skin breaks out.”

I have scant memory of driving to Bloomfield, showering, or getting under the covers. But I must have done all those things, because I was at home, in bed, and smelling unlike rot when my cell phone rang at precisely nine the next morning.

I was in the midst of one of my usual anxiety dreams, the one where I’ve shown up for the final exam in a college French class, and I suddenly realize I don't speak a word of French. So, at first, the phone was ringing in the middle of the dream, just as the professor was passing out the exam.

When I finally figured out who I was, where I was, and that I shouldn't answer with "*bonjour*," my phone had rung three times. I tapped the answer button and tried to say my name, but with my vocal cords still asleep, it came out as, "Carr Rahh."

"Carter, it's Jim McNabb." His voice boomed through my earpiece. He had me on speakerphone, and like most people of a certain age, he felt he needed to yell at it to be heard. It was loud enough that Deadline, who had been pressed up against my thigh and doing his best impression of a stuffed animal, actually lifted his head to investigate. Usually, it would take the Four Horsemen of the Apocalypse having a hoedown at the foot of the bed to stir such curiosity.

"Hi, Jim," I said, propping myself up and stifling a yawn.

"Are you busy?" McNabb yelled.

"Not for a while. I got indefinitely suspended from my job yesterday."

"Oh yeah?" he said, with his usual interest in anything that sounded like scuttlebutt—enough that I could hear the sound of him picking up the handpiece and taking me off speakerphone. "What happened?"

I debated whether I should confide in McNabb, who tended to use information as leverage. But, in this case, desperation outweighed caution. Besides, he was a friendly guy. And sometimes you just need friends.

"Jackman is on to me," I said. "He trumped up some stuff against me and tried talking Brodie into firing me. The old man wouldn't go quite that far, but he did suspend me."

"Really? Wow. Well, I guess it's no surprise that prick plays for keeps. You better watch your back around him. We've already seen what he's capable of doing to an employee who pisses him off."

"Yeah, thanks," I said, making a mental note to look both ways when I crossed the street.

"So how long are you on the bench? A week? Two?"

"Try three months."

"Whoa, that's a big number!" McNabb said, like we were discussing how much I lost on the ponies over the weekend. "See, that's why you need a union behind you. We'd file an immediate appeal, probably throw in a grievance, too, just to complicate matters. If they still didn't want you coming to work while it all got settled, no problem—we'd make sure you were getting a paycheck the whole time. Eventually we'd throw enough stuff at them they'd be begging us to settle. You'd get a free vacation and never be out a dime."

"Well, I don't have a union. So until I can prove to Brodie what Jackman's real motivation is, I'm on a one-way street to the poorhouse. I'm hoping you're calling with some information that will help me get off it."

"Yeah, yeah, actually, I am," he said. "I got something to show you."

"What is it?"

"I don't want to ruin the surprise. Just come into the office. You got to see it in person. It'll be worth the trip. It's something you can actually use—no off-the-record this time."

"Okay. I'll see you in about forty-five minutes."

"I'll be here."

Deadline had slipped back into repose, and with the Four Horsemen elsewhere—probably behind the counter at a Starbucks, screwing up people's orders—my departure from bed did not disturb him. I had a brief debate about what I ought to wear, inasmuch as I was technically off duty. But I settled on my usual reporter's garb, which included my notepad in my right pocket and two pens in my left. That was my armor, after all. And even if this particular knight had lost his liege, it was still what I wanted to wear as I went into battle.

I waved to my neighbor, Constance, as I left my house—she was watering her lawn, as usual—and made the trip to downtown Newark. I found parking outside a dry cleaner on a cramped side street, about eight blocks from my destination. Now that I was no longer on the *Eagle-Examiner's* dime, I needed to keep my expenses down. No parking garages for Citizen Ross.

I got out of the car to find the sun was already starting to beat down on the pavement. The temperature and humidity were doing that mid-July tag team where one slams you to the canvas and the other jumps off the ropes and lands on you. I was already wiping sweat off my brow by the time I finished my eight-block walk and made it to the revolving front door of the National Newark Building.

I went through the routine of announcing myself at security, riding up to the twentieth floor, and pushing through the doors etched with the IFIW logo. At the reception desk, I was greeted by a smiling Jim McNabb, who was again dressed like he was on his way to play in a member-guest golf tournament. Every day must have been business casual for Big Jimmy.

We took what appeared to be the same circuitous route back to his office, winding our way through cubicles and workstations, past the low-rent bleached blonde with the overdone eye makeup. She was standing next to her desk, wearing a tight blouse that, if it could talk, would say, *Hi, I'm trying too hard.*

"Hey, Big Jimmy!" she called out playfully.

"Hey, candypants," he said.

We rounded the next corner and I couldn't help myself.

"*Candypants?*" I asked.

"I don't do that with most of the girls," Big Jimmy said. "But that one actually likes it, you know? Makes her feel good, like she must be doing an okay job because why else would the boss pay attention to her?"

Either that or it made her feel like her ass had just been caramelized.

We rounded one last corner and went into McNabb's office, with its commanding view from Newark to Manhattan and all the Superfund sites that lay in between.

"I'm glad you were able to come in," he said, settling himself into his ergonomically correct chair and sliding a keyboard out of a drawer under his desk. "I got something I want to show you on the computer."

He typed in some kind of password and waited as the machine came out of dormancy.

"I just love the computer," he said. "I'm not real natural with it, but I'm trying. Some guys my age, they need to be dragged kicking and screaming into this stuff. Not me. To me, this is the future and you got to get with the program. So give me the BlackBerry, the blueberry, the iPhone, the mePhone, the youPhone. I'm actually thinking about getting a new one right now. I want to stay current with all of it."

He started working the mouse with the skill of someone who, for all his good intentions, never quite got comfortable with the thing.

"Okay," he said. "I was going to forward you this e-mail, but I wanted you to be able to see it with your own eyes, exactly as I got it, so you didn't think I was monkeying around with it or making it say something it didn't really say."

He turned the flat-screen monitor on his desk toward me. He had highlighted a message from Jackman that had been sent July 1—exactly a week before Nancy was killed—at 10:34 A.M.

"This, as you can see, is an e-mail from Gary Jackman. You can look at the full header later if you want to so you can see it's legit."

"That's okay, I trust you, Jim."

"I know you do. I just know how you reporters are. You guys have to be suspicious of everything and I don't blame you. I want you to know this is for real."

"Got it."

He double clicked on the e-mail and I started reading:

Jackman, Gary [gjackman@eagleexaminer.com]
To: 'McNabb, James'
Cc: 'Porterhouse, Gregory'; 'Koncz, Sophie'; 'DeLillo, Alec'; 'Blake, Michael'
Subject: IFIW Local 117 Renegotiations

Jim,

As you are aware, these continue to be extraordinarily difficult times for newspapers, and the *Newark Eagle-Examiner* has not been immune to the forces that are ravaging the industry as a whole. In short, revenues continue to fall, despite sustained efforts to stop the slide.

As I have told you previously, this newspaper has been operating at a loss for far longer than any business ought to. And while our owners have taken a long-term view and shown remarkable patience, that patience has come to an end. They have informed me that if I cannot return the paper to at least some small level of profitability by the end of the year, they will cease operations and sell all remaining assets.

The only way for us to avoid this dire scenario is to drastically change our business model. To date, our Mailers' union, Drivers' union, and Printers' union have recognized the extraordinary nature of our distress and agreed to substantial givebacks on their contracts. Our nonrepresented employees have also withstood a series of pay cuts and furloughs. Other arrangements with vendors and suppliers have been modified. Your union, our Deliverers, remains the lone holdout. Yet without a new agreement with our Deliverers, we will have no choice but to cease operation. All employees—from your members to this paper's publisher—would be terminated.

This is not an idle threat or posturing for the purpose of negotiation. This is a necessity, and I will be happy to have our COO open our books to prove it to you. Unless we can reach an accord, your union will be responsible for bringing the *Newark Eagle-Examiner*, one of the great remaining American newspapers, to its knees. It is my hope we can work together in good faith to avoid this dire outcome.

Sincerely,
Gary

When I finished, I turned the screen back in his direction. I knew things were real bad at my paper. I didn't know they were *that* bad. It occurred to me for the first time that when my suspension ended, I might not have a job to return to.

"Now, you tell me: Does that sound like a man desperate

enough to commit murder?" McNabb asked. "He's not only going to lose his job, he'd go down as the guy who couldn't save a 'great American newspaper.' He'd never get another job near that pay grade. That's a pretty powerful motive, to me."

I thought about the $2.27 million McMansion, the $35,000 property tax bill, the his-and-hers matching manicures, the pocket squares, all the elitist trappings of a well-financed life that would instantly evaporate if Jackman found himself on the unemployment line next to the rest of his former employees.

"Can I have a printout of that?" I asked.

"I figured you were gonna ask that," he said, sliding a piece of paper across the desk at me. I grabbed what I could tell was a photocopy of the e-mail, albeit with a few identifying characteristics strategically blacked out. "I figured it was cc'd to enough people that any one of us could have leaked it to you."

"Great," I said. "Just curious: Is your e-mail backed up somewhere?"

"Why do you ask?"

"I just want to make sure that e-mail exists somewhere on a server, so if I got a prosecutor to subpoena you, they would definitely find it somewhere."

"Oh. Oh yeah. Well, we do backups, for sure. But I'm not planning on erasing this. And if I got a subpoena, yeah, that'd be great. That would let me off the hook with my board and everyone else, because I could just say, 'Hey, I had no choice.' Why, you thinking about taking this to the cops?"

"Not yet," I said. "At this point, I'd just be a disgruntled employee with a wild theory. I'm still a few facts short."

"Yeah, I guess this could still all be one big coincidence, right?"

He looked at me with a frank, open face. And I once again found myself wondering whether I could trust McNabb with more information. He was a born blabbermouth, the last guy who could be relied on to keep a secret. But the more I thought about it, the more I realized I didn't actually *want* him to keep it secret. Having McNabb working back channels for me might just flush out more Jackman adversaries with heretofore unknown evidence.

Besides, there was that whole thing about no longer having the luxury of caution.

"Actually," I said, "it's no coincidence."

Over the next ten minutes, I recounted for McNabb a distilled version of the story Mrs. Alfaro told me. Naturally, I was careful not to disclose her name, say where she lived, or give identifying characteristics—I wanted to respect the pledge of confidentiality I had given her—but I didn't spare the details. As I spoke, McNabb's mouth set into an ugly pout. I got the sense it was hard for him to hear. He had obviously been fond of Nancy Marino.

When I finished, he stood up and walked over toward the window. He put his hands on his hips and made a loud shushing sound as he emptied his lungs. His eyes appeared to be focused on something far beyond Manhattan. He shook his head a few times, like he still didn't want to believe it, then went back to staring.

"That son of a bitch," he said at last, without turning away from the window. "I know I told you I thought it was Jackman, but I was always thinking maybe I had it wrong. You assume people are basically good, you know? Nancy, she . . . that kid was . . . she didn't deserve anything like this. He killed her because of, what, a few bucks an hour in a stinking contract?"

Except—and I had already done this math—it was more than just a few bucks. Say we had one thousand carriers, as Buster Hays suggested. Say they each worked three hours a day delivering the newspaper and did it seven days a week, 365 days a year. If Nancy was any guide, they were getting paid $18 an hour to do it. But a fifty percent pay cut meant a $9-an-hour savings for the paper. That rounded to about $7 million a year. In a budget where years of ritualized fasting had created negligible fat, $7 million could certainly make the difference between red and black—which would make the difference between Jackman getting to remain as the publisher of a fully operating major metropolitan newspaper and being put out of work.

"It's like you said, Jackman was getting desperate," I said.

"A powerful man facing the loss of his power will do just about anything to protect it," McNabb said thoughtfully.

"Yeah. Yeah, I guess he will."

"So do the cops know about this yet?"

"My source doesn't trust the cops. I think I'll eventually be able to talk her into working with them, when it comes to that, but for right now that's not a priority."

McNabb walked back from the window and sat down, flopping his weight heavily on the chair.

"What *is* a priority is that last conversation you had with Jackman," I continued.

"Huh?"

"The talk you had with him in the bar the night before Nancy was killed."

"Oh yeah. Oh geez, I wasn't even thinking about that. But you don't even need that anymore, right? Your source saw him do it."

"My source saw a large black SUV do it," I reminded him. "She never laid eyes on the driver, and even if she had, it would be a stretch to say she could make a positive ID that would hold up. Jackman had to be going fifty, sixty miles an hour at a minimum by the time he hit Nancy. My source was way too far away, and being on the second floor, the angle was all wrong for her to be able to see the driver's face anyway."

"I guess you're right."

"I'm beginning to think Jackman wasn't actually the driver. He strikes me as the kind of guy who might hire someone to do his dirty work. I'm fairly certain he doesn't own a black SUV himself. I think he either rented himself a killer or rented himself a car."

"Oh yeah? What makes you think that?"

"I, uh, had his garage investigated late last night," I said, throwing in a wink.

"What do you mean?"

"I broke into Jackman's garage and had a look around," I said, leaving out the small detail that Tommy had been the one doing the breaking and looking. "There's a Lexus and a Ford in there, but neither are SUVs."

"You got to be careful doing something like that. You could get yourself in trouble, someone sees you sneaking into garages."

"Yeah, well, I didn't say I got away with it. I spent last night as a guest of the Mendham Borough Police Department."

"No kiddin'! You going to be okay? I know some good lawyers . . ."

"Thanks, I'll figure that out later," I said. "In any event, it's going to make proving his guilt a little more difficult. The case might be more circumstantial than I or anyone else likes. But it also makes that bar conversation absolutely pivotal. Think about it from a jury's perspective. You hear the suspect was drunk and tossing out threats, and then hours later the person they were threatening got killed? Even if we never did find that black SUV, your testimony might be enough to get a conviction."

"I told you, I can't get involved like that," McNabb said quickly, defensively. "What I was doing with Jackman could get me in real trouble with my board. When I told you about that conversation, you promised me off the record. Off. The. Record. Don't you go back on your word."

His big belly had shoved the keyboard back under the desk, and he was leaning toward me, pointing a finger at me with his face flushed.

"I'm not. I'm not," I assured him. "But, at this point, you've got to agree that a murder is bigger than you getting a little jammed up with your board. Be reasonable here."

"So nothing with you is really off the record, huh? You're going to run to the cops and rat me out?"

"Just relax. I'm not running anywhere or ratting anyone, Jim. All I'm saying is, I need your help. There's got to be something you can do for me or give me that will help establish Jackman was drunk and raving that night. Surely some bartender or patron overheard you guys? Then if the cops approach you and ask you, you can just say it was a friendly get-to-know-you drink that went bad, and you can leave out the part about contract negotiations—"

"Yeah, but eventually I'll have to testify."

"That's a long, long way down the road," I said. "Let's worry about getting Jackman arrested first. The fact is, Jackman will eventually realize we got him, but he'll have just enough leverage—because there will inevitably be holes in the case—that he'll get a decent plea deal. You'll never have to testify about anything."

McNabb leaned back and exhaled, closing his eyes and rubbing his temples in a circular motion with two fat middle fingers. Finally he opened his eyes.

"Let me think about it for a day or two," he said.

For now, it was the best I was going to get. I just had to give him that space. He led me out of his office, past candypants, past the reception desk, and out the etched-glass doors.

I was back down in the lobby when my phone rang. It was Tina.

"Hey, how's my favorite ex-editor?" I asked.

"Carter, you need to come in immediately," she said, her voice terse and low.

"What, you can't live one day without me? I'm flattered."

"Stop joking around. Brodie just heard about the incident at Jackman's house last night, and he's absolutely fuming. I've never seen him this mad. If you've got anything to say for yourself before he makes your suspension permanent, I suggest you come here damn fast and say it."

At first, he was both astonished and impressed by his opponent's temerity. He had been around reporters plenty of times. Most of them thought daring was to plunge into an especially large box of documents.

This one obviously had different ideas. Snooping around a house in the dark of night? Breaking into a garage? Being willing to do the dirty work with no thought of the danger involved? It was the rare reporter who pushed that far to get a story.

But his surprise at—and grudging respect for—those tactics quickly gave way to other feelings. Like irritation. And anger. And hatred.

The threat was more serious than ever. A few threads of this supposedly perfect crime had already started to unravel. And even if Carter Ross was still far off in certain areas, he was getting close—way too close—in others. He was starting to know about things no one ought to have been able to discover. And if he had learned that much already, while showing no signs of wanting to pull back, he might just discover even more. Depending on how determined he was, he might figure out the whole thing. And Ross seemed pretty determined.

Under most circumstances, it didn't take much to break a man, especially those soft, white-collar types. A little push here. A little shove there. Men who had worked to achieve a certain standing didn't want to lose it. Threaten them with the loss of something that mattered to them and they backed off. You just had to figure out what was important to them and make sure it became imperiled.

Ross didn't seem to work that way. He was far less risk averse. He wasn't put off by the potential loss of his job, by hits to his reputation, or even the threat of jail. Who knows what else he might put on the line?

Ross had already been through things that would put most men off the case, but it wasn't enough. Not yet. Clearly, a more active approach would be required.

CHAPTER 6

Hurry. I definitely needed to hurry. I pushed through the revolving doors, feeling the muggy embrace of a heat index that had to be 105 already, with the hottest part of the day yet to come. I started power-walking back toward my car, feeling the sweat popping on my upper lip after about four steps. By the end of the second block, the spot where my briefcase strap rubbed against my shoulder had started to soak through. By block four, the perspiration on my forehead was beading and rolling down the side of my face. By block six, a small rain forest had sprouted in my pants.

And then I got to my Malibu—or, rather, the side of the street where my Malibu should have been. But it was completely clear. I felt a surge of panic, which I tried to suppress. Maybe I had gotten the wrong street? I remembered parking in front of a dry cleaner. And, sure enough, the dry cleaner was still there. My car was not.

I stood there, dumbly gawking at the long stretch of naked curb. Less than an hour earlier it had been haphazardly littered with vehicles—not densely packed, mind you, but that's why I had been able to find parking there to begin with. And now, it had either been attacked by a large and unusually well-coordinated band of car thieves or . . .

I looked at the parking sign for the first time: STREET CLEANING WED 10–12. Then I fished into my pocket for my cell phone: "10:41 A.M. Wed Jul 13."

Sure enough, upon closer inspection, there wasn't a scrap of litter on the street, except for the small, dusty parabola where the driver of a street-cleaning machine had been forced to swerve around my Malibu and then, out of spite, reported me to the parking police.

In some municipalities, being towed is merely a huge annoyance. Then there's Newark. New Jersey's largest city is serviced by a variety of companies that have contracts to do police towing, but most of them seem to share a few characteristics: they are headquartered in the swamp by the turnpike, in that smelly industrial crotch pit that unduly odorizes New Jersey's reputation; they are staffed by men who have all the charm of bridge-dwelling trolls; and they are fully empowered by the law to first steal your car, then extort whatever they want out of you before they give it back.

And I just didn't have the time to deal with that hassle, not with Brodie arming for hostilities. By the time I repossessed my car, he would have mobilized his troops, declared war, and completely overrun the small island nation that was me and my career at the *Newark Eagle-Examiner.* I had to make a token effort at building defensive structures while there was still the chance it might do some good.

It was a twenty-minute walk back to the newsroom, fifteen if I hustled. So I started hustling, making my legs churn as fast as I could while perspiration squirted out of every pore in my body. Before long, my feet actually started to feel squishy, my tie had become something resembling a drooling baby's bib, and I was beginning to worry if my white shirt was about to become translucent, turning me into the hairiest wet T-shirt contestant this side of the Atlantic.

By the time I barged through the front entrance to the *Eagle-Examiner,* I looked like I had just run the Borneo High Noon 10K. The rain forest in my pants had become positively Amazonian, with a complex network of streams and rivers feeding into the big, mushy bog that was my ass. Even my knees felt sweaty.

But there was no time to towel off. Brodie was on the warpath and needed to be talked off it. I ducked into the elevator just as the door was closing, next to a woman from the classified department who discreetly took two steps to her left so she wouldn't get wet. I disembarked on the floor for the newsroom to find Tina waiting for me.

"What the hell happened to you?" she demanded. "What took so long?"

"My car got towed."

"Okay, but why did you swim here?"

"I walked. It just happens to be a hundred and fifty-seven degrees outside."

"Well, you aren't seeing Brodie like that. He already thinks you've lost your mind. You can't come into his office looking like you've spent the morning practicing drowning. Come on."

Tina charged toward her office with single-minded focus, and I did my best to keep up, cutting my way through a thick underbrush of curious stares from my (former) colleagues. Everyone, I'm sure, knew I had been suspended and they had probably been gossiping about it ceaselessly. The only consolation was that they didn't know about my escapade at Jackman's house.

Or so I thought. Then I went past Buster Hays's desk. He looked up and with a sly grin let out a "meeeeeeooooow!"

Some of his enablers cackled.

"How you doin', 'Peeping Tomcat'?" he asked.

"What the . . . How do *you* know about that?"

"I read the paper, Ivy. You should try it sometime."

He slid a folded copy of that day's paper toward me. Sure enough, the third item down in the Morris County crime roundup read, "Bloomfield man arrested for peering." I scanned it quickly—it was just a four-paragraph brief—and while I saw my name and the particulars of my crime, I didn't see Jackman's name. It ended with, "Borough Police, who say this is the first known case of cat door infiltration in Morris County, are calling the alleged perpetrator the 'Peeping Tomcat.' Ross could not be reached for comment."

I sighed. Of course I couldn't be reached. I was in jail.

"You got some kind of feline fetish, Ivy?" Buster asked, prompting some barely muffled tittering from the peanut gallery. I grinned—better to laugh it off than show weakness when it comes to newsroom ball-busting—but before I could come up with a retort, Tina charged toward me, grabbed my arm, and pulled me into her office. She snatched her gym bag from behind her desk, then pushed through me on her way back out.

"Follow me," she said.

Tina was wearing a sleeveless navy blue tank top that nicely showed off her arms and a short tan skirt that did even better for her legs. I would have followed her anywhere.

She cut down the back stairwell, past a fire exit whose alarm had long ago been disabled by the newsroom smokers who sneak out for a quick cigarette. We descended into the basement, where she led me to the old pressmen's locker room. There hadn't been presses in the building for at least thirty years—they had been moved out of the city, to suburban facilities close to interstates—but we still had the locker room where the pressmen long ago retreated to wash off the day's ink. It looked like it could have belonged in any high school gymnasium, right down to the communal shower.

Tina locked the door behind us.

"Strip," she commanded.

"What?"

"Strip," she repeated. "Now."

Tina didn't pause to see if I was complying, just went into the shower room and turned on the water. When she returned, she bent down into her gym bag and emerged with a towel, which she placed on one of the benches, then dove back in and came up with a hair dryer. I just stood there, watching her quick and determined movements, still fully dressed in my sopping clothes.

"Come on, we don't have time for you to be modest," she said, pointing the hair dryer at me like it was a gun. "Hop in the shower and I'll do what I can to dry off your clothes while you're in there. Now strip."

"Tina, I, uhh . . ." I stopped, feeling myself flush a little bit.

"What's the matter?"

"Nothing, I just . . ."

"You want me to strip, too? Fine."

The next thing I knew, Tina had pulled off her top and was wriggling out of her skirt. Underneath she had on a plain black bra and matching panties—no lacy underthings for Tina.

I pulled off my tie, then started fumbling with the buttons on my shirt, which had been cemented into place by sweat and were noticeably unyielding.

"Hurry up," she said.

"I'm sorry, I've got more clothing on than you."

"Yeah, you sure do," Tina said, stepping quickly out of her

underwear, then unhooking her bra and laying it neatly on top of where she had piled her other clothes. She shuffled off her shoes, then stood before me, hands on her hips, perfectly naked and, well, perfect.

"There," she said. "That's how it's done."

I was trying to maintain a professional demeanor about the whole thing—this was professional, right?—and resist the urge to attack any one of several very vulnerable, very delicious parts on her suddenly available body.

"You're going too slow," Tina said, exasperated. She hurried over to me and started fumbling with my belt. I felt a muscle somewhere deep in my abdomen, one I didn't use all that often, tighten involuntarily. This was too much.

"Tina!"

But my objection—if you could really call it that—had no effect on her. She had unhooked my belt, unbuttoned my pants, and lowered my zipper. She yanked off my pants with one move, then took my boxers with the next. I had, by this point, stopped moving, having been mentally incapacitated by the flow of blood out of my brain and into other regions of my body. So Tina took over with my shirt buttons, finishing that job quickly enough. Then she shoved my arms in the air and started pulling my sodden T-shirt over my head.

But, my height being what it is, she had to narrow the distance between us and go up on her tiptoes to be able to reach that high. And somewhere during that process, she leaned into me a little bit too closely, causing parts of us to sort of, well, brush. By accident. And then suddenly it wasn't so much of an accident.

The next thing I knew, Tina had knocked me over—I still had my pants around my ankles, so I was easily tipped—and was crawling on top of me. Her mouth hungrily attacked mine, and all that sweating I had been doing was suddenly just lubrication as our bodies slid against each other. She seemed to have at least two tongues, because at one point I swore one was in my mouth while the other was in my ear.

And for as much as I was in the moment—Tina was demanding as much—I was also sort of detached from it all. There had been so many times when the lighting and the music had been just right, when the mood was set and everything seemed preordained for us to consummate our relationship. Yet it had never happened. I just couldn't believe, after all the near-misses, this was where we would finally collide: in the bowels of the *Newark Eagle-Examiner*'s basement, in the pressmen's locker room, under the harshness of the fluorescent lights with the shower running, when I was probably just moments away from getting fired.

If any of this was going through Tina's mind, I couldn't tell. She was moaning too loudly, her throaty voice bouncing off the hard tile, and she seemed intent on grinding me right through the subfloor. Not that I minded. I was beyond feeling anything but pleasure at that point. The world had become one big, slippy-slidey-wonderful funhouse, and Tina was the only person in it. She readjusted herself, and I thought she was getting into one of those positions I've only read about in books.

Then she rolled off me.

"Oh my God, what am I doing?" she said, giggling and smacking her hand to her forehead like it was just some minor mix-up, like putting ketchup on her burger when she meant to use mustard. "Sorry, I got a little carried away."

I groaned.

"Tina, you can't just—"

"Oh, what, a guy could die?" she said, chortling some more and rolling her eyes. "Come on, I haven't fallen for that line since high school. Go take care of it yourself in the shower if you have to."

I lay on my back, breathing hard, feeling the throbbing subside. A woman laughing when you're naked—no matter what the circumstances—tends to have that effect. Finally, I raised myself to a sitting position and untied my shoes so I was able to slip off my pants.

Tina, meanwhile, was back to being all business, plugging in her hair dryer and running it over my shirt. She was still naked, still quite stunning, but was pouring her attention into her task, paying me not the slightest bit of mind. So I stumbled into the shower, which had been running for a while and was hot enough to have kicked up a cloud of steam.

I got in for a second, then realized I was going about things all wrong. A hot shower was the last thing I needed.

I reached over to the nozzle and twisted it all the way to cold.

Twenty minutes later, Tina and I emerged from the locker room, doing our best to look respectable. My clothes were still damp, but at least there was no danger of me dripping on anyone. The shower had cooled my core temperature enough that I was practically shivering in the air-conditioning. Tina had reassembled her clothing and, other than some slight extra color to her face, looked composed.

It felt good to have Tina on my side again. We'd had our ups and downs—among other adventures—but I could tell she was fighting for me now, squarely in my corner. I was whole again.

"So what's our plan?" I asked as we marched back up toward the newsroom, a united front once again.

"That depends. Do you have *anything* to say for yourself?"

"Yeah, as a matter of fact, I do."

"Mind sharing?"

We had reached the landing with the fire exit, the one the smokers used, and I stopped there. I had, up until that point, been consumed by the drama with my car, the moisture in my pants, and, well, other happenings in my pants. It had given me no time to think of how, exactly, I was going to explain myself. But Tina could help me with that.

"You remember Nancy Marino?" I said.

"The papergirl. The reason you were out at that diner in Bloomfield with Nikki Papawhatever instead of bear-spotting with Lunky."

"Right."

I paused to gather strength. Here goes:

"I'm pretty sure Gary Jackman killed her."

"Excuse me?"

"She was killed in a hit-and-run accident, only it was no accident. I interviewed a woman who said someone driving a large black SUV had been stalking Nancy for several days, then intentionally ran her over.

"So I started asking myself, Who would want to kill Nancy Marino?" I continued. "I interviewed her sister, who told me Nancy had taken a very hard line in our paper's negotiations with IFIW–Local 117. Then I talked to Jim McNabb, the union's executive director, who said the night before Nancy was killed, he was having a drink and/or some unofficial negotiations with Jackman. McNabb kept telling Jackman that Nancy wouldn't budge, and then suddenly Jackman went nonlinear and started making all kinds of threats about how he would 'take care' of Nancy Marino. The next morning Nancy was dead."

I stopped to see how Tina was taking all of this.

Unfortunately, she was looking at me like she usually did when I was selling her a story that was still half-assed.

"So to prove all this, you thought you'd get your head stuck in Jackman's cat door?"

"I was trying to peek into his garage to see if there was an SUV in there."

"And?"

"No dice. He must have hired someone to do it for him."

"And the thing with Jackman's secretary yesterday . . . what was that?"

"I was trying to get confirmation that Jackman had been drinking with McNabb last Thursday, maybe learn where they went so I could interview the bartender."

"And?"

"Nothing," I admitted. "But McNabb did give me this. It shows how desperate Jackman was to get Local 117 to renegotiate. Pretty much everything was at stake."

I went into my pocket and fished out my copy of the Jackman e-mail that McNabb had given me. It was a little damp but had otherwise held up okay. Tina pored over it for a second, then handed it back to me.

"This . . . this doesn't prove anything other than that the paper is in trouble, which anyone knows."

"It's a piece of the puzzle," I said.

"Still . . . let me get this straight. You've been harassing the publisher of this paper because you think he killed someone?"

I nodded.

"He's the *publisher*," she said.

"A publisher who once brained a guy with a seven-iron."

"Yeah, but . . . that's . . . I mean, someone came after him. Say what you will about the brutality of the act, but he *was* defending himself."

"So say he and his golfing buddies."

"Look, publishers of major newspapers don't just go around killing people."

"Don't they? Why? Because they live in fancy houses and wear pocket squares? Don't let yourself get blinded by a title."

"I'm just saying, you know how tight Brodie and Jackman are. I don't know if Brodie is going to buy this."

"We can convince him," I said.

"We?"

"Yeah, we. You do believe me, right?"

Tina looked down at the floor, to a corner of the landing where a few dust bunnies had accumulated. It was not the first time in the last few days she couldn't bring herself to make eye contact.

"Tina, I've got to know I have you behind me. For whatever personal history we have and for whatever *that* was"—I gestured in the direction of the pressmen's locker room—"we've still got a lot of professional history, too. We're on the brink of a huge story, and I just need you to have a little faith and a little patience and give me time to prove it. I've told you that a lot of other times before and I don't think I've ever led you wrong. That's got to count for something."

Her head was still down. The dust bunnies were obviously quite fascinating.

"I want to believe you, I really do," she said. "It's just you've been acting so strange. You lied to me about being with the intern. You made a scene at a funeral ho—"

"That was *not* a scene. Jackman is twisting everything. He's obviously trying to get rid of me."

"Was he twisting everything when he said you lied to his secretary? Honestly, Larry from accounting?"

"Ted," I corrected her. "I was Ted from accounting. I was just trying to get a little information. I wasn't really representing myself because it's not like I was going to quote her in the newspaper. I just didn't want Jackman to know I was on to him."

"Well, you sure have a strange way of going about it, showing up at his house and getting yourself arrested like some peeping pervert? Jackman told Brodie his wife had to take two Valium just to settle herself down enough to sleep last night . . ."

"Imagine how tough it'd be if she knew she was sleeping next to a killer . . ."

"Then Tommy has to come bail you out? *Think* about that behavior from someone else's perspective. You've always been on the edge as a reporter, but this is so far beyond that. It's so strange and bizarre. I don't . . ."

Her voice trailed off.

"Okay, but think about it from the perspective of—" I started, then stopped myself.

I am, in general, a fairly easygoing guy. I don't even simmer most of the time, much less reach a boil. But every once in a while, I get hot—and when I do, it's molten. And then it's pretty much Mount Saint Helens time. Which is where I suddenly found myself. I was through with this conversation, through with Tina and her ridiculous games, through with having editors who trusted some empty-suited scrooge of a publisher rather than one of their own reporters.

So I blew up.

"You know what? Forget it. Just forget it. I'm not crawling up to Brodie's office to grovel when he'd rather listen to a bunch of lies from some cold-blooded murderer. Here," I said, handing her my company-issued cell phone, then reaching into my bag for my company-issued laptop and thrusting it into her arms. "Brodie can kiss my ass and you can, too, because I quit. I *quit*. I don't want to work at a newspaper where my editors don't believe in me."

I slammed my weight into the fire exit door, barging through it before Tina had a chance to say a word. She just stood there, juggling my computer and phone, looking bewildered. I heard the door slam behind me but didn't see it. I wasn't looking back.

Not that I knew quite where I was going. This is the problem with my eruptions: they last all of fifteen minutes, after which I'm left with a bunch of soot and ash and a few gassy belches.

For a while, all I did was wander around in a daze, trying to figure out just what had happened to me. At the beginning of the week I had a job, a car, a quasi-girlfriend, a clean criminal record, a phone, and a computer. In the span of two breathtaking days, I had managed to lose all of those things. My life had swirled right down the toilet, and I couldn't figure out when I missed the flushing sound.

Eventually, when heat and hunger overwhelmed me, I stumbled into an air-conditioned pizzeria and settled into my usual two-slices-and-a-Coke-Zero routine, which allowed me to regain equilibrium. Jersey pizza is noted for its restorative powers in that respect.

Midway through the first slice, I had the impulse to call Tina, beg her to take me back, and offer to do the necessary groveling with Brodie. Then, toward the end of the second slice, I talked myself out of it. Tina was right: I sounded like a nut, trying to push some wild theory about a murdering publisher without being able to prove it. Once I had the Jackman story nailed, the old man would beg me to come back—mostly because if he didn't, I'd take it to the *New York Times* or the *Wall Street Journal*. The last thing any newspaper wanted was to be scooped on its own news.

But until such time as I had the goods on Jackman, I was on my own.

Over the next few hours, I got myself back on my feet as a fully functioning mobile journalist. My first stop, after another sweaty trudge through downtown Newark, was an electronics store. There, I got myself outfitted with the latest iPhone, one of those do-everything models that could take phone calls, surf the Web, and dispatch the nuclear arsenals of several small former Soviet Republics.

After setting up a new e-mail account, I used my iPhone to determine which towing extortion racket had stolen my car. I briefly debated unleashing some of my newfound warheads—Chechnya's maybe—on the guilty party. In the end, I decided to call a cab, ride out to the far swampy reaches by the turnpike, and repurchase my car. All told, the transaction took a shade over four hours.

By which point I was hungry again. And while I needed to get on with the work of saving my career, I knew I could serve both needs with a trip to the State Street Grill. I hadn't yet followed up with Nikki Papadopolous, who had left that message that had gotten me in trouble with Tina. Since I had never been given the number Nikki left for me—and wasn't exactly in a position to call Tina up and ask for it—I'd have to make a visit in person. And I might as well select an item or two from State Street's twenty-four-page menu while I was there.

I fired up the Malibu, put the air-conditioning on high, and started trying to find my way out of the maze that was industrial Newark, all the while luxuriating in the fact that I once again had a V6 engine to do the hard work of transporting my tired carcass from point to point.

As I got under way, I decided to continue exercising my new iPhone and call Tommy. I needed someone on the inside to do snooping outside Jackman's office, and being that it was now after six, it was late enough for him to do it undetected.

"This is Tommy," he answered.

"Hey, it's your favorite jailbird."

"Shhh . . . I'm not allowed to talk to you."

"Says who?"

"Tina."

"What?"

"She said you were probably going to call me, looking for help on this Jackman thing, and that I shouldn't take your call."

"But you're going to ignore her, right? I just need one quick favor."

Tommy didn't reply.

"You wouldn't leave a fellow reporter in the lurch, right?" I asked.

"Well, technically, you're not a fellow reporter anymore . . ."

"Ouch. Oh, wow, major ouch."

"I'm sorry. I didn't mean it like that. It's just, well, I guess Jackman called Brodie and got him pretty stoked up. And you know how that goes. Brodie gets a fever and the rest of the newsroom catches cold. So you've sort of been, uhh, banned."

"Banned?"

"Or banished. Or something like that."

"According to whom?"

"Jackman, I guess," Tommy said. "I don't know. It's not like there was a formal memo or anything. Tina just told me it was in my best interests to keep my distance."

"Oh. That's nice of her."

"She also said you were on a self-destructive path and that

I shouldn't enable you. She said if I was a real friend, I'd try to talk you out of going down this path. She's really worried about you."

"She has a strange way of showing it. She fired me this morning."

"She what? She didn't mention that."

"Yeah, well . . . Needless to say, I could really use your help."

He groaned.

"Again," I added.

"Okay, but if you get me fired, too, *you're* the one who's selling his body into male prostitution to support us."

"What, you can't find us a sugar daddy?"

"Oh, I totally can. I just think you should sell your body as punishment."

"Fair enough," I said.

"Okay, can you hang out for a second?"

"Yeah, I'm just driving."

"Good. I can't risk getting caught aiding and abetting a known scoundrel like you. But I've got an idea of someone who might be able to get away with it."

He hung up before I could ask what that meant, and I finally started paying attention to where I was driving. It suddenly dawned on me I had no idea where I was. I had gotten myself tangled somewhere in the endless labyrinth of overlapping exit ramps near Newark Liberty International Airport.

Lost in Newark. It was starting to feel like the metaphor for my existence.

Eventually, after a few more misguided turns, I found my way out and further assessed my situation. To say nothing of my other issues, my clothing had absorbed well more than the

FDA-recommended allowance of sweat, and I was starting to smell a bit like moldering hockey gear. Rather than inflict that odor on the State Street Grill, I made a brief stop at the Bloomfield home of Deadline the Cat for a shower and a new wardrobe.

The only thing I couldn't do much about was my notepad. As I transferred it from my old pants to my new ones, I discovered it had retained some dampness. Still, it was backed by sturdy enough cardboard that it would survive to fight another day.

Was the rest of me as stern? I checked in with my soul for a moment to ponder that question and found that, yeah, it was a little shaken, but it was basically still whole. A reporter without conviction is not much of a reporter at all. My only chance at this point was to stick with my principles and hope they bore me out, just as they had so many times in the past—whether I had Tina's backing or not.

I was just returning to my car when my phone rang.

"Carter Ross," I said.

"Hi, Mister Ross, it's Kevin," a voice replied.

Kevin? Did I know anyone named Kevin? Oh, of course: Lunky.

"Hi, Kevin," I said. "It's after six. Shouldn't you have gone home already?"

"Yeah, I know. But, well, I just sort of like hanging around the newsroom. No one ever bothers me so I get lots of reading done."

Sad but probably quite true.

"Anyway, what's up?" I asked.

"Mister Hernandez said I should give you a call because you needed a favor."

I smiled. Good ol' Tommy. Lunky was the perfect choice. The kid may have been roughly the size of Alaska, but he was invisible as far as the editors, Tina included, were concerned.

"He said I should go out in the parking lot and call on my cell phone and not tell anyone I was doing it," Lunky continued. "So now I'm out in the parking lot, which seems a little strange to me. Do you know why Mister Hernandez asked me to do it this way?"

"Kevin, you said you're into Thoreau, right?"

"Oh, definitely."

"Then let's just say Tommy knows I need you to practice a little civil disobedience. Can you do that for me?"

Lunky responded with enthusiasm. I provided him a brief rundown of how I believed the publisher was a killer, which he accepted without question, comment, or dispute. Then I instructed him how to find the secretarial pool outside Jackman's office, locate the lockbox atop the filing cabinet, and use the key to break into Courtney's desk—where he would hopefully discover Jackman's appointment book and the name of the bar he and Jim McNabb visited the night before Nancy was killed.

"So, really, the only hard part would be getting into that lockbox," I concluded. "You might have to smash it open. But it's pretty flimsy. A big guy like you shouldn't have a problem with that."

"Do I really have to smash it?"

"Well, it's a lockbox, so it's probably . . . locked."

"Oh, that won't be a problem," he assured me.

"Are you sure?"

"Mister Ross, can you keep a secret?"

"Of course."

"When I was young, just a freshman in high school—before I knew better, really—I . . . I . . ." He started to speak but couldn't seem to bring himself to finish. Was Lunky about to confess to a life of juvenile delinquency? A life that included boosting cars and picking locks?

"Go ahead, Kevin," I urged him in my best therapist's voice. "This is a safe space for sharing."

"Okay, okay," he said, taking a deep breath, then blurting out, "When I was a freshman in high school I . . . I read *The Da Vinci Code*."

He paused, like I should be gasping in horror. But really I was just trying to stifle my laughter. Lunky plowed on: "And . . . and . . . I really liked it. Please, please don't tell anyone, especially not my professors. It would forever ruin my standing in the academy. You know how those people are. You're not supposed to read a book like that. And if you do, you're not supposed to admit it. But if you get caught, you're supposed to pass it off as, I don't know, an intellectual lark, like you're trying to understand some misguided pop culture phenomenon from an almost anthropological view. But the truth is, I liked it, and it really got me into the science of cryptography—you know, finding hidden information, cracking codes, that sort of thing. I sort of made a hobby out of it in high school."

"So you're saying you'll be able to guess the combination on the lockbox?"

"It's not *guessing*," he corrected me. "Guessing suggests it's somehow random. There's a system to it. How many digits does the box have on it?"

"Oh, it was tiny. Three, I think."

"Oh, that's child's play," he assured me. "It'll take ten, fifteen minutes tops."

"All right. Well, give me a call when you're done."

"Righto," he said, then disconnected.

I shook my head. A six-foot-five, 275-pound defensive end who had devoured the entire canon of Western literature, considered himself an amateur cryptologist, dead-lifted bears, and finished conversations with "righto." Sure, he couldn't bang out a newspaper article to save his Emerson collection, but it was hard not to like the kid.

As Lunky made like Professor Langdon, I drove toward the diner. I had just found a parking spot—a legal one this time, I checked—when he called.

"So you were able to crack the code?" I asked.

"Not exactly," he said. "I tried opening the desk first. It wasn't locked."

"Oh," I said. Genius cryptographer, indeed.

"I went back to last Thursday, like you asked."

"And?"

"The last thing written down is, 'IFIW Meeting.'"

"What else?"

"Nothing."

"What do you mean *nothing*? There's got to be something else," I said, because it ought to have been easier than this. It was in the Bad Guy Handbook somewhere: Jackman was supposed to leave easy clues for me to follow. Whether he did it before or after he waxed his mustache and donned his black cape was up to him.

"I'm looking at it right now. All it says is, 'IFIW Meeting.'"

"Well, that's still something," I said, knowing it at least proved Jackman and Big Jimmy had been together, even if it didn't tell me where. "Look, do me a favor and make a photocopy of that page then return the appointment book where you found it."

"Sure thing," Lunky said. "Anyhow, this was fun. Thoreau never mentioned civil disobedience could feel like a scavenger hunt. If you need anything else, just let me know. No one else around here ever asks me to do anything."

I assured him I would, and he hung up. I killed the engine on the Malibu and walked toward the State Street Grill, finding myself looking forward to again seeing Nikki and her alluring green eyes.

What I saw instead momentarily rendered me incapable of putting one foot in front of the other. It was two men sitting at a window booth, bent toward each other in what appeared to be an intense conversation. One was the ill-tempered and combed-over owner of the State Street Grill, Mr. Papadopolous.

The other was Gary Jackman.

Not knowing what else to do, I positioned myself behind a tree for a moment. I would say I hid behind it, but this particular tree had only recently been planted and was probably fifty years away from being wide enough to offer a guy my size any real concealment, even if I turned sideways. But I at least wanted to get something between myself and the Jackman-Papadopolous conference.

The questions began pouring into my head. Actually, that's not right. It was really just one question I kept asking myself in different ways: What were *they* doing together? *What* were they doing together? What were they *doing* together?

Or perhaps more pressingly: What had they already done?

I flashed back to when I saw them at the funeral home and replayed it in my mind: Papadopolous waving his arms around frantically, Jackman staying cool and collected—but eventually telling him to bug off, in a way that suggested they would talk again. I had, frankly, forgotten all about the encounter because it didn't seem significant at the time. Besides, I had become convinced Jackman was my villain.

But now? Seeing them together again? It seemed to strain the bounds of anything that could be considered happenstance. I couldn't think of anything that a mighty newspaper publisher and a small-time diner owner would have in common . . . except for the one employee they shared. And she was a woman who happened to be dead at the present time.

Were Jackman and Papadopolous somehow in on this together? Was *that* why there was no dented SUV in Jackman's garage—because Papadopolous was actually the owner/driver of said vehicle?

In my one prior run-in with Papadopolous, he certainly acted like a man with something to hide, throwing me out of the diner because I was a reporter. Here I had thought the golf-club-wielding Jackman fit the profile of a killer. But I had to admit a short-tempered Greek guy—the kind of guy who wanted to corporally remove me from his restaurant—might be just as capable of violence.

But why would they both want Nancy dead? And how would they have discovered their mutual desire for her termination? Was Nancy also causing problems for Papadopolous in some way I had yet to discover?

All I knew was that I didn't know enough.

I now really needed to track down Nikki Papadopolous, who might be my only source on whatever was happening between her father and my ex-publisher. Finding her would obviously require some finesse, inasmuch as I didn't want to alert her daddy to my presence.

I eased out from behind my spindly little tree, casting one quick look at Jackman and Papadopolous, who were still engrossed in their collusion. I rounded the corner and jogged up the front steps, aware I would have to avoid the left side of the restaurant when I entered. Luckily for me, the office was on the right side. Nikki and I might be able to talk there without her father being the wiser.

Entering the second of the front doors, I found a woman at

the hostess stand whom I recognized as being Jen the Waitress, Nikki's friend. I positioned myself so I couldn't be seen from the Jackman-Papadopolous table.

"Hi," she said, smiling pleasantly. "Just one today?"

"Actually, I was here to see Nikki. Is she around?"

Jen smiled again, but this time in a way that suggested it perhaps wasn't unusual for young men to come there and ask for Nikki.

"Sorry, she's not around right now. It's her day off. You're the reporter who was here the other day, right?"

"That's me."

She pointed toward the left side of the restaurant and said, "Is it something Gus can help you with? He's just back there."

Gus? Who was Gus? Then it dawned on me that she was gesturing toward the diner owner. Of course his name was Gus. What else would a guy named Gus Papadopolous do in New Jersey other than own a diner?

"That's okay, actually," I said. "He, uh, had some anger-management issues the last time I tried to chat with him."

"Yeah, he has those a lot. Once he goes off about something, there's just no talking him down."

Noted.

"Actually," I said. "Would you mind giving me Nikki's number? She left a message for me at the office, I just forgot to write her number down"—or, rather, Tina never gave it to me, but I didn't want to get lost in details—"and I feel rude not calling her back. Do you have it by any chance?"

Jen glanced back toward Gus's table for a second. "Yeah, sure," she said, took a phone out of her pocket, pressed some buttons, then dictated ten digits to me.

"Thanks," I said. "I'm Carter Ross, by the way."

I extended my right hand. "Jen," she said, shaking it. "Jen Forbus."

"Thanks, Jen Forbus," I said. "You're a real sweetheart."

She smiled and I gave her a quick salute as I departed. I walked around the corner toward the pizzeria I had visited the day before—I was still starving, after all—and gave Nikki a ring. We established she would meet me at the pizzeria, and before long I was shoveling the first of two slices into my mouth.

I was finished with both slices—and a life-giving Coke Zero—and was starting to get tired of sitting there by the time Nikki arrived. Then I saw her and realized it had been worth the wait. She was wearing a light green, knee-length summer dress made out of some gauzy floral-print fabric. It was wrapped around her and secured at her waist with a little spaghetti string. I had untied that string with my eyes at least twice in the time it took her to cross the restaurant toward my table.

"Hi, there," I said, feeling the smile overtake my face as I rose from the booth.

"Hey, there, handsome," she said, and I accepted a kiss on the cheek. She was lightly perfumed and freshly made up. Her dark hair—which she wore up while at work—was now down just below her shoulders. She looked nothing short of fabulous, and I wondered if the effort had been on my account. One way to find out.

"I hope I didn't interrupt anything," I said. "You look like you're about to go out on a date or something."

"Oh no," she said quickly, then added, "It's just so nice to wear a dress on a hot day."

So it *was* for me. But we were pretending it wasn't. I could play that game. I could play it all day and all night if she wanted.

I tried to remind myself I was there for, you know, business purposes; that she was the daughter of the man who might have helped murder Nancy Marino; that this was potentially an important interview.

I needed to keep my wits about me. I needed to be like those guards at Buckingham Palace. They don't let *anything* distract them from their duty—not goofy, picture-taking tourists; not those ridiculous fur hats they wear; not even beautiful Greek women.

Then I got another eyeful of that summer dress and realized the British Royals would be toast under my watch. I gestured to the opposite side of my booth and said, "Have a seat."

She sat. I smiled. She smiled. It could have been awkward, but wasn't. I have come to believe human interactions are at least partially governed by things we barely understand, things that determine—without our active participation in the process—whether we'll be able to get along with someone or whether it will always be a struggle. There was no struggle with Nikki. It was easy.

"You want anything to eat or drink?" I asked.

She laughed.

"What's so funny?"

"Nothing," she said, "I just spend all day asking people that question."

"Oh right," I said, and I was tempted to pass the next several hours just studying her face and making delightful small talk. But I forced myself to stay on task. "So you called me about something?"

"Oh yeah," she said, clearly a little distracted herself. "My dad interrupted us yesterday before I had a chance to tell you something about Nancy. And I don't know if it even matters anymore or not. But I thought you should know."

"Okay."

"This guy came in last week and was asking my dad a lot of questions."

"About Nancy?"

"Yeah. They went into a booth in the back of the restaurant, and I couldn't hear what they were saying. I just saw my dad getting pissed off like he always does and waving his hands in the air a lot. I asked him what it was about later and he said, 'Nancy.' And I was like, 'What about Nancy?' But he was just fuming about affidavits and subpoenas and stuff like that."

"So your dad was going to have to give an affidavit or else he'd get subpoenaed?"

"Something like that, I guess. Yeah. I'm not a lawyer or anything."

Neither am I, of course. But I've learned enough about the law to know that whenever subpoena power is involved, things are usually pretty interesting.

"So who was the guy?" I asked.

"Well, I didn't know. He just came and left. But then I saw this business card tacked to the bulletin board in the office. I made a photocopy for you."

She pulled a folded sheet of paper out of a small green clutch she was carrying. She handed it to me, and I unfolded it to see contact information for Peter Davidson, regional director of the National Labor Relations Board. It had an address in Newark and a phone number with a 973 area code.

"National Labor Relations Board?" I asked. I knew the NLRB was a federal agency, but I was only vaguely familiar with it from articles I had read. Usually, the NLRB was called into negotiations that had become huge pissing matches between labor and management—sort of like what the *Newark Eagle-Examiner* had going with IFIW–Local 117.

But I was still confused. "What would the NLRB want with your dad? You guys aren't unionized, are you?"

She shook her head.

"So, uh, okay, I don't get it," I said, intertwining my fingers on the back of my head.

"I tried to pump my dad for information, but he told me it was nothing to worry about. He's not the kind of man who likes to unload his problems on other people, even his own daughter. Especially his own daughter. I asked him two or three times, and he just patted me on the head and said, 'Eet's fine, eet's fine, no troubles.' "

But there were troubles. There had to be. And maybe they were substantial enough to turn Nancy Marino into the kind of obstacle that made Gus Papadopolous every bit as interested in her removal as Gary Jackman. All I knew was feds just didn't waltz into your place of work and threaten you with a subpoena unless there was trouble *somewhere*. The trick was figuring out where.

Or maybe, at least for now, the better question was when it started.

"You said the guy was here last week," I asked. "What day?"

Nikki cast her eyes upward and found the answer swirling in an old ceiling fan. "Monday," she said. "It was Monday."

A timeline was assembling in my head. On Monday, a representative from the NLRB waltzed into the State Street Grill to talk about something that had Gus Papadopolous waving his hands in the air. On Tuesday morning, the black SUV began stalking Nancy on her paper route—at least according to Mrs. Alfaro's memory. By Friday, Nancy was dead.

So Gus was involved. He had to be, right?

But did that mean Jackman *wasn't* involved? Maybe yes. Maybe no. But if it was no, why did I keep seeing them together?

It was, potentially, a brilliant bit of criminality: any prosecutor could tell you nothing weakens a murder case like having two suspects, each of whom has an equally strong motive. In the absence of good physical evidence—which this case was unlikely to have—each suspect ostensibly guarantees reasonable doubt for the other, because each defendant's attorney can argue, hey, it wasn't my guy, it was the other guy. Unless the prosecutor can find some kind of reasonable link between the perpetrators—e-mails, phone calls, payment of some sort—and charge them together, there's pretty much no case.

I suddenly wished I had snapped a quick cell phone picture of the two of them sitting at that booth. Not that it would truly prove anything—given enough time, I'm sure they could concoct a reasonable cover story—but it would at least establish that the men weren't total strangers.

Or, for all I knew, they might have another tie. Maybe one everyone—or at least Gus's daughter—knew about already. I focused on Nikki and tried to act nonchalant.

"Hey, this may seem like a strange question, but does your dad know a guy named Gary Jackman by any chance?" I asked.

"Uh, I don't know. Who is he?"

"He's the publisher of my newspaper, which sort of makes him like my boss."

Or ex-boss. But let's not quibble.

"Gary Jackman," she said, pondering it more deeply. "I don't think so. But it's not like I know all my dad's friends, you know? He does a lot of stuff with the Bloomfield Chamber of Commerce, so he's always bothering people about that. Why do you ask?"

"Oh, I've just seen them together a couple of times and I was just . . . curious."

Nikki shrugged and smiled sweetly. Then she asked me a question no guy could resist coming from an attractive woman: "So, you want to get out of here, grab a drink or something?"

And I know that I should have been like those boys at Buckingham. I know it was entirely possible that she wasn't as innocent as she appeared. I know she might well have been an enemy agent sent to seduce me, pry information out of me, and then kill me with some exotic, undetectable poison, like a girl in a Bond flick.

But perfume has a way of clouding my judgment. Besides, doesn't the enemy agent end up falling in love with Bond despite herself?

"I don't know, Nikki," I teased. "What would Gus think about me having a drink with his little girl?"

She grinned. "I don't think Gus is allowed to have an opinion on the matter."

"Then let's get out of here."

Soon, we were riding in my babe-magnet Malibu on our way to a trendy bar in Montclair, the kind of place with low couches and lower lighting where we could spend a little time getting acquainted. We swapped our stories—you reach a point in singlehood when you've got your standard first-date material pretty well down—and the hour grew late. We drank but not excessively. Just enough to have a nice little buzz. It was all quite enchanting.

I found it pleasant talking to Nikki, who laughed easily and told fun stories. She had wanted to be an actress and did the New York audition thing for a while until she concluded they didn't want someone who looked, as one casting director put it, "so ethnic." After that, she returned to school and studied restaurant management and was being groomed to take over the family business.

We were from somewhat different sides of the track—me with my Wonder bread background, she with her pitas—but that didn't seem to matter. I found her refreshingly uncomplicated as compared to game-playing Tina. And maybe Nikki was just a rebound from Tina. But even if that was the case, any basketball coach could tell you rebounds have helped with a lot of ball games. And it was becoming obvious where the evening was heading.

It started with a little hand-patting, which turned into hand-holding. Then I might have started idly stroking her forearm, which she must not have minded because she suddenly scooted quite close to me on the couch we were sharing. She got up at one point to visit the ladies' room, and when she returned, she gave me a kiss on the lips—no tongue, but it was still meaningful—then snuggled herself against me. The smell of her was at least as intoxicating as the drinks we were having.

One thing I enjoy about being a grown-up is that, at a certain point in time, you stop needing quite so much pretense with the opposite sex. When you were in high school, you had to lure a girl out to the park with the ploy that it was the best place to see shooting stars. When you were in college, she came back to your dorm room because you wanted to show her your fish tank. But then sometime in your twenties, all that subterfuge—which never really fooled anyone anyway—becomes unnecessary. So when last call went out sometime short of midnight, I suggested we head back to my place, and she accepted. Just like that.

Before long, we were back in Bloomfield. I turned the Malibu into my driveway. My garage is detached—in the way all garages used to be—and it has become something of a repository for things better left unseen by hot dates. Plus, it's a bit of a tight squeeze. I didn't want her having to crawl past my lawnmower and my Weedwacker on her way out.

I pulled up short of the garage, hopped out of the car, and hurried around to open Nikki's door for her. Then I took her hand and escorted her down the driveway, rounding the corner of the house toward the small set of brick steps that led to my front door. We were walking single file—the path wasn't wide enough to go side by side—and I was in the lead.

It was only later, when I replayed everything in my mind, that I realized this was about the time I heard a car engine coming to life. At the time, with my mind clearly on other things, I can't say I really paid much attention. There had to be at least fifty houses on my block. One person starting their car—even at a late hour like this—was not unusual.

But yes, a car had started somewhere. And I became aware it was traveling rather speedily, but, again, that didn't concern me. Everyone drives too fast in Jersey. Even if I had thought about it, and I'm quite sure I didn't, I would have assumed it was some kid heading home from his girlfriend's house, fired up by a success or dejected by a failure.

The first thing that I noticed for sure was the headlights. They were big and bright and closer to eye level than headlights should be.

The second thing I noticed was that those headlights were coming right at us. Nikki was saying something about how she liked my little house when the SUV veered off the street, using the neighbor's driveway like it was a highway entrance ramp and hurtling across my front yard. I felt my eyes squinting involuntarily as those big headlights suddenly bore down on us.

Then instinct took over. I released Nikki's hand, pivoted, and plowed myself into her, shoving us over the foundation shrubbery next to the front steps. There was no real time to make it gentle or pretty. I just tackled her as hard as I could, hoping I had enough momentum to get us both out of harm's way. We crashed through the shrubs, and most of my weight landed on her. The scream that was starting to escape from her mouth turned into a grunt as I knocked all the wind from her lungs.

I felt the rush of air and exhaust as the vehicle missed us by a few feet. I heard the roar of its engine and the small shriek of its tires as it jumped back over the curb and onto the asphalt. But I didn't see anything. My head was down.

By the time I looked up, the SUV was gone.

He arrived at Carter Ross's house at a quarter to six in the evening, just to have a look around. He was ready with a cover story in case Ross saw him, but that proved unnecessary. The reporter wasn't at home.

So he treated himself to a quick but full surveillance of Ross's domain. He eyeballed angles and imprinted the layout of the property in his head as best he could. He noted the detached garage. He studied means of access and egress—a front door and a back door, nothing on the sides. He looked for signs that might tell him what Ross's patterns were.

He was searching for vulnerabilities, of course, for potential ways Ross might be attacked. He quickly concluded Ross entered and exited exclusively through the front door. The back door, which opened onto a small deck, simply wasn't as convenient to the garage. And it didn't seem to be used frequently—the grass in the backyard appeared undisturbed, as if no one had walked on it in several days.

That was good. He wouldn't have to use his gun. Ross would be an easy target for the Escalade. He paced off a few distances, counting the seconds it took to walk them, coming up with a likely range of times. It was the same sort of mental preparation he had made for Nancy Marino, and he expected the same results.

Having made the necessary determinations, he didn't allow himself to linger. He knocked on the front door, making himself seem like just a casual friend who had stopped by for an unannounced visit and, finding the master of the house not at home, left just as quickly. He didn't think any of the neighbors had taken note of him. The only person he saw was a woman outside watering her lawn, but she didn't seem to be paying attention.

Then he settled in to wait, parking just down the street. He had a place in his brain where he went at times like this—a small cerebral refuge that allowed him to keep himself physically dormant yet mentally alert. It was the place where he told himself his life story, as if he were dictating a memoir. He loved going there, and he had learned he could stay there, quite contentedly, for hours.

He changed some of the details, of course, especially ones that pertained to his father. Everyone lies in their memoir these days, right?

He had both a quick version and a slow version of the story. And since he knew he might be waiting for a while, he went with the extended edition, pacing himself. He was still only in his late twenties when he saw a car roll down the street and into the appropriate driveway.

Instantly, his body came to life. He looked at the clock, which read 12:17. The car crept past the house, on its way to the detached garage. He began a small countdown, turning his ignition key midway through. The car came alive, illuminating the street in front of him. He had hoped to go dark—all the better to catch his target unawares—but the Escalade was equipped with daytime running lights and he didn't know how to disable them. So he opted to go for the next best thing: high beams. If he couldn't sneak up on Ross, at least he'd blind him.

With the countdown complete, he shifted into Drive then hit the gas. The house was on the right side of the street, so he stayed on the left side, giving himself a better angle from which to swoop onto the front yard. He had decided he would enter via the neighbor's driveway. Going over the curb might slow him down or knock him off track.

Everything was going exactly as he hoped, right until the last moment. The first thing that surprised him was the presence of another person. His assumption had been that Ross, who appeared to live alone, would be coming home alone. Yet there Ross was with a young woman. Did she look familiar? There was no time to even consider it. Not at that speed.

The second thing he hadn't remembered to factor in was the slight upward slope to the front lawn, which slowed him down at a time when he should have been accelerating. It gave Ross enough time not only to get himself out of the way but to rescue the young woman as well.

He watched in frustration as Ross and the young woman dove toward the house, into the safety of some shrubbery. He yelled as he passed them by—like that would do any good—but didn't dare to slow until he was out of eyeshot. He just had to trust that his high beams, to say nothing of the element of surprise, had rendered them incapable of seeing anything that would identify him.

But that, he knew, was a poor substitute for his real plan, which was not to leave a witness in the first place.

He drove in circles for a while, aggravated at himself. Eventually, he realized he might as well make the best of a botched situation. After all, if Ross could be dissuaded from continuing to investigate Nancy Marino's death, it would be as good as having Ross dead.

It just had to be made clear to the reporter what awaited him if he persisted.

CHAPTER 7

For a long moment, I just lay there, panting. I had rolled off Nikki and was pinned between the shrubs and my house's foundation, with a bug's-eye view of a few small weeds that had crept up in the bare dirt. I began taking inventory of what might or might not be broken, dismembered, or paralyzed, but quickly determined I still had all my parts and they seemed to be functioning as would be expected. Except for a few scratches and perhaps a bruise or two, I had done nothing more serious than perhaps use up one of my nine lives.

I looked over at Nikki, who was crumpled at an awkward angle, with her head resting against the house, her torso on the ground, and her legs up in the air, supported by the shrubs. Her dress, with its thin fabric, was bunched up around her midsection, exposing her strong, rounded thighs and green, seamless underwear. It struck me she ought to be tugging the dress down. But Nikki wasn't moving.

"You okay?" I said.

No reply.

"Nikki?"

Nothing.

I scrambled toward her on my hands and knees, then stopped. Even in the shadow of the shrubbery, there was enough light from a nearby street lamp that I could see her hair was wet with blood. There was a red smear mark, vivid on the painted concrete, leading in a short arc from where her head had crashed into the foundation to where it was currently propped.

"Oh, Nikki," I said. "Nikki, honey, can you hear me?"

It was a stupid question. She couldn't hear anything. Her eyes were closed, and it was difficult to tell if she was even breathing.

Or alive.

A small jolt of horror surged through me. I wish I could say I was one of those cool, calm, collected types, capable of blocking all but the essential facts, processing them, and acting accordingly. But that's why newspaper reporters make lousy emergency responders: we're trained to take in everything, leaving nothing out. So there I was, noting the cut and color of Nikki's underwear instead of saving her life.

I forced myself to think back to a thousand first-aid classes taken a million years earlier, when I was a Boy Scout and a camp counselor, doing things responsible kids do, getting certified in this or trained in that. You weren't supposed to move someone with a potential spinal cord injury. That part came back to me quickly. But, then, wasn't oxygen the first priority? Didn't I have to make sure she was getting some?

Then a long-ago video appeared in my mind, where some perfectly calm woman came across an inert body, bent down to assess it, then turned to the equally composed person with her and, in a totally inflectionless voice, said, "No breathing, no pulse, call Eee-Emm-Ess."

I pulled my iPhone out of my pocket, brought up the dialing screen, and shakily punched the nine key, followed by the one key twice. Then I hit Send.

"Nine one one, what is your emergency?" a voice queried.

"Please," I moaned into my phone. "Please come quickly. A woman is hurt badly."

"What is your exact location?"

I faltered—because for a moment I couldn't remember I was in my front yard—then recovered and gave my home address. The operator started asking me questions about the nature of the woman's injuries.

"No time. Just come," I said, and planted the phone back in my pocket, returning my attention to Nikki.

I got as close to her as I dared without jostling her, then made myself very still. I couldn't see any breathing, so I reached out toward her arm, which was splayed on the dirt, and grabbed her wrist to check her pulse. To my relief, I could feel a small thumping—weak but extant. Then I looked at her chest and saw it rising and falling slightly beneath that summer dress.

My next concern was the blood. There seemed to be a lot of it, too much of it. I couldn't tell where it was coming from, and I didn't dare touch her. I tried as best I could to get close to her scalp and see if I could locate the wound, but all I could see was wet, blood-matted hair.

It was about that time I heard the first siren. Then I heard several. They were crying out at varying pitches and rhythms, everything from the long, low fire engine's blast to the short bleep-blipping of an ambulance. We had to be the only emergency in Bloomfield that night because they seemed to be coming from everywhere. I grabbed Nikki's hand.

"Help's coming," I said. "Just hang with me."

The ambulance got there first. A short, stout guy and a tall, thin guy, both in tight T-shirts and multipocketed pants, hopped out of the back of the truck, with one of them carrying a duffel bag laden with even more pockets. I released Nikki's hand, stood up, and shouted, "Over here, she's over here."

"What's going on?" the short one asked, as he walked up my lawn.

"A car tried to hit us," I said. "I had to push us out of the way and she hit her head."

The short guy glanced at his partner and they shared some silent agreement on the subject—something along the lines of, *Sounds like the worst excuse for domestic violence we've ever heard, but let the cops sort it out.*

"She's breathing and has a pulse," I continued, trying to be helpful. "But she's bleeding from the head. I tried not to move her."

"What's her name?" the second one asked.

"Nikki."

"Nikki, are you okay?" he started yelling. "Nikki, are you there?"

She was about as chatty with them as she was with me. So they got to work, stabilizing her neck, rolling her onto a backboard, mauling my shrubs in the process. One of them started raking his knuckle down her sternum, which looked like it must have hurt like hell. I couldn't discern the medical purpose of it—unless they were now encouraging torture in CPR—but Nikki didn't stir.

A second ambulance had showed up by this point, as had a fire truck. I kept getting shoved farther out of the way. I could see they had gotten a breathing mask on her face and a collar on her neck. They seemed to be doing other stuff, too, I just I couldn't tell what. Then they lifted her into the back of the ambulance.

I was just sort of tagging along at that point, and they weren't paying much attention to me until the tall guy turned and said, "We're taking her to Mountainside if you want to follow us in your own vehicle. Just don't follow too close. Nikki doesn't need any more trauma right now."

The next few hours at Mountainside Hospital were a blur of antiseptic corridors, stiff-backed waiting room chairs, interrupted naps, and at least two less-than-fun conversations.

The first was with a lady from the admissions staff, to whom I had to explain that I knew next to nothing about the young lady I had accompanied to the hospital. No, I didn't know her address. No, I wasn't sure if she had insurance. No, I didn't know how to contact her next of kin. No, I wasn't really her boyfriend. Before long, the woman had decided I was some guy who hired a hooker, then decided to throw her around a bit, and so she was treating me with all the warmth and kindness you might expect.

The next uncomfortable chat was with a pair of young Bloomfield cops, who came to ask me questions. I told them what happened, giving them as many details as I could—which, admittedly, were quite few. They were noticeably unimpressed by my version of the events and were debating whether to arrest me or just take me out back and rough me up a bit. Guys who hurt nice girls like Nikki are not looked upon fondly by the law enforcement community.

The only thing that saved me was my insistence they would find tire marks on my lawn. I also dropped the name of Detective Owen Smiley at least four times, promising he would vouch that I wasn't a total scum bucket. They still weren't entirely convinced, but they eventually left me alone, making vague noises about how I shouldn't go on any extended trips, in case they had more questions. They never asked if I thought someone might be trying to hurt me, which was probably good. It would have been tough explaining that one of the potential suspects was the injured girl's father.

Sometime toward dawn, Nikki was considered stabilized enough that I was allowed to enter her room. I glanced at her, lying sedately with gauze wrapped around her head, but mostly had to focus my attention on a guy in blue scrubs who didn't introduce himself but was likely a doctor. He had that full-of-himself air about him.

He explained to me what I probably could have figured out myself: Nikki had sustained what he called a "mild traumatic brain injury" (what they used to call a "concussion") and might be out for a few more hours. The gash on her head turned out to be superficial. It just bled like crazy, as head wounds tend to do. They had given her an MRI and determined there was no "intracranial hemorrhaging" (what they used to call "bleeding") or "cerebral contusions" (what they used to call "bruises") inside her skull. Her respiration was fine, her oxygen level was adequate, her blood pressure had started a little low but was improving. When she came to, she might be disoriented, confused, or suffer from short-term memory loss. But even if she seemed fine, I should summon a nurse.

The doctor asked if I had any questions, but he was already inching out of the room, so I let him go. I didn't need medical science to explain to me that Nikki had bumped her head. Bad. And she needed some time to rest and give her body a chance to make itself better.

I pulled a chair next to Nikki's bed and held her hand for a while, because it felt like the hospital thing to do. Then I thought maybe I should talk to her a little bit. Isn't that what you're supposed to do with people who have lost consciousness? Give their brain a little bit of something to chew on in hopes you could make it hungry for more?

"You looked beautiful tonight," I said, sounding hoarse and throaty. "I was planning on telling you that when we got into my house, but I sort of got interrupted."

I looked at her, her chest rising and falling steadily, her color surprisingly good. Then again, she was Greek and this was the middle of the summer, so I suppose that shouldn't have been quite so remarkable. I stroked her hand a little bit.

"That SUV that tried to run us over is probably the same one that got Nancy. I didn't really get a look at it. Or the driver. But I think I know who's behind it."

And it might be someone you know pretty darn well, I thought. But that hardly seemed the right thing to say to whatever small part of Nikki was still processing information.

She breathed some more. I babbled some more.

"You have to understand, I'm coming out of this *thing*—I'm not even sure I could call it a relationship—with someone who was basically my boss," I continued. "It was pretty messed up already. And then she fired me. Yeah, I got fired yesterday. I didn't want to tell you that. Because what girl wants to think she's on a date with some unemployed loser? So I guess you could say it's over now. The relationship. My job. Yeah, all of it is over.

"Anyhow, I don't think this thing with you and me is some kind of rebound situation. But it might be. I probably should have warned you about that. I usually try to be up front about my emotional baggage. But you were so nice to talk to. And you looked so damn hot in that dress with that little tie on the side.

It's like you were some kind of present, and all I wanted to do was pull the string and unwrap it so I could see what was inside."

I looked over at the clock. It was quarter past five in the morning.

"Oh yeah, and I'm sorry I tackled you," I said. "You should know I'm generally not that rough with women."

Suddenly, a smile crept across her face, and she croaked out, "That's too bad."

"Nikki? Nikki! Are you awake?" I said, standing up, as if I was in the presence of a miracle. I had never been around a person as they regained consciousness—or around someone who lost it, for that matter—but it had the feeling of rebirth. She coughed and opened her eyes.

"I actually woke up when the doctor was still in here," she said in a stronger voice. "But you guys didn't notice. And then I just sort of felt like resting for a while."

"So you, uhh, heard everything I said just now, huh?"

"It's fine. I'm glad you liked my dress."

I felt my face getting red.

"And sorry you lost your job," she continued. "You don't have to feel bad about that. It doesn't matter to me."

"Yeah, about all that rebound stuff . . ."

"Don't worry about it. It was just a first date."

"And *some* date it's been," I said, gesturing to the surroundings. "I want you to know, I don't take just *any* babe to a classy joint like this."

She smiled and closed her eyes again. I took her hand and let her relax for a while.

"Nancy's funeral is this morning," she said, her eyelids still shut.

"Yeah, I guess it is."

"I want to go."

"I'm not sure that's the best idea. In any event, I don't think they're going to let you out of here."

Her eyelids opened, and she fixed those two lovely green eyes on me.

"Can you go for me? Tell her I'm sorry I couldn't make it."

I patted her hand and assured her I would. It seemed to be the least I could do.

I fetched the nurse, who did the necessary poking, prodding, and assessing, then left us in peace. Mostly, I just hung around as Nikki dozed. I might have caught a small nap myself, bringing my evening's sleep to a grand total of perhaps three hours. Then I had to go home and ready myself for a funeral.

When I returned to my house in daylight, it was difficult to tell what might have happened there the night before. I expected the SUV would have left deep, vivid tracks. But it had been so dry and the ground was so hard, it was difficult to make out where it had been. The trampling of my lawn and shrubbery was more from the EMTs than anything else.

Upon entering my front door, I was greeted by Deadline, who had not been affected by the previous evening's folderol, except for one important disruption to his daily routine: he hadn't gotten his morning kibble. And he was rather frantic about this. He took one glance at me, walking in the front door, then ran to his food bowl in the kitchen. When he realized I wasn't getting the hint, he came back and looked up at me, impatiently, as I thumbed through some mail. Then he dashed to the kitchen, because clearly I would fall in line and follow this time. He returned again, his anguish so pronounced—*why doesn't this moron take the hint?*—that I finally walked toward the kitchen to remedy the situation.

That's when I noticed Deadline was leaving bloody paw prints on the hardwood floor. There were three distinct sets of tracks—one for each trip—and I followed them into the kitchen, where they became even more vivid on the off-white tile.

Then I saw a brick, sitting in the middle of the room. There was broken glass scattered all about, which explained why my cat was bleeding. A strip of paper was wrapped around the brick.

"Oh, what the . . ." I started to say.

But I interrupted myself. The paper had block lettering on it:

MESSAGE FOR CARTER ROSS

Deadline, sitting by his food bowl, let out an urgent meow. I walked over to him, crunching on the broken glass, and scooped him up so he couldn't frolic through any more of the wreckage. He allowed me to inspect his paw, which had a small cut in one of the pads. I know even less about feline first aid than I do about human first aid, but the wound didn't seem mortal.

Nevertheless, I couldn't have my cat bleeding all over the place. The police were probably already looking at me hard for assault and battery. I didn't need to add animal cruelty to my booking.

I dumped some food in the bowl, then took it and the cat into the bathroom, where I unrolled a length of toilet paper and wrapped it as tightly as I could around his bloody paw. Then I set him down and observed. He attacked the kibble, unconcerned about his injury, so I closed him in the bathroom and returned to the mess in the kitchen.

The brick looked old and well used, like it had been tossed around a lot in its day. The paper, which appeared to have been torn off a standard 8½-by-11 sheet, had been tied tightly to the brick with two pieces of twine—one lengthwise, one widthwise—in a very neat, tidy little package.

I bent down and studied the "MESSAGE FOR CARTER ROSS" up close. The lettering seemed to be self-consciously anonymous, as though the writer wanted to make sure it could not later be identified by a handwriting expert. It had been done in black ink, probably a disposable ballpoint pen.

"You couldn't have just sent me an e-mail?" I said out loud.

Picking up the brick, I pulled on the first string, then the second, then the third, letting the twine fall to the floor. I unfurled the paper and turned it over to find the same block writing on the backside:

BACK OFF. OR YOUR NEXT.

I stood there for perhaps a minute, brick in one hand, note in the other. Oddly, what really bothered me about it was not that they had brought my cat into this fight or that I had to replace a broken kitchen window. It was that either Jackman—or Gus Papadopolous, or the rent-a-goon they were using—didn't know the difference between "your" and "you're." It's one thing to be threatened. It's quite another thing to be threatened in grammatically incorrect fashion. I felt like some basic right as a literate American had been violated. I folded the note and tucked it in my notepad.

So, obviously, the drive-by had been a scare tactic, with the ol' brick-through-the-window routine tossed in to make sure I didn't miss the message. What I couldn't figure out is why I was being left alive at all. Whoever I was dealing with didn't place much value on human life. Maybe he just couldn't figure out a way to kill me and make it look like an accident, and he thought frightening me off the story would accomplish the same purpose.

I crunched across the glass, grabbed a broom from my pantry, and began sweeping, trying to make sure I found every last shard, shaving, and splinter—because if I didn't, Deadline would. Somewhere around the third dustpan full, I started feeling strangely heartened to know I was still considered trouble. It gave me new hope there was something out there—maybe at the National Labor Relations Board—that would make this all come together, with or without confirmation of the threats Jackman had made in Jim McNabb's presence, with or without evidence of the nefarious link between Jackman and Papadopolous.

I just had to stay alive until I found it.

My transformation from hospital-weary caretaker to spit-polished funeral-goer took fourteen minutes. On my way out, I remembered to let Deadline out of the bathroom. Though, really, he probably wouldn't have minded spending the day in there: when I opened the door, he was passed out on the rug, having gorged himself on Iams Weight Control. The toilet paper that was once on his paw was now a shredded mess on the floor, but the bleeding had stopped. So I left him alone. Never disturb a happy cat.

The funeral was held a short drive away in Belleville at St. Peter Roman Catholic Church, a beautiful Gothic-style stone building that had been erected back in the days when people still knew how to make churches—not like these days, when so many of them can be confused with warehouses or big-box stores. Just to the right of the church was a cemetery, where a plot had been dug, draped, and made ready to accept a new resident. A row of white plastic chairs had been set up, giving close family members a graveside seat for the interment.

I parked in the lot across the street, which was filling up like it was Easter Sunday, and walked toward the front entrance. I stopped and looked at the marquee, which told me St. Peter offered a Sunday Mass in Spanish. I'm sure some of the old Italians in the area probably griped about a bunch of Spanish-speakers coming in and taking over their church. What they didn't remember is, once upon a time, the Irish who founded St. Peter probably griped about the Italians. And someday the Ecuadorians and Peruvians coming into the area would grumble about someone new.

And really, they were all worshiping the same God; living the same American story; experiencing the emotions of thousands of births and baptisms, confirmations and communions, weddings and funerals. And it was tempting, standing in front of a church built by people who were long dead, to be so humbled by one's own insignificance as to wonder what any of it could possibly mean. What's one more life—or death—when we all just end up in the cemetery next door anyway?

But I suppose at a certain point you have to resign yourself to the simple fact that while you don't get many years on this planet—in the grand scheme of things—you sure do get a lot of days. So you might as well get on with the business of doing with them what you can.

And maybe someday, someone wandering through the cemetery would see Nancy's headstone, do a bit of quick math on her dates of birth and death, and wonder what ended her life after just forty-two years. And if they got real curious, I wanted to make damn sure that if they typed the name "Nancy Marino" into some supercomputer of the future, the archives would be waiting for them with the real story. Because that's what I had chosen to do with *my* days on this Earth.

I was standing there, still stuck in this thought, as Jim McNabb came strolling up.

"Good morning," he said solemnly. "Am I interrupting anything?"

"Nope, just pondering mortality," I said, staring up at the steeple. "And the things that really matter."

"Oh yeah? And what really matters?"

"Getting the story. Finding the truth. No matter what it costs."

He stuck his hands in his pockets and looked down at the steps.

"What's it cost you so far?" he asked.

"Well, my job, for one. After I left your place yesterday, I got myself fired. My girlfriend, for another. She and the job sort of went hand in hand. I might lose my house, too. I don't exactly have a lot of savings to cushion being out of a paycheck. But all of that stuff is just, I don't know, fleeting."

"You don't give up, do you?" he said, taking a hand out of his pocket and clapping me on the shoulder affectionately.

"Not if I can help it."

He nodded thoughtfully.

"Well, I don't know what your beliefs are. But I'm going to go in there and spend a little time on my knees," he announced. "For Nancy and for me. We could all use a little confession now and then, you know?"

"Yeah, sure. I guess you're right," I said, and followed him inside.

It was five minutes to ten, a little later than I liked to arrive for a funeral, and the place was already near capacity. I recognized many of the same people from Monday's wake, including an odd pairing three-quarters of the way back, sitting on opposite sides of the same aisle: on the left, a foppish-looking man with ash-blond hair and, on the right, a mostly bald man with thin strands stretched across his pate.

Jackman and Papadopolous. Together. Again.

I wanted to confront them, make a scene even. But this was hardly the right setting—especially when I wasn't entirely sure what was really going on. Yeah, they were probably in cahoots. But for all I knew, Nancy's murder had been entirely Gus's doing and Jackman had nothing to do with it. Or it was just as possible it was all Jackman and no Gus.

Nevertheless, the brick-through-the-window thing needed to be answered. I had to do something to show these guys that I wasn't cowed by bullying. So I did what writers do: I composed a snarky note.

I pulled out my notepad, opened to a clean page, and in the same big, anonymous block lettering my brick-tosser had used, I wrote:

MESSAGE FROM CARTER ROSS

Then I tore out the sheet, turned it over, and continued:

"YOUR" IS A POSSESSIVE PRONOUN.
"YOU'RE" IS A CONTRACTION OF "YOU" AND "ARE."
PLEASE LEARN THE DIFFERENCE.

I made another copy of the note, then walked the short distance up the aisle to where they were sitting. I turned and faced both of them.

"Hello, gentlemen," I said, plastering a fake smile on my face.

I then stuffed my pieces of paper in the breast pocket of each of their suits. Gus was so stunned by the assault he didn't even move. Jackman physically recoiled, though he was more taken aback than anything—I had mashed his pocket square. I gave each of them a final head nod, then turned and walked toward the front of the church without looking back.

It wasn't the big scene I was really aching to cause. But, as juvenile as it was, it felt nice to be on the offensive for a change.

The only open seating that remains two minutes before the start of a crowded funeral is, inevitably, up front, close to the casket, where no one really wants to be. And that's where I landed, in the row directly behind the pews that had been reserved for family.

I hadn't been seated for more than a minute when Jeanne Nygard was escorted in on the arm of her husband, Jerry. She had managed to find herself a black dress—no hippie-dippy floral pattern, for once—but was still wearing Birkenstocks. She was immediately followed by her stern sister, Anne McCaffrey, who had on another totally sensible charcoal gray skirt suit that, to the unschooled eye, was indistinguishable from all her other totally sensible suits.

Jeanne slowly made her way down the row until she was directly in front of me. She sat but turned immediately, peering at me through those photochromic lenses that were still dark from the sun.

"I've been trying to call you," she said in a voice that was just a bit too loud.

The stern sister pounced before I could answer.

"Jeanne, no!" Anne hissed.

Jerry wasn't far behind. "Hon, we talked about this," he growled.

"I've been trying to call you, but your phone has been off," she repeated, making a point of twisting a little farther away from her sister and husband as if to emphasize that she was ignoring them.

"Sorry about that," I replied softly. "I have a new phone number."

Jerry turned around, pointed at me, and whisper-shouted, "You leave her alone! This is none of your business!"

Jeanne was still disregarding her family's protestations, focusing on me as she said, "I need to talk to you as soon as possible."

"Jeanne!" Anne barked.

"Come to Nancy's house after the funeral," Jeanne continued. "We're having a reception. We can talk there."

"That'd be fine," I said, while Anne was saying something along the lines of "Don't you dare!"

Satisfied, Jeanne turned back around. Anne glared at her sister while Jerry was trying to shoot me dirty looks. But any further hostility was cut short by an organ sounding the first mournful notes of a funeral procession.

I spent the next hour or so fathoming the mystery of Christian death in the light of the resurrection, observing as the rite of committal was administered, trying not to screw up any of the prayers. Then it was off to Nancy's house.

Which, naturally, got me thinking about potato salad. A motivational speaker I heard once—can't remember his name—had a monologue about potato salad. His conclusion, basically, was that life is all about what happens between birth and potato salad. And you have to accomplish what you can before the potato salad. Because after the potato salad, it's all over.

The joke, of course, is that after you die, your family and friends spend a few days saying wonderful things about you—things they might never have said when you were still alive—and then they take you out to some grassy spot, leave you there, and go back to your house and eat potato salad.

And before long, that's what we were all doing: eating potato salad at Nancy's place.

Her house turned out to be a small, white 1950s ranch with a sunken garage beneath the main floor. There were folks congregating on the front lawn, which had a decent-sized tent on it. Jerry Nygard was among them, and he put his hands on his hips when he saw me, like I would be scared off when I realized how offended he was by my presence. I thought about going up to him and offering him a Coke.

Instead, after a morning of mourning, I needed to find myself a bathroom. So I invited myself inside the house.

The front door opened into a small living room. There was some food set out on the coffee table, but it had yet to attract any visitors, who were all still under the tent. At the far end of the room was a swinging door—probably to the kitchen—and a hallway that cut down the middle of the house and led, I hoped, to a bathroom. I started walking in that direction and was just about to take a left when I heard what sounded like Anne's voice coming from behind the swinging door. I caught her midway through a sentence that ended:

". . . a spectacle out of our sister's death."

Then I heard what was unmistakably Jeanne replying, "What do you propose? That we let the *legal system* work it out?"

Anne: "Well, obviously not. She can't very well testify now, can she?"

Jeanne: "So what do you propose?"

Anne: "Drop it. Just let it drop."

Jeanne: "I'm not going to let a murder drop."

Anne: "It wasn't a murder."

Jeanne: "You don't know that."

There was a momentary standstill. I heard the rattling of a pot, the running of water, the clicking of a gas stove being ignited, and then the soft whooshing of the flame coming to life. I kept myself perfectly still, not even daring to swallow, lest it make too much noise.

"Do you really trust this guy?" Anne resumed.

"He seems like a nice young man," Jeanne answered.

"Yeah, but would he, you know, blow things out of proportion?" Anne asked. "Reporters do that, you know."

By "reporters" I realized, of course, they were talking about me. But bursting into the room and insisting I wasn't like all those other lowly journalists—who skulk around people's houses and eavesdrop on their conversations—was clearly out of the question. So I just hung on and hoped Jeanne would do my fighting for me.

"I don't think he would," Jeanne said. "He seemed very reasonable to me."

Attagirl. Sure, I might have worded it a little more strongly, but that would do.

Jeanne added: "If anything, he seemed more reserved than I thought he should be. He talked about the need to be prudent."

"He did?" Anne asked.

I did? Then I remembered I had. Well, actually, Jeanne had used the word "prudent," and I just repeated it. But if she needed me to be Mr. Prudent, I could keep my speedometer at fifty-five, my seat belt fastened, and both hands on the wheel.

"Oh yes. He said there might not be a story, and he wouldn't charge around throwing out false allegations."

Yes, yes I had. I heard the scraping and jostling of cookware, then Anne finally said: "You know, I suppose there's no harm in showing it to him. If I'm right and there's nothing to it, there's not a story. And if you're right, I guess we have to do it."

"Good," Jeanne said.

Great, I thought. Of course, now I was intensely curious as to what "it" was.

"But can we ask him to come back later?" Anne asked. "I just don't want to do it now. This is a funeral, for goodness' sake."

"You *promise* we'll show it to him?"

Anne hefted a resigned sigh. "Yes, I promise."

I heard the suction of a refrigerator door being pulled open and the soft ringing of bottles clinking against each other. "Do we have any mustard?" Anne asked.

"It's out in the tent, I'll get it," Jeanne said.

"No, just relax. I'll get it," Anne replied.

I heard footsteps coming toward me and quickly backed several steps away down the hallway, then pulled on the first door handle I saw. Anne swung open the kitchen door just as I was pulling on a handle that, it turned out, led down into the basement.

"Hi, I'm sorry, I was looking for a bathroom," I said, as apologetically as possible. I was just a guest in need of relief, not a guy who had been helping himself to her private conversation.

I had caught her by surprise, and she just said, "Next one down."

"Thanks."

I closed the door to the basement, pivoted, and started making toward the bathroom. I was almost home free when she finally recovered enough of her senses to ask, "Were you outside the kitchen just now?"

I turned back toward her. She was wearing a denim apron over her sensible suit, but it didn't diminish the feeling that I was suddenly on the witness stand under cross-examination. Which meant it was in my best interest to play as stone-dumb as possible.

Luckily, I'm good at that.

"Uh, that depends, which room is the kitchen?" I said, looking around like it might be hiding in the crawl space above me.

"It's . . . never mind, forget it," she said. "Look, I know this may sound rude, and maybe it is. But can I ask you to leave when you're done? I'm just . . . I'm not comfortable with having you here right now."

"I'm sorry, did I do something wrong?" I said, as if I was still quite perplexed.

"No, it's just that . . . It would really just be better if you came back later."

"Later? I'm not sure I understand . . ."

"I have a document I'd like to show you," she explained. "But it's not appropriate for right now, with all these guests here."

So the aforementioned "it" was a document. That was good. Documents are *always* good where a reporter is concerned.

"Sure," I said. "Later. Later is fine."

"Could you come back at five today? I think my sister, Jeanne, wants to be with me when I show it to you."

"Uh, yeah, five is fine."

"Good," she said. "Now, if you'll excuse me . . ."

"Definitely. Go, go," I said, waving her away. "I'll see you back here at five."

I did what I had come inside to do, then showed myself out. I cut across the lawn, past a tent full of people eating potato salad.

• • •

In a way, Anne had done me a favor in kicking me out. I didn't really have the time to be hanging around, trading empty bromides about death with Nancy's friends.

I got in my car and started driving, mostly to get the air-conditioning going. I thought about the to-do list rattling in my head and decided the first item was to place a call to Peter Davidson of the National Labor Relations Board and learn what his business had been with Nancy. I got his voice mail, and just as I was leaving the end of my message, another call came through on my phone. I switched to the new call.

"Carter Ross."

"Smiley here," I heard back.

"Hello, Detective. I thought I might be hearing from you. I nearly wore out your name with a couple of your colleagues last night."

"Yeah, that's what I'm told," he said. "I just started my shift and I got this note from two guys on patrol saying you threw a woman into a concrete wall and then made up some story you were really saving her from a hit and run? Please tell me that's not how you roll with the ladies."

"It's not, it's not," I assured him. "And, unfortunately, the story about the hit and run is true."

"Oh yeah? For real?"

"Yeah, and the damsel in distress could have told your officers as much last night—she just happened to be unconscious. She's awake now, so she could give you a statement if you need it."

"Oh. Wow. That, uh, changes things."

"How so?"

"Well, there's someone out there who should have some pretty heavy charges against him."

I don't know why, but I hadn't considered that attempting to run someone over with your car was probably frowned on by the law.

"At minimum, he could be charged with aggravated assault," Owen continued. "We could also hit him with possession of a weapon for an unlawful purpose—in this case, the car. Depending on how good our evidence is and whether we could prove he was actually trying to hit you, we could even go at the guy for attempted murder. Trying to hit someone with your car and missing is the same thing as firing a gun at someone and missing. Just because you're a bad shot—or, in this case, a bad driver—doesn't make you any less culpable."

"Right, of course."

"Did you see anything?"

"Nothing other than a big set of headlights trying to run my ass down."

"No plates? No description of the vehicle?"

"Sorry."

"Too bad," he said. "Well, in any event, I need to get that statement from your lady friend. Those patrol officers were ready to charge you, and they wrote you up in their report. My bosses are going to think I'm playing favorites with a friend if I don't give them something."

"I hear you. Can you meet me at Mountainside Hospital in fifteen minutes? I should pay her a visit anyway."

"Yeah? You, uh, getting a little some?" he asked.

"Why, Officer, I do believe kissing and telling is unlawful under New Jersey Criminal Code."

"So that means you haven't sealed the deal?"

As usual, the sex-deprived, married father of three—or four, or however many kids he had now—was in search of titillation. I felt bad disappointing him, but I said, "Afraid not."

He clucked his tongue. "Too bad. I'll see you at the hospital," he said, and we hung up.

So, despite my previous intentions not to take this to law enforcement, the police were now involved. I asked myself how I felt about that, and I realized pretty quickly that I felt relieved. I needed some allies, especially ones who were trained in the use of firearms.

Detective Smiley and I pulled into the Mountainside Hospital parking deck at the same time and found spots next to each other—me in my Malibu, him in a brown Ford. If the stereotypical cop is a big, lumbering, doughnut-munching guy with a flattop, Owen is pretty much the opposite. He's small, quick, and hard-bellied, with dirty blond hair that's long enough to get in his eyes on occasion. I guess police grooming standards were relaxed for detectives.

"So," he said as soon as he got out, "this victim. Would you describe her as . . . attractive?"

"You're asking strictly as an investigator, I assume?"

"Oh, of course."

"Actually, you might know her: Nikki Papadopolous. She's a hostess at the State Street Grill."

"The one with the sweet bod?"

"Yeah, that's her."

"Go, lady-killer!"

He stuck out his fist for a bump, and I reciprocated, all the while feeling like I was back in high school gym class, talking about who "put out" and who didn't.

"Yeah, you might want to be careful about how you use the phrase 'lady-killer' if you end up writing a report about this."

"Fair point," he said, and we entered the hospital, taking the elevator up to see the patient.

I stopped outside her door and said, "Let me just make sure she's up for receiving visitors right now. Give me a second."

Owen nodded, and I knocked lightly on the door, entering when I heard Nikki say, "Come in."

She was sitting up in bed and smiled when she saw me. But there was something reserved about it. And I soon understood why. I was about to be dumped by a woman in a hospital bed—a first, even for me.

She gave me a variation of the old "it's not you, it's me," line. Except it wasn't me *or* her. It was Gus. Her father, she explained, "totally flipped" when he learned his daughter had been in my company the previous evening.

That's because I'm on to him, I wanted to say but didn't. Instead, I allowed her to explain that while she knew she needed to live her own life, she didn't want to aggrieve her father too greatly. And if being with me was *that* difficult for dear Babba, it probably meant our relationship was doomed because her family would always be important to her.

Given that our one and only date ended with her unconscious and upside down in my shrubbery with her underwear showing, I couldn't exactly launch a compelling argument as to why she was making a bad decision. Plus, there was the small complicating factor that I was very possibly in the midst of an investigation that would get her old man thrown in jail.

So I let her off easy and we agreed, if nothing else, it had been a memorable first (and only) date. I gave her a kiss on the cheek before I left—her perfume had finally worn off, so I was able to do it without getting dizzy—and told her Detective Owen Smiley of the Bloomfield Police Department was waiting to take her statement.

Then I bid her farewell and slid back out into the hallway, where I waved Owen in.

"She's all yours," I said. "I'll be down the hall in the lobby. Let's chat when you're done."

I camped myself on a couch, whittling away the next half hour or so fiddling with my iPhone. Like most new technology, it was simultaneously a great productivity enhancer and a total time waster. Then again, I suppose most of the microchipped gizmos and digital doodads we've developed in the last thirty years or so pretty much fall into that category.

So it was I ended up in an extended e-mail conversation with Lunky. I had configured the e-mail settings so that instead of appearing as "Lungford, Kevin," his messages came in as being from, simply, "Lunky." Oh, I do amuse myself so.

Lunky was trying to convince me that Philip Roth really should have won the Pulitzer Prize for *Sabbath's Theater* ("his true masterpiece") and not *American Pastoral* ("a brilliant but slightly lesser work"). If anything, he informed me, *American Pastoral* and *Sabbath's Theater* were opposites of one another—in one the protagonist is too optimistic to live, and in the other he's too cynical to die. In Lunky's opinion, the Pulitzer committee rewarded the former rather than the latter simply as an acknowledgment it had goofed.

Just to prod Lunky, I wrote back that I thought *Portnoy's Complaint* was Roth's finest work, prompting a long screed from Lunky that while Portnoy showed glimpses of Roth's genius, it was essentially "rudimentary"—really just "the crude sketching of a man who was later to become a master artist." In particular, "having Portnoy masturbate with raw liver is, to say the least, unrefined."

Naturally, I hadn't read any of those books—and since I wasn't fond enough of liver to cook and eat it, much less pleasure myself with it, I can't say I was planning to put *Portnoy* on my reading list. Lunky was just beginning to uncork his thoughts on why *Human Stain* was the last worthwhile Roth composition—and why everything since only evinced a once-great writer who had slowed a step or two—when Owen came walking down the hallway.

"Well, it turns out you're the hero after all," he said.

"I'm so relieved, Officer," I replied, wiping the nonexistent sweat from my brow.

"But Nikki in there is the star."

"Oh yeah? Why?"

"While you were playing middle linebacker, she managed to get a description of the vehicle."

"She . . . wow," I said. "I didn't even think to ask her."

"That's why you pay all those taxes to the town of Bloomfield, so the genius detective can pose the pertinent questions."

I thought about the mechanics of it and realized she had had a much better chance at seeing something. I had turned and faced her as soon as I became aware something was charging up my lawn, whereas she had remained facing it for much longer.

"So let me guess: we were nearly run over by a large black SUV."

"A Cadillac Escalade, yeah. Nikki said the last thing she saw was that big grille plate with a Cadillac crest on it," he said. "Wait, how'd you know? You told me you didn't see anything."

"I didn't."

"So, what, you suddenly recovered a lost memory? You know that won't play on the witness stand. It's in the patrol officer's initial report that you couldn't ID the vehicle. Defense attorneys shred people for stuff like that."

"Just call it reporter's intuition."

Owen grunted, clearly unconvinced. I gave myself one final chance to churn over the ramifications of allowing the long arm of the law to reach all the way into my story. But I realized it was already in there.

"Okay," I said, releasing a large breath. "The person who tried to run us over is the same person who killed Nancy Marino, that hit and run I called you about the other day. I spoke to a witness on Ridge Avenue who said she saw a large black SUV intentionally run down Nancy."

"You . . . how is that possible? We talked to everyone on that block."

"You didn't talk to these folks. Trust me."

Owen got a faraway look for a moment, then said, "That red house. The one on the high side of the street. I thought it was abandoned. That house was right in front of where the accident happened. The people there would have been able to see everything. I knew I should have tried that house again."

"No comment. My source spoke to me on the condition that I wouldn't go to the police."

"So they're illegal," Owen said.

"No comment," I said again. "My word is my word. All I can tell you is that I'll go back to my source and try to convince her to cooperate."

"Well, tell her we don't care about her family's immigration status. Not when she's a witness to a crime. That's department policy."

Owen pushed his hair back away from his eyes and was pacing around the waiting room, working hard on all this new information. He was carrying the notebook he had used to take Nikki's statement and periodically slapped it against his hand.

"Let's talk hypothetical for a second," I said. "Just say we got that witness to cooperate and tell you what she saw. Now, let's say I have another witness—who, again, is not quite in a cooperative mood just yet—who would say he heard a man making threats against Nancy Marino the night before she was killed—"

"This clearly isn't hypothetical," he interrupted.

"And let's say the man who was making threats had an adversarial business relationship with Nancy," I continued. "And that it's possible he was conspiring with another man who *also* had a good reason to want to be rid of Nancy. Would that be enough to arrest both guys?"

"Well, I'd have to talk to the prosecutor's office, obviously, but we've arrested people on less than that," Owen said. "That's the beginning of a pretty strong circumstantial case, especially if you've got the threats. And obviously, we'd be able to get some search warrants and do some more investigation and try to make it less circumstantial. Can you really deliver all those things?"

"I think so."

"Why didn't you tell me about any of this earlier?" he asked, shoving his hair back again.

"It's complicated," I said.

"What's complicated?"

I took a deep breath, then said, "Because one of the suspects is that girl's father. He owns the State Street Grill." I jerked my thumb in the direction of Nikki's hospital room. "And the other is Gary Jackman."

"Who's Gary Jackman?"

"He's the *Newark Eagle-Examiner*'s publisher."

"When you say publisher, you mean, like, *the* publisher?"

I nodded.

"Ah," he said. "Well, I can see how that would make your life complicated. But it doesn't affect mine one bit. Suspects are suspects. How do these guys know each other?"

"Well, I haven't quite figured that out yet. But I saw them chatting at Nancy's wake. Then I saw them sharing a table at the diner, talking about something pretty intensely. And they were sitting near each other again at the funeral this morning."

He frowned. "That's a start, I guess. Maybe when we pull phone records, bank accounts, and e-mails, we'll start to see more. How soon do you think you can get these hypothetical witnesses in line?"

"Hopefully within the next six hours," I said.

"Okay," he said. Then before departing, he added: "Give me a call if you need any help. And keep your eyes open when you're on the sidewalk."

In my younger, dumber days, I might have just puttered over to the Alfaros' house, knocked on the door, and relied on a well-considered logical argument—make that: logical *to me* argument—to carry the day, as if I were trying to win a Lincoln-Douglass-style debate at Millburn High School. I blame my WASP upbringing for the overreliance on things like logic and my underappreciation for, well, everything else.

But one of the things I had (finally) learned is the importance of having friends whose worldview was substantially different from my own. For all the politically correct halfwits who defined "diversity" in terms of skin color or ethnicity—things that might just be window dressing, depending on the individual—the real value in diversity is having people around who think differently from you, friends who can tell you when your logical is someone else's crazy.

In this case, I needed a friend who could tell me how to overcome a natural suspicion of the police. And that friend was Reginald "Tee" Jamison.

I had written a story about Tee—a burgeoning T-shirt entrepreneur, hence the nickname "Tee"—a few years back. And we had become buddies, for however unlikely we looked together. Tee is about five foot ten, 250 pounds, with lots of braids, tattoos, and muscles. If you put him in tony downtown Millburn, he'd be the kind of black guy who would make white people subtly reach for the car door lock button.

What they didn't know is that while he came packaged as a thug—in dress, speech, and manner—he had the soul of an artist and the emotional sensitivity of a woman in her third trimester. I once caught him in the back of his shop with a tissue in one hand and a Nicholas Sparks book in the other.

Having lost his cell number, which was stored in my other phone, I Googled the number for his T-shirt shop and dialed it.

"Yeah," he said, which is how he always answered any phone, home, work, or cell.

"Hey, Tee, it's Carter."

"How come your name didn't pop up on my caller ID? I almost didn't answer it. You got a different number or something?"

"No, I've gone into business as a major dope dealer, so now I use burners."

"You see that on *The Wire* or something? Because you know it don't work that way no more."

Tee is constantly explaining the ways of the hood to me. He sees it as his duty to educate the ignorant. Tee is a strictly legitimate businessman, but he remains familiar with the methodologies of those who aren't.

"I'll make a note of it," I said. "In the meantime, I need your input on something."

"Go."

"Okay, where to start. So . . . in your neighborhood, people don't like the police that much . . ."

"Is that so?" Tee said, making himself sound like a white New Englander with a head cold. "This is the first I'm hearing of this. Somebody ought to write a stern letter and put those unruly Negroes in line."

"Nah, we don't write letters about You People anymore. We call in the National Guard and tell them you've just looted a liquor store."

I was glad the waiting room was empty. Someone overhearing this conversation might take it just slightly the wrong way.

"Good point," he said, returning to his usual voice. "Anyway, go on."

"Okay, now let's just say there was a circumstance where you needed someone in your neighborhood to cooperate with the police. What would you do?"

"I wouldn't do nothing. Didn't I tell you about the time—"

"Yes, but let's not get into that," I interrupted. Police were constantly harassing Tee on account of his fitting a certain profile. Tee kept his friends close and his lawyers closer.

"Let's just say that despite your past experiences, you really needed someone to cooperate with the cops," I continued. "How would you convince them?"

"I'm not sure you could. People hear you talk to the police around here, they start calling you a snitch and the word gets out. And you're pretty much done, you know what I'm saying?"

"Okay, but let's say you really, *really* needed someone to talk to the cops. Like, your life and livelihood were at stake. What would you do?"

"Oh, that's easy," he said.

"Oh yeah?"

"Yeah. Money."

"As in reward money?"

"Yeah. You got to make sure a brother gets paid," Tee said.

"When the police are coming with money, it ain't just about what you can do for them no more. It's about what they can do for you. As long as you're ratting out someone who wasn't no good anyway? If people hear you got paid, they okay with it. They figure you probably got some bills or you need it for, like, a family situation, you know what I'm saying?"

Reward money. Owen had mentioned it early on, and I had completely forgotten about it.

"What about with Hispanic people who might be concerned about their immigration status?" I asked.

"Money looks just as green to Spanish people as it do to everyone else," Tee pointed out. "You just need to, you know, position it in the right way."

"And how's that?"

"Like it ain't coming from someone like you. No offense."

"None taken."

"I'm not saying black folks and Spanish people get along great or nothing. But they see someone like me, they're gonna know it ain't no trick, you know what I'm saying?"

"Yeah, yeah. So, uh, what are you up to this afternoon anyway?"

"I'm already grabbing my car keys," he said. "Where are we going?"

I gave him the address on Ridge Avenue, then said, "But cool down for just a bit. I may need a little more time to round up all the necessary elements. Can you give me a half hour?"

"This ain't one of those things where you really mean an hour, but you're telling the black guy a half hour because you figure I'll just be late anyway. Is it? Because I'm on to that trick."

"No. A half hour. I mean it."

"Okay," he said. "See you then."

• • •

My iPhone buzzed at me just as I hung up, telling me I had another e-mail from Lunky. But I didn't have time just now to hear about why Nathan Zuckerman wasn't *really* Philip Roth's alter ego.

I had to assemble my team to approach the Alfaros. First, I rang Owen, asking him if he could quickly hustle some reward money from his bosses. He asked for fifteen minutes to get the proper approvals.

Then I called Tommy, giving him a brief rundown of all that had occurred—laying heavy on the part that Jackman would be in handcuffs by the end of the day—and telling him his translation skills were needed. I also told him if he helped me, I'd give him two tickets to a Broadway show of his choosing. I expected griping and moaning about being under orders from Jackman and all that. But he readily agreed. Tommy is a sucker for Broadway.

With my Alfaro Attack Team assembled, I turned my attention to the other critical piece: Jim McNabb. Judging that he had been allowed enough time to eat his share of potato salad and clear out from Nancy's place, I called his cell phone. We exchanged greetings, and then I got to the point.

"Jim, you in a place where you can talk for a second or two?"

"Yeah, sure. I'm in the car. What's up?"

"Well, I didn't want to tell you about this at the funeral, but someone tried to have me run over last night."

"Oh yeah? No kidding!" he said, sounding more excited than concerned.

I should not have been surprised this would have piqued Big Jimmy's easily addled curiosity. So I gave him a full accounting of the previous evening, Nikki's injuries, our trip to the hospital, and the visit from Detective Owen Smiley.

"So the cops are in on it, huh?" McNabb said, when I was through.

"They are now, yeah."

"And that girl said it was a Cadillac Escalade?"

"Fancy killer, huh?"

"Yeah, real high class, this guy," he chortled. "So what are the cops going to do?"

"I think they're getting ready to make some arrests," I said. "And it's not just Jackman. There might be another guy involved. It looks like they both might have had a reason to want Nancy eliminated."

"Yeah? Really? Who's the other guy?"

"Gus Papadopolous. He owns a diner in Bloomfield. Ever heard of him?"

"No. How did he help Jackman?"

"I don't know. It just seems like Jackman didn't act alone, and I think Papadopolous might be the XFactor."

I had reached my Malibu, still waiting for me faithfully in the parking garage, and started the engine.

"Jim, this thing has gotten . . . Well, it's always been serious. But now it's getting really serious. I know we said 'off the record,' and I intend to honor that as far as the newspaper is concerned. But this is a lot bigger than the newspaper, and it's a lot bigger than you getting some heat with your board. At some point, we stop being a reporter and a source, and we start being responsible citizens with a duty to perform under the law. We're talking murder charges, here."

"You really think they're ready to press charges?"

"Well, yeah . . . If I can establish that Jackman made those threats. I didn't tell the cop about you by name, but I'm not going to be able to keep a lid on this forever. The cop told me the threats might be the key to the case."

I had pulled out of the parking garage into daylight, turning back in the direction of Ridge Avenue.

"Yeah. Yeah, I see that," he said, and I felt some relief. Logical arguments didn't work with everyone, but they did work with guys like Jim McNabb.

"Look, I still want to be as sensitive as I can to your needs here. So let's do it like this: you give me the name of that bar, and I'll get a bartender who will be willing to tell the cops what he overheard. Then the cops will come looking for you. But in the meantime, you can lawyer up a bit. Your lawyers can insist that the cops only question you on very specific areas—basically, confirming what the bartender has already said. That way, the parts of your conversation with Jackman you'd rather not be known stay unknown. You follow me?"

I pulled onto Broad Street, which was getting sluggish with mid-afternoon traffic. I could hear McNabb breathing through the phone, so I knew I hadn't lost the call. But I also knew I hadn't won him over just yet. If I really needed to, I would threaten to give his name to the cops. He would know as well as I did the prosecutor's office would hit him with a subpoena, and that would be the end of it. But I didn't want to have to haul out that stick just yet. I wanted to give him a few more nibbles at what was, relatively speaking, a carrot.

"Jim, I need the name of that bar," I said.

More breathing followed a sigh that had the full force of his gut behind it.

"Okay, okay," he said. "Look, let me take you there. I'd still rather handle this as quietly as possible. I don't want you mucking around, making a lot of noise. I'm pretty sure the bartender who was there that night is working again tonight. How about you meet me after work and we'll go there together?"

"Sure. That sounds fair."

"Five o'clock okay?"

I thought about my date with the Marino sisters and their supersecret document, whatever it was.

"Better make it six," I said. "I've got something else before that."

"Okay. Six o'clock. You sure about all this? Them charging Jackman and everything? I can't be sticking my neck out if they're not charging him."

"Yeah, Jim, I'm sure. Just relax."

Soon, I hoped, we would all be able to relax.

The brick-throwing had been pure improvisation. He happened to have a few bricks rumbling around in the back of his SUV, left over from a landscaping project. He always kept twine in his glove compartment. The idea developed from there.

He debated whether to even bother but eventually decided it couldn't do any harm. It might have been the final piece to convince Carter Ross to back off. What said you were dealing with an old-school tough guy—the kind who wouldn't be afraid to follow through on his threats—better than a brick through the window?

He should have known better. Ross just didn't scare that easily. Seeing Ross at the funeral—as apparently resolute as ever—made that altogether too obvious. This was the one reporter who wouldn't quit until he was in the grave.

It was finally time to make arrangements for that. His first task was to find a place. He had a few spots in mind and the second one he scouted turned out to suit his needs. It was deep in the swampy reaches of the Jersey Meadowlands, the kind of spot where the mob had been stashing bodies for decades.

His next task was to retrieve his weapon. The Bureau of Alcohol, Tobacco, Firearms and Explosives once estimated 87 guns a day are "lost" by gun shops—or stolen from them—putting an estimated 31,755 untraceable guns on the street every year.

He didn't know what happened to the other 31,754 untraceable guns from last year. But he knew one of them had ended up in his possession: a Smith & Wesson M&P Compact .357 Sig, billed by the shady thug who sold it to him as a perfect firearm for personal protection and concealed carry. When he bought it, he hadn't known what he would even use it for. But he figured it would be nice to have a little insurance, just in case.

Now it was time to cash in the policy. After the funeral, he drove home and clambered up to his attic, back to the medium-sized box in the corner labeled "Dad Sentimental" that he knew neither his wife nor children would ever disturb. He slit open the tape, pulled out some dusty photo frames and nicked award plaques he no longer needed, until he found the wad of old T-shirts he had used as a swaddle for the gun.

His old hunting knife—long and cruel and still sharp—had been wrapped in the same bundle, still in its sheath. He took that out as well, just in case, then continued digging until he found a box of bullets. The same thug who sold him the gun told him these rounds would have "the stopping power" he needed.

That assurance came back to him now, and he hoped it was true. He needed Carter Ross stopped.

CHAPTER 8

The call from Peter Davidson of the National Labor Relations Board came in just as I was arriving at the Alfaro residence. I slid my notebook out of one pocket and a pen out of the other as we went through the necessary exchange of hellos and gee-it's-hots.

"So what can the National Labor Relations Board do for you today?" he asked in a friendly tone.

"Well, I understand you guys are investigating a case involving Nancy Marino."

"What makes you think that?"

Oh great. It was going to be one of *those* interviews.

"Because you recently paid a visit to one of her employers, Gus Papadopolous at the State Street Grill in Bloomfield."

"I see. Can I ask what your interest is?"

"I'm a . . . freelance journalist," I said, which sounded strange coming out of my mouth after years of identifying myself as being a proud representative of the *Eagle-Examiner.* "I'm working on a story about Ms. Marino."

"Okay," he replied, without adding more

"What can you tell me about the case?"

"Not much at this point. We're still waiting for certain elements."

"What elements?"

"At this point, I'd really rather not say."

"Does it involve Mr. Papadopolous or a fellow by the name of Gary Jackman, by any chance? Or someone else from the *Newark Eagle-Examiner*?"

"Again, I'd rather not say."

"Why not?"

He paused. I watched the weeds outside the Alfaro household waving as a slight wind stirred. It was the first thing resembling a breeze in at least two days.

"Have you ever dealt with the National Labor Relations Board before?" he asked.

"Nope. This is my first dance with you guys."

"Well, some background: the NLRB was created by Congress to uphold the National Labor Relations Act and see that it's being properly enforced. We also enforce existing collective bargaining agreements. We've really got a fairly narrow mandate and this . . . this may be something that falls outside our purview."

"Why is that?"

"I'm not sure I can say."

"Oh. Can you at least give me some clue here? I don't want to have to waste your time playing twenty questions."

As I waited for Davidson to formulate his answer, I watched the white-haired busybody—the one who had warned me about the eee-legal ale-eee-ans living in the red house—walking along with a skittish white poodle, clearly a case of a dog resembling its owner. I wondered if the poodle was wary of nonpapered Chihuahuas.

"This may be something that ultimately involves another agency," Davidson said at last. "And if that's the case, I want to be respectful of that agency's rules and procedures. And, frankly, without looking them up, I don't even know what they are. But I don't want to hand them a case that's been damaged by media attention in some way."

Another agency? Why, that must mean . . . Actually, I didn't have the slightest idea what that meant. I was getting a whole lot of nothing and taking it exactly nowhere.

"Can you tell me what other agency?"

"Not . . . not without giving you too much of a tip about what's going on."

"Can you at least tell me why you threatened to subpoena Gus Papadopolous?"

"Who said I threatened to subpoena Mr. Papadopolous?"

"He did," I said, leaving out the part that I only knew this because he told his daughter.

"Well . . . I won't speak to any specific conversation I did or didn't have with Mr. Papadopolous or any other witness. But I will say in general that when an employee makes a complaint, I try to investigate all aspects of the employee's history. I like to get a sense of what kind of person I'm dealing with. It helps me understand where the complaint might be coming from."

"So Ms. Marino made a complaint?" I said, latching on to the first bit of decent information he had given me. He forced out a dry laugh.

"I probably need to end this phone call," he said. "I'm not trying to be evasive. I usually cooperate with the media. But in this case, I really just have to be careful about what I say."

"Okay, do you have to be as careful with what you write down? Is this anything I can FOIA?"

The Freedom of Information Act—the most wonderful piece of legislation enacted by Congress since the First Amendment—had been a friend to me many times over the years.

"I can't stop you from filing a request, obviously," Davidson said. "But I have to warn you I would probably deny the request on the grounds that it might be used in an ongoing criminal investigation."

"Criminal investigation?" I said. "What crime?"

He laughed again.

"You're good. I really have to stop talking to you. You're getting way too much out of me. I'm going to end this call now. If the National Labor Relations Board can be of future assistance, please do call again. But I just can't help you this time. So I'm hanging up now."

And, sure enough, he did.

Not long after the line went empty, I saw Tee's boxy Chevy Tahoe roll up behind me. The first part of my attack team was in place. I got out of my car, feeling the heat envelop me, and went over to Tee's driver's side.

"I told you the black man could be on time," he said, as his window rolled down.

"Yeah, you're a real credit to your race," I joked. "Mind hanging loose for another second or two? We need to wait for our translator, and I have another phone call or two to make."

"Yessuh, Mistah Ross, suh," he said, doing his Sambo impersonation. "You knows I's a just happy to do whatever you be tellin' me to do, boss. Whoooweee!"

"That's a good boy," I said, playing along. "Now you sit tight, hear?"

"Can I dance fuh yuh now, boss?" I heard him saying as I walked back toward my car. "I's just love to dance fuh yuh!"

He rolled up his window, and I got back in my tepid air-conditioning and placed a call to Lunky.

"Hi, Mister Ross!" he said, with proper intern enthusiasm.

"Shh. You're not supposed to be talking to me, remember?"

"Oh yeah, right," he said, having hushed himself by at least fifty percent.

"Are you doing anything right now?"

"No," he said glumly.

"You up for more civil disobedience?"

"Sure!"

"I need you to go over to the National Labor Relations Board office," I said, giving him the address I had copied off Peter Davidson's card. "File a Freedom of Information Act request for any documents pertaining to a complaint made by Nancy Marino."

"I'm not sure that's what Thoreau had in mind when he advocated—"

"Kev, I gotta run," I said as another call clicked through on my phone. "Just trust me: all those transcendentalists would have been big FOIA fans. They just didn't live long enough to know it."

The new caller was Detective Owen Smiley.

"You said fifteen minutes," I teased. "It's been at least twenty-four."

"Yeah, well, what I got is worth waiting for."

"That's not what Mrs. Smiley tells me."

He snorted. "Yeah, I wish. Just wait until you're married with three kids under the age of five. Even a lady-killer like you will be striking out."

I didn't bother informing him I'd struck out plenty of times already, even without kids to blame it on.

"Anyhow," I said. "What do you have for me?"

"Good news. We get a grant that gives us a certain amount of reward money each year. The chief tells me we're well under budget so far, and if we don't use it, we lose it. So he authorized ten large."

Ten grand was a nice chunk of change for that family—for any family. I thought about the sparseness of the furnishings, the folding chairs, and the disco-era couch. Ten thousand dollars would make them feel like they had hit the lottery. Maybe they could even buy a lawn mower for all that grass in front of their house.

"I'll have to send your chief a thank-you note," I said.

"You'll have to do more than that. If we take a statement from these people, we'll have to shift Nancy Marino to a homicide in our UCR numbers. We don't get many of those in lovely Bloomfield, so each one makes a big difference in our annual clearance rate. If I don't close this one, it'll mess with our numbers."

"You'll close. Don't worry."

"Okay, okay. Now, the deal with the reward is the information has to lead to an arrest and conviction. That's how it works. You be sure to tell these people that."

"Got it," I said.

"And I know they don't want the cops around. But I just might be in the neighborhood should they find ten thousand reasons to have a change of heart. So give me a call if that happens. I want my chief to know he's not wasting his money."

Tommy's car rolled slowly past me and parked two houses down. The final piece of my team was now in place.

"Fair enough," I said. "Let me go work my magic."

Except, of course, it wasn't really my magic I was counting on. I knew it was Tee and Tommy who were going to save this part of the day, if in fact it could be saved.

Tommy was walking up the sidewalk as Tee and I got out of

our cars. We congregated in front of the house, and I did the proper introductions. The three of us were, to say the least, ill-matched. There was Tommy, the wispy, nattily dressed Cuban who accessorized his tight-cut shirt and pants with the latest Dolce & Gabbana sunglasses; Tee, the muscle-bound black guy, wearing winter camouflage pants, a black sleeveless shirt that showed off his biceps, and a matching black skullcap, from which his braids sprouted; and me, the tall, well-scrubbed white boy wearing a charcoal gray suit along with the world's most boring shirt and tie combination.

The Alfaros wouldn't know what hit them.

"So here's the deal," I continued. "The Bloomfield Police have authorized a ten-thousand-dollar reward for information leading to an arrest and conviction in the hit-and-run death of Nancy Marino. We need to convince them it's in their best interest to do what is required to claim this reward."

"All right. Ten grand. I can work with that," Tee said, then pointed at me. "Your job is to keep your mouth shut."

"Agreed," Tommy said. "Let's do it."

We walked up the driveway, three men intent on their mission, ascending the concrete steps with Tommy in the lead. As we were knocking on the door, our attention turned toward the house, we didn't notice that Felix Alfaro had walked up behind us.

"Hello," he said.

We turned to see Mr. Alfaro, wearing a T-shirt that said TICO'S PAINTING in a script meant to look like brush strokes. Underneath, in a plainer font, it said, RESIDENTIAL/COMMERCIAL and INTERIORS/EXTERIORS. The entire T-shirt was flecked with paint splatters, and Mr. Alfaro, while smiling at us, looked properly spent from a long day of work. It was around three o'clock. At Tico's Painting, they probably started at six and quit at two, to spare themselves working during the hottest part of the day.

"Buenos dias," Tee said. "My name's Tee."

"Buenas tardes," Mr. Alfaro replied.

Tee turned to Tommy. "Tell him we just here to talk a little bit about what his missus saw."

Mr. Alfaro nodded like he understood, but Tommy said the appropriate words in Spanish anyway. Mr. Alfaro said, "Okay."

Tee began addressing Mr. Alfaro directly: "Look, I'm going to break it down for you real straight. You and me, we ain't got a lot in common, right?"

Tommy began translating. Tee waited until he stopped, then went on: "But we got one thing we definitely got in common, and that's that we don't trust the cops, right? What cops do to my people, I don't even want to get started. And what cops do to your people ain't too cool neither, you know what I'm saying?"

Another pause for Tommy to catch up.

"Now, I know he look like a cop"—Tee pointed at me—"and I know he look like he *might* be a cop"—Tee gestured to Tommy—"but I ain't no cop, you feel me?"

Mr. Alfaro waited for Tommy, then bobbed his head up and down. "Yeah," he said, grinning. "You no a cop."

"All right. And I'm telling you they ain't cops, either," Tee said. "They newspaper reporters."

Mr. Alfaro appeared to be growing befuddled about where this was all going. But Tee plowed on.

"So—and here's where I'm just laying it on the line for you—I want you to know that we don't care if you got any problems with your green card or nothing, you know what I'm saying? We ain't here about that, and we ain't going to let no one near you who cares about that. We'll protect you and your family. You got my word on that. And this brother's word is solid."

Tee pounded his big, meaty chest when he said "solid." I'm not sure how precisely Tommy was able to put all of what Tee had said into Spanish—a lot of it seemed fairly idiomatic—but Mr. Alfaro was again smiling.

"I show you something," Mr. Alfaro said, reaching into his back pocket, pulling out a well-worn wallet and producing a small, white piece of paper.

It was a perfectly legitimate Social Security card.

Over the next few minutes, we fell over ourselves to offer apologies for the misunderstanding, and Mr. Alfaro graciously accepted them. Of course, I couldn't help but wonder, If he and his wife were here legally, why were they so leery of the police? Why hide from them? Why talk to me with the insistence of "no police"?

Mr. Alfaro had been on the landing of his front steps the entire time we had been talking, and he finally walked up them toward his front door.

"Give me minute," he said.

As he disappeared behind the front door, we looked at each other sheepishly.

Tee turned to Tommy. "I know why *he's* ignorant," Tee said, jabbing a thumb in my direction. "What's *your* excuse?"

Tommy was about to return fire when the door reopened and we were invited into the Alfaros' threadbare living room. The shades were drawn, as usual, but I now recognized that not as an attempt to hide from the world but as an effort to keep the house cool. There was no air-conditioning.

The children were on the floor, contentedly playing—the little boy with a train, the girl with a doll of some sort. They looked up at us with big, dark eyes, regarded us for a moment or two, then returned to their toys. Mrs. Alfaro was taking a basket of laundry upstairs and said something involving "*momento.*"

My keen language skills told me that meant she would be a moment.

She came back downstairs and went into the kitchen to do the whole coffee thing again, I thought. But no, she returned to the living room and we all sat—Mr. and Mrs. Alfaro in folding seats, Tommy and I in mismatched chairs that had been dragged in from the dining room, and Tee on the disco couch. Mrs. Alfaro had a folded-up Spanish-language newspaper, which she occasionally used to fan herself.

Without being prompted, Mr. Alfaro launched into the backstory of their immigration status, which Tommy patiently translated. During the El Salvadoran Civil War, when his family was booted from its coffee plantation, he was still just a boy, but he realized his future was no longer in El Salvador. When he was old enough, he applied for political asylum in the United States, but that application had been rejected, for reasons he either didn't accept or didn't understand. So he applied for a green card. He waited nine years for his name to finally rise to the top of a waiting list. His wife was able to come over three years after that. And they held off on starting a family until they were in the United States, so their children could be born here as full-fledged citizens.

"He says he could have come here years earlier, but he wanted to do it the right way," Tommy said.

They still sent money back to El Salvador. They spoke of their family there as if they still lived in poverty. And I couldn't help but think, *And you're living in the lap of luxury?* But I suppose it's all relative.

After enough of the get-to-know-you stuff, I caught Tommy's eye and gave him a small "let's get on with it" hand gesture.

"Mr. Alfaro, I'm sorry, I just have to ask, why do you have these feelings against the police?" I asked.

Tommy translated the question, and Mr. Alfaro looked directly at me for the first time since we darkened his doorstep.

"Do you know of the Organización Democrática Nacionalista?" he asked.

I shook my head. He glanced over at his children, to confirm they weren't listening, then turned to Tommy and began speaking in a low, rapid voice.

"They were the national police of El Salvador," Tommy translated. "They were . . . brutal thugs . . . like terrorists . . . They roamed around the countryside with their death squads . . . They had a network of informants . . . All it took was one accusation to ruin someone's life . . . One night they . . . a death squad . . . came for my grandfather . . . He was accused of being a Marxist sympathizer . . . He insisted he was no such thing—he was just a coffee grower who wanted to live in peace . . . They killed him and mutilated his body . . . And they made my father watch the whole thing."

It was difficult to know what to say. Part of me wanted to proclaim that he was in the United States now and things were different here. Except that, in all likelihood, those death squads had probably been either financed or trained by Uncle Sam. We did a lot of shady stuff back in the seventies and eighties in the name of propping up democracy in Central America. I'm sure it felt necessary at the time—we couldn't allow the Communist menace to get a foothold in our backyard—but it was hard to imagine how the senseless death of a coffee farmer had aided that cause.

"I was two years old," Mr. Alfaro said. "I don't know him, my grandfather."

"Mr. Alfaro, I'm very sorry," I said, and I tried to slow my speech just enough to give him some help following it but not enough to be the dumb American who talks loud and slow to be understood. "Our police here aren't perfect. They make mistakes like everyone else. But they are, by and large, very good people who try their best to uphold the law. You can trust them."

Mr. Alfaro swiveled his head toward his wife, then back at me. Finally, Tee—who had been squirming on the disco couch for a while now—lost his patience.

"Man, I'm getting bored," he burst out. "Did you tell him about the ten grand? Just tell him about the ten grand. Never mind, I'll do it."

Tee scooted himself forward on the couch and began using large gestures as he spoke.

"If your wife here talks to the police about what she saw and they end up sending the dude that did it to jail? The cops will give you ten grand. That's ten thousand dollars. *Mucho dinero.* You feel me?"

I think Mr. Alfaro followed what Tee was saying. But, just in case, Tommy talked him through it in Spanish. The Alfaros conversed briefly—actually, it seemed like Mr. Alfaro was doing most of the talking and Mrs. Alfaro, in between waves of her newspaper, was doing the agreeing. At the end, they were both smiling nervously, and Mr. Alfaro delivered a small monologue to Tommy.

At the conclusion of it, Tommy said, "Mr. Alfaro wants you to know he's not doing this for the reward money. He's doing it so his children can see that things are different here. He says they're American citizens, and they need to learn to trust their government."

"So they're going to cooperate?" I asked.

"Oh yes," Tommy said. "They're going to cooperate."

I summoned Detective Owen Smiley from his hiding spot, and he arrived ten minutes later, with another officer there to translate for him. Mrs. Alfaro made some coffee, and my little trio stuck around long enough to make sure the ice was broken and everyone was getting along okay.

Then, when it was time to get down to business, Owen announced, "Okay, the reporters go bye-bye now."

I protested briefly—after all, I wasn't even technically a reporter anymore—but the fact was I had places to go, people to meet, and perhaps leftover potato salad to eat.

Tommy, Tee, and I spilled out onto the sidewalk. The day had gone from hot to hotter, and the humidity reminded me of the inside of a dog's mouth. I looked to the sky, which had a few puffy clouds that might form into something like a heat-breaking storm. But for now the forecast called for a ninety percent chance of *shvitzing*, with a strong possibility for continued swampiness.

"Thanks for the help, guys," I said.

"You needed it," Tee replied. "See you around."

"They say the neon lights are bright on Brooaaadwaaaaay," Tommy crooned, dreadfully off-key as usual.

"Yeah, I'll pay up," I said, cringing. "Your singing is an embarrassment to gay men everywhere."

"Yeah, well, that suit is an embarrassment, period," Tommy shot back. "When did you buy it? Nineteen eighty-four?"

"Yeah, wanna see the skinny leather tie I got with it?" I said, then switched gears. "Tommy, seriously, thank you. I know you're risking a lot to be here, and I appreciate it. You're a good friend and I'm lucky to have you."

"Cut it out. I'm the one who's supposed to get overemotional, remember? Just watch your back until the arrests go down, okay?"

"You sound like Tina."

The skin around his eyes crinkled and he said, "Yeah, maybe there's a reason for that."

Before I could ask what he meant, he was gone, back to the

comfort of air-conditioning, which is where I soon returned myself.

I still had a half hour before meeting with the Marino sisters, just enough time to return home and check on my wounded cat. In an unusual show of initiative, Deadline had managed to remove himself from the bathroom and trek all the way into the living room, where he had taken up residence on a windowsill. Only my cat would feel the need to bathe in sunlight on the hottest day of the year, thus sparing his body having to expend any energy to heat itself.

"No, that's okay, don't get up," I said as I entered. When I saw he had heeded my command perfectly, I added, "Good cat."

Then I went upstairs to change. I had spent enough time in my monkey suit for one day. And it was just too hot to muster the enthusiasm to don my normal uniform. Slacks and a polo shirt would have to be good enough.

Returning to my car, I noticed Constance at her usual spot, watering a lawn that was—even in the throes of a July heat wave—lush and green. Last summer I found myself rooting for water restrictions so she and her emerald island could be knocked down a few pegs. I gave her my usual I'm-going-somewhere-no-time-to-talk wave, but she stopped watering and dragged herself and her hose in my direction.

"There was some excitement at your house last night," Constance said, showing her usual mastery for telling me things I already knew.

"There sure was," I said.

"There were ambulances. I was so surprised. I was worried you had a fall."

"Oh, everything is fine, thank you," I assured her, unaware that falling at home was a potential concern for able-bodied thirty-two-year-old men. Mostly, I was trying to formulate a polite way to extricate myself from a rehash of the "excitement." I decided if I just laughed at whatever she said next and dove into my car, that would do the trick. My car door was already open when she said something that made me a little more eager to stop and chat:

"There was a man looking at your house last night."

"A man? What do you mean?" I asked, closing the door and walking a few paces toward her.

"Well, I wasn't really paying attention. I was just watering my lawn"—and minding her own business, to be sure—"but I saw this man walk up your driveway, look into your backyard, then come back around front and ring your doorbell. You weren't home."

"About what time was this?"

"Well, I had just gotten back from the soup kitchen"—Constance volunteered and wanted to make sure everyone knew it—"so it was probably about six?"

"What did the man look like?"

"Well, I wasn't really looking. I was watering my lawn," she said again.

"Well, sure, but you must have gotten some sense of him. Even if you just saw him out of the corner of your eye?"

She put down the hose and crossed her arms, pursing her lips, as if this was all necessary to summon the proper concentration to answer the question.

"Well, he was . . . thick," she said.

Hired killers often are.

"Is he a friend of yours?" she asked.

"Not that I . . . no, definitely not."

"Well, then I would say he was a little fat. I didn't want to be unkind, in case he was a friend of yours."

"Tall guy? Short guy?"

"About medium."

"White? Black? Hispanic?"

"White."

"Old guy? Young guy?"

"It was hard to tell. I didn't see his face. He definitely wasn't young. But I don't think he was old, either."

"How was he dressed?"

"About like you're dressed right now," she said.

"Did you see anything unique about him? Any tattoos? Jewelry? Odd mannerisms?"

"Well, I was watering my lawn," she said, just in case I had missed it the first two times.

"Right, right. Sorry. Did you see what kind of car he was driving?"

She paused again and looked toward the street.

"He parked it right over there," she said. "It was a big SUV, one of those gas-guzzlers."

"Was it black?"

"Yes, I would say it was. It had a very shiny paint job."

"Was it a Cadillac Escalade, by any chance?"

"Well, I'm trying to think if I saw the Cadillac emblem. Those are pretty distinct, you know. It was definitely big and boxy, like an Escalade would be. But I didn't really see. I was—"

"Watering your lawn," I said. "Thanks. I think I might know who it was, after all."

"Oh. Is it a friend of yours? I'm sorry I called him fat."

"No, no, that's okay. He, uh, sells magazine subscriptions. Those guys can be very pushy."

"I know. Sometimes, I can't bring myself to say no."

Constance turned and picked up her hose, like she didn't want her parched lawn to have to go much longer without quenching.

"I know what you mean," I said before walking back to my car. "Sometimes you just have to get a little tough with them."

The man Constance described didn't sound like Gary Jackman or Gus Papadopolous. The obvious conclusion was that they had been outsourcing the ugly stuff to a hoodlum-for-hire who had come to my house to scout things out ahead of time, so that when it came time to embed me into his grille plate, he'd know the best way to go about it. I thought about Constance's account of him: a thick and/or fat white man, medium-sized, middle-aged, dressed in slacks and a polo shirt, with no identifying marks. A quarter of the men in New Jersey probably fit that description. And if Constance didn't see his face, she was effectively worthless where the police would be concerned.

About the only thing that made it useful, I thought as I drove across town toward Nancy's place, is that after the authorities made their arrests, they could subpoena financial statements and look for sizable, unexplained withdrawals. Or checks made to the order of any local crime families. If this was going to be a circumstantial case—and it just might have to be—either of those things would bolster the cause.

Pulling up in front of Nancy's ranch house, I saw the tent was still on the front yard. But other evidence of a large gathering had been tidied up and cleaned away. There were still two cars in the driveway, including what looked like an airport rental, so I knew Jeanne was still around. Anne must have been there, too. But the aggrieved sisters had retired inside. Tough to blame them: the house had central air.

Getting out of my car, I labored through the heat up the front steps, then rang the doorbell. And waited. And waited some more. I pressed the button again, holding it down longer this time. More waiting.

Unreal. If they were going to pretend not to be home, they could have at least moved their cars. Who did they think they were hiding from? Helen Keller?

I knocked on the door, rapping it hard enough to make my knuckles smart. I could already feel the moisture forming on my upper lip and brow. Sometime real soon, I was going to have to lock myself in a refrigerated room for a week.

My knuckle-knocking had done no good, so I switched to a fist and boomed on the door with the fat side of my hand. I was starting to have the thought that I should have pressed a little more to get the document when I had the chance—yet another example of hindsight acing an eye exam that foresight had flunked. The time for lying back and being patient with Nancy's family had passed. The supposedly prudent reporter was done being patient.

I was about to shift my knocking to something more like thumping when Nancy's oldest sister opened the door. She was slightly disheveled, with one side of her bob flattened. She was dressed in the skirt of her sensible suit but not the jacket. Her white blouse was wrinkled. Her heels were gone and she had also ditched her panty hose. Yes, Anne McCaffrey had definitely gone native.

"I'm sorry, I lost track of time," she said. "We were napping."

I believed her. The crease of a pillowcase was pressed into her cheek.

"Sorry," I said, then tried to come up with a hasty fib. "I just thought maybe you couldn't hear me over the air-conditioning."

She stood there in her bare feet, holding the door in one hand, undecided about whether to invite me in. I could see the inside of the house had not yet been cleaned, and I decided that, in addition to being groggy, she might have been hesitant to invite me in because things were still a mess. So I sought to reassure her that I could have cared less about dirty dishes, empty cups, full ashtrays, or whatever else I might find lying around.

"I know this has been a crazy day for you. I can't imagine how you found the time to clean up out there."

She turned to the side and covered a yawn with her non-door-holding hand. My iPhone bleeped its new mail ring tone at earsplitting volume—I had yet to fiddle with the settings to change it to vibrate—and my hand dove into my pocket to silence it. But it was too late. The noise seemed to wake up Anne just enough to want to be rid of me.

"Mr. Ross, I'm sorry, but I'm going to have to ask you to come back another day. I'm just . . . I'm not up for this right now. And Jeanne is asleep. She needs her rest. Are you free next week? Maybe we could set up a time when we could all meet in my office."

Yes, it was definitely time for Mr. Ross to get assertive.

"I'm afraid I can't do that," I said. "My investigation into your sister's death has . . . reached a critical point. Time is of the essence. You mentioned you had a document for me. Why don't you just give it to me and I'll be on my way."

"I . . . I don't have any copies."

"I'll run to a Staples and make you ten sets," I countered.

"That's not the point," she said, running her hand through her hair in a gesture of frustration. "It's complicated."

I realized that Anne McCaffrey, who was all about staying in command of things, was trying to keep what little control she had over this situation. I also recognized a woman at the frayed end of her rope. And yet I felt I had no choice but to keep tugging on her.

"Ms. McCaffrey, with all due respect, a lot of situations get pretty complicated. I've been a newspaper reporter a long time. I've never met anyone whose life comes in a neat package with a bow on top. I don't expect yours does, and I wouldn't expect Nancy's did, either. Why don't you just show me what you have and we'll sort it out together."

"Well, I'm a lawyer," she said, as if I didn't already know. "So I don't expect things to be neat, either. It's . . . I don't want this to be something that becomes . . ."

She exhaled forcefully and winced, covering her face with her hands.

"My mother is so devastated by this, and I . . . I just don't need this to be . . . bigger than—"

"I'm afraid that may be unavoidable," I said.

"What do you mean?"

"Ms. McCaffrey, I know this might not be what you want to hear," I said, as evenly as I could. "But by the end of the day, it's entirely possible two men will be arrested for conspiring to murder your sister."

For a newspaper reporter, delivering bad news to people is part of the job, something you find yourself doing with enough frequency that you get accustomed to the range of reactions.

There are the deniers, the people who immediately insist what you're telling them couldn't possibly be true. There are the displacers, the people who channel that immediate rush of hurt and anger at you and hold you personally responsible for whatever you're telling them. There are the crumblers, the people who collapse into something resembling a catatonic state, to the point where they become useless. There are the bawlers, the people who immediately start crying on you or anyone else who happens to be around.

Then there are the stoics, which is the group Anne McCaffrey fell into. She was a tough nut, and she had no plan on showing me whatever emotion, if any, she was experiencing. If I had to guess, I'd say it was resignation more than anything—like this was news she feared might be coming, and therefore had braced herself to receive.

But that was just a guess. Outwardly, all she did was run her hand through her hair again, then step aside from the doorway.

"You'd better come in," she said wearily.

I followed her into a living room still cluttered with the detritus of Nancy's funeral reception. Anne gazed at it like it was just one more thing in life that disappointed her. Then she looked my way, as if she was placing me in the same category, though she wouldn't be able to clean me up as easily.

"Have a seat," she said. Nancy's living room had a couch against the far wall, flanked on either end by two sturdy armchairs, with a coffee table in the middle of the three pieces. I selected one of the armchairs.

"Would you like something to drink?"

"No, thank you," I said.

"It's no trouble. I'm going to get a glass of water for myself."

"I'm all right, thanks."

Just then, Jeanne came into the living room. She was wearing her black funeral dress and had been inside long enough that her glasses were actually clear.

"What's going on?" she asked. "Why didn't you tell me he was here."

"He just got here," Anne said, trying not to sound defensive. "I didn't want to wake you."

"I wasn't sleeping. I was just resting," she said, then turned to me. "Hello, Mr. Ross."

"Hello," I said. "And please call me Carter. I think we're going to be getting to know each other a little bit."

"What do you mean?" Jeanne asked.

Anne eyed her sister nervously and began trying to herd her toward the couch.

"Jeanne, why don't you have a seat, honey?"

"Why don't you stop telling me what to do?" she snapped.

Another sister spat was not what I needed at this (or any other) moment. So I interceded before this one got any momentum.

"Anne, on second thought, I'd really like that glass of water," I said, and she rolled with it.

"Jeanne, would you like one?"

"No, thank you," Jeanne said testily.

While Anne was in the kitchen, Jeanne took a seat on the couch—of her own volition, of course, not because her sister suggested it. Anne returned juggling three water glasses with a grace that would have made her waitress younger sister proud. She arrayed three coasters on the coffee table—Anne was a coaster-using kind of woman—placed the glasses on the coasters, then chose her spot on the opposite end of the couch from Jeanne.

"So, Carter," Anne said in her most diplomatic tone, "can you please repeat to my sister what you just told me?"

I not only repeated, I elaborated, narrating for them the full rundown of what I knew, from the NLRB visiting Papadopolous to Mrs. Alfaro's statement to the police. I tried to keep the level of detail high enough that I didn't leave anything out, yet sparse enough that I didn't bog down the story. Still, it took me about twenty minutes to finish it all.

When I was done, Jeanne actually looked pleased, like she

had been vindicated and was waiting to whip the world's biggest I Told You So on her older sister. Anne was still stoic.

"Gary Jackman," she said, at last. "You said that's one of the men's names?"

"That's right."

"Well, that answers that," she said.

"What do you mean?"

"I'm sorry, Carter," she said, shaking her head. "You've told us a lot, but I . . . we haven't told you everything. Or anything, really. There may be more to the story. Or it may be a different story entirely."

"There was a lot my sister was keeping from me," Jeanne interrupted. "They were things I would have told you when we met, but I didn't know them myself at the time."

"I felt it was privileged information," Anne explained, and Jeanne steadied her head just long enough to glare at her sister. This had clearly been an argument from recent days, and I just hoped they weren't going to rehash it in front of me.

"I called you when Anne finally started telling me," Jeanne said, "but your phone was dead."

"Yeah, I, uh, had to switch phones," I said. I could tell them about my employment status later. "Anyway, what about this story is going to change?"

"I should probably just show you," Anne said. "I'll be right back."

She rose from the couch and walked out the front door, keeping it ajar behind her. Jeanne swayed gently. We both took sips of our water. Anne returned, bringing a burst of muggy air back into the house with her. She was carrying a brown accordion file folder. It was stiff and new and mostly empty, but she had selected a large one, obviously thinking it would expand with time. She unwrapped the band that secured the flap and handed me a sheaf of paper that had been stapled in the upper-left-hand corner.

At the top of the first page I saw: "IN THE SUPERIOR COURT OF NEW JERSEY, ESSEX VICINAGE, CIVIL DIVISION."

It was, obviously, a complaint for a civil lawsuit, with the usual captioning. There was no case number, which meant it hadn't been filed yet. The plaintiff was listed as "Marino, Nancy B."

There was only one defendant. He was listed as "Caesar 710."

My eyes began poring over the document. Its first assertion was that at all times relevant to the complaint, Nancy Marino was a resident of Bloomfield, New Jersey. The subsequent facts were similarly banal stuff—that she was an employee of the *Newark Eagle*-Examiner, Inc., that she was a shop steward in IFIW–Local 117 and so on. I was into pages 4 and 5 before I got to the meat of the thing, and on page 7 before I started having an inkling about what was going on.

"This . . . this is a complaint for sexual harassment," I said, feeling my head cock to one side.

"That's right," Anne confirmed.

"But . . ." I said, then let my voice trail off as I refocused on the paper and continued reading.

Actually, I should say I was skimming. It usually takes me three or four trips through a document like this before I really absorb it. During my first run-through, I have a hard time keeping myself from speeding to the end.

But I was getting the highlights. It started with Caesar 710 making remarks about Nancy's appearance, including comments about her breasts. One quote that jumped off the page was, “On several occasions, the defendant stated the plaintiff should wear tighter clothing to ‘show off your body more.’ ”

Then he began asking her out on dates. At first, it was just invitations to drinks, which “plaintiff rejected as being inappropriate.” It escalated from there to sexual advances, descriptions of proposed encounters that became increasingly lurid. At a certain point, the complaint alleged, Caesar 710 started initiating physical contact, fondling her thigh under a table. The complaint referred to this as assault and battery.

“Assault and battery?” I asked. “He hit her?”

“Those are legal definitions,” Anne said. “Assault is any attack that causes the defendant to fear physical harm. Battery is simply touching without consent.”

I thought of what I had learned about Nancy, how she didn’t really date or seem all that interested in it. Every description of her made her sound fairly asexual. What was it that Nikki said about her? That while all the other waitresses gabbed about a hot guy coming into the restaurant, Nancy didn’t treat them any differently from the old ladies.

I could only imagine how she would have reacted to Caesar 710’s behavior. She would have been shocked, horrified, humiliated. She probably wouldn’t have known what to do about it at first.

But eventually she would have decided to fight back. Nancy Marino was no pushover.

And this complaint was part of that fight. There were other names mentioned, also in code: Caesar 413, Caesar 168, Caesar 1224. But Caesar 710 was clearly the star of the show.

“Wow,” I said, looking up from the document when I reached the end. “So who is ‘Caesar 710’?”

“I don’t know,” Anne said.

"What do you mean?"

"She wouldn't tell me."

Anne continued: "She said Caesar 710 was vindictive and violent. We were e-mailing this document back and forth, and she said there was a possibility it would be, I don't know, intercepted by someone. She thought if she put the real name in there, it would get reported back to Caesar 710. At the time, I just thought she was being paranoid."

Or, more likely, she was using her *Eagle-Examiner* e-mail account and feared someone loyal to Jackman would have access to it.

"But . . . what's the significance of 'Caesar 710'?"

"I have no idea. It's a little riddle she came up with," Anne said.

It was a riddle that had me stumped. Because, on the one hand, "Caesar" could be a reference to Gus Papadopolous—with the subtle switch from Greek to Roman, because "Pericles 710" would have been too obvious. Then again, it could also be Gary Jackman, who as publisher of a major newspaper was a Caesar-like figure.

"But you're her attorney," I protested. "How could she not tell you?"

"No, I'm her *sister,*" Anne corrected me. "I never would have represented her in this. I'm a real estate attorney. Workplace discrimination is pretty far from my area. I prepared this document as a kind of guide for another attorney, just so Nancy wouldn't have to walk into someone's office cold. I think it helped her organize her thoughts."

"So who's her lawyer?"

"She didn't have one yet. She was planning to put an attorney on retainer to pursue this claim. She had even applied for a home equity line of credit so she could afford to pay for it."

So that explained the $50,000 loan Tommy found in his background check.

"She said she was prepared to take this thing as far as it could go," Anne finished.

Jeanne, who had managed to sit quietly through this whole exchange, was itching to add her input.

"Can you think what it would have been like to be Nancy?" Jeanne said, with tears welling in her eyes even as her voice stayed flat. "With this . . . this animal saying those things? And putting his hands all over her? You're a man. I'm not sure you know what that would feel like."

I get this a lot, of course. People assume that because I'm a privileged white male, I am utterly incapable of understanding discrimination or persecution in any form. It's tough to convince them otherwise without sounding totally disingenuous—"but I have a *friend* who's Jewish" doesn't get you very far—so I ignored Jeanne and turned back to Anne. Somehow, she *had* to know something that would confirm the identity of Caesar 710.

"Had Nancy told you about her complaint to the National Labor Relations Board?" I asked.

"Well, yes . . . sort of. When Nancy first came to me about this—and, mind you, she wouldn't tell me who it was—I said her first step was to take it to her employer's human resources person. But I don't think she got a very satisfactory response."

"Well, yeah, if the problem was at the diner, I can't imagine she would have," I said. "A mom-and-pop restaurant like that doesn't exactly have a human resources department."

"Well, whatever happened, I told her the next step was the Equal Employment Opportunity Commission—the EEOC. But Nancy was very union proud, as you know. And I think she wanted to feel like she was getting some kind of solution that way. So she insisted on taking it to the NLRB. But I don't know if she heard back from them before she was killed."

That pointed the arrow back at Jackman because Nancy was a unionized employee of the *Eagle-Examiner*. There was no union presence at the State Street Grill. But why would the NLRB visit there?

"Well, the NLRB isn't being very forthcoming," I said. "I had a Freedom of Information Act request put in today, but I'm not optimistic that's going to get them to open up."

I returned my attention to the cover page of the complaint and found myself staring at the captioning on top. I wind up reading a fair amount of legal documents, and something about this one struck me as a little sparse. Then it hit me: it was the lack of codefendants. Generally, with these kinds of lawsuits, the plaintiff at least starts off with a big pile of targets, whether they're named individuals, corporations, or just John Does.

"If Caesar is Gary Jackman, why not sue the paper as well?" I asked. "Even with times as tough as they are in the newspaper business, the *Newark Eagle-Examiner* still has much deeper pockets than Gary Jackman personally. And if Caesar is Gus Papadopolous, throw in the diner. It's not as rich as the newspaper, but it's something."

"I told her the same thing. Nancy said she didn't want to hurt Caesar's business, just Caesar himself."

I tried to stop the alphabet soup—NLRB, EEOC, IFIW—that was sloshing around in my brain and instead concentrated a bit more on the "Caesar 710" riddle. Clearly, the "Caesar" part wasn't leading me anywhere. But what about the 710? Was it a date—July 10? An address of some sort? In the old movies, wasn't it always a locker number at a bus station?

"I'm still trying to untangle this 'Caesar 710' thing," I said out loud.

"I thought Nancy would tell me when the time was right, so I didn't give it a lot of thought. I just assumed maybe it was initials of some sort."

Initials? Of course. Initials. I started writing "A, B, C . . ." down one side of my pad, then "1, 2, 3 . . ." next to it. The *7* lined up with *G*. The *10* lined up with *J*.

"GJ," I said. "Gary Jackman."

There was more to discuss with the Marino family, but the mini grandfather clock in Nancy's living room—big hand on the VIII, little hand nearing the VI—told me there was no time to do it right now. If I was going to make my date with Jim McNabb at six o'clock, I had to clear out. I made my apologies, and the sisters Marino said they understood, practically shooing me out.

"I know you said you didn't have copies of this," I said, handing the complaint to Anne. "But do you have a file you could e-mail me?"

"Sure. I think Nancy has it on her computer here. It might take me a few minutes to find it on there, but I'll send it to you."

"Great," I said, giving her the e-mail address connected to my iPhone.

Outside, the temperature had actually backed off slightly, mostly because the sun had been blotted out by an ominous-looking line of dark clouds. The thunderstorms that would hopefully break the back of the heat wave were rolling in from the hills of Pennsylvania. After a brief bit of fireworks, it would be a nice night in New Jersey. In more ways than one.

As I drove into downtown Newark, I began working out some things. Jackman, faced with a sexual assault lawsuit from an already difficult employee, had decided he could rid himself of both problems with one action. Gus Papadopolous's involvement was, admittedly, still unclear to me. I'd have to leave that to Owen Smiley to sort out.

At the first light I hit, I picked up my iPhone, which I had stashed in the Malibu's cup holder, to see if Anne had sent me the file. She hadn't. There was just an e-mail from Lunky, telling me the NLRB had, as expected, denied his FOIA request.

I returned the iPhone to the cup holder. The NLRB would be a battle for another day. Assuming I could get myself reinstated at the paper, it would probably be fought by the very *Eagle-Examiner* lawyers who were used to doing Jackman's bidding. They'd probably enjoy the task of prying loose evidence of Jackman's guilt.

I was just a few blocks away from the National Newark Building when my iPhone began singing out its new mail song. At the next light, I grabbed my phone to have a look. It was the file from Anne McCaffrey. Someday, I thought, a printout of this file would likely be marked as evidence in a murder trial—if it ever went to trial. Maybe Papadopolous would admit to helping Jackman and agree to testify against him in exchange for less jail time. Jackman would know he was done for and grab the best plea deal he could get.

Jackman might end up with something short of life in prison. No matter. He would be ruined all the same.

At precisely six o'clock, I pulled up in front of 744 Broad and called Jim McNabb's cell phone. He answered with an ebullient, "Hey, Carter Ross!"

"Hey, I'm outside your building."

"Great, I'll be right down."

I used my short wait to forward Anne's e-mail onto Lunky, my amateur cryptographer, just to see how long it would take him to crack it. I wrote "Et tu, Brute? Then fall, Caesar!" in the subject line, figuring he'd appreciate the Shakespeare reference more than most. In the body of the message, I wrote, "Professor Langdon: A code for you to crack. Who is Caesar 710? See enclosed."

As I hit the Send button, Jim McNabb came strolling out of the building, still dressed in the same suit he had been wearing at the funeral. I stowed the iPhone back in the cup holder.

"Jim, I just want you to know, I really appreciate this," I said as he sank heavily into the passenger side of my car.

"Well, I gave it a lot of thought," he said. "And I just decided this is the right thing to do."

"Good. This thing might move fast. Have you been in touch with your lawyers for when the cops come to question you?"

"Not yet. I'll worry about that later."

"Okay. Where are we heading?"

"Just start driving north on Broad Street. We're getting on 280."

I did as instructed, pulling into traffic that was moving quickly out of town. Everyone was trying to beat the storm home. The sky was now some combination of green, black, and blue, the kind of sky that makes you want to take the kids and the hogs down into the cellar. And I don't even have kids, much less hogs. Deadline isn't *that* fat.

"Hey, did Nancy ever mention anything to you about a sexual harassment complaint against Jackman?" I asked as we merged onto the highway.

"Sexual harassment?" he said.

"She was about to file this civil lawsuit against the guy."

"Against Gary Jackman?"

"Looks that way. She referred to him as 'Caesar 710' in the complaint, like some kind of code in case someone intercepted the document. But it's him, all right. Sounds like he was a real dirtbag, hitting on her, not taking 'no' for an answer, putting his hands in places she didn't want them."

"You don't say? Isn't that something. I had no idea."

"Yeah, I guess she was pretty secretive about it."

I let it go at that. We drove in silence for a while, passing over the Passaic River.

"What about the NLRB?" I asked. "She ever say anything about going to the NLRB with a complaint?"

"Not that I heard. But it's not like I was her closest confidant, you know?"

We neared the entrance to the New Jersey Turnpike, and I got into the left lane, thinking that's where we were heading. But McNabb corrected me.

"No, no, stay to the right," he said, pointing to Exit 17A, which went toward Jersey City.

The end of his sentence was partially interrupted by the insistent screeching of my iPhone, telling me I had a new e-mail.

"Is that the new model?" McNabb asked, eyeing it covetously.

He went to grab it, then stopped himself short. "You mind?" he asked.

"No, go ahead."

It was so dark, it was almost like nighttime. And my headlights were only doing so much good. We were driving through an industrial stretch of Harrison—or possibly Kearny, you never quite know. We were about to pass under the eastern and western spurs of the New Jersey Turnpike. I couldn't imagine what bar we'd find this way. McNabb obviously hung out in some old blue-collar dive.

"I got the older model, but I've been thinking about upgrading," he said as he fondled my phone. "I told you, I just love all this technology stuff. Here you are, driving along at sixty miles an hour, and you just got an e-mail from . . . Lunky?"

"Oh, that's just what people call him around the office. He's one of my colleagues, Kevin Lungford. Would you mind opening that?" I said. "Lunky likes puzzles, so I sent him the sexual harassment complaint and told him to figure out the whole 'Caesar 710' thing."

"Yeah, no problem," McNabb said, cleared his throat and began reading:

"Mister Ross, this is almost too easy. The 'Caesar' is a reference to the Caesar cipher, one of the oldest cryptology methods known to man, so named because Caesar used it to communicate with his generals. It's really a simple form of alphabetic substitution, but with a three-letter shift down. So while '7–10' would make you think *G* and *J*, it is actually *J* and *M*. The person in this complaint has the initials J.M."

"J.M.," I said out loud. "Who's J.M.?"

There was only one person in Nancy's life I could think of whose initials were J.M., and that was Jim McNabb.

Who was now pointing a gun at my head.

McNabb trained the barrel of the Smith & Wesson an inch above Ross's ear. All the idiots who watch too many movies always stick the gun at the target's temple. But while that might do the job, it also might send a bullet racing through one soft part of the head and out another soft part without ever hitting anything hard enough to make it expand. It was only when expanding that a bullet did the full, flesh-tearing damage that would guarantee killing a man.

McNabb felt the tension of the trigger against his right index finger and reminded himself to stay calm and take deep breaths. He didn't think Ross would make any sudden moves. Ross didn't seem like the type to do anything that irrational. But McNabb wanted to make real sure that if the guy tried anything, he wouldn't get very far.

What amazed McNabb—thrilled him, actually—is how thoroughly unaware Ross had remained, right until the very moment the gun came out. Ross knew about the sexual harassment, the NLRB, even the Cadillac Escalade. Yet for all his supposedly honed reporter's instincts, Ross had never been able to put it all together.

McNabb had played a role in that, of course, having spun

that marvelous bit of fiction about Gary Jackman and the threats. None of it had ever happened, of course. Oh, there had been a meeting between the Eagle-Examiner's *publisher and representatives from the IFIW that Thursday afternoon, and it spilled into the evening. But it had just been another negotiating session. It was not followed by any trip to any bar. That one fabrication had kept Ross off track.*

But McNabb knew it wasn't going to work forever. All those twisted little lies were eventually going to get straightened out.

So he spent the afternoon preparing for a visit to "the bar," finding the ideal place for everything to go down, planning the route, thinking about what he'd say, anticipating how his adversary might react. They were only a few hundred yards away from their destination when the e-mail came in.

The e-mail was, admittedly, a wrinkle. McNabb couldn't simply make Ross disappear now, as he had planned. There was too much of a trail that might be followed—if someone started looking at Ross's e-mail, if someone plied answers from the NLRB, if someone pulled all those loose strings . . .

But no, Ross was the only one who was even close to tying them together. And the poor sap wasn't going to be alive to tell anyone about it.

So McNabb—aka Caesar 710, J.M., Big Jimmy, whatever anyone wanted to call him—just needed to improvise a bit, to orchestrate the reporter's death in a way that made it look like it was something other than what it really was. Just as he had done with Nancy.

A new scheme was already forming in his mind. And the more he thought about it, the more he liked it. He relaxed and reminded himself to breathe again. He was the one with the gun. He was in control. Total control.

CHAPTER 9

It's surprisingly difficult to look at a gun out of the corner of your eye while driving, especially when it's being pointed at the side of your head. But from what little I could see, McNabb's piece was short, black, and made for the express purpose of ruining someone's day. Gun enthusiasts go back and forth all the time about the merits of various calibers and bullets, chamber types and trigger actions. Not being a gun enthusiast, all I knew is this one would likely leave a significant portion of my brain splattered on my driver's side window.

In my previous thirty-two years on this planet, despite brushes with some unfriendly people, I had never had a gun aimed at me from this short a distance. Or any distance, for that matter. I tried to keep walls, or at least bulletproof glass, between me and anyone inclined toward discharging a firearm in the general direction of my person.

Now here I was, with nothing but three inches of air between this gun barrel and some body parts that I preferred to keep unsplattered.

And perhaps it should have been unnerving. Or disconcerting. Or at least mildly off-putting. I certainly don't fancy myself some kind of big tough guy impervious to bullets. I'm not especially brave in the face of danger. I have no illusions about my own fragile mortality.

Yet the only thing I felt was this strange calm. Maybe it's just because it was all so foreign, I didn't know how to react.

A few raindrops—big, fat, heavy ones—thwapped on the roof of the car. Then a gust of wind lashed us with another band of rain. The storm had arrived.

"Keep it nice and steady," McNabb instructed. "Don't try anything silly. If I feel even an ounce too much brake or accelerator, I'll shoot."

Up until the moment he had pulled the gun, McNabb had been his usual gregarious self. Now he seemed jumpy, on edge, neither of which were qualities I appreciated in a man with a gun.

I studied him, as best my peripheral vision would allow. His mouth had gone into the same ugly pout he had worn when I first told him that Nancy's hit and run was no accident. At the time, I thought the reaction was because of his friendship with Nancy. Now I knew it was because he realized he had not gotten away with his crime.

He almost did. If not for one El Salvadoran woman who liked to watch sunrises, neither of us would be in this spot right now.

McNabb had turned his body toward me, his eyes staring a hole in the side of my head where a fast-moving projectile might soon follow. I could see, now that he was twisted slightly, that he had been wearing a small shoulder holster. I'm not sure how I missed it before, except of course that it had never occurred to me to look.

Had he been unbelted, I would have simply jerked the wheel and crashed into the railroad trestle we were approaching. At sixty miles an hour, I'd take my chances. But he was wearing his seat belt. Crashing the car wouldn't necessarily improve my situation. Sure, it might make it more likely he would get caught for killing me, because the crash would attract attention, and he might be incapacitated enough he wouldn't be able to escape. But he'd probably shoot me as soon as he figured out what I was doing. And while it might be some small consolation for my loved ones that my killer got caught, it wouldn't do me a whole lot of good from six feet under.

So I kept it steady. Like the man with the gun said.

"Slow down. Take a right here," he said as we passed under the railroad. "Right after the bridge."

There was an entrance to a warehouse about a hundred feet ahead. Just short of it was a small, packed-dirt road.

"Right here?" I asked.

"That's the one," he said.

"I'm braking now to make the turn," I said, because I didn't want to get shot until it was absolutely necessary.

The Malibu, not exactly an off-road vehicle, left the pavement with a jolt.

"Keep it slow," he said. "Nothing cute."

"You got it, Caesar."

I used the name to try to get a small rise out of him—to see if he would rattle a little—but he didn't show any reaction. As I gently pressed the brake pedal, the first peal of thunder boomed from somewhere nearby. I didn't see the lightning strike that preceded it, but the storm was definitely close. Then, just as suddenly as the thunder, the rain came, hammering the car from every direction, like I had driven into a car wash.

"Can I turn on the windshield wipers?"

"Do it slow."

I eased my hand to the side of the steering wheel and turned the wipers on the highest setting.

In the meantime, all the mistakes I had made were raining down on my head as well. Some of them were now so obvious. Example: McNabb told me Jackman made those threats against Nancy on Thursday night. But Mrs. Alfaro said the killer started stalking Nancy on Tuesday morning, two days earlier.

"There never was any meeting at a bar with you and Jackman on Thursday night, was there?" I said, raising my voice to be heard over the rain. "There were never any threats."

"Nope," he admitted, without changing the position of anything but his mouth.

Of course there weren't. That's why McNabb would never tell me the name of the bar, why he was always so guarded about the whole thing—there was no bar. Jackman's appointment book just said "IFIW." It had been a negotiating session, nothing more.

"I can't believe I thought it was Jackman," I said, mostly to myself. "Maybe I just wanted it to be Jackman."

That had been another massive mistake, of course. I had allowed my bias against Jackman to cloud my judgment, never stopping to think that merely being a jackass and a foppish, non-newspaper-reading hatchet man didn't necessarily mean he was a murderer—even if he had once used a seven-iron in a way not endorsed by the United States Golf Association. Tina tried to tell me that. I hadn't listened.

Then there was Gus Papadopolous. I still had no idea what business he and Jackman had together, but it hardly mattered anymore. I mean, sure, Papadopolous went a little short-fused when he found out a reporter was in his office. But a lot of people didn't like reporters hanging around. Heck, maybe he sensed I had the hots for his daughter, and had kicked into overprotective daddy mode.

But there were more mistakes. I had badly misjudged McNabb, assuming that because he had one obvious agenda—

positioning his union in its renegotiation with the paper—he didn't have any other agendas that he kept hidden.

McNabb said it himself, in a small bit of conversation that was now coming back to me: *a powerful man facing the loss of his power will do just about anything to protect it.* I thought he was talking about a different powerful man, but he was talking about himself.

More than that, I had allowed myself to rely on his information too much, without stopping to scrutinize it that extra layer. I definitely subscribe to the "one great source" theory of reporting—that all it takes is that one person on the inside to illuminate a subject for you. Of course, you still have to make a good decision about who that one great source should be. And at risk of stating the obvious, I had chosen poorly.

And shouldn't I have known? McNabb was constantly asking me about what I had or hadn't told the cops, always pumping me for information. I had dismissed it as an outcropping of his dirt-mongering personality, never thinking that I was keeping the murderer fully apprised of my investigation.

There was also some bad luck and lousy timing involved. If I had gotten more immediate cooperation from Anne McCaffrey—or if Anne had put Jeanne in the know earlier—I would have discovered the sexual harassment sooner. I would have had time to read the complaint a little more carefully and come to some different conclusions, ones that would have led me away from Jackman.

One example that was suddenly obvious: the complaint said Caesar touched Nancy under a table. When would Jackman ever have been sitting close enough to Nancy to do that? The only time he would have ever seen her was during a negotiating session—when he would have been on the *opposite* side of the table.

For that matter, Caesar was asking her out on dates. There was no way the publisher of a major newspaper, locked in a tense negotiation with its largest union, would have done anything that outrageous with one of the union's shop stewards.

And there was Jim McNabb, calling one of his employees "candypants," right in front of me all along. But I still couldn't see it.

Yep, I had screwed up every way but good. And because of it, it might be the last story I ever worked.

We bounced along the dirt road, splashing through flooded ruts and potholes, going no more than fifteen miles an hour. The lightning flashes were providing more illumination than my headlights. The wipers beat furiously but still couldn't keep up with the torrent of water gushing down from the sky.

On our left, we passed the loading warehouse and a parking lot, then a small trailer on our right. Then we were in no-man's land. Beyond the waist-high weeds that lined the road, I had a railroad track to my right and some sort of retention pond to my left. It was a body of water that had probably been the recipient of enough heavy-metal-laced runoff and landfill leachate to make it glow in the dark.

I briefly considered yanking the steering wheel to the left and taking us for a swim in that yucky stew—I could take my chances with the elevated cancer risk two decades from now. But we were moving too slowly. McNabb might be a little surprised, but he'd have ten chances to shoot me before the water closed over the car and forced him to bail out.

No, the simple fact was, in the middle of the most densely populated metropolitan area in America, I had managed to find myself in a totally isolated spot with an armed killer. Yet another genius move on my part.

"Okay, stop here," he said.

I pressed the brake until the car halted.

"Put it in Park," he instructed.

I moved the shifter up from the Drive position.

"Now put your hands on the ceiling, palms up."

I did as instructed. A thick lightning bolt lit the sky, followed quickly by an enormous thunderclap. I could briefly see a large power transfer station perhaps a hundred yards ahead, then the elevated road surface of the New Jersey Turnpike a few hundred yards beyond that. Traffic was probably crawling in a storm like this. I wondered if any of those drivers could see me, this strange little car parked along a railroad access way. But I doubted it. The visibility had been reduced to nothing. We might as well have been in an underground bunker.

"Why don't I just drive us down to the Pine Barrens," I said. "I know a spot that's got to be ten miles from anywhere. You dump me off there, and by the time I get out, you could be a hundred miles away in any direction."

"And live like some damn runaway the rest of my life? I don't think so."

"Jim, you're not going to get away with this," I said.

"Yes I am. You didn't tell anyone about me. You told me so yourself."

"Someone else is going to figure out who 'J.M.' is. That complaint makes it pretty obvious."

"Yeah? If it was so obvious, how come *you* didn't figure it out?"

Because I'm a total moron, I wanted to say.

"I didn't, but Kevin Lungford will," I said. "He's a brilliant,

Princeton-educated reporter, one of the smartest guys I've ever worked with. He's probably already put it together."

I put as much force behind it as I could, but McNabb wasn't fooled.

"Yeah, that's why you call him Lunky, huh? Because he's so smart?"

Natch.

The rain slacked off for a few seconds, then pounded on the roof with renewed intensity, like a thousand tiny percussionists all doing a drum roll at the same time. The windshield wipers thumped from side to side, with little effectiveness. Our breath had fogged over the inside of the windows.

"Look, killing me is only going to make things worse for you. You could spin Nancy as manslaughter. They'd give you ten years, and you'd be out in five for good behavior. You kill me and it's a double homicide. First degree. They'll put you away for the rest of your life."

"I'm not going to kill you," he said, and I felt myself getting hopeful until he finished: "You're going to commit suicide."

"And why would I do that?"

"Because, Carter Ross, at this point, you have one choice to make in what is left of your short, miserable little life. You can die quick and painless—and I'll make it look like a suicide. Or you can die the slowest, most agonizing death you could possibly imagine."

"No, thanks," I said. "I'll take the mystery prize behind door number three."

In one fast move, McNabb chunked me on the head with the butt of his gun. He didn't have enough room in the car to get any momentum behind it, but it still wasn't the most pleasant feeling in the world.

"Ow," I said.

"It's going to hurt a lot worse when I blow off both your kneecaps. And that's only a start. You see that trailer we just passed?"

"Yeah?"

"It's open. And it's abandoned. I checked it out earlier today. After I do your kneecaps, I'll take you in there, and we can have a real good time all night long. I left some rope in there to tie you up with, and I have a hunting knife strapped to my calf. I'll carve off a piece of you at a time until there's nothing left. Or we can get it over with quickly. Now what's it going to be?"

I thought about dying a messy death in that railroad trailer and about all the blood I'd leave behind. McNabb didn't have any cleaning products with him. If someone ever did enter that trailer, they'd be sure to notice that it looked like a calf had been slaughtered there, and maybe let the police know about it. Then again, it still fell into the category of Things That Don't Matter When You're Already Dead.

"No one will believe a guy like me committed suicide," I said. "I'm too happy-go-lucky."

"Oh yeah? I don't know about that. You just lost your job. Your girlfriend dumped you. You're probably going to lose your house. That sounds to me like a guy who's pretty down on his luck."

"The detective investigating Nancy's death is Owen Smiley, a friend of mine. We play on the softball team. He knows me too well. He'll never believe I killed myself."

"Oh, he'll believe it."

"How you figure?"

"Because," McNabb said, pressing the barrel of the gun against my head. "You're going to write a suicide note. In your note, you're going to say you've lost everything that matters to you and decided to end it. Oh, and one more thing."

"What's that?"

"You're going to admit to killing Nancy Marino."

• • •

The condensation on the inside of the car had grown thick enough that small beads of sweat were rolling down the windows. My palms were still pressed against the roof of the car, and my shoulders were starting to ache from keeping them there.

"That's absurd," I said. "Why would I kill Nancy Marino? I didn't even know her."

"Yes you did. You live in the same town. You met her at the diner and fell in love with her. You finally summoned the nerve to ask her out. She rejected your advances. You're a love-struck loser. If you couldn't have her, no one could have her. Why else would you have written an obituary about her? It was your guilt coming out."

"That's . . . that's, like, the worst episode of *Law & Order* I've ever heard. That doesn't even sound like me. Besides, everyone knows I drive this crappy old car—not a pimp-daddy Cadillac Escalade. How would I have gotten my hands on a ride like that?"

McNabb eased the gun back so it was no longer directly touching my scalp, but kept it aimed at the same spot.

"Maybe you rented it, maybe you stole it," he said. "I'm not trying to get you found guilty beyond a reasonable doubt. This thing isn't ever going to trial—you'll be dead. I'm just throwing people off the trail. Don't you get it yet? People are easily distracted. You give them a story that makes sense, that fills in just enough blanks, and they accept it and move on. Look at how well it worked on you. I told you one lie about Jackman that seemed plausible, and you just ran with it."

"Not everyone is as dumb as me."

"No, most people are much, much dumber. And a whole lot less persistent. You just kept coming at me, kept digging. So what did I do? I distracted you some more, with that e-mail from Jackman."

"Was that real, by the way?"

"Sure was," McNabb said, and turned his gun toward my right knee. "But, of course, you were nice enough to let your overly active imagination run wild with it. Then somehow you thought that diner owner was involved. That was great. I didn't even have to do anything to get you spinning on that one. That was fun."

He chuckled, then abruptly stopped.

"Now, you've got five seconds to decide. You want to die quick or slow? Suicide or torture?"

Some choice. Then again, I wasn't exactly enamored of dying in that little trailer in the middle of a swamp, alone and in agony, tormented by this horrid man. He'd toss my mutilated carcass into that retention pond where my softer parts would get gnawed on by various critters. I'm not saying I needed to leave behind a corpse worthy of the V. I. Lenin treatment. But if this was the end, it would at least be nice for my parents to have something to bury.

"Okay. Suicide it is," I said. "How are we doing this—this note thing? You got a pen and paper for me?"

"Nope, you're going to draft an e-mail on that shiny new iPhone of yours. I want to be able to edit this thing, and I can't do that if you handwrite."

"Okay, e-mail. Mind if I take my arms down now?"

"Go ahead."

My shoulders felt instant relief. Sort of like when you stop hitting yourself on the head with a hammer.

"I'm going to grab my iPhone now," I said.

"No, let me give it to you."

McNabb kept the gun trained on me and bent slightly to grab

the phone, taking his eyes off me for a split second. Maybe this is the point where a real tough guy—like an ex-military cop or something—would exploit the one small moment of his opponent's weakness to execute some kind of quick, devastating backhanded karate chop that severs the spinal cord between C-4 and C-5. Alas, that's not something they teach newspaper reporters.

He hastily tossed the phone in my lap, then, before I knew what was happening, he hit the unlock button, exited the car, and reentered in the backseat. Again, the tough guy would have been alert enough to turn the situation around. But by the time I even knew what he was doing, he was behind me, with the gun still firm in his right hand.

"Hit the lock button," he said, and I did as I was told. "Now, start writing. I'm watching everything you do, so don't try anything."

"Okay. To whom am I addressing this farewell missive?"

"Send it to that Lunky fellow, if you're really that fond of him. And you better make it good. You're a writer. I expect to see some real inner torment being expressed."

I inhaled and let the breath out slowly. Compose Your Own Suicide Note. It had to be the worst creative writing assignment ever, even worse than Compose Your Own Obit.

I turned on that tiny little iPhone keyboard, opened up a new message, addressed it to Lunky, and began typing.

> Dear Kevin,
>
> It is most unfortunate that I find myself writing these words. As you know, being a reporter was everything to me. And now that I no longer have that, I find life isn't worth living anymore.
>
> Please tell Tina not to blame herself for what hap-

> pened. She begged me to marry her many times, and perhaps if I had said yes, none of this would have happened.
>
> But the fact is, I couldn't marry Tina when I was in love with someone else. Her name was Nancy Marino. I never let on to anyone about my true love, but my heart burned for her every day. She wouldn't have me, and I honored that choice. But

I put down the iPhone for a second and said, "Wait, what was that line you wanted me to use?"

"Something like, 'If I can't have you, no one could,'" McNabb said.

"Right, right, of course," I said, then continued:

> if I couldn't have her, no one could. I can't wait to join her where the angels soar.
>
> And now it is time for me to go to a place that is deeply meaningful to me. Where Philip Roth began is where I will end. The man who gave the world *Sabbath's Theater* will help set the stage for my final act.
>
> Sincerely,
>
> Carter
>
> P.S. Please find my cat Deadline a good home, perhaps a farm in the country where he can continue to lead his active lifestyle.

I reviewed my effort, deciding that fertilizing day at the organic farm couldn't have stunk worse. But, of course, that was the point. If nothing else, I hoped the fans of my writing would recognize I would never allow my last words to be so painfully trite. But even if they didn't pick up on all the clichés, the purely comical line about Tina, or the nonsense about Nancy, the part about Deadline would throw it over the top. Deadline's slothfulness is that legendary.

"You should be a little more direct about the Nancy thing," said McNabb, who had been hovering over my shoulder the whole time. "You need to come out and say 'I killed her.' "

"Nah, come on, think about it: the love-struck loser on *Law & Order* is never that straightforward," I said. "If I really was that loony, I'd probably be too nuts to even realize what I had done."

He grunted and continued to study my note, breathing hot exhaust in my ear—which wasn't quite as painful as torture but had to be at least as annoying.

"What's this Philip Roth thing?" he asked.

"It's where you're going to kill me."

"What are you talking about?"

"You're going to kill me—excuse me, I'm going to commit suicide—outside the house where Philip Roth grew up. That's why I wrote 'Where Philip Roth started is where I will end.' It's a bit obscure, I know. But it'll make sense when that's where my body is found. Everyone who knows me knows I'm the biggest Roth fan there is. You want this to be believable? There's got to be a Roth connection."

"Roth, huh?" he said, and I could tell he was rolling it around in his head.

"You can scroll through my sent messages if you don't believe me. Earlier today I was trying to convince Lunky that *Portnoy's Complaint* was Roth's greatest work."

"That's the one where that sick bastard whacks off with coleslaw or something like that?"

"Raw liver," I corrected him, as if I were the most learned of Roth scholars.

McNabb breathed some more, mulling over whether to permit me my literary license. I took advantage of his indecision.

"You said you wanted this to be convincing, right? And you said you wanted it to distract people. Think about it: a frustrated writer commits suicide outside a famous writer's childhood home? That's nice, easy symbolism."

"Okay," he said. "Philip Roth's house it is."

I quickly hit the Send button on the message.

"Hey, I didn't say to do that!" he said sharply.

"Sorry, I thought you—"

"You want to go in that trailer?" he shouted, grinding the gun into my head hard enough that it bent my neck forward and plowed my chin into my chest. "Is that what you want?"

"Just take it easy. Lunky goes home at six. Most of our reporters work ten to six. You know that. He won't get this until tomorrow morning."

"Never mind. Just give me the damn phone," he barked.

I passed it back to McNabb, who promptly rolled down the window and tossed it outside. Even through my hazed windshield, I could see it sail over the weeds in the direction of the retention pond, where it would spend eternity stewing in toxicity.

"You won't be needing that," he said before I could offer comment. "Now let's get moving."

I reached forward with my arm and swiped a clean spot in my thoroughly fogged-over windshield, then started blasting the defroster so it would stay clear.

"How am I getting out of here?" I asked. "I'm not sure backing up is the best idea."

"Drive down to the power transfer station and turn around," he said. "Now, here are the rules: two hands on the steering wheel at all times, and keep them nice and high—ten o'clock and two o'clock. Nothing too crazy with the gas or the brake. If I don't like what I see, I'm putting a slug in your kneecap, and I'm going to shoot first and ask questions later. So let's not get cute."

I eased the car back into Drive and began splashing my way forward. The road was waterlogged, and even at twenty miles per hour, we were tossing up spray like a powerboat under full throttle. The rain had slackened—it was now just a gentle drizzle—but the sky was still bruise blue, like it hadn't yet released all its fury.

"You're going to die tonight, Carter Ross," he added. "You stick to the script, you die easy. You make it hard on me, I make it hard on you. That's how it works."

I didn't know how this lunatic thought he'd get away with this. Except, of course, he had nearly pulled it off with Nancy.

"You know where you're going?" he asked, when we made it back to the paved roadway.

"I told you, I'm a huge Roth fan," I said.

Keeping my hands at the mandated position, observing all posted speed limits, and generally acting like I was taking my driver's test all over again, I pointed us toward the turnpike—which was, as I suspected, trudging along well below the speed limit. The rain had all but stopped, though another line of storms was bearing down on us, putting on an impressive fireworks show in the distance.

Rolling along just above stall speed gave me time to start placing recent events in their proper order and to make sense of everything for the first time. As a newspaper reporter, I am trained to think in narratives. And narratives are best understood when you start at the beginning. So how had this started?

Mrs. Alfaro said a man—who I now knew to be McNabb—began stalking Nancy on her paper route the Tuesday before she was killed. What event precipitated that? Peter Davidson of NLRB stopping by the diner on Monday.

But, of course, the diner probably hadn't been his only stop that day. Davidson said he tried to investigate all aspects of an employee's history. So the diner would have been a side stop, but if the complaint was primarily lodged against McNabb and the IFIW, that would have been Davidson's main destination.

"It was the NLRB, wasn't it?" I said. "The NLRB visited the State Street Grill on Monday. They came to you the same day, didn't they?"

"Are we on the record, Mr. *Eagle-Examiner* reporter?" he taunted.

"Hell yes. The least thing you can do is grant a reporter his last interview."

"Okay, I guess there's no harm now," he said. "On the record: yeah, that pencil-pushing prick from the NLRB came to my office on Monday, asking me questions about allegations made by Nancy Marino."

"And what happened?"

"I stalled him. It was all crap anyway."

We were picking up speed as traffic diverged into the enormous mixing bowl of roadways at Newark Liberty International Airport. I followed the signs for Route 78.

"Oh, come on, you're not really going to deny sexually harassing her, are you?" I said. "Your union probably represents a couple hundred employees a year in sexual harassment cases. You know the rules."

"Damn straight I do," he said. "There's two kinds of sexual harassment. One is quid pro quo, where your boss asks for sexual favors in return for a raise or a promotion. The other is creating a hostile work environment. Well, guess what? I'm not her boss—I'm just an employee of the union to which she belongs. Hell, if anything, she's my boss, because she votes for the board that hires or fires me. So there could be no quid pro quo. And I couldn't have created a hostile work environment for her when she doesn't work for the union."

There were at least a hundred holes in his argument, not the least of which was that union negotiations easily fit under the umbrella of a "work environment" as the courts had defined it. Besides which, you're not allowed to grope a woman's thigh without her permission *outside* the work environment, either. But I wasn't arguing legal technicalities with a man so obviously deranged. Or so armed.

"So why did Nancy take all that to the NLRB anyway? Shouldn't she have gone to the EEOC?"

"Because her complaint to the NLRB didn't have to do with the harassment," he said. "She was saying her harassment complaint had not been properly heard by the union."

"Was it?"

He chuckled, like he was enjoying this. "Hey, it's not my fault our human resources people didn't see things her way," he said. "She got a thorough exercising of due process."

More likely, she got the runaround when McNabb cajoled and threatened his horsewhipped employees into ignoring her complaint. This was all becoming clear to me.

"So, if you were so much in the right," I said, "why kill her?"

He actually laughed. "You ask good questions, you know that? In some ways, it's a shame I have to kill you, too. You were one of the best reporters in my Rolodex."

"Yeah, and I'm a good enough reporter to know when someone is dodging my question. So, again, why kill her?"

"Because I was tired of dealing with her," he said. "She had gotten to be too much of a headache, and I realized she was never going to shut up. I just tried to give the bitch a few compliments and she went and made some big thing out of it."

The line of storms I had been watching in the distance hit Newark just as we got off Route 78, while I was on the ramp for Exit 56. It reduced visibility to the few feet in front of my windshield, but that bothered me less now that we were back in Newark. I may be the whitest man alive, but Newark is still my hood. I could find my way to 81 Summit Avenue in a blizzard if need be.

So I hydroplaned my way into the Weequahic neighborhood that Philip Roth once called home. The Jewish population that dominated this area fled in the fifties and early sixties, not long after Roth himself left for college and never came back. The street names and some of the old houses might still look familiar to Roth or any of the other aging Jews who still had a memory of the place. But it had changed in just about every other way. The Weequahic they knew was long gone.

We kept hitting red lights all along Elizabeth Avenue and on Chancellor Avenue. It occurred to me the storm had significantly improved my chances of being able to make a break for it at a stoplight. I just couldn't figure a way to get out of the car. The Malibu kept the doors locked as long as it was in Drive, so I couldn't just roll out. There was too much my hands had to do: unclick the seat belt, unlock the door, pull the handle. It was impossible to even attempt such a move while white-knuckling the steering wheel at ten and two. Not even Houdini could have pulled that sleight of hand.

We passed Weequahic High School and I glanced at the Malibu's clock. What should have been a fifteen-minute drive had taken us closer to thirty. I just hoped it was enough time for Lunky to do something other than prepare a lengthy reply message about how Roth really intended for suicide to be used as an allegory.

But as I turned onto Summit Avenue, I didn't see any kind of welcome party, just a long, wet, empty street teeming with raindrops. Up until that moment, my faith in Lunky had been total, perhaps inexplicably so. I thought for sure he'd still be hanging around the newsroom, like he was every other night, see my message, get the reference to Roth's home and call in the reinforcements.

Instead, my life was going to end because Lunky either wasn't reading his e-mail or didn't understand it. He was a kid who couldn't find his way out to South Orange Avenue without me holding his hand and who thought he could wait until the next morning to write a story for a daily newspaper. Just because he was well read and knew how to translate a Caesar cipher didn't mean he had been handed enough street smarts to be of any real use.

I slowed as I approached the former Roth family home, which was on the right side. It was a three-family house with brick front steps and little in the way of a yard. Someone had added stone facing to the first floor at some point after the Roths departed. There was also a plaque marking the house's significance.

"We're here," I announced as we approached. "I don't suppose we could just call this quits, could we? You know, I'll let you skate on Nancy if you let me walk away? I don't need to tell the police anything. And I can forget I ever met a guy with the initials J.M. What do you say?"

But McNabb either wasn't listening or didn't feel like answering. I turned slowly to face him and saw that his eyes were scanning the street.

"This is good. This is perfect," he said. "Now do exactly as I say. Park the car."

"Okay. There's no parking on this side."

"Fine. Turn it around. Just pull a U-eey in this intersection."

I followed his instructions. There were several parking spots available opposite the Roth house, and I stopped in one of them. Just then, a shock of thunder rattled the car with a sound wave so powerful it seemed to alter the air pressure as it passed.

Something about it jolted me out of the numbing sense of calm that had gripped me ever since McNabb pulled the gun on me. It finally occurred to me, *This is it. I'm really going to die.*

More than anything, I felt pissed. Joan of Arc was, what, sixteen when she died? Half my age, and she led armies. Jesus? He was thirty-three—only a year older than me—and look at all he managed to get accomplished in that time. I'm not saying I had delusions of grandeur, like anyone ought to be basing an entire religion—or a television miniseries—on my life. But dammit, here I was thirty-two and all I had to show for it was a few decent newspaper clips scattered across the course of a not-even-half-finished career. Now here I was, working my last story, and I'd never even get to write it.

At the very least, I was through with being obsequious. If he was going to kill me, it would be on *my* terms.

"Come on, let's get this over with," I said, ripping my hands from the steering wheel, hitting the button on my seat belt, shoving open the door, and swinging my legs onto the street.

"Hey, what are . . ." McNabb began to protest, but I was out of the car before he could finish.

I heard the back driver's side door opening up behind me, and McNabb was already in midroar: ". . . ass back here. Stop right there."

But I marched across the narrow street to the sidewalk in

front of 81 Summit Avenue, and just as I was about to turn around and face my end, it suddenly occurred to me:

What do I mean, die on my *terms? Why am I waiting around for this guy to kill me? Run, you dumbass. Run for all you're worth.*

"Stop. I haven't cleaned my prints off the gun yet," McNabb yelled, as if this was somehow my concern.

No, my concern—my *only* concern—was putting more distance between myself and McNabb. I felt my right thigh muscle flexing, then my left. Strides one and two were a bit of a misadventure, as my dress shoes slipped on the wet pavement. Strides three and four went better, with my feet gaining traction, enough that the sides of my vision began blurring. I was starting to move. Fast. Hey, if I could outrun a bear, I could certainly outrun a fat lump like McNabb.

I looked for something resembling cover, but there was none. Summit Avenue was just this long, straight street with nowhere to hide. So I concentrated on making it to Chancellor Avenue, my best chance to find a cop, a hiding spot, something. My arms were pumping. My legs were churning. I was going to make it.

I heard another thunderclap, only it was even closer than the last one. Then something tripped me and I went sprawling.

Only it wasn't thunder. And I hadn't tripped. It was McNabb's gun firing. And he had shot me in the back of the leg.

For a moment, I saw nothing but wet, time-worn asphalt in front of my face. I was down. I tried to scramble up but couldn't seem to get my left leg underneath me. It didn't hurt or anything. I just couldn't make it move.

All I could do was roll over. The rain was pounding me so hard I was losing track of where it was coming from. Now that I was faceup, there was so much water gushing on me it was almost like I was trying to open my eyes under a running showerhead. I propped myself on my right elbow and used my left hand as a shield, just so I could see McNabb marching toward me, scowling and red-faced. My mad dash had gotten me all of three doors down from the Roth residence.

"You want to do this the hard way? You want to do this the hard way?" McNabb screamed, keeping the gun aimed at me.

I had no answer for him. I just lay back down and started to feel an otherworldly pain emanating from my left hamstring, like a bad cramp, only fifty times worse.

At least I had tried, I told myself, no matter how lame the attempt was.

"I told you to follow the script," he bellowed, now standing over me. "How are you supposed to commit suicide with a gunshot wound to your leg? How is *that* in the script?"

He steadied himself with his legs spread wide, gripped the gun in both hands, and pointed it down in the direction of my head. I didn't want to watch anymore. So I looked up at the sky and tried to concentrate on something other than the growing agony coming from my lower half. I found myself tracking individual raindrops as they fell into my eyeball from a seemingly impossible height, watching as they cascaded down through space that seemed curved. And I waited for the lights to go out.

I've heard it said the moments before death are slow ones, stretching out far longer for the soon-to-be-deceased than they do for anyone else. This, at least, is what those who have experienced near-death come back to report—life flashing before their eyes, tunnels appearing, that sort of thing.

But I wasn't experiencing any of that. I just suddenly became aware the lights *hadn't* gone out and the guy who was trying to kill me suddenly wasn't upright anymore.

A large, fast-moving shape had barreled into the small of his back, sending his chest thrusting forward in a parabolic shape, his arms flying out at his side and his head tilting back. An explosion of air escaped from his lungs in a barely formed grunt. And then he disappeared.

I propped myself up on both elbows to look for him. But he was gone. All I could see was Lunky—Lunky!—and he had apparently executed an absolutely textbook tackle: head down, arms wrapped, body low for maximum leverage. He finished by landing squarely on top of McNabb, momentarily obscuring the smaller man. It was a quarterback sack that would have made any NFL Films highlight reel. McNabb had been thoroughly blindsided.

He wasn't done fighting, of course. No, he was struggling against Lunky, wriggling and cursing and wriggling some more, trying to at least get himself turned over to face his assailant. But he couldn't get any momentum. Lunky was so much bigger and stronger, he easily kept McNabb pinned, long past a ten-count. McNabb would have stood a better chance against a mountain gorilla. Lunky actually seemed to be taking it easy on the guy, like he pitied him.

I began opening my mouth to warn Lunky not to be too blasé, that McNabb was armed. Then I saw the gun had come to rest a good ten yards away. McNabb had no more chance of reaching it than I did of standing up and winning *Dancing with the Stars* on one leg.

Lunky maneuvered into a sitting position atop his quarry, with his powerful legs keeping McNabb's arms pinned. With one giant paw, Lunky smothered the side and back of McNabb's head, keeping it pressed down into the street. Lunky could have kept McNabb there all night if need be, and McNabb seemed to resign himself to it. Either that or he had run out of energy for his struggle, because he was finally still.

The pain was starting to make it hard to think, so I lay back down and stared up at the rain some more. Soon, a head of curly brown hair was poking into my frame of vision and a very concerned-looking Tina Thompson was gazing down at me.

"Are you okay, honey?" she asked,

I wish I could report my reply had been something valiant, funny, touching, or memorable. But it was, in fact, a little more candid: "It hurts."

"You've been shot," she informed me, like I didn't already know. "It's okay. Tommy is here. He's calling an ambulance."

"Just hang in there," Tommy said from somewhere in the neighborhood of my feet. "I'm on the line with 911 right now. They're coming. The other good news is the EMTs will probably cut those ugly pleated pants off you."

I may have attempted a smile, but I was aware it came out as a grimace. Tina was still looming above me, tucking a piece of hair behind her ears in a way that, even in my agony, I couldn't help but find adorable. I wanted to be mad at her, really mad, for not believing in me, for bailing out on me in my time of need, for siding with the publisher over her own reporter—even if, as it turned out, she was sort of right about the whole thing.

But I just felt so grateful to be alive. There was not the least scrap of anger in me. Only relief. I let my lungs fill with air, then released it, then repeated the process a few more times. The air was wet but, I swear, it had a flavor to it. And it tasted delicious.

There was a moan—it was probably coming from me—and I tried to concentrate on breathing some more. And I also heard a voice that sounded like it belonged to Detective Owen Smiley. But I couldn't be certain.

The rain was finally tapering off into a light sprinkle. After having been hammered by globules the size and weight of quarters, the smaller, needlelike drops actually were pleasant by comparison. Besides, it gave me something to think about other than my leg.

Tina had repositioned herself and was now kneeling at my side.

"Don't die on me," she said. "You've got a story to write."

"I don't work for you anymore, remember?" I said.

"Sure you do."

"Don't mess with a soon-to-be-dead man. You fired me."

"No, you quit," she corrected me. "And I never accepted your resignation. As far as the *Eagle-Examiner* is concerned, you were on suspension, but it has been revoked."

"All I had to do was get shot, huh?"

"No. Actually, your part-time translator and full-time co-conspirator returned to the office this afternoon, telling us you were on the trail of a pretty amazing story and that we'd be idiots not to bring you back in the fold and let you work it. I took it to Brodie, who backed you immediately. You should have told us about the eyewitness."

"I didn't think you'd believe me."

"Sorry," she said, stroking my hand. "I'm so sorry, Carter."

"I'm cold," I said.

"I don't have a blanket. Just hang on a little longer. Is there anything else I can do?"

I heard a siren approaching from somewhere. I was getting a little disoriented. Tina's curly head was starting to spin.

"Tell that bastard," I said, then got hit by a surge of pain and had to stop.

"That bastard over there," I said. "Remind him."

"Remind him what?"

"That we made our last interview on the record."

Then I'm fairly certain I passed out.

• • •

If I had to choose one city in the world in which to get shot, I would pick Newark, New Jersey, above all others. No matter where you are, from Weequahic to downtown all the way up to the North Ward or out to the Ironbound, you are no more than a short drive away from one of several trauma centers that rank among the country's finest. There, you will find a team of doctors more experienced with gunshot wounds—and more skilled at treating them—than you will in any of the world's standing armies.

I ended up at Newark Beth Israel, just a few blocks away. When I came to, my parents were there, as was a rather unimpressed doctor. He informed me the bullet had passed clean through my leg, coming close to nicking both a bone and an artery—either of which injury could have been disastrous for various reasons—but missing both, rendering my wound neither very dangerous nor, to his mind, very interesting.

The night was a blur of bothersome nurses and rounding doctors, buzzing in and out through the evening and into the small hours of the morning. They made it damn difficult for a guy to get a decent night's sleep, which is what I needed most. I may have grumbled about this, perhaps even created a few profane word combinations in expressing my displeasure. Eventually, my father took over, posted guard at the door, and made it clear to any and all—including my mother—that I was not to be disturbed. Dads are good that way sometimes.

By the next morning I was feeling pretty good. Though, admittedly, my mood may have been aided by the wonders of Percocet. Around ten o'clock, I assured my father I was sufficiently well rested, and he relented, allowing a stream of flower- and balloon-bearing visitors to begin entering my room and paying homage to the wounded hero. Dad only let them in one at a time, so I had to hear the story in bits and pieces—and all out of order, since my visitors were not thoughtful enough to arrange themselves chronologically—but I eventually assembled a fairly thorough account of the evening.

It started with Lunky, who had received my e-mail shortly after I sent it. He said I caught him at a good moment—he had finished Emerson and was just about to plunge back into Thoreau when my e-mail came—and he realized fairly quickly that something was amiss. The tip-off for him was that, apparently, *Sabbath's Theater* has nothing to do with the stage.

"I was sure you knew Mickey Sabbath is a puppeteer, not an actor," Lunky informed me gravely. "I considered it a cry for help."

So while the part about suicide didn't grab him, the bungling of Roth did. And he was thus inspired to take my note to "Missus Thompson," perhaps not fully realizing she was one and the same as the "Tina" who was referenced in the note. Tina recognized the entire e-mail as gibberish and acted accordingly.

"I decided you had either lost it completely or you were in real trouble," Tina told me during her first visit of the day. "Either way, I needed to intervene."

Tina didn't have my new number, so she couldn't call me. And, in any event, my phone was already sitting at the bottom of a Hudson County retention pond, next to some radioactive fiddler crabs. So she asked Lunky for a translation of the Roth stuff, and he remembered our first conversation, where he had mentioned Roth's childhood home at good ol' 81 Summit Avenue.

Tina summoned Tommy, and the three of them decided fairly quickly to hightail it down to Weequahic and figure out what was going on.

On the way, Tommy had put in a call to Owen Smiley. Unfortunately, while Tommy remembered Smiley's name, he didn't have the detective's cell number. So he had to go through the Bloomfield Police Department switchboard. And Smiley, whose gun just might have come in handy, didn't get the message for a little while—which is why I only heard him on scene after the shooting had already happened.

But it didn't matter, because Lunky was my secret weapon. The lady who lived at 81 Summit Avenue remembered him fondly and invited him and his friends in from the rain. They were huddled in her house, trying to figure out what to do, when they saw my car pull up.

I guess everything happened pretty fast from there. But Lunky said as soon as he heard the gunshot, he knew I needed help—he's a quick study, that Lunky—and he bolted out the door and bounded down the steps. He saw McNabb walking toward me, ready to shoot, and went in for the tackle. The noise of Lunky's rapid approach was drowned out by all the rain and thunder.

From there, all ended happily for those not named McNabb.

None of my visitors were allowed to bring in the Friday paper, which was deemed "too stressful" for me in such an early and tender phase of my recovery, but I managed to get the details of what we had printed. The *Newark Eagle-Examiner* reported that Jim McNabb, IFIW–Local 117 executive director, had been arrested for the murder of Nancy Marino and was being held without bail. A spokesman from the prosecutor's office said McNabb could also expect to be charged with two counts of attempted murder, and a variety of weapons charges for both his use of an illegal handgun and his use of a Cadillac Escalade, which, it turned out, he happened to own and have registered in his name. A reference was made to an "outstanding local citizen" who would be receiving a $10,000 reward for her cooperation with the Bloomfield police.

They had put my byline—and mine alone—on the story. It was accompanied by an editor's note, explaining to readers that the story had been primarily the work of staff writer Carter Ross, who had been injured during the course of doing his reporting. Tommy Hernandez and Buster Hays had completed the reporting and written the piece.

Since Hernandez and Hays were only beginning to untangle the mess with "Caesar 710" and the sexual harassment angle—and didn't want to put guesses in the newspaper—they had left the matter of motive fairly vague. It was only in the morning, when Tommy got Peter Davidson of the NLRB on the phone, that things started becoming a little more clear to them. Now that Davidson knew Nancy Marino was dead—and therefore he didn't have to worry about spoiling an EEOC complaint—he relented on the FOIA request. By lunchtime, Tommy had a small handful of documents, all of which named Jim McNabb as the target of Nancy's complaint.

Gus Papadopolous's "involvement"—if you could call it that—turned out to be minor. Nancy had listed the State Street Grill as one of her places of employment, so Davidson had paid a visit there, just to get a sense for what kind of worker she was. Davidson said that Gus had been a little leery, repeatedly saying he "didn't want no trouble." But Davidson was ultimately just looking for a character witness of sorts. And the affidavit Gus supplied extolled Nancy's long history as a loyal, reliable worker.

As for the Jackman-Papadopolous conspiracy I had created, it turns out that the Bloomfield Chamber of Commerce, of which Papadopolous was the president, was one of several chambers partnering with the paper on a new initiative aimed at driving consumers back to downtown shopping areas.

Which is what Tina had just finished explaining to me during her second visit of the day, during the midafternoon.

"So there's another daily story going in tomorrow's paper, I assume," I said.

"Yeah, with a sidebar about McNabb's long tenure atop IFIW–Local 117 coming to a close. The union board convened a hasty meeting this morning and voted to terminate him."

"Who's writing all this?"

"Hernandez is doing the main. Hays is doing the union stuff."

"Uh-huh. And who is doing the big, beautiful Sunday story that makes sense of it all?"

"I didn't think you would be up for—"

"Get me a laptop," I said, before she could finish.

Over the next four hours, I let it pour out of me, indulging my penchant for overwriting, knowing the desk wouldn't dare take it out. Reporters who have been shot in the line of duty get special dispensation. And since I hoped this would be the only time in my career I could claim that exemption, I enjoyed it thoroughly.

It was definitely better than writing my own obit.

ACKNOWLEDGMENTS

By now, you're probably accustomed to reading author acknowledgments that say something like "This book wouldn't have happened without . . ." And, most of the time, the words that follow are as fictional as anything else in the novel.

But this time it's actually true. This book—and Carter Ross as a character—was on life support, perhaps doomed to a premature death, when my agent, Dan Conaway of Writers House, and Minotaur Books executive editor Kelley Ragland conspired to give him new life. I'm a fortunate beneficiary of their many talents.

While I'm at it, I'd like to thank some of the other folks in the Flatiron funhouse who help make Minotaur the true beast of crime fiction: Jeanne-Marie Hudson and Matt Baldacci, who do the dirty work; Hector DeJean, who is as kind as he is tall; Andy Martin, who steers the ship; and Matthew Shear and Sally Richardson, without whom the ship would likely sink.

Thanks are also due to:

My former colleagues at *The Star-Ledger*, who unwittingly provided much of the color for Carter's world and whose camaraderie and collegiality I still miss.

Teresa and the rest of the crew at my local Hardees, where

large portions of this book were written, thanks to them keeping the soda fountain well stocked with Coke Zero.

Joe Hefferon of the Essex County Sheriff's Office, a fellow writer who helped with some cop questions.

My beloved readers, in particular Dolly Thrift. She knows why and she'll never tell.

My author buddies, including Julia Spencer-Fleming, Marcus Sakey, and Sean Chercover, who helped me out in a pinch a while back; and Sophie Littlefield, Carla Buckley, and Hilary Davidson, who are just lovely ladies.

The bookstore owners who have given me a boost, in particular Gayle and Ron Harris of Books and Crannies, who showed me what Texas hospitality is all about.

All the library scientists who make literacy their business, including Lesa Holstine of the Glendale (Arizona) Public Library, who has done so much to promote the mystery genre; and Lindsy Gardner of the Lancaster (Virginia) Community Library, who withstands my friendship even as it sullies her otherwise sparkling reputation.

Jen Forbus. That's all I can say about her.

David J. Montgomery, who has done me more favors than I'll ever be able to repay.

Jorge Motoshige and Leslie Jennings, who are never-ending friends in times good and bad; Scott Colston, who is generous with his fellowship and his furniture; and Tony Cicatiello and James Lum, who always put a roof over my head.

I also can never stop thanking my family: in-laws Joan and Al Blakely, who have been saviors too many times to count; my brother Greg, who remains my best man in every sense of that term; and my terrific parents, Marilyn and Bob, whose ceaseless cheerleading for my career probably gets tiring to their friends but never gets old to me.

Finally, I am tremendously blessed to have an endlessly supportive wife and two brilliant, beautiful children (they take after their mother in these respects). Every writer needs an inspiration. They're mine.